HYDE'S LAST STAND

Suddenly, eyes staring, startled and dazzled by searchlights, ears deafened by the noise of rotors and engines, he looked wildly around him—three —no, four helicopters, one a big MiL transport. They whirled, then settled around the lake, one near the wreckage, careful not to disturb the scene, another at the mouth of the knife-cut valley where the river ran out of it. The fourth skimmed the lake, searchlight glaring down, without pause.

Troops spread out cautiously, sealing off the lake, preserving the scene for those who would come later to analyze, investigate—*believe*. Torches wobbled; voices snapped orders, called positions. The crackle of R/Ts.

He was trapped. Hidden but trapped. The valley was sealed. He was imprisoned.

His hands and arms began to quiver.

Also by Craig Thomas

EMERALD DECISION
FIREFOX
WOLFSBANE
SNOW FALCON
SEA LEOPARD
JADE TIGER

Published by
HARPERPAPERBACKS

CRAIG THOMAS

THE LAST RAVEN

HarperPaperbacks
A Division of HarperCollins*Publishers*

This is a work of fiction. The characters, incidents, and dialogues are products of the author's imagination and are not to be construed as real. Any resemblance to actual events or persons, living or dead, is entirely coincidental.

HarperPaperbacks *A Division of* HarperCollins*Publishers*
10 East 53rd Street, New York, N.Y. 10022

A hardcover edition of this book was published in 1990 by HarperCollins*Publishers*.

Cover illustration by Bill Schmidt

First HarperPaperbacks printing: July 1991

Printed in the United States of America

HarperPaperbacks and colophon are trademarks of HarperCollins*Publishers*

10 9 8 7 6 5 4 3 2 1

≡

for
EDDIE and JUNE
—for the fun

ACKNOWLEDGMENTS

I wish to express my gratitude for assistance with this novel to the United States Department of Agriculture Forest Service, especially to those responsible for the health and long life of the Shasta-Trinity National Forest in northern California, and to the Convention and Visitors Bureau of the town of Redding, also in northern California.

Craig Thomas,
Lichfield

*Two Ravens sit on Odin's shoulders
and bring to his ears all the news
they see and hear; their names are
Thought and Memory. Odin sends them
out with each dawn to fly over the
world, in order he may learn everything that happens.
Always, he fears that the raven named
Thought may not return, but every day
his deepest concern is for Memory.*

—*Snorri Sturluson,* The Deluding of Gylfi
(from the Icelandic)

THE LAST RAVEN

PRELUDE

To see one raven is lucky, 'tis true,
But it's certain misfortune to light upon two
And meeting with three is the devil.

Matthew Lewis, Ballad of Bill Jones

Early November

There had been that awkward, hesitant moment as he was helped off with his overcoat—the momentary, reminiscent pain in his arm, still in a sling; and his umbrella dripping on the carpet before it was thrust into a stand made from an elephant's foot. He thought of Longmead's insensitivity in allowing that monstrosity of Empire to remain there. Then he was being ushered into the cabinet secretary's office, where the net-curtained windows overlooked Downing Street, and where they were all present and all smiling—and he was back; returned, promoted and congratulated, and with work, *real* work to do!

He brushed his remaining hair flat and tempered the smirk of satisfaction on his face. His thoughts rushed warmly. Everywhere, on every face—Geoffrey Longmead's, Clive Orrell's, the PM's parliamentary private secretary, Peter Shelley's—there was satisfaction and amnesia. He was welcomed back as chairman of the Joint Intelligence Committee, not as a former outcast or pariah. He might have left his leper's bell in the elephant's foot together with his umbrella.

"Kenneth—my dear Kenneth!" Longmead, hand extended, came towards him, beaming, the lights glinting from his heavily rimmed spectacles, his waistcoat bulging just above his trousers. Aubrey took the hand offered him and, smiling inwardly, observed that he did not bite it. He *wanted* to be back!

He glanced beyond the cabinet secretary's shoulder but, no, there were no sullen loyal sons who resented the prodigal's return and the killing of the fatted calf. They were all consummate actors...except perhaps Peter Shelley, whose pleasure seemed alloyed. The look in Peter's eyes disturbed the wholehearted pretense of the room. Aubrey realized that the cancellation of his appointment with the prime minister, and his being offered his new post by the foreign secretary instead, was not the only small cloud in the sky of his inwardly sunny day...

...Patrick, of course. Aubrey discovered a flush of guilt that enveloped his body, hearing once more in his head—as he had done repeatedly in the car all the way from Earl's Court—Ros Woode's shrill and vulgar blame yelled through her entry phone as he stood in Philbeach Gardens in the rain. Accusing him of having as good as killed Patrick Hyde; at best creating the circumstances of Hyde's death by his indifference. It simply couldn't be true—!

But the look on Peter Shelley's face confirmed that it was. Patrick, to whom Aubrey owed his life and his probity, had been killed in some Godforsaken corner of

Afghanistan because . . . because of him, he admitted bitterly. He had loaned him out to anyone who cared to use him, like a book he had already read and recommended to others.

He had called at Hyde's flat on his way from the airport, just as a courtesy, simply wishing to make certain, now that he had returned from Nepal, that Patrick was all right. Ros's accusations had exploded like a parcel he had been opening in all innocence. Patrick Hyde was—dead.

"Thank you, Geoffrey," he murmured, shaking Longmead's hand, smiling into his face, into the other faces there. Early evening lights sprang out along Downing Street and leaked from Whitehall. Yes, Whitehall: his place—*his* place. A whiskey was being pressed into his hand, its soda fizzing. As chairman of the Joint Intelligence Committee, Aubrey was now the most powerful individual in the room, with the exception of the cabinet secretary. Even Orrell realized it and was hastening to make his peace. And yet Hyde . . . he sipped the whiskey, toastlike to the room, and again heard Ros's strident Australian voice.

The whiskey went sharp and cheap on his palate and his stomach lurched. His arm ached, too, reminding him of other things, recent dangers, making a pattern of it all. Hyde was—

—*dead*. Shelley's look had not given the lie to it.

"All right, Kenneth?" Longmead murmured, holding his elbow firmly, impatient to guide him into the center of the room, the center of attention.

"What?" he all but snapped. Ros's accusations echoed overlappingly in his head like some tricksy recording. Then: "Oh, yes, Geoffrey—a little overwhelmed." He smiled disarmingly and moved forward with Longmead.

He shook hands with Orrell, who was deferential in a minuscule, important way. Then a brief exchange ensued with the PM's PPS, whose lugubrious young face displayed the *probationary* reality of Aubrey's new appointment, its perhaps unfortunate necessity. Which, no doubt, was why the PM had not seen him personally. She had landed the foreign secretary with the task at the last moment. Evidently, her Puritan sensibilities, her inflexible rectitude, allowed her to retain some smidgen of mistrust as far as he was concerned.

"Giles!" He greeted Giles Pyott warmly.

"My dear, dear old boy!" Pyott replied, his eyes actually misty with pleasure. Aubrey looked up at the tall, erect soldier as his arm was pumped up and down. A real friend . . . reluctant, less imaginative, but there was always a debt of gratitude towards Giles.

Yes, he decided, continuing pleasantries with Giles, with Longmead, with Orrell and even with the PPS, the PM regarded him as something of a cardsharp, a conjurer. Clever, but don't hand over a ten-pound note and allow him to tear or secrete it! Too clever by half. The irony of it all was that *he* trusted *her*!

Shelley seemed reluctant to join the group in the center of the cabinet secretary's faded, intricate Persian carpet. His features had something of the grave lack of indulgence exhibited by some of the Victorian prime ministers who looked down on them from the walls. Aubrey smiled and nodded and chaffed and demurred, all the while aware that Shelley was at the edge of this new, beaming, content circle. Then, soon after his second whiskey and soda was handed him, Shelley was there as Giles Pyott moved aside, in conversation with Longmead.

"Peter . . ." Aubrey could not conceal the hesitant guilt in his tone. His whiskey glass masked the weak, loose expression on his lips.

"Sir Kenneth." Shelley, he realized, was as reluctant as he to begin, as if it was a dangerous journey that confronted them rather than a conversation. "I'm—delighted at, you know, the chairmanship . . ."

There was a shared sense of guilt, Aubrey decided. And Shelley, having known for longer than he, had already encountered something akin to loss, even grief. Patrick just wouldn't be there any more.

Aubrey blurted: "It is true?" His voice was shocked, maidenly prim.

Shelley nodded, his face lengthening. "I—I'm afraid so. Alison's very upset. I didn't think she even liked him much. You—want to know, of course."

"But *how?* Patrick . . . ? I mean—" Now, the others seemed to be studiously ignoring them, even providing a background of jollity, discussing in raised, lubricated voices cabinet changes, money supply figures, matters in a dozen countries. Aubrey's attention returned to the narrow, darker business of Hyde's death.

"His whole group was wiped out. Look, I know they haven't recovered the body, but no one's really in any doubt. I shouldn't hold out any hope, frankly," Shelley said.

"What were they doing?"

"He was with one of the mujahideen groups, inside the USSR. It was just surveillance, a monitoring operation, nothing more." Shelley shrugged.

"Where, precisely?"

"Only *just* across the Soviet border, reporting to Langley as well as to us. As things are in the Moslem republics of the—"

"It had nothing to do with that other business?" Aubrey blurted, lurid headlines filling his imagination. He referred to that aircraft accident, the one with the potential impact of an earthquake shivering around the world.

"You mean—? No. Hyde might have been in the area—I suppose he might have been caught by the increased army presence there." Shelley rubbed his chin, then became angry in his attempt to shuffle off guilt. "Look, Sir Kenneth, he was on loan. He was familiar with Afghanistan. He was monitoring the volatile situation in Tadzhikistan—it just *happened.*" Shelley's cheeks were flushed. Behind him, Orrell was approaching, conciliation on his features like a large-scale map. Suddenly,

Aubrey wanted the distraction of talking to Orrell, talking business—anything but *this*.

"I see," he murmured. "The CIA knows nothing more?"

"No more than they've told us—than I've told you." Shelley seemed to sense that the conversation was all but concluded and appeared relieved.

It was easy, so easy, for an agent to have lost his life in the violent, unsettled circumstances of the Afghan border after the Soviet withdrawal. So easy.

"Excuse me, Peter—I want a word with Kenneth," Orrell interposed, smiling, exuding affability like an actor with a new script from which he was still learning.

"Oh, yes," Shelley mumbled.

"Thank you, Peter," Aubrey said heavily. He at once beamed up at Orrell, even took his arm like someone hurrying a companion away from unpleasantness. "I think we must have lunch as soon as possible, don't you?"

Aubrey deliberately turned aside from Shelley's reproachful look. The conversations seemed to surround him quickly, and they proved narcotic; he was able to fend off the admission that Hyde was dead.

PART ONE

THE KILLING
OF
THE DOVE

*Censure acquits the raven, but
pursues the dove.*

Juvenal, Satires

1

RETURN OF
THE JEDI?

Late October

He began crying helplessly with huge, shuddering sobs, his body quivering with its now-perpetual weariness. He stared at the Sony Walkman in his shivering hands, cursing it. His tears fell on his hands, on the portable cassette player. His shoulders heaved. Fucking thing, fucking bloody useless *thing*—!

He stood up shakily, sniffing loudly, wiping his grimy, stubbled face with the sleeve of his loose, filthy shirt. He stared down into the narrow knife-cut of the valley, down to where the river was stony gray. The wind buffeted and chilled. His cheeks hurt where his tears were drying. He stared once more at the Walkman, which he had broken presumably when diving for cover earlier that day, or perhaps the previous day—or week. It was broken. He could neither suppress nor control his exaggerated reactions, the tears and shuddering, the weakness, even a thin anguish. Its being broken seemed to signify something as huge as the loss of his remaining sanity. It was another fingerhold on reality gone. With a bellow, he lifted his arm and threw the Walkman, its headphones still attached, in an arc out over the valley, then watched it descend until it was too small to distinguish. The small canvas bag filled with cassettes followed, accompanied by a second enraged cry. Then he slumped once more into a hunched sitting position, his spine curved against a rock, his head in his hands as they made constant, hard washing movements over his face and hair and neck.

Patrick Hyde knew he was without reserves, close to collapse. At any moment, he might break, as easily as the cassette player had, against some slight, future impact. The impact of anything that belonged *here*, to *this*—! Dead Petrunin had called it a shithouse and he was right. This had been Petrunin's heart of darkness ... fucking useless bloody useless fucking thing, he went on mindlessly repeating somewhere in the dark back of his head, as if he kept an idiot twin locked up there. Aware that he might have been describing himself... useless fucking thing. He was buggered, finished, close to breakdown. He needed to get out. Christ, how he needed to get out!

It was days ago he'd realized he could no longer control his temper, that his judgment was suspect, irrational; more than a week ago he'd started smoking the hashish the mujahideen always carried with them. Its effects were hardly noticeable. The tranquilizers he'd been issued were all gone. He squeezed his eyes shut. He did not want to look at the place, not at any part of it. Fucking *mountains!* There was no noise of helicopters or jets on the wind. They were in the Soviet Republic of Tadzhik-istan but the bloody place was identical to bloody Af-ghanistan. Heart of darkness.

The weary repetition of the same expletives tightened his throat, made his forehead thud. If he reached out his arms to each side, long before they were at full stretch his palms would encounter the limits of his mental cage. He knew that with a sick, churning certainty. So he hunched closer into himself, shoulders bowed, arms wrapped across his stomach, legs drawn up. The wind plucked and niggled at the thick sleeves of his shirt; ruffled the sheepskin lining of his jacket where it showed at shoulders and hem; flapped the loose trousers he wore. He wasn't even dressed as himself; he wasn't himself in any way. The distance to London, even to Peshawar, was to be measured in light years rather than miles.

He had been used . . . that didn't matter. It was being used *up* that he hated—the knowledge that he was all but finished. This shithouse of a place, the hundreds of legless children, the chemically attacked faces and limbs of men and women, the empty, bombed or flame-throw-ered villages. The whole catalog of horrors. He was an inventory man. He'd seen everything they'd done to each other, Afghan and Russian, logged it all, noted, reported, itemized. Now, he had sickened of it; he was not merely sick of it, that had happened months ago. He was sick-ened of it; was ill because of it. This heart-of-darkness shithouse that had gone quiet and unbloody for maybe six months then simply folded its tents and moved north; so that Russian soldiers burned and bombed and ex-ploded and gassed and poisoned and booby-trapped their own Muslims now, *inside* the great and glorious

USSR! He lay his forehead on his forearms as if in supplication or apology.

And the Soviet Moslems in Tadzhikistan, Uzbekistan, Turkmenistan had learned or were learning. Shoot down the helicopters, disembowel the prisoners, use the Stingers and other missiles . . . fight! Jihad. The Moslem Holy War against the infidel had come north over the border, into the Soviet Union, as Brezhnev might even have suspected, in 1979. The mosques were full, the armories and the bomb caches were full. The mullahs were urging. There was even *Hezbollah,* the Party of God, because the Iranians were involved—prompting, whispering, backing, sending money and missiles.

Find out, he'd been told. Keep watch. Report back. Tell us the truth, what's *really* going on . . .

. . . *we know Kabul's involved, we know what the Russians think, there may be a timetable . . . give us the facts!*

So, he had watched and noted and reported, learned and inwardly digested. And it had infected him: all those bodies without hands; all those corpses with dicks cut off and shoved in their grinning mouths as if they enjoyed the idea; all those kids on crutches, and all those silent, cloaked women; and all of the starving hordes, and all of the old people left behind, rounded up and executed. Oh, *Jesus Christ*—!

He realized his eyes were leaking again as the wind began to freeze-dry his tears before they reached his chin and throat. Oh, sweet-Jesus-Christ, get me away from here!

It would be another Afghanistan, going on for another decade at least—unless the Russians stopped it by nuking the Moslems out of existence, turning their own southern Asian border into a wasteland.

It was time to go.

They didn't trust him, not even this pro-Western group he was with. They knew he was on the edge, maybe over it. He'd lost whatever respect and trust they'd ever given him. It was time to go, before they began regarding him as a risk, and put an end to him.

The wind was icy, the valley below funneling it, and the mountain to his left throwing the cold air up towards him. He shivered, his teeth chattering, but still he did not move, hardly looked up at the voice hailing him. Slowly, it penetrated his awareness. His name. But, when he looked up, he saw only the mountains. The Pamir, snow-covered, stretching away coldly to the east, into China, the Alai range to the north. The roof of the world, the arsehole of the world. With difficulty, he snapped away and slowly felt the insidious, always-present cold sunk deep in him. He rubbed his arms and stiff legs, watching the mujahideen with his flat, pancakelike cap climbing the last few yards towards him, Chinese-made Kalashnikov slung across his chest. One of Masood's people, from the Panjshir Valley. Hyde shrugged indifferently. Perhaps if the regime hadn't at last succeeded in killing Masood, things might have been different. Unlikely, but possible. A few less bodies.

"What is it?" he asked in awkward Pashto, which the man would understand despite not being Pathan. Once, they would have made this mujahideen learn it in school. His lean, dark features were excited, his eyes gleaming.

"Hyde—" There was no respect, but they still used his name and came to him with reports. "Less than two miles—" He was pointing with the rifle. "Russians."

"Coming this way?"

"No. They remain where they are."

"How many?" The mountains loomed and stretched away in a seemingly endless, diminishing perspective of snow and lifelessness. "What are they doing?" he added, indifferent.

"They are at ease—though busy." The man had switched to an English that was fractured and strangely bookish. "About thirty. A perimeter of guards. A vehicle. And one gunship—" He spat, as if religiously. "One big helicopter . . . transport."

"What is it transporting?"

"One big truck." The Afghan shrugged. "It carries a small aircraft." Then he added: "There is an American with them. You know him."

Hyde felt puzzlement sting like a half-regarded insect, then his feeble concentration focused once more on the man now squatting in front of him. Like most from the Panjshir, the man, called Nur, was Tajik. Like the Moslems this side of the Soviet border. In the aftermath of Masood's death, his people had adhered to the Americans, even the British, because there was a debt of weapons between them. Masood's fame as a mujahideen leader had ensured the supply of Stingers and Blowpipes and guns. The Afghan Tajiks were looking for a cause, seeking to extend the war against the Russians inside the Soviet Union. People like Nur already resented their use by people like himself. They wanted to fight the Russians again, not observe them. Once they found a new Masood, their assistance would end . . .

. . . long after Hyde's demise. He knew that, quite certainly. As Nur did. The mark was on him. His fatal error was waiting around the next turning on the next goat trail. And he didn't much care.

"What do you mean, a small aircraft?" he asked, knowing he should be concerned. A truck carrying an aircraft? An American he would recognize? He groaned, expelling the air from his lungs in a huge sigh, shaking his head, rubbing his hair, then his sunken cheeks. "What American?" he asked, concentrating.

"He has been in the Panjshir—also Peshawar. He supplied missiles. I forget his name."

"CIA?" Nur nodded. "With *Russians?* Bullshit!"

Nur shrugged and tugged at his short beard. Hyde could smell the man's unwashed skin and clothes. His eyes gleamed with offense, but he murmured: "It is as I say."

"Have you taken photographs—with the long lens?"

"That is your task," Nur replied.

Hyde felt his concentration slip once more, and felt the persistent weariness slide over him like a cloak. His awareness was like a loose electrical contact lighting something. Flashes of weak light, periods of darkness.

"Shit," he muttered. He rubbed his face once more. Then looked up as keenly as he could. "You're *certain?* You've seen this bloke before and he's CIA? He's with Russian soldiers *now?*"

Nur nodded slowly, patiently, as if conversing with a child.

"OK—*OK!* Get the others ready!"

Nur nodded one final time and rose to his feet. It was as if he had left a door wide open, through which the wind sprang with renewed energy. Hyde looked at his quivering hands, with their dirt and broken nails, and at once clutched them against the gun in his waistband.

Nur scrambled sideways like a crab down the scree slope to where the other seven in the group were eating. He did not look back at Hyde. The sky was shredding into cloud and blue because of the wind, like cloth being torn. The high vapor trail of an aircraft, heading for Tashkent or even Moscow, drew a thread across the largest patch of blue. The mountain flanks gleamed suddenly gold as the chilly sun emerged from cloud. The landscape did not warm, merely shone more icily. Ponderously, Hyde got to his feet. His legs were weak and aching. Movement nauseated him, because it was the first small step towards more killing. Going with the Tajiks, observing the Russians, taking photographs, identifying the American and what the truck carried, all brought the killing nearer.

Young soldiers, mere children, these Panjshiris below him...

The high vapor trail was dragged out of shape, pushed into a vague cloud by the wind. He scrabbled his way down the steep scree slope, pebbles and dust rising away from him, rolling ahead. When he reached the narrow, twisting goat track, they were already waiting for him. Eight of them, dressed like motley extras for a cheap movie; turbans, pancake caps, a leather Soviet paratrooper's helmet from God knew where or who. Baggy trousers or Afghan army fatigues; sheepskin jackets, combat jackets, bandoleers, grenades, Panjshiri scarves of blue and white. Bearded, silent, watchful. They were ready for more killing. Nur's report of an American in Russian company, across the border, made that certain. He sensed their impatience, like the sting of ice against his skin. If he did not respond, *now*, they might even begin with him. They were thoroughly tired of him. They'd leave at best, at worst leave his body, and head back to the Panjshir Valley...or link up with Tajik mujahideen on the Soviet side of the border.

With a vast effort, he checked the Kalashnikov one of them handed him. The safety was off. They never applied the safety catches to their weapons; which was unnerving in itself. Someone offered him a hashish cigarette and he shook his head. The Afghan was unimpressed.

"You're sure you've seen this American before?" he asked Nur.

"Yes. In the Panjshir, two, three years ago. In Peshawar also."

Hyde nodded and arranged his features to suggest deliberation, then finally decision.

"OK, let's go." He hefted the backpack so that it rode more comfortably on his shoulders. "Nur, you lead the way." The Afghans moved off immediately, eager as children seeking a game. The wind bullied about Hyde, slapping him into half-wakeful attention as he trudged along the narrow, rock-strewn track behind them, back bent, eyes narrowed against blown dust.

American . . . ? It was as if he understood for the first time as someone in intelligence might and should. An American—CIA. Consorting with Russian soldiers. He sighed, slowly realizing that his interest was not professional at all. The presence of the American might be enough to keep him going for another day, two days . . . but it wasn't that. He shook his head. With photographs, he could get out of Tadzhikistan straight away. He would not have to endure the week that remained before this patrol was scheduled to return. He could go back tomorrow.

The idea moved in his bloodstream like a sluggish stimulant. He could get out of this awful place.

The apartments overlooking the Kutuzovsky Prospekt were by no means modest. They were luxurious, Pyotr Didenko thought to himself as one of the KGB bodyguards removed his overcoat and took it away somewhere; into one of the rooms he had probably never seen. Nikitin was standing in the doorway of the main drawing room, the gilded handle of a door in each large hand. Aleksandr Aleksandrovich Nikitin, general secretary of the Soviet Communist Party. There was a delicate, glowing icon near his head on the flock-papered wall. Didenko paused, waiting for his apprehension to subside. It did not really matter, he told himself, and gradually the sharp little moment of contempt and suspicion faded. Most of this luxury was Irena's doing, after all. Even *Pravda* ridiculed her for it. *Krokodil*, now available on the streets, always called her the Tsarina. There were icons, delicately gilded, carved tables, paintings she had borrowed in Moscow and even from the Hermitage, thick carpets, flowers. Nikitin ushered him into the drawing room, then closed the double doors behind them.

"Sit down, Pyotr. A drink? Of course . . . Scotch?" Nikitin was grinning, as if he could see the mental lip-pursing of Didenko's momentary reaction. Why did Didenko feel that their reforms should always bear the seal of approval of some dreadful Puritanism? Vodka not Scotch, plain wooden tables, threadbare rugs? Why did he imagine—*still* imagine—revolutions needed austere, even impoverished surroundings? He did not doubt Nikitin's sincerity, not for a moment. "There!" Nikitin handed him a tumbler all but full. "Drink up—your best health, as always, Pyotr!" Even Nikitin's habitually bluff heartiness seemed at odds with *perestroika,* their bloodless revolution. How to turn the clock forward, as Nikitin phrased it. The unremarkable hero, as *Pravda* had dubbed him; meaning unlikely!

Nikitin swallowed half his glass of cognac. A nervous tic began in Didenko's wrist, as if to turn the face of his plain watch towards his glance. He resisted looking at the time. Nikitin was smiling, his glass raised as if Didenko had forgotten a toast.

"To Irena's success," Didenko blurted, raising his tumbler. Its facets caught the autumnal brightness from outside, flashing specks of light on the ceiling. Nikitin nodded and murmured *Irena* almost under his breath. He emptied his glass and refilled it.

With his back to Didenko, he said, "What are her chances, Pyotr? Honestly, now!" The last words were almost growled. Again, there was that sense in Didenko's mind of pretense, of role playing, something he found distressing, unforgivable. It did not matter how clever Irena was and how *led* Nikitin! It was happening. Things *were* changing. Their reforms were embedded—transplanted and flowering. They could begin to claim that they would succeed. The conservatives were on the retreat, everywhere. Nikitin, as the American newspapers said of him, *meant business*.

"I thought you wished to talk about the Central Committee," he began, but Nikitin was already shaking his large head. Wisps of hair—too little for a man in his fifties, too little for a hero, *Krokodil* had observed!— fell across his forehead. Nikitin brushed them away and sat down opposite Didenko, his armchair sighing luxuriously as he did so.

"Come on, Pyotr—you're one of less than a dozen who know and the only one whose judgment I trust absolutely! Do *you* think Irena's stuck her neck out too far, expecting agreement with Kabul?" He had almost finished his second large cognac. The bottle was dated and of plain glass. Another of the countless, mocked little luxuries.

Didenko put down his own glass and spread his hands on his thighs. Then he looked up.

"I—I'm not certain what to think, Aleksandr. I want to say no, she hasn't..."

"*But?*"

"But..." He looked up at the high ceiling with its ornate frieze and plaster ceiling rose above the crystal chandelier. There was nothing more than the faintest hum of traffic along the Kutuzovsky Prospekt coming through the double-glazed windows and tall French doors leading onto two balconies. He looked down again at Nikitin. "But I can't see the mullahs backing down!" he stated emphatically, all in a rush, waving his hands. "There are hardly any moderates left, apart from the king himself—and he's virtually a figurehead. They've listened to the beguiling noises from Teheran and they *like* what's happening in our Moslem republics!" He sighed, then shrugged, shaking his head mournfully. "I wish I could be more optimistic, Aleksandr."

Nikitin looked grimly at him, staring into the painful but unflattering truth, it seemed. He was nodding silently. He stared at his empty glass, then at the sideboard and its bottles, and put down his glass. A circle of reflected light appeared on the pale blue of the ceiling. Nikitin leaned back heavily in his chair.

"I wish I didn't agree with you, my friend...but *Irena!*" He threw up his hands. "She definitely thinks she has a chance of calming the situation." His face darkened. "Which *has* to be done, otherwise we'll have a bloody civil war to accompany our quiet little revolution! I don't want that. The adventure in Nepal I was persuaded into, against my better judgment..." He looked for reproach. Didenko smoothed his features and merely nodded. "I don't want the army making a *second* Afghanistan out of parts of the Soviet Union! That *would* finish our plans. But, I just can't see what Irena expects, even with the concessions we've made, the promises of aid. I don't think those fanatics will listen to her!" He rubbed his forehead. "But, she has to succeed, doesn't she? Unless I can show the Politburo and the army something conclusive, then I'm going to have to agree to at least increase the pressure to the level of a *limited* offensive in Uzbekistan, Tadzhikistan and Turkmenistan..." His eyes gleamed. "And don't remind me it wouldn't be the first time in Soviet history we've put down internal *religious dissent,* either, because it won't make the pill any sweeter to swallow!"

At once, he lapsed into a profound silence, gloomy and introspective. His face was gray as his eyes roamed the carpet near his feet. His shoulders were slumped, defeated.

"I agree," Didenko offered. "It must not happen. It's unthinkable...it will ruin everything."

"Now you know why I agreed to let Irena go to Kabul with a list of promises like a schoolgirl with an imposition! Why I made myself at least half-believe her idea." Again, his hands were raised in a kind of surrender. With justification. The remaining conservative faction on the Politburo would pressure him; the army would offer him a solution he could not ignore; and a suspicious, half-hearted Soviet public would begin to stop believing in Nikitin and *glasnost* and the reality of recent change, together with the rest of the world, which had already accepted Nikitin's apology over the Nepal fiasco, in which two loaded military transports had *accidentally* veered off course, and been forced to make an emergency landing. What had followed had been regrettable, even tragic. Certain army generals had been retired. The world had shrugged and looked the other way. Nikitin did not intend to make a similar mistake by trusting the army's answers to problems again. He wouldn't let them shit on his own doorstep!

Yet, here was Irena off on another of her secret visits to Kabul, that new hotbed of Moslem fundamentalist fervor, ever since the mujahideen had finally brought down the Kabul communist regime. Could even she snatch something out of the fire? Didenko did not know.

The "Tsarina" was clever, and strong. None of the mockery, the satire, the suspicion when Nikitin made her minister of culture had dented her confidence or determination. But *this* . . . ? This was something even she might fail to bring off—

"What time does her flight arrive in Kabul?" he asked, deflecting Nikitin's intent stare.

"Oh." The general secretary looked at his gold Rolex watch, the luxury of which set off in Didenko that ingrained, habitual mental tic, as if he had clicked his tongue against the roof of his mouth in disapproval. "In just over an hour." The afternoon sun had dulled towards evening beyond the pale shimmer of the lowered net curtains. The traffic breathed homewards outside. Nikitin rubbed his forehead, and sighed loudly. "She *has* to succeed!" he growled. "She has to bring something back this time, some agreement not to interfere in our internal affairs." He paused, then snapped: "Brezhnev's precious legacy, eh? Everything we're doing here might very well rest on the whim of the mullahs in Kabul! We have to placate the bloody Afghans!"

The Afghan's bent back quivered like that of an animal held on a leash, then stilled. Hyde rested the long, bloated lens of the camera across the hardly-more-than-boy's spine, and adjusted the focus. The scene emerged more starkly and more monochromatically than through the binoculars. He moved the camera, the view sliding like something submerged beneath clean oil.

The tip of Communism Peak in the northern distance was bright gold, lower mountain tips and flanks surrounding it white-to-gray with permanent snow. A glacier loomed fuzzily. The riverbed was salty white below them, the two helicopters like dark green insects, the group of men tiny—he stretched and rubbed his eyes, then refocused. The men sprang closer through the big lens, the helicopters took on bulk. The truck was ... it looked like an old V–1 flying bomb on the back of a furniture van. Or a toy airplane. The truck and its crew waited beside the hurrying, narrow river. There were men wearing padded jackets working on the rotor head of the Hind gunship. The other helicopter was huge, its shape skeletal, cartoonlike, the huge rotors sagging and quivering in the wind. Its landing gear was exaggeratedly tall. A MiL flying crane. It had brought the truck and its cargo to this roadless, empty part of Tadzhikistan.

Why?

As he took his eye away from the camera, waterfalls became dribbles once more, the machines tiny and the men insignificant. He was more aware of the wind. He motioned the Afghan to get up. He had used the first roll of film on the tableau below. He rubbed his eyes. Why? The question did not insist, rather nagged, like a piffling task requiring to be done before sleep. Once he was no longer using either the camera or the glasses, he became aware of the proximity of the Afghans, their movements and scents and tension. Now that they were watching their enemy down there, in the army duvet jackets and boots and greatcoats with caps and shoulder boards indicating senior rank, he was just another white face, another heathen and atheist like the Soviets.

The single American ...

He did recognize him. That was the burr irritating old habits, old instincts. His name was Harrell. He *was* CIA, ostensibly based in Peshawar before the Soviet withdrawal, then much later he'd been posted back to Kabul. Assistant station chief. Harrell. The name, the recognized features, rubbed saltily against his worn curiosity, stinging it. Harrell's presence was like aversion therapy, shocking Hyde out of his numb, weary self-absorption.

Why was he here, with Red Army and KGB officers—including, by their shoulder boards, two colonels and a general-lieutenant? Why? Whatever it was, it was important.

He lifted the binoculars to his eyes, adjusting the focus. There was activity around the truck and its toy airplane. Harrell had moved across the rock-strewn riverbank and was next to it, together with the—yes—most senior KGB officer and the army general. Arms gesticulating, charts being consulted, glances above the mountain flanks towards the deepening blue of the late afternoon sky. Clouds massed to the west. The long van was unmarked, daubed with desert-style camouflage. The small, winged machine sitting on its back, on what was presumably a short—too short?—launch rail, was unidentifiable, strange. There were footprints and small, rotor-blown creases in the salty flat sand beside the river.

They were still working with a small furiousness on the Hind's rotor head. Evidently, the thing couldn't fly, for the moment. The transport helicopter, sketchy as an early Disney cartoon, squatted by the water, oblivious. The truck had become the focus of the scene. He picked up the camera again, reloaded it, refocused, and felt that the group of men which included Harrell had become sped up in their gestures, comic and purposeful. Harrell in good profile despite the light...speed of the film to balance that—the Russian faces, the gestures of urgency, the sense of quarrel...debate...agreement. He picked off their faces like a sniper. Eventually, the second roll of film was exhausted. He reloaded quickly, obeying the tempo they seemed to be setting against the white salt-sand beside the river. Nur watched him assessingly while the others watched the enemy. He felt their collective shiver of anticipation as clearly as the excitement and nerves running through the Afghan's spine when he first

rested the camera lens across it. The boy glanced at him
and dropped onto all fours once more when he nodded.
The lens rested like a black cannon on the curve of his
spine. Hyde checked the light and opened the aperture
further. The gold had dimmed on the flanks of Communist Peak. The clouds were hurrying from the west,
eating the darkening blue sky.

Men climbed into the truck. It was really most like
an armored security van with drab-and-yellow daubs on
its sides. The toy airplane was insignificant, modest. Yet
Harrell was watching a duvet-jacketed soldier tinkering
with it, fussing over it. Then the soldier jumped down
from the back of the truck.

Aerials now. Jutting from the white sand, little dishes,
long waving fronds. Men set them down, wired them
up. Hyde became absorbed, occasionally operating the
camera. Quicker tempo. The launch rail rose from the
back of the van, angling up towards the sky. More men,
fiddling, checking. Plumes of vapor from the toy airplane
. . . fire.

It was enveloped with smoke, then appeared, tiny and
unimportant, beyond the launch rail and the van, higher
and rising quickly. The glow of orange was from some
kind of jet assistance. It rose rapidly. Hyde dropped the
camera, moved the bent-backed boy, picked up the
glasses. The Afghans muttered, as if envying some new
weapon. He trained the glasses, sweeping them across
sky and cloud and dark mountain flank.

He picked out the toy airplane, diminishing, rising.
Up, up, smaller, smaller, tiny . . . an eagle, a crow, a sparrow, then a dot before disappearing into the already
failing light. He thought he caught it once reflecting
sunlight like an ice crystal, then returned his attention
to the floor of the narrow river valley.

Men with headphones, the little dishes of the radars

being adjusted, a dish aerial jutting now from the roof of the van, the launch rail retracted. He glanced at Nur. Puzzled now, the Afghan had reacquired respect. Hyde grinned cynically, contemptuously. What the hell *were* they doing?

The Afghans seemed pressed close, even though they were spread out along the rock-strewn ledge in separate concealment. His skin prickled despite the cold, his cheeks quivered with more than tiredness. An unmanned vehicle, something remotely piloted, operated from inside the van, monitored by the dish aerials, signaled to by the waving fronds of other aerials. That's what the bloody thing was! A remotely piloted vehicle (RPV) with a camera on board, able to stooge around at anything up to twenty thousand feet, perhaps for four or five hours on its tiny motor.

Looking for what?

It did not explain the presence of Harrell, only the van beside which he was now standing, headphone pressed against his ear, the general sharing the set, head bent, face set. Hyde reloaded the camera, focused, judged the light, and the motor began whirring. Their urgency was infectious, his puzzlement propelled by the spur of memory. Eventually, he would understand.

He looked up at the sky, as they did frequently. He could hardly smell the Afghans now; their voices did not impinge. There was nothing visible up there. It must be twenty thousand feet, maybe more. Then he remembered, the Russians did not have that kind of compact, truck-launched RPV. Harrell was explained. His presence, at least. It was an American RPV, on loan.

Why?

What did it have under surveillance?

Hyde returned his attention to the men on the riverbank. The Hind was still under repair, the flying crane immobile and comic, the van anonymous. The general and Harrell and the two colonels were all—

—using binoculars now. There were powerful cameras focused upwards, too, and a big portable telescope. The fronds and dishes of aerials seemed to twitch like the noses of dogs. The scene, as the glasses slipped over it, making it jumpy like his nerves, expressed tension, expectation. Almost reluctantly, he raised his glasses and swept their focus across the empty, birdless, machineless sky; across the dulling glow of mountains.

Another high vapor trail, turning pink in the late afternoon. Delicate and out of place. Heading south towards Afghanistan or even India. A silver fleck. Probably Russian, possibly an Ilyushin; he had no idea whether civilian or military. The trail extended across the faded blue of the upper atmosphere, soporifically, confidently.

He glanced down at the valley floor. Dark figures against the salt-sand that seemed even whiter. Van, gunship, flying crane, men, radars. Tension—

—he looked up, as they still did. In time to see the silver speck turn orange and spread, the vapor trail interrupted and changed into smoke that billowed, rolled. He looked down. Hands raised, vibrant emotions of pleasure on the shadowy faces—up again. Smoke, flame, the sagging of something out of the sky, the broken vapor trail, the thin stream of smoke coming from the orange tear in the sky. A tear that moved like a sullen bird, leaving the long rip of smoke behind it. The rip slowly became a spiral as the aircraft lost height and momentum and began to whirl like a slow sycamore leaf.

He focused on the men again. They believed they had caused it. They were congratulating each other; urgent rather than tense. The van was on the move towards the flying crane. Men scattered to collect the aerials.

Up again. Searching for a few seconds then finding the ruin of the vapor trail, the spiral of descending smoke. It was coming almost straight down—*near*...

...mere thousands of feet, dropping out of the sky ...how? Nothing had been fired, no missile, there was no other aircraft up there!

Van...RPV. Not a camera...a warhead. It had stooged around up there waiting for the aircraft to pass, then homed in, directed by—

—them, down there, scurrying to get away now, happy as children knocking a crow out of a tree with catapults. The crane's rotors were turning already. The greatcoated officers were arguing near the gunship as if over the destination of a bus. Mechanics protested from atop the blunt, ugly machine. Harrell was placatory—

—up again. Coming down fast, spiraling, its smoke trail a fingerprint on the pale sky. He could hear it now. The Afghans were insecure in their excitement. To them, it did not matter who had killed the aircraft, only the effectiveness with which it had been done. Harrell and the Russians and an American RPV had killed it.

Its noise came back out of the steep-sided valley like the roar of a wounded animal. Hyde could see the broken fuselage now—Russian military flight...*military?*—with flame and smoke streaming behind it. It leveled, no more than a thousand feet up, still dropping helplessly, passing southeast, towards the lake. He swung the glasses after it as it dodged a mountainside like a toy, and disappeared.

Down again.

No time for self—

—or the Afghans.

Harrell was arguing with the general, pointing towards the flying crane which now hovered like some great black spider above the van, which was being attached by a sling to its belly. Reluctantly, almost dragged by the two KGB officers, the soldier moved towards the flying crane, which set down again, harnessed to the van as if it had trapped it. Harrell was still waving them——explosion.

He felt and heard it a moment later. Close. The splash of orange against a reflecting glacier, then the new light dulled. Harrell was ushering the flying crane away, shooing it like a chicken. Then he was berating the mechanics on the gunship. Lurching heavily, the flying crane helicopter rose into the air, dragging the van after it. It swung like a watch fob beneath a dark belly. Upwards, then leveling along the valley, heading towards the north, away from the crash site. Scuttling away guiltily.

Harrell and one of the KGB colonels remained beside the gunship, with three armed soldiers or KGB men. He couldn't distinguish uniforms any longer in the failing light. The flying crane's noise diminished, its size a speck, before it turned a bend in the river and disappeared. Harrell and the colonel continued to berate the mechanics atop the Hind. He had the illusion of hearing thin, distant, angry voices.

It couldn't fly, not now, not yet. He gripped Nur's arm, making the man wince. Hyde's teeth ground together and he felt the skin on his face tighten.

"Get them moving, Nur!" he growled. "On your feet, the bloody lot of you!" There was a sensation of huge, cold shadows and departing daylight urging him on more than any other factor. A retinal memory of the flash of light from the airliner's impact gleamed on the map that he tugged from inside his thick shirt. His finger, dirty-nailed and grubby, traced across the map's contours ... There. His finger tapped. Nur glanced at the map, then up at the landscape, and nodded. "It must have crashed in or near the lake—now, let's get on with it before they repair that fucking gunship down there!" There was a reaffirmed and temporary subordination in Nur's eyes, the respect of fear.

Hyde held the Afghan's gaze for a moment, then forced a narrow smile. As he rebuttoned his shirt after thrusting the map back against his chest, he felt drawn by the crash into an old, familiar pattern. It was a magnet, he was being reshaped like iron filings. The self-pity—he saw it only as that now—and the weariness were still controllable. What the hell was Harrell *doing*, playing footsie with the KGB and the Red Army, inside the Soviet Union?

"Come on, you buggers," he snapped, thrusting his arms through the straps of his pack and adjusting its weight across his shoulders, "get bloody moving!"

Dmitri Priabin's mood of well-being, supported by memories of the previous evening's Covent Garden performance of *Tannhäuser,* dissipated at the first chirrup from the telephone on his desk. His hand slid across that morning's *Times* to reach for the receiver. The music correspondent had been caustic about the production, but Priabin had rather enjoyed it, despite some of the shadows of painful memories evoked by the death of the heroine. The telephone call was expected, and, he suspected, unwelcome. The call had assumed an importance much like that of a patch of slippery oil, or a banana skin, on which he might at any moment set his foot, only to go tumbling down from his upright career. His mentor, Kapustin, was in trouble in Moscow, and the man was both his promoter and protector. Bad news now from Stockholm—Aubrey's people had been over there for days, goaded on by that cripple, Godwin. Would he go down with Kapustin?

An autumnal wind was pulling and tearing at the leaves of the trees along Kensington Palace Gardens. In his large, second-floor office, he coldly heard the creaking of the branches outside.

"Yes?" he snapped. He had been, he admitted, a prey to hundreds of small, nagging doubts over the past weeks. Perhaps—he hoped so, devoutly at that moment—he gave too much credence to Aubrey's efficiency. But then Kapustin, who knew Aubrey well, had warned him against the man. *A terrier,* he'd said. *A small dog, but a vicious one that hangs on to your trouser legs, whatever you do to kick it away.*

It was Stockholm on the line. "Yes, Boris—good to hear you, yes!" Would it be, though? The pleasantry with which Boris followed his greeting was hollow. "Yes, well . . . restaurants, opera, the usual bore," Priabin replied, forcing himself to laughter. "And you? The family well? Good . . . and, our business?"

"The shipment got away on Aeroflot, no problem about that."

"But—?" he asked, too quickly, aware of the reservation in his counterpart's tone.

" . . . arrests—sorry about that, but they were right on their tails—no, no one important, but with definite links to us. I'm on the first plane home, to explain, I'm afraid. The people they got shows they know the whole setup, how we've been doing it from start to finish. I'm sorry, but I think the game's up as far as using Stockholm as a staging post is concerned."

"They got that close?"

"That close. They obviously understand how the pipeline works and they probably know who the others are. Maybe even who *you've* got inside—maybe you'd better warn your man—?"

"I'll consider it." *A terrier,* Kapustin had said.

Priabin's secretary entered and placed a decoded signal on his desk, together with the transcript of the original message and that day's one-time pad. He rarely checked for mistakes. He nodded. It was from Moscow Center. He did not wish to read it, for the moment.

"Damn it," he murmured. "You're certain we can't go on using Sweden?"

"That's what I'm telling the center, anyway."

"Takes some of the heat off you, doesn't it?" he sneered.

"Maybe." There was a shrug in Boris's voice, and a knowingness. Priabin willed himself not to read his coded signal, and swiveled his leather chair with a slight, branchlike creaking so that he was staring out the window at the swaying boughs and the torn-off leaves. Earlier vandalism was compounded by the wind as leaves were scuttled across the lawns of the embassy.

"That bastard on crutches, Godwin is it? Well, he was out at the airport, pointing the finger, almost shaking his fist at the flight as it took off—"

"How far back down the pipeline do you think the British can reach?" Priabin interrupted.

"No idea. A long way, is my guess. As far as back into the factories?"

"No doubt you'll tell Kapustin that, as well!"

"Not if I don't have to. It depends how nasty he gets in his turn. I'm not carrying the slop-out pail for anyone else, Dmitri, you can be assured of that."

"No. I'm sorry, no reason why you should. But I'm going to have to know how awkward it's going to get over here, in London. The shipment you sent off was intact, though, was it?"

The branches moved hypnotically; or perhaps he was attempting to tranquilize himself by staring at them. It felt hot in the office.

"Sure. I've got the invoices here." The receiver chuckled drily in his ear like the irritating buzz of an insect. He all but wafted his hand at it. "As of now, the innards of the battlefield computer are the property of the peoples of the Soviet Union, *glasnost* be damned!" A pause, then: "Look Dmitri, they can't be that hard on either of us. We've had a good run out of this smuggling pipeline—there's an impressive list of high-tech items we've supplied over the past year ... cheer up?"

"Maybe—oh, yes, you're probably right. As long as Kapustin's reasonable in his assessment—"

"—and still has the clout to look after us?" Boris added.

Priabin whirled in his chair and snatched up the decoded signal from Moscow Center. From Kapustin, he corrected himself with an inward collapse, as if his stomach had slid into a watery pit. *Return immediately,* was all he needed to read. Yes. Get on the first flight to Moscow ... just like Boris.

"I've just been recalled," he muttered. "Like you. *For consultations in the light of today's events.*"

"Imaginative, isn't he?" Boris's voice was thin and nervy. "Just the same words, exactly. See you in the corridors of power, then—?"

"Looks like it ... OK, Boris, I'll do some checking and dam-plugging here and catch the first flight I can."

"Do you want to meet up, uh, *before*—?"

"I don't think that would be wise, do you? Who knows who might be looking?" Distance yourself, he thought, arriving at the cunning of survival circuitously and late, but with enthusiasm. Boris recognized his change of mood.

"And stuff you, too, Dmitri!"

"No, no ... Look, if we both tell the true story, we'll be bound to agree—won't we?"

"I'm not taking the shitty end of the—"

"Why should you? Our record's good, as you pointed out. Let's leave it at that, eh?"

"OK. See you outside the headmaster's study, then. And don't expect any favors. 'Bye."

His brow was prickling with perspiration and, as he put down the receiver, he realized that his palm was slightly damp. He pushed the decoded message away from him, flinging up his arms in a gesture of exasperated surrender and dismissal.

"That's that buggered, then!" he exhaled, swiveling the chair. All of Kensington, even the whole expanse towards the West End, seemed to crowd into the frame of the window. Saying goodbye, he snorted silently. *Youngest general in the KGB stumbles in cushy London posting and is never heard of again.* He rubbed at his forehead in anger and impotence. *The best, the most secure pipeline for the smuggling of Western high technology, civil and military, has just gone down the toilet! Aubrey and Godwin have just flushed it away and your career with it!*

"*Shit!*" he yelled at the top of his voice, but the expletive brought little or no relief to the tight feeling in his chest and even—for God's sake—the prickling behind his eyes! He'd be held responsible. Aubrey and Godwin had done months, maybe even years of damage! "Oh, *shit!*"

From where he had first seen the water, as he had come around a high, narrow ledge of rock, the lake had looked like the flank of a zebra, striped by white sandbars; the pieces of the aircraft's wreckage had been hardly more significant than flies on the lake's flank. Now, scuttling across the sandbars or through the shallower water, camera pressed to his face or against his chest, he thought the lake seemed immense. The darkening mountains pressed close and loomed above him. The sun streamed along the river valley that fed the lake, making the water shiver with cold, gold light.

The Afghans were looting as he took frame after frame of film, fumblingly changed rolls, adjusted the focus and the aperture to compensate for the worsening light. They hardly attended to the entirety of the wreck, but scrabbled and muttered and laughed around the single broken cigar of what remained of the fuselage, rag-picking among the recently dead. There was no one alive now. Hyde thought there hadn't been, couldn't have been judging by the wreckage, but nevertheless he had winced against the first howls, the expected cries of pain wherever Afghans encountered Russians.

Russians. Uniformed or suited, soldiers and civilians. The flight deck of what had once been an Ilyushin military transport was tilted into the lake from the lip of a gouged sandbar, and they had all been dead in there. The RPV's warhead must have driven home just behind the flight deck. The crew all burned; all identification lost like their skin and flesh. There had been nearly twenty people on board—and guns enough to please Nur and his companions. And R/Ts and radios and ammunition and money and useful documents. They picked it over like insects on a carcass.

Shot, shot, shot...a colonel's uniform identifiable against the white of the sandbar where the fuselage had come to rest, after plowing its dark furrow. Hyde still felt detached from his circumstances; he felt little or no reaction to what he photographed. There was only the wind's noise and the sound of his harsh breathing. He raised the camera, refocused, then photographed the setting: stunted, twisted trees on the lakeshore, the strips and kidneys of sandbars, the ruffled, steely water. Then he lowered the camera and watched the low, streaming sun and the slowly darkening sky. Still empty. But the gunship could appear in an instant. They'd got the flying crane and its cargo away as quickly as they could, but the gunship must come to check what had happened.

He shook his head. No time. The Afghans were dragging the bodies from the wreckage now, solicitous, as if concerned with decencies. Then they began stripping them of boots, jackets, trousers. One of the Afghans carried a stack of prepacked meals, grinning. Hyde turned away, staring at the sky and the icy water and the shadows slipping down the flanks of the mountains. He shivered at the immense isolation of the place. To feel dwarfed was his only reaction. Even the wreck was reduced to insignificance. He fiddled with the camera, looking for something he had not yet photographed, some further evidence. A CIA field officer had contributed to this, was perhaps behind it. Why? Who the hell *were* these people? Significance seemed to emanate from the corpses and the wreckage like a mist; from the one wing floating in the water like a huge surfboard, from the other buried upright in the sandbar like a great blade. It was *important* . . . at least, these people had been.

The woman's body was floating facedown in the water, her small, high-heeled shoes jutting back onto the sand. The figure was small, doll-like. As he knelt beside the legs, he realized her torn suit was expensive. A long gash in the left calf, a hole at the base of the skull where something had embedded itself then fallen loose. Up-caught dark hair, graying where not matted with blood, strayed out around the head, drifting like seaweed. He reached out hesitantly—glanced up at the sky, still empty—then gripped the woman's sleeve and turned the body over.

Immediately he recognized the face, which had not

been damaged. The mouth and nostrils were clogged with wet sand, the only distortion. The drawn-back lips grimaced, but he still recognized her. Irena Nikitina, the "Tsarina" they called her . . . Nikitin's wife.

He had consciously to still his hands, and it took him time to refocus the lens, then he was able to photograph her. Time after time. Fascinated, appalled . . . the sense of the place slowly crawling across his back like a chill, his hearing attendant beyond the Afghans' noises to the empty sky. Empty, still empty. Irena Nikitina. Military flight, coterie of officers and advisers. Direction towards Kabul. Shot down, murdered, inside Soviet Tadzhikistan. By Harrell.

His hands were shaking too much for him to continue with the camera. He let it hang by its strap from his neck. The briefcase chained to her wrist was locked. He could not—*not!*—cut off the hand to free it, and looked around with a renewed, desperate haste for a stone, a rock. He scrabbled one up and smashed at the locks, springing them.

Sodden papers, a row of pens, a novel soggy and coming to pieces, spectacle case, a picture of Nikitin, framed. Bulky, sealed envelopes. Hurriedly, he thrust them into his shirt, their chill striking his chest. Pictures of two children. A small bag of rings and a gold necklace, notepads . . .

He stood up, aware of the sky, then looked down at her again. *Her!* Here, and dead. The envelopes were icy inside his shirt and he pressed them with his hand. The lake was noticeably colder, its surface no longer gray but becoming an inky blue. The sun was retreating down the river valley like a curtain.

Was there anything else? He had to get out now. Anything else? He felt held by the wreckage, the woman's corpse. *That* woman. Christ, they'd killed *her*—!

He remembered suddenly a cartoon in the *New York Times*. It was the fixed stare, the grinlike set of the sand-filled mouth that struck the similarity. A line of Bob Dylan's had appeared beneath the caricature of her and Nikitin at breakfast, as she appeared to lecture him. *Everybody says she's the brains behind Pa*... And Harrell had conspired to murder her.

Was there anything else? he raged at himself, still mesmerized by the dead woman's face and his recognition of it. It was as if he must *do* something, find something, perform some ritual...

... flight recorders. The aircraft's black boxes! Nose and tail. The pilot must have seen something, tried to contact an air base, spoken. Get the tapes out of the boxes or just drag the boxes away—anything, just *do* it!

He turned away from her, galvanized. He raised his hand to wave, then opened his mouth to shout at the Afghans—

—and the gunship appeared as a speck against the evening sky, caught the setting sun and became golden, approaching quickly. The Afghans heard its noise and looked up, at once reaching for weapons. The Hind drove down after hesitating for a second, almost in the hover as it scanned, assessed, decided. It skimmed the lake towards them, like a black stone, churning water behind it.

"Get out! Get out! Scatter!" he heard himself shouting, beginning to run himself as he did so, stumbling over the woman's legs, righting himself, his body heaving at the first noise of the gunship's undernose machine gun, his eye catching a tic from the flare of the rocket pods under the stubby wings and then the fountains of sand and flame flung into the air. The sandbank was uncertain, like quicksand under his feet. "Get out, get out!" he still seemed to be screaming with a dry, aching throat, but the noises might have been in his head.

After the first pass, the Hind whirled like a matador to attack the scattering Afghans again. It became a still, stable gun platform in an instant as its machine gun and rocket pods opened up once more. The wreckage was a doll's house in which adults could not hide. Smoke and sand enveloped Hyde, but not before he saw Nur flung like a bundle of rags through the darkened air to lie still; he saw at least two others go down, dancing and twitching. Like a huge dog sniffing, the Hind began to move slowly over the scene, through the clouds it had created.

He was up to his knees in water. He heard someone screaming, too intensely to be helped, in too high and inhuman a way. The gunship was all but obscured. The Hind could not see him. He ran on through the icy water, stumbling on the glutinous sand beneath, then skirted another sandbank—no footprints, no footprints!— keeping to the edge of the water, his breathing labored, his heart thudding. Then a thin, gnarled branch slapped him across the cheek and he clung to it, sagging against the slim bole of a birch, silver and black. He felt the nausea well, and swallowed desperately. He wiped his eyes and shook his head.

There were only uniforms moving back at the wreckage. He fumbled the glasses from his pack and focused them. Harrell leaped into view, his lips grinning. Hyde knew the American was looking down at Irena Nikitina's body. With a conscious effort, he swept the glasses across the scene. Huddled bodies in Afghan clothing. He recognized the color of Nur's shirt and his headdress. A KGB officer kicked the body casually and turned it over with his boot. Armed soldiers checked each of the bodies. They were all dead, then . . .

He had to know what they would do. Looking about

him, he retreated further into the straggling trees. Almost immediately beyond them, the flank of a mountain rose in a nearly sheer cliff. Twisted trees and stunted bushes dotted its lower slopes, leaning drunkenly out from the rock. He began climbing, twitching at the noises behind him, audible now that the Hind's rotors had stilled. A single shot rang out.

His fingers grasped desperately, slid; his feet lost purchase, then he held on, groaning at the ache in his arms, his feet scrabbling for new holds. He found them. His body shuddered against the rock. Another shot sounded. He winced.

He reached the cover of a spreading, stunted juniper and settled on a narrow ledge behind it, concealed from sight. He had to wait until his body ceased shaking and his heartbeat settled; a long time, it seemed. The weariness choked and cramped him, dulled his mind. Angrily, he focused the glasses. A third shot cracked.

More Tajiks appeared. Prisoners. Local, Soviet Tajiks, they had to be. Harrell was waving his arms, directing the piece of theater on the sandbank. They had brought a group of Soviet Tajiks with them—! To plant ... to kill them and *arrange* their bodies. Almost reverently, someone laid on the sand beside one of the dead Tajiks a long, bulky tube ... an SA-7 surface-to-air missile launcher. Hyde's breathing was shallow as he lowered the glasses and reached for the camera. It might be too dark now, but *this* ... He had to try. This proof, this frame-up. The scenario was unmistakable: The Tajiks shot down Irena Nikitina's aircraft in the mountains, then were surprised and ambushed by a Hind gunship while looting the wreckage.

There was a Russian photographer down there now, capturing everything. Hyde aped him. Minutes passed. The sky was dark blue, and the fat three-quarter moon showed like a ghost of itself. The wind soughed, rattling and creaking the juniper bush. Snow on high mountainsides turned coldly blue.

For half an hour the set-dressing went on. Four more dead Tajiks were strewn about the wreckage, their costumes sufficiently different from those worn by the corpses of his group. Harrell seemed pleased by the effect of the scene as he watched beside a KGB colonel. The Afghan bodies were left where they had fallen. They must have been a bonus, a real *pleasure*—! The frameup proved not only that Tajiks killed Irena Nikitina but they had planned and executed it together with Afghan mujahideen from the Panjshir.

He did not know the ultimate motive, only that it was the effect they intended. *Proof* that Soviet Moslems had killed the general secretary's beloved and domineering wife. He had to live, get out, report this fraud.

It was fully dark before they left, the Hind gunship lifting quickly away from the sandbank and slipping into the river valley. Down on the sandbank, four guards had pitched a tent around a flickering fire, near the wreckage and all the bodies. Irena's had been placed in a black zip-up bag and flown off; the others remained. In another half-hour, he decided, he'd leave another half-hour.

He tried to rid his mind of the mutilations they had systematically carried out on the Russian bodies from the crashed Ilyushin. Harrell had supervised that process as coolly as every other detail of the set-dressing. Hyde tried to forget. Unsuccessfully . . . the images flitted in and out of his awareness as he flitted in and out of consciousness. Castration, penises in dead mouths, hands cut off for stealing Moslem land. These images darted like obscene, sickening fish in his mind. His head drooped.

Suddenly, eyes staring, startled and dazzled by searchlights, ears deafened by the noise of rotors and engines, he looked wildly around him—three—no, four helicopters, one a big MiL transport. They whirled, then settled one around the lake, one near the wreckage, careful not to disturb the scene, another at the mouth of the knife-cut valley where the river ran out of it. The fourth skimmed the lake, searchlight glaring down, without pause.

Troops spread out cautiously, sealing off the lake, preserving the scene for those who would come later to analyze, investigate—*believe*. Torches wobbled; voices snapped orders, called positions. The crackle of R/Ts.

He was trapped. Hidden but trapped. The valley was sealed. He was imprisoned.

His hands and arms began to quiver.

2

THE CLOSING
OF A DOOR

He was too cold to shiver. The shaking in his hands and
wrists as he held the glasses to his eyes was caused by
a need for hashish, not a reaction to the cold. Below
him, they moved like pale ghosts in the night glasses,
enlarged and bleached into negative. The water was
black, the sandbanks dirty gray, the soldiers and crash
investigators gray-white, the glaring hard lights mere
gobbets of brightness.

He could climb no farther up the cliff because there
was no shelter of trees up there. He would be like a fly
on a clean white wall. And the overhang just above the
twisted juniper behind which he squatted would be almost impossible to negotiate, even if there was cover.

And there was the lack of will to move. He was an animal skulking in a corner of a cage it had learned to accept. He lowered the glasses and rubbed his eyes. There was a vague, milky paleness in the sky now, above the reddish aura thrown off by the lamps. The investigators had arrived before midnight, flown in in a big MiL transport, all of them army or KGB. It was a convincing setting for make-believe: pieces of wreckage, the bodies, hundreds of photographs, marker tapes, diagrams and measurements, and evidence collected in black bags. It was almost as if they really intended to discover the cause of the crash. Maybe they did. They didn't have to be in the know, none of them down there now, with the exception of the colonel who was in command.

He rested his head on his arms, which hung limply across his knees. It was all but impossible to envisage escape—even moving from that concealed spot. With his eyes closed, he felt vertigo arise from his perch on that narrow ledge. His eyes snapped open, blinking. His stomach heaved, then ordinary hunger made it rumble.

The dawn seeped into the sky. Scraps of cloud to the east acquired a penciled outline of orange-pink. He took up the night glasses again, scanning the lake and its shoreline. The only exits from the place were the two narrow valleys where the river entered and left the lake. There were troops at both points. Campfires were white-gray hotspots in the lenses; the bulky, warm-clothed soldiers glowed like shadows as they moved, wavered and flickered like thin, gauzy curtains stirred by a breeze.

They had made no search of the area. They were unaware of his presence, anyone's presence. With daylight, they would find him. He couldn't squat like a statue indefinitely. When he moved, they'd see.

The realizations were like distant, dull drumbeats, hardly a threat.

The night had been endless, punctuated by the flare of cutting torches, the hammering of already damaged metal, the shouts and whispers of the crash investigators, the oily clicking of weapons, if he was awake, rather than awoken by them, for he dozed again and again, slipping into blackness as if falling drugged into dark water. Now—he was dully grateful—the mountain peaks were white-glowing-pink, golden already in the distance, and the sky was gray-blue, the small clouds whitening. The noises from below were less loud now that he could discern the size of the mountain bowl in which the lake lay, striped with sandbanks—the sand white, indented heavily with countless rows of footprints and the neat row of black bags which contained the bodies of the dead Russians. Nur and the others lay in a deliberately untidy heap, as if waiting for petrol and a spark; which might yet come, he realized.

The KGB colonel who commanded the detachment of troops emerged from the main door of the gunship, stretching, pulling on his duvet jacket. Hyde picked up the glasses—the larger daylight binoculars, the strap catching on a twig of the bush and the twig snapping loudly, terrifyingly, as he tugged it free. He adjusted the focus to observe the colonel, unshaven, bleary-eyed, impatient. Vaguely, the Russian scanned the scene then tossed his head, thrusting already chilled hands in his pockets. Hyde's own cold reasserted itself at the gesture, and he shuddered.

Soldiers moved like slow, undersea beasts. The smell of cooking wafted upward as the campfires dimmed in the daylight. As the soldiers emerged from tents and sleeping bags under camouflage netting, or drifted in from guard duty, each one sparked a tiny, electrical shock that jumped in Hyde's wrists and hands. It was only his exhaustion that prevented a surge of impatience from driving him out into the open in an attempt to escape.

The colonel, smoking a cigar, gestured broadly with his hands and arms as he discussed the wrecked main fuselage with one of the investigators. Hyde heard their laughter ...

... out of which the noise of a helicopter, banging off the cliff faces, rose and dominated. Faces turned towards the now-blue sky; binoculars were raised. The MiL–24 gunship—the same one?—hurtled like a gray stone out of the narrow valley down which Harrell's aircraft had disappeared before darkness, carrying Harrell and Irena's zipped-up corpse. It shivered the water, threw up white sand, then settled on the sandbank. The colonel ducked beneath the rotors, though it wasn't necessary, and then the door opened.

Hyde recognized Harrell, despite the KGB uniform he wore. Unsurprising. They weren't all in the know; Harrell had to be taken as Russian, then. He and the colonel shook hands, the colonel directing Harrell towards the wreckage—where Harrell, pretending it was all new to him, displayed interest, shock, with much head-shaking, and a lugubrious expression. It was a bloody *play,* an endless bloody play! Harrell was introduced to the army officers of the investigation team, then taken on a short, brisk stroll around the sandbank. More head-shaking over the black body bags ... then they came to the heap of dead Afghans and Soviet Tajiks.

Harrell ordered photographs. He turned over one of the bodies with the toe of his boot, then another. Nur's cold face flopped towards Hyde accusingly.

Why had Harrell come back? Mistrust, nerves? Hyde automatically photographed him in the even more incriminating Russian uniform. Harrell bent over Nur's body intently. Must have missed him the day before, when the light was poor. Then he stood up, quickly, angrily, and turned on his heel, arm waving, pointing at Nur, then encircling the landscape in one gesture. He'd *recognized* Nur. He *knew* him—knew he was from the Panjshir, and which groups he had worked with, and which—agents. The realization dripped slowly, as certainly as water, despite Hyde's awareness being blunted like that of a weary man on a motorway, where the distance between himself and an accident diminished in sudden, ugly, frightening jumps.

After going through Nur's pockets, his pack, Harrell stood up. He was pointing as if holding a gun at Nur's face, waving his arms, and then he was using binoculars.

Hyde raised his own binoculars and refined the focus on Harrell's face. Realization. Conviction. Collision. The accident had happened to the weary motorway driver almost without his realizing. He could hear Harrell's shouts, then Harrell and the KGB colonel hurried towards the small, scouting MiL helicopter, idle near the broken, twisted cigar-tube of the wreckage.

A magnified, distorted voice blurted from the loudspeakers mounted on the MiL. The colonel's voice. Orders. A search.

Hyde lowered the binoculars and tried to concentrate. His heart was thudding with fear, yet even so his awareness stuttered with blank moments of exhaustion and utter indifference. Men moved, shuffling into duvet jackets, picking up weapons, running. Those on the sandbank converged on the MiL while the colonel's voice ordered a search of the shoreline by the other, more scattered units. Hyde forced himself to lift the binoculars with quivering hands and scan those troops being organized by their NCOs. He began to count them, gave up, and instead concentrated only on their movement, direction, thoroughness. *A body, maybe—maybe still alive,* he heard booming back off the cliff behind him. A captain was relaying the orders by R/T to the farthest units, down at the other end of the lake, almost a mile away.

Hyde tried to take comfort from the size of the area to be searched, and the small number of men, no more than thirty. Two men were shrugging themselves into frogmen's suits on the sandbank. Oxygen tanks were carried towards them. He simply could not find their numbers and preparations ridiculous in relation to the area of the search. All he could consider was that Harrell was looking for *him* now; not just anyone, him. Nur had done that. Harrell knew Hyde led Nur's group. Simple arithmetic. There was one tiddlywink missing. Find it.

Hyde looked almost with longing at the narrow fold in the cliffs where the river entered the lake, the way he and the Afghans had come. The way out. A transport MiL sat on the shore like a huge beetle with ant-men scurrying around it before they moved off, coming along the tree-scattered shore towards his hiding place. The colonel's voice stopped bellowing and the two turbo-shafts of the reconnaissance MiL shattered the momentary silence. The rotors began to turn stiffly, then gathered speed. Hyde returned his wavering attention to the nearest troops, moving into the stunted, thin trees, scanning the ground and the rocks above them. It looked perfunctory, but it had hardly begun. Harrell would make certain, search over and over, until—

A small bird perched on a branch of the juniper bush and pecked assiduously for insects, oblivious of Hyde. He held his breath as relief shivered through him. If the bird didn't notice, didn't see him—

It flew off after hopping to another twig. It had not noticed him. He exhaled noisily, gratefully. In the sky, a griffon vulture staggered upwards in the early thermals like a scrap of vegetation dislodged from the face of the cliff. The small helicopter quivered, the sand shivering around it, beginning to cloud. Harrell and the colonel had moved away, towards the frogmen. The MiL lifted into the air and dodged sideways, banking away towards the far end of the lake. Again, his breath sighed out. The MiL slipped over stunted birch and fir, diminishing, then over the water, disturbing but not flinging into the air a small convoy of geese drifting between sandbanks.

The first bulky frogman flapped into the water, less elegant than the geese. He waded out, his frame only slowly being swallowed by the quivering gray surface. Eventually, he disappeared, a line held by two soldiers who walked along the edge of the sandbank indicating his progress, together with a faint, rippling glow from his lamp. The second frogman waddled towards the farther side of the sandbank—

Hyde jerked the glasses dizzyingly across the scene and picked up the soldiers closest to him, mere gray and padded smudges under the trees, moving beneath the branches. He could now hear their desultory voices and the instructions of their NCO. His breathing quickened. He returned the glasses to the sandbank, picking up Harrell almost at once.

He was uptight, his features clouded. He was avoiding the investigators now, who had returned to their examination of the ruined flight deck and the tail section. Only the KGB colonel, R/T against his cheek, was close to him. Harrell was leaning on a foldaway table, a map spread out, his head constantly lifting to orient him, to assess, to confirm. Harrell *believed* Hyde was out there. Somewhere. And alive.

Harrell glanced occasionally towards the heap of corpses, which had been made less untidy and like rubbish because he had had all of the bodies and their clothing and packs searched again, as if he might find some definite clue to Hyde's exact location. Harrell's attention to the bodies seemed to confirm that he was looking for someone still alive. Otherwise, Hyde would be there, with the rest of those bundles of rags.

Hyde's heart jumped. Rough laughter, close below. He lowered the glasses with exaggerated caution, looking down. Another small bird flew startled out of the juniper with a cry, as if raising some alarm. A soldier looked directly up at him—

—and saw nothing, merely shrugging, his eyes following the tiny bird. Another man moved into Hyde's line of vision, bulky as a Michelin man in his padded clothing.

Then a shot. Hyde scrabbled for the binoculars as they slipped in his damp grasp, catching them up by the strap. The men below were similarly startled. Harrell on the sandbank, a distant figure for the first time, it seemed, turned his head in quick shock towards the noise. Hyde saw a fawn-and-brown something that looked like a ball of knitting wool with its appropriate needles sticking awkwardly out slide down the cliff only hundreds of yards away. Then he realized what it was. A horned ram, legs splayed, tumbled outwards as the slope of the cliff steepened, then fell into the sand of the shore. The young soldier who had killed it seemed stunned with shock as it lay near his feet. His Kalashnikov was still aimed at it.

The soldiers moved out of the trees, pointing, laughing. The ram killer was disconcerted, afraid of the animal's corpse. Harrell returned to his map, while the colonel nodded to the voices coming over his R/T. The NCO below him lit a cigarette and pointed up the knife-thin crevice towards the juniper bush and the narrow ledge. Hyde remained motionless, only his hands and lips quivering and an icy perspiration running on his forehead and behind his ears. He smelled his clothing, felt the cramps in his crossed legs, and the sharpness of rocks through his sheepskin jacket. He could hear the corporal's voice quite distinctly. The accent might have been Ukrainian.

"Up you go, then, shithead...it's good exercise, that."

"Corp—!" the soldier whined.

"Look, the officer says check everything—so *you* check that bush up there, and that ledge." The corporal exhaled a plume of leisurely smoke which hung above his head in the windless air. "Come on, get on with it, dickhead!" He was smirking.

Reluctantly, the soldier handed his rifle to the man beside him and removed the padded jacket, then regained the weapon and slung it across his chest. Watched by smirking faces, he moved to the foot of the cliff. Other cigarettes were lit, two men sat down, backs against a thin birch. The corporal watched with idle, certain power as the soldier began climbing awkwardly up the sixty or more feet of the crevice towards Hyde.

Nikitin had been seated on the same upright chair, too fragile-seeming for his bulk, for most of the night, staring at the drawing room curtains. Now that Didenko had tugged back the heavy shot silk, Nikitin studied the whiteness of the net curtains with the same blank expression. He had crossed in front of Nikitin while doing so, but there was no registration of the fact on his strained, blind face. His whiskey glass was empty again. He had drunk continuously, monumentally. Didenko had begun by counting and only very reluctantly refilling the tumbler, then had abandoned the idea and indulged the mostly silent Nikitin. He was troubled now not by the alcohol but by Nikitin's appearance. He could not reconcile the endless, unchanging blankness with any idea he had formed of personal grief. Memories of Irena had flitted in and out of his own head like moths, smiles and a dampness in his eyes alternating—as surely should be the case. But *this* . . . ? This noiseless, voiceless, dull blank of a man.

The telephone calls, the necessary meetings, the funeral arrangements—the demands of the Politburo, army, KGB, the press, the world—had all piled up outside the door like mail through the letter box of people long on holiday or even dead. He had broached the most urgent—embarrassingly just before Didenko had slipped into a light, dozing sleep—but Nikitin had been devoid of response.

"Aleksandr . . ." he murmured after clearing his throat. A vein throbbed in Nikitin's neck and his eyes seemed to bulge like those of a toad, but there was no acknowledgment of Didenko's voice, or even of his presence. "Aleksandr—!" The head twitched. "Aleksandr, *please*—!"

Nikitin half-turned on the creaking, frail little chair and stared at Didenko as at an intruder. Then he blinked and stretched his eyes, attempting to focus them.

"*What?*" Nikitin snapped angrily. He used the tone of Didenko's ancient mother whenever she was interrupted while watching television.

"You—you . . ." Now, Nikitin was staring at him as though into a void; staring through him, rather. "We must begin to deal—deal with this."

Cold sunlight from the tall windows fell on gilded clocks; fell on dusty gilded chairs made warm with richly embroidered seats and backs. Didenko shivered. Irena was everywhere in the room.

"I'm trying to deal with it!" Nikitin snarled, his eyes red and staring, his mouth working loosely, his whole frame hunched with what seemed like threat. Then the air pressure in his frame seemed to collapse and he became loose, unaggressive, drunk. He waved one hand limply at the windows. "I'm *trying* to fucking deal with it!" he bellowed, and Didenko saw, to his embarrassment, the gleam of tears on Nikitin's cheeks. "I'm trying to deal with it." It was a sobbing noise now. Nikitin's head lolled forward onto his chest and he slumped against the tiny, creaking chair.

Quietly, Didenko got up from the sofa and lowered his long-empty glass onto a small table, cushioning its tiny impact by holding it in both hands. Then he went to the doors, opened them silently, slipped through the gap and closed them once more. He had glanced back once, as at a sleeper.

In the elegant, mirrored hall, he picked up from a Catherine the Great table the secure telephone, and dabbed out the number with an uncertain forefinger. He was breathing quickly and heavily. The telephone rang, taunting his impatience, arousing his awareness of the man he had left in the drawing room. Then the other receiver was picked up.

"Yes?" A hesitant voice—it was like a badge everyone would be wearing today, or a cold they had all caught. "Yes?"

"Yuri? Listen..."

"Pyotr, what's happening? I'm trying my best to hold the fort, but—!"

"No time for that...he's—uh, crying now." It was as if he had committed some small betrayal of confidence. "Look, you'll have to call a full meeting of the Politburo today, that's inevitable—"

"I realize that much."

"But first, our people—bring them *here*," he continued with sudden, awful inspiration.

"What? After the way you described him in the middle of the night?"

"Bring them here!" He wished for a deeper, more commanding tone. "It may be the only way—shock him out of it. I can't do anything with him, he just stares!" He swallowed, embarrassed by the alto register in his voice. "Yuri, I've *tried*. Get everyone here this morning. Eleven-thirty. Full Politburo for three this afternoon. If we can't get him out of it by then, we can expect trouble from this moment on!"

"That's the truest thing you've said so far. Is he really that bad?"

"He is. As if the Serbsky Institute had had him for a fortnight—in the bad old days, naturally." It was *no* time for joking!

"This could really encourage those reactionary bastards, if *he's* lost his grip."

The thought struck like iron on iron, loudly, for the first time. They could seize on this to make trouble, that was the problem. So easily, too.

"Very well," he announced primly, "then we'd better do what we can. If everyone's here, then he might be made to see he's got to—to be himself, despite what has happened." He paused, then asked softly: "You agree?"

"I suppose so. I'll tell *Pravda* to run the obituary and a short account, sanitized—and *Izvestia* can do the same. TV can cobble some eulogy together by tonight ... but he'll have to *say* something soon. If he wants to play grieving husband, fine—but in *public*."

"Yes, yes—! Eleven-thirty, then?"

"Very well, eleven-thirty. Goodbye."

Didenko put down the receiver as if it were heated metal. The foreign minister's gruff, blunt cynicism jarred even at the most relaxed, unpressured moments. Now it seemed defeatist. Were they lurching, as his tone seemed to suggest, like drunks towards some crisis or other because of Irena's death? Staggering out into the middle of a busy road only to collide with an oncoming truck? Surely they couldn't be, not here in Moscow? In the Moslem republics, perhaps... but here?

He stood in the hall, narrow chin cupped in his long fingers, abstracted and gloomy, until he was startled into attention by the noise of glass meeting glass in the drawing room. A drunken man pouring another drink. Aware of the time and moving as if the hall were already crowded with opponents, he hurried towards the doors of the drawing room.

She stood by the small window of the houseboat, smoking, as they carried her father's stretcher noisily along the planking of the jetty on which the houseboat had been built, towards the ambulance. Alan Aubrey's face was ashen, thinned, his nose pointed and pale as an icicle. She shuddered and wrapped her arms across her chest. Then the view was again that of the jumbled masts and rigging against the green yet somehow baked hillsides of Sausalito, dotted with bright houses. Out beyond the kelp, in the slanting sun coming across the harbor, she could make out a sea otter calmly smashing abalone shells on its stomach with a stone. She listened. Doors slammed, an engine roared and a siren recommenced, rapidly fading along the waterfront. She shivered once more. It had seemed hours—endless—while she had waited to hear the siren approaching, bending over her father's shuddering, corpulent frame and that suddenly narrower, gray face with its loose, wet mouth and noisy, desperate breathing.

She sighed out smoke, as if to drown noises from her

father she was still able to hear. The tide sloshed beneath the polished wooden floor. She turned away from the window and saw at once, as always, the litter of an unplanned, disorganized, uncoordinated life, and turned back to the dying light outside. The sea otter had lost form now, was no more than a bobbing speck. The noise of the siren had faded. The remembered noises of his struggle for breath, his gasps of pain, were tolerable.

It had been a massive heart attack. The paramedics from the expensive ambulance had been dubious, reluctant to comment. She had shaken her head when they had asked if she wanted to *travel with the old guy* ... adding, *It couldn't be long, lady—suit yourself* ... as they hurried him through the still-open door of the houseboat, wrapped in a red blanket; red and gray, wool and flesh.

Her hated, despised, beloved father, Alan. Her cheeks were wet and she could not see the otter now. The window was a fluid reddish glow. Her analyst had explained everything—naturally. *You're an achiever, a liberated woman ... you want to tidy him up, give him the same kind of purpose you have ... and yet he's achieved too* ... She hated this room, Sausalito, the hot-tubbed Jacuzzied Marin County, the glitter and insecurity of it! The sunset gleamed on the outline of a saxophone, on the reddened stave paper and the yellowish keys of the upright piano against which she was leaning. *You haven't forgiven him for his wives, his life, his not being there for a whole lot of your life* ...

Smartass, she had replied, lighting another cigarette in her prim analyst's office—it offended him, doing that. She lit another now. Her father's butts remained in the large glass ashtray with the legend KEYSTONE KORNER almost obscured by ground, dark ash. She quelled the desire to empty it; to straighten the litter of stave paper.

What she could not do, she realized, was pick up the scrawled-on stave paper lying on the floor where he must have dropped it as he clutched at his chest and fell. The rug remained thrust into a heap against the legs of the dining table. His body must have pushed it there. She could almost see his hands clutching at the fringe, convulsively tightening on it ... *If you hadn't gotten here when you did, lady, he'd be dead right now*.

She was deeply cold. Lights began to stand out on the hillsides and along the waterfront. Laughter flowed from a neighboring boat, from people she did not like and usually ignored, and now would have to inform unless she could avoid them when she left. A painter and his too-young companion. Gays on the other side of Alan's houseboat. This was foreign country, so unlike San Jose. Keystone Korner. A jazz club.

A month ago, a white French dwarf who played the piano and a black bass player had duetted a group of Alan's tunes in their second set of the evening. He'd been invited up onto the small stage to take a bow and enjoy the applause. She had not enjoyed the music but she had felt pleased for him, almost without qualification; an almost simple moment. Now, it *was* simple, stark. He was a shape on a stretcher with a gray, dying face. He was, for good now, removed from this untidy, symbolic room she hated, removed from his persistent lifestyle and the too-young third wife newly divorced, removed from everything except his rediscovered identity as her father. She furiously stubbed out the second cigarette, then wiped at her eyes and cheeks with the sleeve of her business suit and sniffed loudly; swallowed, lifted her chin as if about to face a hostile gathering, then nodded to herself.

He'd enjoyed the applause at that hot, smoky club with a quiet, modestly dignified satisfaction. The dwarf-pianist's embrace had seemed genuine, even respectful. It had been a strange moment of insight, unsettlement, which had only been erased by returning to this room with him afterwards, the evening foggy.

She ducked closer to the window, looking for the painter and his almost-hippie girlfriend. The girl was brushing long, golden hair, her back to the window, like some clichéd lithograph of a mermaid. The painter was not in sight, but she thought she could smell spicy cooking. It was clearly time to leave.

She reached the door, then the telephone rang. She stepped onto the planking of the jetty outside the door and heard the slap of the water against the wooden piles before snapping her lips tight and returning to the room.

"Yes?"

"Kathy? Kathy—thank Christ for that!"

"John? Is that you? Daddy's had a heart attack, a big one—where *are* you, for Christ's sake?"

"—ringing all over for you. I need *help!*" His voice was pitched high and she could hear his ragged breathing, as if he had been running.

"Didn't you hear me? I said, Daddy's had a heart attack. I found him on the floor—Jesus!"

"Kathy—*listen to me!*" It was the peremptoriness of desperation. Strangely, she recognized it; it was as taut and penetrating as some of the voices in her head only minutes ago.

"What is it—what's wrong?"

"Look, you have to meet me, bring a car. I have to get away from here!"

Her concern faded. "Didn't you hear me? My father's dying, for Christ's sake! Doesn't that *mean* anything to you?"

"Does it mean a whole lot to *you?*" he snapped back. His voice was at once more distant, accusative. She felt hotly angered as some trapped pocket of fresh guilt was released.

"It does!" she shouted at him. "I can't help it, but it does!"

"I'm sorry..." he murmured. "Sure I understand. Christ, I only saw Alan three days ago, no, four—"

"You called here? Without telling me?"

"Yes! He was fine." Something she recognized as fear returned to his voice. "Listen, Kathy, I'm up in the high north, near Lake Shasta—no, just listen to me, for God's sake! I'm ten miles from Red Bluff on Interstate 5, you understand? They ran me right off the highway. They tried to kill me, for Christ's sake!" He seemed exhausted, as if engaged in some painful confession.

"John, John—they've taken him to Marin County General. I have to be there now, in case..." Up in the north of the state? Why? Driven off the road? Puzzlement at once became irritation. "John, I have to go now," she warned.

The blonde from the neighboring houseboat appeared in the doorway. Her eyes were bright with good humor and something ingested. The long purple dress clung to her small, narrow figure, to her girlish breasts and hips. She enraged Kathryn for no reason that was comprehensible.

"Alan isn't here?" the blonde asked. Christ, hadn't she heard the siren? "He was coming over to dinner. Bill sent me—" Her smile was vacuous, but without malice. Her eyes *were* brightened by something she had drunk or smoked; round and slow and expressionless like her voice. "—to tell him to come on over for early drinks, or something. But, he isn't here." She seemed childishly disappointed.

"He's been taken to the hospital. A cardiac arrest." Had his heart stopped by now, already, before she could—? She must hurry. She looked at the girl and at the receiver with her hot, damp hand clamped over John's desperation. "Didn't you hear the ambulance?" Her voice was calmly acidic.

"Funny, I said to Bill I thought . . ." The girl appeared to think, frowning, looking down at where her sandaled foot stirred near the crumpled rug. Then she looked up again. "Gee, I'm sorry. Alan, he was sweet, y'know." Past tense. Cardiac arrest. Stop. "I gotta tell Bill right away." The purple dress removed itself from the doorway.

Sweet . . . ?

Her cheeks were wet and it was difficult to see clearly. She could hear someone choking, sobbing. That brainless girl! That *bimbo!* Guilt possessed her; she was shaking violently. John's voice called her distantly, a highpitched, insistent chirruping like that of some bird. Her father, his pointed nose disappearing, she remembered now, under the semiopaqueness of the oxygen mask they had slipped over his features as the gurney passed the window. Oh Christ, she thought, desperate and guilty. Oh-sweet-Jesus . . .

She pressed the receiver to her wet face. "John, I have to go. Call me at the hospital, but right now I *have* to go!"

The ridiculousness of it, she thought, the bedside reconciliation, the erasing of past years, the wiping the slate. But she had to do it; and he had to be alive still—now, this moment.

"Kathy, for God's sake, you crazy bitch, they're trying to kill me! They're going to kill me because I know how they did it—what went wrong, how the crash happened. I know, *damn* you. Get me out of here!" It was a wail rather than a demand. More quietly and quickly, he went on: "I can't rent a car here, it could be traced. I can't stay here, either. You have to come tonight—are you listening? You could be here by morning. There's a place you could—"

"Not now, John!" she screamed at him.

There was a strident sense of enclosure about the room, of being trapped, which his circumstances only added to. She was menaced more strongly by guilt than he seemed threatened by—whatever it was. Take her car, drive two hundred miles? Lake Shasta? She could not remember why he was there or recall the precise nature of his—his growing *obsession* of recent months. His words over the telephone from God-knew-where were no more real than those whispered messages passed around a circle of children only to end up garbled, nonsensical. She understood that he meant what he said, that his fear and desperation were real to him. But not to her. It wasn't *his* danger that bullied her; thrust her into motion and evoked this helpless, guilty pity.

"Kathy—!"

"Call Marin County General, John—*please!*" she wailed. The sunset struck highlights from the saxophone; the bright, scattered cushions seemed to gleam in the room's dusk. The place had shrugged off the contempt she held for it. "John—I'll be there in ten, fifteen minutes—call me there!"

She thrust the receiver down on some cry of his, shuddering. She snatched up her purse and hurried to the open door, towards her car. She knew she should have gone with him, in the ambulance. Should have—

The Russian soldier was wedged into the crevice now and Hyde couldn't see him—not without leaning into the branches of the juniper and making a noise, becoming a visible shadow to the others beneath the trees. Cigarette smoke hung, then rose slowly, fragrantly. The corporal's bulk he could pick out still, despite his having moved to lean against a narrow, slanting birch. And the shapes of three other soldiers . . . and the scrapings and the loosened stones rattling and even the labored breathing of the climber. Hyde saw a bobbing head in a fur cap, a pair of broad, heaving shoulders, white, ungloved hands scrabbling, clinging.

He had to remind himself to breathe. His chest felt sunken, narrow; it seemed to whistle like a windy street corner. His hands clasped each other as if for warmth— at least that way they were still. Gripping the pistol tightly—the old Heckler & Koch with the personally fitting grip, knowing it was useless as a weapon but needing to hold it, squeeze its warm metal and plastic— he sensed his eyes widening, as if he were paralyzed, rabbitlike, in the middle of a road at night. The soldier was cursing audibly now, though his voice was little more than a whisper intended to remain secret from his NCO below. There were shouts, desultory and smug, and the climber answered them—occasionally shouting down, more often in his grunting, labored whisper— with a stream of obscenities and blasphemies. The language had no effect in reducing Hyde's sense of danger. He simply waited, tense as an overwound spring, a quiver running through his shoulders and cheeks, for the blunt young face he had glimpsed to appear through the leaves and branches of the juniper.

Each noise wound the spring tighter, and tightened, too, the shrinking thong that seemed wrapped around his forehead. Sweat seeped from beneath his arms, dampened his forehead, making it prickle. But he could not move.

The corporal's yell made him shiver, his heart lurching.

"You got your glasses with you?" Something clinked appropriately against rock.

"Yes Corp," the soldier shouted back—*his voice so close!*—then muttered, "Yes, fucking Corp, yes you fat fucking bastard, yes..."

Above the stream of expletives, Hyde heard the NCO's voice.

"Then have a good look round before you climb back down, son!"

"Yes, Corp...." Then the voice continued in its nearing, maddening grunt: "Yes-fucking-Corp, anything-you-say-fucking-Corp..." On and on. The rustle of leaves, the snapping of a twig. Hyde could not catch his breath.

From below, someone he could not see asked: "Who's that KGB officer giving the orders, Corp?"

"Who know, son—who knows?" The climbing soldier was forcing himself through the last of the branches that overhung the crevice, to reach the ledge. Hyde stared as if mesmerized at the spot on the narrow ledge where his hand would appear. "Some Moscow creep—no need to worry as long as you keep in with me," the NCO continued. "Some asshole armed with a clipboard, nothing more."

A white, gripping hand appeared, the right one. Broken, dirty fingernails. Then the left hand shot into view, followed by an explosion of breath and cursing, then the broad, blunt-featured face still in its twenties thrust through branches and stared at Hyde... and at his pistol. Sunlight gleamed off weapons below; there was a haze of cigarette smoke.

Hyde heard the drone of the small MiL, returning up the lakeshore, as they stared at one another. The soldier's mouth became a surprised then ready-to-shout round black hole, his tongue pink as a dog's. Hyde felt restraints, as if he was bound with cords or bandages—

—then he leaned forward and gripped a wrist with his left hand and brought the barrel of the gun down across the forehead and nose of the wide-mouthed soldier. Bone cracked, blood splashed on Hyde's wrist and sleeve. His arm was dragged almost into dislocation at the shoulder and he winced audibly. Stones rolled and bounced away from the soldier's scrabbling-then-still boots. He held on, supporting the man's unconscious weight. The pebbles and debris ceased rattling. He could hear the grinding of his teeth against the tearing ache in his arm, louder than the rotors of the small, approaching helicopter. He thrust the pistol into his shirt. The soldier's face, lolling up at him, was smeared with blood from his temple and broken nose. Hyde shifted his weight and felt himself teeter forward, beginning to overbalance like a round-based doll without any ability to bob upright again. He grabbed the man's collar with his right hand, holding on, feeling the stitching strain.

"Where are you, fuckface?" the NCO shouted up from the edge of the trees, his back still comfortable against the thin birch, cigarette in his hand. Hyde looked for the soldier's trunk, then his legs, which were concealed by the juniper. The noise of the MiL was louder now than his grinding teeth. He and the soldier were hidden. "What are you playing at?" The NCO was vaguely curious. "Where are you?"

"Twisted my bloody ankle!" Hyde cried in Russian, filling his mouth with saliva, yelling out the muffled words, comic, pathetic, silly. "Slipped—hurt myself, Corp—oooww!" Someone below laughed unsympathetically, acceptingly.

"You clown. Never mind your ankle—what's happened to your voice?"

He looked at the unconscious, bloody face and strained against the tearing pain in his arms.

"Sat down on my goddamn balls!" he roared. General laughter followed at once. The NCO was smirking, his features clear through the tangle of the juniper. The soldier's body slipped.

"What a fucking racket! Can you see anything up there?"

"—nothing..." He groaned convincingly, using the pain and effort of clinging to the unconscious man. "No one here."

The MiL made the water of the lake ripple as it passed over the frogmen, returning to the sandbank as if being slowly reeled in on their safety lines. Then the helicopter nipped sideways and headed away from the cliff. His hands were becoming numb, his arms like rods of pain. The NCO was standing in the sunlight now, hands on his hips, squinting upwards at the spreading, untidy, obscuring mass of the juniper. The sun struck gold from the leaves of the birches.

"Are you dogging it up there, son? 'Cause if you are..."

"No, honest, Corp!" he shouted back, groaning in punctuation, his voice distorted with his own, unpretended pain. Sweat filled his eyes, made his body cold. "I can't walk!"

"I think I'd better come up myself and have a look. I'll give you first aid or a swift kick in the ass!" Laughter and indifference.

Christ...

The soldier's eyes opened, wide, staring, slowly comprehending, the lips beginning to work, the brain understanding, the eyes narrowing, as if prompted by the first scrabbling of boots in the crevice below them.

Hyde released the collar and moved his right hand to

his belt. Scrabble of boots, scratch of an R/T in the still morning, a shout of encouragement to the NCO, snickering laughter, the retreating helicopter drone, the soldier's lips opening, perhaps to yell in pain as his awakening brain recognized the shattered nose for what it was—

—the blade of the knife flashed quickly and then was red as Hyde cut the jugular and blood splashed on his hands and into his eyes. Breath sighed out through the severed windpipe like a weary accusation. The body became heavier. He gripped the front of the uniform with the hand that still held the dull, red knife, and blinked away the blood. He watched as it drenched the front of the uniform, dyeing his gripping hand evenly red.

The R/T crackled from below. The climbing noises had ceased. It seemed important that he listen, too.

"No, sir, not hanging about—checking out these trees, sir, and the cliff...*sir!*" Yes, sir, right away, sir—doing what I thought...*yes, sir!* The NCO cursed indecipherably, then shouted, descending noises accompanying his voice: "Right, you bastards—on your feet! The officer thinks you're slacking—so do I!" Grumbling protest, the clinking of metal. "You up there—Kissin!"

"Yes, Corp," Hyde muttered through clenched teeth, his stomach churning at the smell of blood.

"You'd better catch up with us in half an hour, or I shall want to see your medical certificate!"

"Yes, Corp."

"Right, you cunts, fan out, get moving!"

Hyde was aware of himself only as queasiness and pain. He was becoming dizzy, his hands without feeling, his arms racked. The first soldier moved out from beneath the pines and birches, along the shoreline. A second one stopped to poke into a gnarled bush with his

Kalashnikov. The corporal, equanimity restored, sauntered behind them. Groaning, with a vast, slow, inadequate-seeming effort, Hyde dragged the soldier's dead face level with his own, and slid the dead buttocks onto the ledge...laid the body down slowly, shaken with exhaustion. He wiped his hands nauseously on his sheepskin jacket and leaned back against the cliff, his eyes blinded by salty sweat. He hugged his arms across his stomach. He could not stop shaking.

Gradually, the nausea subsided. He swallowed sharp bile at the back of his throat, then wiped at his eyes, clearing them eventually. He ignored the body. And waited...

The uniform was bloodstained. It would have to do. He shuddered at the idea of its wetness against his skin. He would keep the clothes he was wearing, for later. Films and envelope. Fur cap, trousers, jacket. Boots! He'd leave the body on the ledge, wedged against the juniper's roots.

It would take him ten days to reach Kabul, once he got away from the lake, even if he could manage to keep going, keep out of their hands.

And he couldn't even bring himself to undress the body and change his clothing!

The shaking slowly subsided. Eventually, he could hold the binoculars steady. Harrell and the KGB colonel were drinking something from large mugs, standing beside the map spread out like a cloth on the folding table. Harrell in closeup. Harrell trying to kill him, looking for him now. Harrell. Once, he'd almost liked the man. Now, he hated him. Harrell, having killed Irena Nikitina, wanted to kill him.

Finally, he started to undo the buttons on the body's uniform. If he could steal supplies without being seen, good. If not, then he'd find help over the border, once he'd changed back into Afghan clothing. He heaved and tugged the dead, heavy arms out of the sleeves of the jacket. He'd eat when he could, sleep when he must. Crouching over the body, he pulled off the boots. Not too small, big if anything. Then the trousers. He looked in Harrell's direction often, to remind himself, to make survival his only imperative.

3

PRODIGAL SONS AND OTHERS

Early November

Aubrey's brother's death was a strange, ugly little cloud sitting on his pleasure's horizon. It troubled him with his own mortality, with a sense of time and distance he had done nothing to repair—a kind of guilt—but most vividly it evoked irritation at its inappropriateness. Just *now*—! Two days after he had first occupied this spacious room in the Cabinet Office, mere hours after the last of his secure telephones had been installed, he must fly off to San Francisco or somewhere equally exotic and unreal to attend Alan's funeral!

He lowered his gaze from the ceiling rose while keeping his fingers linked behind his neck and his body slumped back in his leather chair, and frowned at the monarch's photograph on the wall and inwardly at his own . . . well, cheap selfishness, he supposed. Yet somehow it was that aloof, distant, grieving woman—Alan's daughter—who had made him selfish in the first place. Her—what? Detachment? Being somehow possessive with her guilt, as if it was newly discovered and therefore precious, and demonstrably not caring whether he attended the obsequies or not. Indeed, telling him his brother had hardly inquired after him of late, while suggesting he should have known, perhaps by telepathy, that Alan was dying. Aubrey sighed. Had Alan's last hours had that preternatural brightness about the eyes, that transparency of skin, they had both witnessed in their mother when she died? His eyes prickled mildly.

But, he would go . . . must go. He and Alan's three wives would attend, and perhaps some of the black men he had played music with. And that strange, terse daughter of his, whose personality seemed to squeak in protest at the slightest contact, like something stretched too tight over an unstable bulk. A rope on a badly loaded truck.

He looked across the room at his small suitcase and the smaller locked briefcase. Then he glanced at his watch. The car would be brought around to take him to Heathrow in ten minutes. He and his shadow . . . which evoked unwanted thoughts of Patrick Hyde, now dead. He suddenly became impatient for the car. His imagination seemed a minefield of small, explosive guilts this morning; Patrick's meaningless, futile demise the largest of those detonations. His group wiped out in Soviet Tadzhikistan. His body unrecovered. At the bottom of the lake where the others had been killed by a Soviet gunship, presumably. He sighed more loudly, as if blowing to dispel smoke. If he was still alive, he was sought for interrogation by the CIA as well as SIS. Privately, Orrell and even Peter Shelley hoped he was dead. They needed *no* links, however, strained or remote, between the service and Irena Nikitina's death. Officially, Hyde must have left the group of mujahideen to their own devices. He had not been, *could not* have been, involved in looting the Soviet general secretary's wife's body!

The truth was, no one wanted him to be alive, or his body found.

Thankfully, Aubrey's intercom buzzed and his new secretary announced Godwin. He sat up, adjusted his waistcoat and rubbed his eyes quickly. His fingertips were dry but the sense of prickling remained around his lower eyelids. Weak sunlight slanted across the room, highlighting the maze of the old carpet. And yet Tony Godwin was another reminder of his past! He sniffed. Patrick was dead, probably before the plane crash.

Godwin's plump, ruddy features, still red-nosed from the cold in Whitehall, appeared around the door. He shuffled in on two sticks—sticks, not crutches now, but he would improve no further—moving with a slow, heavy weight that swung loosely, distressingly. Aubrey stood up, took the hand offered the moment one stick tapped against his desk, and motioned Godwin to sit. He collapsed sacklike into the chair, breathing heavily, his eyes accommodated to his disability. His glance was eager and satisfied. After all, he had thwarted Priabin in the Stockholm business. He was rising again in the service, after a long decline.

Aubrey glanced at his watch.

"I haven't long, Tony—is this important?"

"Sorry to hear about your brother, sir—well, yes, it might be important. About the pipeline we closed down, to Stockholm, onward to Moscow." There was an undisguised, ingenuous smile of lingering satisfaction, which caused Aubrey to smile, too, warmed as he was by Godwin's presence and his reassignment to the JIC Office with special responsibility for investigating Soviet high-tech smuggling. In that, Godwin had found an area of expertise and tenacity which made him necessary, elite and scarce within the service. In a word, modern. The knowledge of his value was a source of permanent satisfaction to Godwin.

"Yes, Tony?"

"I need to go to the States, sir—for at least a week, probably two. To liaise with the FBI and NSA people working alongside our efforts." Aubrey was already nodding as Godwin shifted heavily in his chair. "There were sixty to seventy subcontractors involved with that battlefield computer Priabin managed to get out. Even if we take the other recent items they've either got hold of or gone after, there are still more than a dozen in common. I need to be on the spot, sir, if I'm going to find the UK length of pipe the Russians have been using.

"Of course. When?"

"ASAP, sir."

"Then go ahead. Tell Gwen to type up the proper authorization. But tell me, Tony, you don't think we're just providing an overnight stay, a sort of B&B for this smuggling?"

Godwin shook his head firmly. Thin, fair hair fell across his frowning brow. "Definitely not. There are producers here, I'm sure. One gets glimpses of things but nothing definite. It's not just consignees, a change of plane, the use of a port. It's more than that. Some Ferranti and Plessey stuff has turned up in Moscow— but not directly from them... like the battlefield computer the Americans lost. No prime contractor—where we've concentrated investigations—has been naughty."

Aubrey held up his hand, forcing himself to smile. Godwin could be—well, obsessive, encyclopedic, even something of a bore, on this subject.

"I see," he murmured, very obviously consulting his watch.

"Sir, if you could persuade—order?—MoD to be a little more helpful?" Godwin pressed, leaning forward in what might have appeared to a stranger to be threatening. "They keep putting us off with murmurings of entrepreneurs and quick-buck merchants—Yuppie treason, someone called it. But it's not just smart, greedy people selling something they're personally working on. It goes deeper. It's better organized."

"Yes, Priabin is a very clever young man." Godwin snorted angrily and Aubrey frowned.

"And MoD and the DS and a dozen other groups take it no more seriously than you do, sir!"

"Tony—" he warned, abashed.

"Sorry, sir." Godwin was unrepentant.

"Very well," Aubrey accepted ungraciously. The lack of cooperation with Godwin, the usual pigeonhole secrecy of English organizations, he admitted, almost shamefacedly, was at this moment no bad thing. Godwin had become a zealot, a firebrand. And, just now, precisely now—while the paint of his new gloss was barely dry and certainly not hardened—Kenneth Aubrey had no wish to rock the boat. "Very well, Tony. Hare off to the States and see what you can come up with. When we *both* get back, this—" He glanced at his *IN* tray. Godwin's full report on the Stockholm affair and its whole background lay in it, unread.

Godwin had noticed its pristine, undisturbed presence, too.

"A priority, as soon as I'm back," Aubrey soothed. Back from my brother's funeral, he silently added, then thought of Hyde, too, but only for an instant. The present, as it had done insistently since he had moved into this office, immediately crowded into the gaps left inside him by those deaths. The present in the form of Godwin's affairs, his new stewardship of intelligence, with its power, respect, honors—all of this barged in and crowded out his private self.

The intercom buzzed. "Yes, Gwen. Thank you, I'm ready to leave." He stood up.

Godwin lurched himself to comfort on his sticks. His movement passed like a cloud across Aubrey's face. Then Aubrey composed his features, took Godwin's hand awkwardly and began to usher him from the office. Power, respect, honors—a *place* of his own, it all insisted on flushing him with contentment. Perhaps Godwin saw his contented excitement as some kind of supercilious complacency, because he turned at the door and said: "Pity we can't both go to James Bondi's funeral, sir." And stared levelly, with no hint of embarrassment, into Aubrey's face.

"Ah, yes," Aubrey murmured. "Things are hotting up in the Moslem republics. We could have trusted *his* reports if no one else's." Godwin's eyes burned. "I've just received a digest of material on Tadzhikistan. Bombings in Dushanbe, Islamic fundamentalists speaking openly. Nikitin has his hands full there, I think."

They passed Gwen, sedately large, neatly attractive in a striped blouse. She offered a quick smile, full-lipped. Aubrey sensed himself pushing Godwin towards the outer door and removed the pressure of his hand from Godwin's back. At once, Godwin turned on him.

"You don't really think he was *there*, do you?"

"Um—you mean—?"

"When they looted that plane?"

"No, of course not."

"Pity. It's Century House's current witticism—old Hyde, tearing off Irena Nikitina's clothes after she was dead!" There was a moment of restraint, then Godwin added in a hardly modified voice: "Still, we shall never know, sir, shall we? The poor Australian sod's dead, after all." Godwin turned at the door to stare almost helplessly at Aubrey. His gaze was doglike, rather lost, but unwavering. "Shame . . ." he added. Aubrey looked beyond Godwin's overmuscled shoulders along the not yet familiar corridor towards the baize-covered door through to Number Ten. When he looked back at Godwin, his gaze seemed to have become accusatory.

"Thank you, Tony." He held out his hand once more and Godwin took it firmly; any disappointment he felt had vanished.

"I'll make arrangements, then—sir. Have a—well, a good flight, anyway."

"Yes."

He watched Godwin collect his overcoat and shrug himself into it, then stump off towards the doors leading onto Whitehall.

"Yes, yes!" Aubrey snapped impatiently at the hurrying, mother-hen look on his secretary's broad features.

". . . reached the Panjshir after a bloody week of it . . ." At the back of Julian Gaines's imagination there had been a kind of awe which had succeeded the shock and urgency he had experienced in the first minutes after Hyde's arrival. It *was* Hyde, alive . . . almost incredible. But awe had quickly given way to secretive nerves and a wrinkling of his nose against the vile smell of the man. Gradually, during his seemingly endless narrative, Hyde had turned into little more than his red eyes, his beard, his matted hair, his filthy clothing, his ashen, deadlike skin beneath hair and grime. His odor filled Gaines's office as it looked out over Kabul towards the snow-peaked mountains to the east.

Hyde scratched himself infectiously, or rubbed his arms and chest repeatedly, something he had begun doing when he reached a description of putting on the dead Russian soldier's blood-soaked uniform. He rubbed as if he were cold, but far harder and more obsessively. It unnerved Gaines, as other considerations did. The man was believed dead, and luckily so. It had been his group who had been massacred while looting the aircraft carrying Nikitin's wife. No one, not in London or indeed Langley, wanted Hyde to be found. Certainly not alive.

"... rested—oh, a day ... came on, then." There was a casual intensity, a monotonous darkness about Hyde's story and his expressionless tone. *Supped full of horrors,* Gaines thought unbidden, but distancing himself from the man on the other side of his desk, nevertheless.

Hyde looked haunted, exhausted—but still driven, presumably because of the stained, grubby linen package he clutched in his dirty, scabbed hands with their black fingernails. It contained undeveloped film and sealed envelopes. Gaines had quashed any speculative interest in himself. It would be best—*really* for the best—if he remained distanced from that grubby package. He sensed its explosive capacity, even from the tight little hints Hyde had let fall.

"... I'm here ..." Hyde simply ceased speaking and slumped farther forward on his chair, staring blankly at the edge of Gaines's desk. Gaines's eyes flitted towards the windows and the cold sunlight across the mountains and the city being rebuilt. And a sky clean of transports and Russian gunships. Then Hyde recalled his concentration, sighing: "This goes to London. To Aubrey." Hyde seemed almost to snarl the name.

"Ah, but Aubrey's now chairman of JIC, Hyde. Not his responsibility, not directly, at least." Gaines cleared his throat. "Not London's really, you see. More Langley's concern." He reached quickly for the telephone. Routine, shuffling-off, putting-in-motion...things he could thankfully do; had been instructed so to do.

The dirt and grime of Hyde's hand was more electric and shocking than the fierceness of his grip. He could smell the man's breath, a wave of unwashed clothing, feel the dig of his filthy fingernails in his wrist. Hyde was shaking his head, wet-mouthed, red-eyed.

"London," he croaked. "*Aubrey.*"

Gaines let the telephone drop back onto its rest. Hyde let go of his hand. He looked at it, as if infected by the dirt.

"I can't do that, Hyde. You must know that, see it from my point—"

"London. Cunt. London."

Gaines leaned forward and snapped: "Look, Hyde, even you must realize how important your—survival is? It's ten days since the—accident. You were *there*. You have material found there. You were almost an eye-witness. Langley will demand to talk to you, to see what you've brought out."

The shaking of Hyde's head became hypnotic, then irresistible, and Gaines faltered.

"*No* CIA. Just Aubrey. Understand, prick? It goes to London, EYES-bloody-ONLY Kenneth-bloody-Aubrey! Have you got it? Understand?"

"Look, do you know what it is? How important it is?"

"Important. Yes, I know."

"Then tell me what you saw!" Gaines shouted, feeling his cheeks become hot, his collar tighter. His slim hand made a fist on the desk but did not move. "This isn't a debriefing, it's your holiday home movie, for heaven's sake! Get to the *intelligence* content of your story, *please!*" His sense of the man waiting in the adjoining office increased. Distancing himself might be wiser, but playing only a walk-on in this would not be a clever career move. He should get Hyde to talk to him before he called in—

"I'm not telling you. I want the organ grinder, not his fucking monkey."

"Hyde, you are bloody impossible! We're supposed to be on the same side! Haven't gone a little too native, have you?" He nodded at Hyde's Afghan costume.

Hyde cracked a laugh, dry-throated, tossing his head.

"Don't be a jackass, Gaines. You've been here five minutes, you know fuck all. I *know* Langley runs the show out here. We both work for *them*. Just this time, I'm doing a foreigner. Understand? Tarmac your drive while I'm not on shift at the Fire Station. Got it? Just get through to Aubrey. Now. Get him out here or get me back there. I don't mind which. Just do it."

"Are you refusing to debrief me, Hyde?"

"No."

"Then begin, if you please."

"Now I'm refusing. Now you've asked me."

Gaines threw his hands in the air. Sunlight moved across Hyde's face but his skin took no color or warmth from it. Gaines felt nervousness become paramount. Thank God Hyde had surrendered the pistol to embassy security. He looked quite capable of using it, now or in a few moments.

Get rid of him, Gaines told himself. At this rate, he could only go on looking more and more foolish and inadequate; as well, he might be overheard being at more and more of a loss. He pressed his intercom button, leaned forward and simply said: "Very well!"

Hyde's hand had twitched at his belt and found nothing. His head snapped around towards the door from the next office, which now opened. Gaines saw Harrell's neatly suited, bulky figure in the doorway with unalloyed relief. Until Hyde, seeing him too, turned back to Gaines with an animal snarl on his face, his chair tipping backwards, his whole body crouched as if to spring or flee. There were two others with Harrell. They crowded into Gaines's office immediately behind him, both of them heavily built. They were all three armed, but there were no weapons in evidence.

Harrell grinned at Hyde. There was a bulk of knowledge, anticipation and anger between them that nonplussed Gaines. Hyde stood rigid, still in his crouch.

"Hi, Patrick—long time no see, huh?" Harrell said.

Hyde's small frame shivered. All three Americans were only feet from him, their bulk diminishing him further. Then, inappropriately, Hyde cracked that same dry laugh, shaking his head.

"Thanks, Gaines. You were a lot of help. I'll remember that," Harrell said mockingly, indifferently. His eyes were eager with a kind of desire every time he looked at Hyde. The enmity chilled Gaines. "Well, Patrick, how's tricks? Where did *you* spring from?" Harrell continued. Hyde was leaning forward as if delivering some urgent, silent message or song. The veins stood proud in his neck. He was sweating; and smelling. "I think, old buddy, you have some kind of story to tell, huh?" Harrell was taunting him. And—well, reveling in what now seemed suddenly more like Hyde's capture than the first moments of his debriefing. If he could have ignored Harrell's *pleasure*, Gaines might have believed more easily that Hyde had been somehow involved in what had happened in Tadzhikistan; been one of the looters; gone native as it were...but that fierce delight on Harrell's face!

"Fuck off, Harrell," Hyde muttered.

Harrell clicked his tongue. "Come on, old buddy—let's go talk some back at my place—huh?"

Harrell's smile, too, seemed inappropriate.

The cypress trees and the more distant cedars were like severely regular stains on the hard blue sky. The lawns were lividly green, as if dyed or diseased. Headstones and more ornate memorial statuary were all, without exception, of glaringly white marble. Winged angels, pinnacles and towers, scale-model mausoleums mostly in the Greek fashion; the whole place was like the wreck of some vast, old Florentine palazzo. The flowers decorating the graves were splashes of misplaced tropical color, and the voice of the minister was little more to Aubrey than the buzzing of an insect. The dark trees, he decided as he attempted to escape from his jet-lagged thoughts, were like shadows created by a detached retina.

I'm simply tired, he told himself. This appalling jet lag won't release me. Like the shade of Patrick. Not while I'm here, witnessing my brother put in the functional ground.

The dark suit he was wearing was too hot, too wintry in the strange Californian beginning of November. The fog had rolled away during the morning. He felt dizzy, almost damaged by the heat of noon. Even the breeze seemed hot, though it came from that hazy, brilliant blue pencil line along the horizon that marked the Pacific. His bare head seemed to sound like a drum, and he longed for the air conditioning of the chapel, its chilly, artificial cold, so daunting when he had first entered the low, Spanish-style whitewashed building.

He was unreasonably and inexplicably moved by the occasion, the funeral of a brother for whom he had learned not to care and of whom he knew even less. Moreover, a brother he had not seen for fifteen years. Past tense easily acquired. More easily than for Patrick Hyde. Godwin's face appeared as if summoned from the back of his mind; accusing him. His left hand moved feebly at his side, as if fending off the unexpected sorrow and unlooked-for guilt. In his strange, tired state, he could quite easily feel guilty even on Alan's behalf. His hand continued to move, as if now warding off the entire scene of unfamiliar primary colors and hard light.

The coffin, silver-handled and of rich, dark wood, struggled into the grave in little jerks as the cords were paid out. The hole seemed inky in the midday light. His niece, Kathryn, stood beside him, dry-eyed but with facial muscles tautened by severe restraint. Her mother, face tautened by surgery and masked by a heavy veil, was on Kathryn's other side. Both members of *his* family? What was the phrase they used . . . ? Immediate family, that was it. Opposite him, across the grave, was the young widow, to whom he was also in some way distantly related. She was the third woman his brother had married. The middle wife was dead or out of the country, he was not certain which. A blond young man, too muscular to appear quite at ease in his lightweight suit, held the young widow's elbow as she sniffed audibly. Aubrey had gathered from Kathryn that she and Alan had been separated recently.

This whole bizarre scene served only to prove that his brother was a complete stranger. A *jazz* musician, three times married and living in some quaint artists' colony once a fishing village and called Sausalito, in a wooden bungalow on the end of a short jetty that Americans called a houseboat! Wildly improbable. As improbable as the idea that he was standing beside a thirty-two-year-old woman to whom he was related by blood and nothing else and whom he had met the previous evening for perhaps only the third or fourth time in his life.

Earth rattled on the coffin lid. Aubrey was drawn reluctantly into the moment, forgetting even Hyde. Kathryn, moving forward, plucked up a handful of dry soil and cast it loudly. She was a tall young woman, profile sharp and even arrogant, made-up cheeks still pale, eyes a dark, disturbing blue, hair black. He saw no family resemblances, nothing that accounted for her striking appearance. The young widow shuddered, glanced down, was led away sobbing by the muscular young man.

Aubrey stumbled forward and felt Kathryn's firm grip on his elbow. He did not resent its implication of infirmity. He looked at her. His own eyes, dyed darker, stared back at him. There was some familiarity, after all. Her mouth appeared relaxed now, though strangely inexpressive; as if she had read only part of a textbook on the art of smiling. He nodded to her, hastily scuffed up earth and dropped it rattling on the coffin. Then other strangers moved forward.

Business associates . . . not of Alan's, of course, but those of his daughter. There were a handful of black men around the graveside, their sadness real. Aubrey assumed they were fellow musicians. Shapiro, sweating profusely, dropped earth; Kathryn's employer, president of Shapiro Electrics. Paulus Malan next . . .

. . . then the silent, solemnly assured black men and others. Aubrey turned away, Malan's authority most vividly impressed on him. He possessed an arrogance greater than that of a man merely born in South Africa and white, the authority of the heir to Malan-Labus-chagne Consolidated. Malan dealt on behalf of his country with the Narodny Bank in Moscow, talking the price of gold and diamonds; fixing them. In contrast with the day's garish light, Aubrey saw monochrome film of Malan in Moscow—SIS film; Malan at the Bolshoi, Malan in Red Square, Malan on his way in a Chaika limousine to fix things, to arrange the price of things.

It was uncharacteristically polite of Malan to be there, presumably because Shapiro was there—except that Malan's proprietorial inspection of Kathryn during the service and around the grave suggested she was the reason for his attendance. Neither his role as negotiator between his country's mineral wealth and that of the Soviet Union nor his interest in Kathryn was Aubrey's concern.

The circle of people around the grave wavered and broke into fragments. Kathryn seemed tight, straightened by grief, but Aubrey suspected muddy emotions beneath the surface. He heard Malan exchanging platitudes with her just as he did likewise with Kathryn's mother. His heavy black shoes crunched on the weedless gravel. Heavier shovelfuls of earth thudded like the noises of a far-off storm. Aubrey shivered, though the sky was still enameled, cloudless. Then Malan turned back from Kathryn's side, leaving her to Shapiro, moving towards Aubrey lightly and certainly, more like an athlete than a businessman. What was he now? Forty-five? Certainly no older. Aubrey embraced assessment as a palliative.

What was it about him? Was it the *certainty* with which he occupied space? He made both companions and surroundings seem less substantial, more shadowy.

"Sir Kenneth Aubrey," Malan murmured, smiling, his accent evident but smoothed, just as his father Jeppe Malan's had always been. Jeppe Malan, from forty-five years before. Did this man know Aubrey and his father were known to one another? Aubrey took the offered hand, which was firm and cool, relaxed in its grip. "I'm sorry," Malan continued, "that we meet at last on—this occasion."

"Ah, yes—your father . . . spoke of me, of course."

"Naturally. Especially during your—recent problems. He never believed it of you, not for a minute."

"Thank you. It's a long time ago, North Africa, when we . . . I could have changed very much in the intervening years." Aubrey smiled self-deprecatingly.

Malan was shaking his head at once. "He didn't believe so. He said you couldn't change, however hard you tried."

"And your father—I read he'd—?"

"Resigned as chairman of the companies? It's true. Cancer." Malan's confident, quiet assertiveness deserted him, then he added: "Six months, the doctors say." He seemed embarrassed, if only for an instant, by his circumstances; then he shrugged his shoulders. "I'll let him know we met. He'll be interested."

Aubrey felt himself weighed, studied. All but discounted. There was a rich vein of suspicion in Malan— why? He seemed aware of Aubrey only in his professional capacity, as if his attendance at his own brother's funeral was a deception.

"Please convey old friendship, well remembered," he said primly. "And my—sympathies, of course."

"I will." His tone had become edgily bland. Malan glanced at Kathryn, with her mother, then back at Aubrey. "Yes, I will." Again that gleam of suspicion. "Excuse me," he murmured, then nodded and walked away towards Kathryn.

Aubrey could not avoid the sensation that something important had occurred, despite the intrusive sense of the glaring white chapel in the distance and the dark cypresses and pines; and the litter of sparrows intent upon the clipped grass. It had been more than just a meeting. He watched Malan move possessively towards Kathryn and her arrogant recognition of him appear for an instant on the tight, pale mask of her face. They knew each other well. Other recognitions appeared in her eyes and on her cheeks, though the arrogance remained. Intimately? Carnally? He was aware of an old-fashioned primness in himself, but he could not avoid the thought.

He quashed memories of the war and Malan's father and the likeness of build between father and son and Jeppe Malan serving with the South African army's intelligence corps in the western desert. He quashed them in order to consider the son, Paulus . . .

Then Alan, perhaps aged no more than six or seven, seemed to be saying in his ear in a hot, breathy whisper, *I don't like him.* As if of a bullying schoolmaster or an older boy meaning either or both of them harm. Immediately, ambushed by loss, his throat bobbed full and his eyes stung wetly. He truly realized Alan was dead. He had *lost* him. And realized, too, that there was no longer any time in which he might reconcile or renew. All that was left to him was to recall.

He was uncertain of how much time passed before the hopping, intent sparrows realized themselves once more out of the damp, misty curtain that seemed to have draped itself across the hard-bright day. Kathryn was still engaged in some murmured dialogue with Malan, who no longer interested Aubrey. Unsteadily, using his stick heavily, he moved jerkily towards the black limousine beside which they stood. He could see Kathryn's mother's starched features dimly through the tinted glass. Shapiro hovered weightily and hot near a long white Cadillac. The cypresses were like dark, drilled soldiers in the heat beyond, and the Pacific was bright

as an ache against his eyes. He paused and looked back
to where two men were filling the grave. The mound of
earth was no more than a molehill. Squirrels hopped
beneath cedars or skittered along low branches. He
heard rock music, jarringly, attendant upon another funeral, bright-garbed and crowded. Alan might have ap-
preciated the irony of his peace being so quickly
disturbed. To his ears, it was shudderingly out of place
and taste. Dark birds rose on high thermals against
bleached, dry hills. Aubrey's nerves jangled and he
sought the air conditioning of the funeral limousine.

Malan's firm grip handed him inside. Leather uphol-
stery sighed under his weight as he sat facing his niece
and her mother. Malan hesitated, then climbed in and
sat beside him, closing the door. At once, the car moved
off, gravel crunching beneath its tires. Aubrey attempted
sympathy in a slight smile, and saw the snail-gleam of
tears on the faces of both women. They stifled the quiet,
slurring, blubbing murmurs that might have accompanied the tears, but made no attempt to wipe them
away. Jazz, drugs, three wives and a dozen mistresses,
a houseboat for a home ... the footprints of a man capable of evoking this helpless grief on pallid faces.

To break the tension their tears invoked, he turned to
Malan and remarked: "I presume you're here on business, Paulus?" The effect, for an instant, was alarming.
Suspicion shone out of Malan's cold, pale eyes. There
was a moment of indecision, then Malan merely nodded,
as if not trusting himself to speak.

Beyond the tinted window, over Malan's large shoulder, sparrows twisted and fluttered from the cemetery
lawns in pursuit of passing insects. Glancing into Malan's face once more, Aubrey saw himself reflected as a
danger. Why? He had no interest in Malan, apart from

an unexpected stirring of protective paternalism towards Kathryn, no interest whatsoever.

And yet Malan expected such an interest. But *why?*

"You can't just drop me from the first helicopter you find."

"It'll be some kind of accident, Hyde," Harrell replied. "A bad one." One of the Americans between whom he was squeezed on the car's rear seat chuckled. "You don't realize the current state of your reputation in London, Hyde," Harrell continued, lazily turning the wheel of the long, cream-colored American limousine with tinted windows, his head turned in profile as he spoke. "They think you were there. You know, where *it* happened. You're an embarrassment to London, Hyde. They'd really like not to see you again." He smiled like a parent soothing a backseat, irritable child on a long journey.

Hyde clenched his hands together between his knees and maintained the rigid immobility of his shoulders; he feared the beginning of some quiver along his arms. His body must display the same lack of expression as his voice and eyes as he stared at the back of the leather driver's seat or at his knees. Never at any of them. Yet he seemed to require physical movement to allay the slowly mounting panic in his stomach and to shake his thoughts into fluidity.

"I'm tired of it, Harrell," he continued as if the prospect of his murder had not arisen, "tired of the killing, I mean." It was the voice of a passionless lecturer; even, dull, empty. For the moment, it did little more than arouse their curiosity, yet he scented the beginnings of irritation in the car. His unwashed smell helped, of course.

"You said."

"You blokes want to screw the world for fun. You

have to kill people." His body had absorbed the admission of imminent death. He glanced up. Harrell, in profile as they turned into a narrow, crowded square filled with stalls and wandering animals and Afghans, seemed to retain his detached, confident amusement. Yet the American on his left stirred and rubbed his cheek, wrinkling his nose to observe: "Come on, Harrell, let's move it, uh? This guy *stinks* back here!"

Hyde looked slowly sideways and breathed towards the man on his left, who scowled at Hyde's halitosis. "Jesus," he muttered. Hyde's eyes were wide like those of a sick pet realizing the purpose of the injection. Then he looked away, as if cowed.

"Don't let him get to you," Harrell soothed, remaining amused. A donkey watched them with infinite wisdom as the limousine slid through a narrow street. The American embassy? No, some—ironic—*safe* house. He breathed steadily. His hands were not tied or manacled but they pinned his arms against his side. He could move just once, quickly, before they were alarmed. Their guns were holstered awkwardly beneath their arms.

But he felt so bloody *weak!* The car jumped forward into another of Kabul's squares. It still struck Hyde as strange not to see the tanks and the trucks and the BMPs, olive-drab, and the crowded uniforms and khaki fatigues and those strange almost Australian hats the soldiers had worn. The Russians had gone ... replaced by the Yanks! So bloody weak, irresolute. And ... he tried to shy away from the idea, but it had gained admittance in his increasing desperation ... the idea that he almost wanted it. An end to it.

Shops gaudy with Western fashions clashed with the black drab of the hooded women. Only the men seemed to belong to the Kabul of the war, together with the still-shattered buildings and the unrepaired roads of the last days. It was still easy to recollect the tracer in the night and the helicopters against the sky like broken insects on a windscreen; and easy to recollect the bodies in the streets, the mutilated Afghan soldiers, the crass panic of negotiation and ceasefire, the explosions and revenges. He gripped his hands together tighter, feeling a tremor in his arms.

It could have been a square, then a wide road, in Teheran rather than Kabul. After Najibullah's fall, with Masood dead and all the moderates ousted, the fundamentalists had poured in and the women had adopted the veil and the funeral wrappings and, in the end, it hadn't been worth a toss after all. Just another Islamic state hurtling back towards the Middle Ages. Masood must be laughing somewhere.

"You can't stop fucking about with the world, can you?" Hyde continued. The American on his left shifted on the leather seat, snorting. The man to his right stared out the window. The interior of the car seemed hotter, more confining. "You just *have* to kill people . . . just like scientists. Throwing live birds into aircraft engines just to find out how many sparrows it takes to choke the bloody thing." They were puzzled now, attentive. Where had he heard that, about some engine manufacturer somewhere? "That's your world. Let's stuff bodies in our engine, see how many it takes?"

"Christ almighty!" It was the other American. Harrell, on a straight, almost empty road, turned his head quickly, suspicious of Hyde. Hyde stared at the back of Harrell's seat blankly, and Harrell turned back to his driving.

". . . the body count—the hardware. Here, Nicaragua . . ." Hyde murmured without pause. His own temperature was rising. Even so, the survival instinct seemed reluctant, the adrenaline he would require dribbling like saliva. Come on, they're going to kill you! Reluctance. Oh, Christ, *come on*—!

The car halted at traffic lights. At once, they tensed against him, pressing close, hands hovering at lapels for the quick comfort of gun butts. They *were* unsettled, but they were too alert. Try silence? No. Talk.

Harrell spoke as two hooded, masked, black-garbed women passed in front of the windscreen and a camel stared with eyes smaller, it seemed, than those of the boy between the women. "Hyde, you've been all washed up for a long time. Dead, only you didn't realize it. We won't really be killing you at all. Just burying the corpse." The man on his left guffawed.

Hyde said: "I don't understand how it's always arse-holes like you three who get to run the show." But he was shivering at the acuity of Harrell's remark. Parts of him *were* dead; he suffered from a kind of gangrene of feelings, of sensibilities. He stared out the window at the white-peaked mountains of the Hindu Kush, as the man on his left growled and Harrell quieted him like a guard dog. Dark clouds were being dragged across the pale winter sky, a strong wind moving them like huge, gray, invading vessels. "Arseholes," he repeated quietly, without menace. Harrell seemed to relax his shoulders. "Certifiable, Inexcusable Arseholes—C, I, A."

"You've done the dirty things, too, Hyde. Don't moralize."

"I don't do it for laughs."

The car drew away from the traffic lights. The wide-eyed boy in a bright yellow anorak and long white socks was still watching the car from between the black enclosure of the women's dresses. Harrell turned left and the street narrowed, became almost at once crowded. They were close to one of the bazaars, one he knew. The warren, could he—? He slipped lower towards his knees, hunched and apparently defeated. He yawned, rubbed his unshaven face loudly; then sighed, swallowing saliva. His fingers tingled. Neither of the Americans penning him seemed alerted. The sun vanished and snow pattered against the windscreen. Harrell turned on the wipers. They flicked intermittently like tongues at the splashes of snow.

"Rambo's world at last," he murmured lifelessly. "Here we go, guys—shoot the bastards, shoot everyone." He swallowed. Keep your bloody *arms* still! He had to talk now to further unsettle them and calm himself. "You're playing footsie with the Russian army and the KGB—Nikitin's opposition—because you don't want a nice quiet Russia. Or maybe you want them to reinvade this dump."

The wipers, continuously flicking, were almost hypnotic. The snow became heavier. The car threaded its way towards the narrow alleys and streets around the bazaar.

"Nearly there," Harrell drawled, glancing around at him. A donkey bumped off the radiator, seemingly unhurt. Its owner raised a fist, spat against the window. The American to his left flinched. "Pity we can't hear the whole of your theory, Hyde. No time. Sorry." He smiled.

An Afghan soldier, Afghan police. Robed, masked women, white-shirted, pancake-hatted men. Guns carried as casually as shopping bags. Traffic lights ahead, strung like Christmas lights above the narrow, twisting street. The daubed colors of dozens of stalls and narrow, dark shops.

"Another fine mess you're getting into—*Ollie,*" Hyde observed in the same listless tone.

"This guy's beginning to annoy me, Harrell."

"Easy. He hasn't got long."

The traffic lights were green. He knew this row of shops, knew the alleys behind them, the rubbish stacked or littered there. The warren. *Green—*

A small portrait of Khomeini like an omen stuck to a shop window. Black-garbed women like burnt scraps of paper hurried along the narrow street by the sudden snow. The force and significance of the game Harrell and whoever was behind him were playing struck against him like icy water. Khomeini's wrinkled, austere, bearded face in a second window, and a mullah accosting a woman, turbaned and robed, her face exposed and frightened. Harrell and the Russians; the traffic lights green as the car eased and inched through the rubbish, the animals, the people and the flying sleet. He slipped forward in his bent, defeated posture, testing the feeling in his fingertips, the weight of the two men against him. Green, green, *green—*

Red.

Harrell hooted the horn at a cart that slewed across his path then tugged on the rasping hand brake. The noise seemed unnaturally loud in the small, confined, hot interior of the limousine. People rubbed like waves against the flanks of the car. A woman's snow-wet black robes wiped along the tinted window. Impatience, irritation in the two on either side, and in the stiff set of Harrell's shoulders. He had been dismissed. They were traffic-angered now, he was irrelevant, merely to be disposed of.

Red—Harrell's neck taut, red, the arms untensed against his—red. The flick of the wipers measuring the time. *Red*—tick—*adrenaline*—shiver through his arms, alerting them. The doors weren't locked from the inside—*red.*

Take the one to the left, the right hand can move more freely. Leave the knife where it is, too awkward to use effectively. He stared at the dusty carpet between his feet, the slight movement of his body sliding his arms against the material of their suits. Green any moment now—

His elbow was free of the pressure down his left side. His silence made them dismissive. He controlled the renewed shiver of adrenaline, contained the tension mounting in his forearms; moved his left elbow slightly. It was not in contact with the man on that side. The window darkened behind the American as a cart or truck drew alongside—still *red*. The smell of an exhaust, the shudder of an old engine ticking over alongside the limousine. Harrell's neck, as he glanced up, taut.

The truck had made it impossible to use the door to his left, it wouldn't open now! He caught his breath, calming it, and heard the sigh of the heating. His right elbow was folded, acquaintancelike, beneath the arm of the man to his right.

Nevertheless, *right*—looked up, Harrell half-turning to say something, still *red*, then amber on the lights strung across the street. Amber, the release of the brake clicking off, the tense unsteadiness of the car—

Right. His elbow jabbed into the American's neck, blunt and sudden into his windpipe. Surprise and the movement of the man's hand—moving upwards, then, as if he were gagging prior to vomiting, his mouth wide, his eyes wide as if he might breathe through them. A hand on his left arm, Harrell's surprise, then his hands reaching across the back of his seat towards Hyde. Hyde turned and butted his head into the other American's face, jerking his neck taut. He heard and felt the crack. His arm was released and he grabbed at the door handle. Harrell's grip was slippery on his clothing. The door swung open. He dug again at the choking American with his elbow, kicked out behind him as he lay across the man, connecting with the other guard. *Green* flashed at the periphery of his vision as he wriggled half out of the swinging door and a shiver of acceleration ran through the car. Glazed eyes, then the sough of dragged-in air near his ear. Harrell was jerking the car away from the traffic lights, abandoning any attempt to restrain him. The street ran like dusty mercury just below his face, then he tumbled out of the car as it swerved violently, and rolled away and into someone's legs as he heard the screech of brakes, then the almost immediate noise of the limousine reversing. Someone shouted above him. The pattern of the car's tires spinning into a blur of dust and noise. He rolled aside and the car drew level with him, the choking American leaning out of the rear, his hand inside his coat reaching for a gun, Harrell's face glaring in the driving seat.

Hyde scrambled to his knees, dizzy and coughing in the upthrown dust, then blundered a black-shrouded woman aside to the protests of the man standing beside her. He heard the squeal of some animal, high as the noise of the car's tires as he flailed through the small crowd that had immediately gathered like a fence to contain him. The American who had been on his left was already out of the limousine, its cream roof smeared by the blood streaming from his broken nose. His pistol was shakily aligned. Hyde swam against the small tide of children—a donkey—two women, stumbled across a beggar's casual limbs, then blundered off-balance a man on crutches whose legless torso slumped back against a wall.

He heard the first shot and was aware of the thinness of the vulnerable skin across his shoulder blades. The American voices were drowned in a rising clamor, the wail of the beggar and the curses of the legless ex-mujahideen.

He rebounded from a rough plastered wall, gripping talonlike to its unevenness for a moment before he clattered against a low shop sign and sent a copper urn rolling away back down the alleyway. Then, as he ran, the alley twisted, doubled back, jigsawed, then became emptier and safer.

The conjunction of his brother's death with that of Patrick Hyde was like the outcome of some malignant horoscope. Aubrey felt the sudden, weighty movement of an ill-ballasted cargo. Where had this loose freight of pity and guilt and a genuine sorrow sprung from so readily? The small dots of sea otters bobbed like a row of corks beyond the kelp line, the afternoon's light rendering them starkly black and unreal. The sea slopped just beneath the floorboards of the room, unsettlingly.

And what was he to do with her?

Kathryn Aubrey's tension, as she stood erect, smoking a cigarette beside the square of the window, was palpable and disturbing. He had thought she wished him there for Alan's sake or his own; but it was something else that concerned her. She seemed to require his *professional* presence. And that he wanted to avoid. It was an intrusion, while all he wished was to make his final orisons and a quick, tactful departure! Kathryn was coiled like a spring about to snap. Her guilty grief was evident even as she dealt with the small traps of cellophane opening a pack of cigarettes.

And there was the thought of Malan. His carnal intent towards Kathryn made Aubrey protective—foolishly, since there had obviously been some liaison in the past that only Malan wished to revive. The South African confused Aubrey. Malan had a holding in Shapiro Electrics. Kathryn and Malan had met at the Paris Air Show that summer. No! Consider Malan objectively, he instructed himself. Shapiro's company was on Godwin's short list. He'd seen that on the flight coming over. Malan was obscurely afraid of Aubrey's *job*.

Aubrey considered the problem in the tense silence the woman created, as the light fell on the upright piano, the stave paper, the saxophone hanging on the wall. He squinted into the window's pearly light, hardly able to make out the otters now in its haze. Kathryn was shadowy in the corner of the room. Strangely, Alan's home embraced him in an immediate, warm manner; most of his own places had not done that. Contentment was like a legend beside the door, DUNROAMIN' or CHEZ NOUS. Alan had been happy, content in this place, and he felt obscurely envious of his dead brother.

Kathryn announced in a small, tight voice: "I need your help—your advice."

"Yes?" he answered quickly, startled.

She blew smoke theatrically, an arm crossed over her breasts, one hand cupping the other elbow. He saw her eyes glitter but could not make out whether the brightness was that of tears.

"What is it?" he felt obliged to add. "How can I help?" he continued in a stronger, gentler tone.

"It's a friend..." Inwardly, he shrank. Not some ridiculous ménage à trois with Malan, herself and another? Was he to be an Agony Aunt to this unknown niece, for heaven's sake?

"Yes?" He gestured to one of the dining chairs, but she shook her head. Wearily, Aubrey sat down.

Silence, then the trickle at once became a small flood of words.

"He's missing—his name's John, I live with him— and have for months..." It was like a distant, interrupted radio broadcast. "His obsession with it, whatever, I didn't *understand!* Up in the north of the state

somewhere...some   accident...when   Alan—when
Alan had his cardiac arrest...he called me." She was
staring blindly out across the pearly water to the indistinct horizon. Her face shone wetly, gilded with tears.
"Hiding...on the run...I couldn't help him. We quarreled, but I couldn't *leave* Alan, could I? Not when he
was dying. He'd have been alone." She ignored the tears
in her voice and their trickling evidence on her cheeks
and struggled to continue: "I can't find him now, he
won't get in touch with me. I talked to him that night,
but I *couldn't* leave—! Then he...he didn't call back.
I don't know what's happened to him and I'm scared
for him. Really scared, I mean, like he was in some kind
of danger."

"Was he?"

She seemed startled by the reminder of Aubrey's presence.

"He said so."

"What was he doing there?"

She pressed the heels of both hands against her temples
as if the effort of memory hurt her. The smoke lay flat
like thin clouds across the sunlit room.

"He—it was an airplane crash there, last spring. He
always said the investigation was a cover-up, there was
something going on."

"Why was he interested?"

"He—he's in the FAA, the Federal Aviation—"

"I see. And he felt something had happened which
was..."

"*Criminal*. That's what he said."

"What else did he say?"

Again, her hands pressed against her temples, against
the dark, dragged-back hair and white skin. Then: "He
said—he knew how they'd done it, what had really happened." She nodded. "Yes."

"And you believe he was in danger?"

She merely nodded. Aubrey gripped his lower lip between thumb and forefinger. The tension in the room had dissipated. Kathryn seemed somehow released. As for himself . . . it might be anything or nothing. He could put inquiries in motion with Langley, as a favor. It was difficult to treat this with any seriousness beyond the personal level. A distraught, strained, guilty young woman who had quarreled with her lover and was perhaps in the course of drifting back towards another man. The light through the window was less opaque now. Houses bright as buttons climbed the hillsides, and masts in the harbor dipped and swayed with the incoming tide. The houseboat now seemed littered with the evidence of a chance existence, an untidy, ill-disciplined life. There was something shudderingly *bohemian* about it, he decided. Yet there was that sense of accrued satisfactions and contentment. His brother had been a happy man; whereas he, perhaps, had been little more than a dutiful one.

What to do about Kathryn?

He said: "How long since he was last in touch?"

"Not since the night I went to the hospital."

"And you've heard nothing of any—accident? They would contact you; would know to do so in case of an accident?" She nodded. "Then, perhaps . . ." He sighed. "This preoccupation with the aircraft accident? How has it been concerning him?"

"Like it was driving him crazy. I mean, an obsession. Stinging him all the time like a bee."

"I wonder why?"

"It was—oh, that airplane disaster in Russia. The one where Nikitin's wife got herself killed."

"He thought there was some connection?" Aubrey asked in disbelief. The woman shrugged, not knowing.

"I doubt that...an obsession, indeed," he remarked. Then he added soothingly: "I will put some feelers out, among my community, my friends in this country." He stood up. "I'm certain there can be nothing in this to have worried him so desperately. It may be no more than..." He trailed off, seeing her wide, somehow nakedly desperate eyes and the chalky tiredness of her face. "Shall we go?" he asked softly, and she nodded at once.

He ushered her to the door, and saw as he looked back a final time into the room the precariousness of his brother's life and the meagerness of his possessions. He had lived largely on the royalties accumulated by perhaps a dozen tunes that had become secondary standards, recorded a number of times successfully by jazz luminaries. Precarious...

...enviable, too.

His dismissiveness failed to catch light. What accident to an aircraft in northern California? Some connection with Mother Nikitina's death? Surely to goodness not.

The aura of contentment, of a life fulfilled, emanating from the room insisted that he had let too much of life pass by unheeded. He sniffed at Kathryn's lover's obsession and inhaled the scent of the ridiculous.

But, he would initiate a few discreet, soothing inquiries. A small family debt...

4

EXISTENTIALISM

The bazaar shopkeeper's skin was as gray and wasted as if he had swallowed cordite, yet he moved the crutches and his thin body with the indifferent strength of long usage. His left trouser leg flapped emptily. The muscles in his arms were overdeveloped. Hyde watched him blearily, encouraging the steam from the bowl of hot, spicy food to come between himself and the Afghan like a thin curtain. Pictures of the man's dead son hung on the wall, black-draped still; victim to a chemical attack in the Panjshir three years earlier. The son's young widow, properly mummified in black robes, crouched in one corner of the earth-floored room, poking at the open fire from which puffs of smoke climbed to the slit in the low ceiling, like signals...

...to Harrell's Apaches, who were out there, broken out of whatever reservation former rules and practices of the CIA had held them in. They'd killed Irena Nikitina. Did they want Tadzhikistan to boil over like milk on a stove; a new war? Did they want what Kabul's fundamentalists wanted, to spread the jihad, the Holy War, north into the Moslem republics of the Soviet Union? Why, for God's sake? They couldn't be working with the mullahs and the mujahideen who formed the Afghan government—at least, *they* wouldn't work with the Yanks.

But Harrell *and* some ranking KGB and army people were doing their work for them. Why?

He continued chewing on the tough, expensive, curried lamb, picking at the flat, doughy, baked bread, dipping it into the stewlike mess in his bowl. The shaking had deserted his arms, the shiver had deserted his shoulders. His stomach was leaden, but his thoughts flickered like artillery fire along a broad horizon, in quick, glaring bursts. Now that they had taken the rolls of film and the documents and he had no shred of proof against them, he could not stop thinking of that valley in Tadzhikistan, of the long slow spiraling of the plane, of the lake, of the search for him and his escape—and what it *meant!* And Gaines at the embassy—was he in it? HMG, too?

Chewing, he choked on the idea that he could trust no one but Aubrey. Bloody, fucking old Aubrey who'd left him in that shithouse of a country until he was as good as dead. Reported dead. Only him...

The tremor had returned to his arms. He scraped the spoon in the stew, swallowing the hot meat and sauce quickly, repetitively, crowding out the thought of Aubrey from where it twisted in his stomach like a virulent worm. Bloody, bloody Aubrey! For Christ's sake, *him*—

Then he abandoned his recriminations, for they only sucked at his remaining strength, draining him more than the vague, unreal thoughts of the man he had killed ten days ago. His spoon scraped on the bowl's empty bottom and he threw it down on the table. The Afghan watched him from a shadowy corner, standing before a hanging rug of great intricacy. Hyde rubbed his cheeks, his eyes, smelling the dirt on his hands and suspecting the smell of blood, despite his having washed himself under the ancient pump in the narrow, foul yard at the rear of the shop. Then he held his head up, his nostrils away from his body and clothing, inhaling the scents of the spices, fruit and vegetables stored beyond the curtain, in the one back room and the cramped sleeping room above it.

Then he said: "The girl? Is it safe to send her into the streets?"

"Why?"

"I want to know where they are, what they're doing."

The Afghan spoke rapidly to the girl, whose kohl-outlined eyes seemed at once defiant and sympathetic; then she rose from in front of the small fire and rustled through the curtain. Hyde heard the shop door bang shut.

They know about Mohammed, he reminded himself. He's on a list somewhere as a safe house, from the old days. If he's at the top, they'll be here tonight. If at the bottom, tomorrow. The food turned in his stomach, rose and filled his throat, at the thought of more flight, of real pursuit. After the border crossing, there had been no pursuit—by Harrell or anyone. He'd been at one with a landscape he knew better than they. They hadn't bothered because they had known he would make straight for Gaines at the bloody embassy waving whatever he'd salvaged from the aircraft wreckage! And they'd been right, guessing how tired, how exhausted, how *simple* his thinking would be. And they had just waited for him. They hadn't even gambled, they'd known.

The Afghan shuffled to the table on his crutches and laboriously sat down opposite Hyde. His face was that of someone known and still entirely a stranger. There was a distance that had nothing to do with the lost limb and everything to do with the Soviet withdrawal. This was *his* country now. Hy... vas a foreigner; a heathen. The Islamic Republic of Afghanistan—how long before they declared that? Next year, this? This man, once a pro-Western follower of Masood, now dressed his son's widow in black, veiled her and wore his contempt in his eyes.

"Why do the Americans want to kill you?" he asked. "You were their donkey."

"I was. It's better you know nothing."

The man radiated indifference. He was detached from Hyde's danger, unaware of his own. He, Harrell, all of them were no better than dogs scratching in rubbish. Godless heathens.

"How long will the girl be?" Hyde asked, his nerves beginning to jump in his hands, quieted until now by his fierce grip on the spoon and the rough edge of the wooden table; and in his feet, too, shuffling to be gone from there.

He looked up. The Afghan's sharp, dark eyes watched him secretly, but also with the detachment he might have revealed watching insects crawling on a blind in his shop. Hyde breathed in slowly, then exhaled, again and again. Soft, calm, unthinking breaths. The thinking had been done. Harrell had to have him dead, the British embassy was compromised in a way he did not understand, the Afghans would do no more than feed him. He had to get out of Kabul, then out of the country. And that meant Pakistan. Peshawar. And then, Aubrey...

He could not forgive the old man for abandoning him to—to *this!* But he could trust him.

He sat in silence, then. The Afghan made him some bitter, strong coffee and he sat inhaling its fumes rather than sipping it, listening to the evening tumult of the bazaar outside, half-listening for a door banging open behind them or scrabbling in the yard a moment after the thin, black dog's warning bark. There was nothing. He imitated rest. There wasn't really any choice except to survive...no choice...none...

The girl's return startled him from a doze, his face jerking away from the cold coffee in the cup. His eyes were blearily aware of her but somehow more aware of the two stubs of the hashish joints the man had sold him, crushed into a cracked, stained saucer on the table. The hashish had calmed him; been necessary. Now, its fogginess angered him, his head as smoky as the lamplit room. He shook his head. A chair tumbled behind him. The girl's black shadow was huge and moving on the wall. Her words were too quick, too breathy and he caught few of them. Translation from her heavily accented Dari—Afghan Persian—was difficult; his slow thoughts stumbled in his head.

But he saw the man's eyes begin to move, to watch the curtain through to the shop and the passageway to the rear door out into the yard. *That* close?

The girl had brought the alien and the familiar with her as palpably as the speckles of melting snow on her headdress and shoulders. She made the place no more

than another in the succession of earth-floored huts in
the Panjshir where he had been fed and had rested. But
the urgency in her voice and eyes, perhaps something
close to panic, wakened him to the knowledge that the
place was alien, these people were strangers, and it was
a trap. Her rapidly moving eyes watched him, the curtain, the passageway, her father-in-law's crutches, the
ceiling where the smoke disappeared, the lamp, him—

The man's eyes glittered now. Either the girl's words
or Hyde's face had made the searching Americans real,
dangerous.

"The gun you promised—quickly!" Hyde snapped,
dismissing the man, attempting to dominate the girl.
"Where? How many?" His mind was loose now, but
rushed like ether, emptily. "Quick, the gun!" His hands
had begun to quiver as he stared at them. He banged
his fists on the table. "Speak *slowly!* How many? Where
are they? How close?" He pulled a bundle of soiled,
gaudy notes from inside the sheepskin jacket and
dropped them on the table, knowing the money would
draw their eyes immediately. "How many?"

Instead of answering him, as if she divined his real
priorities, she pulled a stubby Kalashnikov, an old AK-
47, from beneath the narrow cot along one shadowy
wall. It hardly caught the light of the dying fire or the
lamp, but it smelled of oil—it would work, he assured
himself as he inspected it. Two spare magazines. He
nodded, and the girl snatched up the money.

"Four—six," she answered. "Akbar's vegetable stall,
two shops that way." She tossed her head, then pointed
towards the back door through the narrow passageway,
wanting him gone. The man passed between them, the
moth she had disturbed from beneath the bed fluttering
near his head before settling back towards the lamp's
neck. Like him, the moth was out of season in that place.

"Go! If Akbar saw you, he will tell them so." The man passed through the curtain, which admitted a cold draft, towards the front of the shop, his crutches thumping dully on the packed earth.

"What's beyond the yard out there?" It was difficult to remember. But she had already turned towards her father-in-law and the shop, ignoring him.

He looked around. Two smoked joints, a cracked saucer. The rustle of long, black cloth, the moth singeing at the mouth of the lamp. The utter weariness, the fragility of his awareness, dim as the shadow, poor light in the room. Nausea and uncertainty, brought on merely by clasping the rifle, pressing it against his cheek, hard.

He shivered like a dog emerging from a stream. He was shouting at himself silently, shouting, yelling.

All the way along the passageway to the rear door.

He opened the door and listened above the noises of the bazaar. It was difficult to tell anything. His vision was difficult, too, because of the snow making shadows deeper, itself lumped and shaded and contoured by the litter of rubbish it covered. Cold air. His smoky breaths like signals of distress. His head clearing of hashish. His body shivered with the new cold, with renewed, tense, alert nerves. Were they already here?

It was noiseless back inside the shop as he ducked his face into its relative warmth. Outside he could hear the bazaar's cries and haggling, its laughter and radioed or performed music, but all other sounds were confused or masked. A donkey brayed, then a stick or a whip fell, close, making his whole body twitch with nerves. The thin, black, unalarmed dog near his legs snuffled.

The yard was safe.

He moved along the wall, turned at its angle, shuffling close to the heaped stones, his body ducking away from forming an outline. Looking back, he could not discern his own smeared footprints in the darkness. Thin light leaked from the rear door of the shop but outlined no figure. He watched the door, his back sliding along the rough stones of the wall until he reached the gap, and ducked his head through it. A passageway no more than a yard wide, winding almost immediately out of sight; blind alley. He listened again. He felt less weak, less exhausted. The few moments of darkness and isolation had returned a sense of advantage to which he had become unaccustomed. Four, six, she had said. She had no idea, not really. But no more than six, for certain. Not if they were searching through an inventory of his contacts, safe houses, old haunts. There weren't that many Americans in Kabul to be trusted and mobilized, not quickly... three or four then. Harrell? His hand tightened on the barrel of the rifle, his finger crooked near the trigger guard. The cold metal of the gun, the cold plastic, no longer made him dizzy or nauseous.

He watched the door. The dog muttered and snuffled, its padding the only marks on the clean snow. The dim light from the room behind the shop was a slab of pale yellow in the darkness. He relearned patience, awareness, feline sensitivity as he leaned against the wall, breathing calmly. The donkey—or another donkey— was goaded and slapped again and protested as loudly. Music, the thin reeding of pipes, the thudding of a small drum. The gossip and hawking of dozens of stalls and narrow shops. A child crying as if teething.

The slab of light darkened, but there was no thumping of crutches in the moments before the shadow occupied the rectangle of dim yellow. Snow blew across the brighter yard as the door was softly, gently opened wide. Blew across the shadowy figure. Hyde could hear the patter of snow against his sleeve, against the bulk of the Kalashnikov; could almost hear the man in the doorway breathing. He heard the dog snuffle, then growl casually at the stranger. Wearing a Western topcoat, and a Russian fur hat, the man looked out, seeing nothing, eyes still adjusting to the evening gloom of the shabby room behind him. His night vision would come soon. Too late to slip away unnoticed, Hyde thought, face filthy enough, unshaven enough to be invisible, but sleeves too light.

"Anything out there? Look for tracks, man!"

American English.

The man did not turn his head, preserving his new night vision, the fur hat tilted forward almost jauntily as he peered out into the darkness-becoming-lighter.

"No tracks!" he called back. "Nothing I can see."

Hyde's nerves were taut in his chest, muscles cramping in legs and arms. Finger remeasuring the movement from guard to trigger, thumb tickling the catch to ensure the gun would fire single rounds. Breathing almost stopped.

Where was the bloody dog? He twitched, afraid it was around his legs, but there was nothing but the faint slap of cloth against skin in the stiff breeze. The dog—?

The American's head turned at the snuffle, then returned. He refocused his vision, which was clearing, adjusting quickly. Uncertain, the American stared, uncertain—

—certain. Hyde leveled the AK-47 and fired. The stock bucked against his pelvis. The American buckled, then seemed to trundle backwards. The rectangle of light was empty of shadow, as he heard the body crash into boxes, against a door; then silence.

Hyde had seen the gun fall into the snow and the dog, only faintly alarmed, sniff at it before retreating into the passageway. He shook himself and slipped through the gap in the wall into the narrow alley. The first exclamations of shock followed him, a bellow of surprised rage, the babble of momentary panic. The silence of caution seemed to echo in the slush-filled, slippery alleyway. His boots splashed in what must have been an open sewer, but cold killed its smells. The exhilaration of movement and killing hurried him forward, assured his footing.

"I thought this place might suit us," Didenko remarked, aware that his smile was both brief and suspicious. "Hardly anyone bothers to come here any more." They were in Lenin's private apartments in the Kremlin, just two rooms; a gloomy, rather shabby place after the arcades between the Kremlin Palace and the Armory, the snow blowing fitfully between the buildings. The room was cold, abandoned, with dust lying thickly everywhere, rising in puffs and breaths as they moved. The rugs were dulled and the wallpaper darkened.

"Indulging your taste for the dramatic, my friend?" Valenkov asked. Didenko smiled as he stared down at the table on which lay an old, folded newspaper, an old-fashioned pen beside it, and a handwritten manuscript. He touched it, and the whorls in the polished wood underneath margined the manuscript. "Are we already in a conspiracy?" Yuri added.

Didenko turned, bursting out: "He wrote his pamphlet, *Immediate Problems of Soviet Power*, in this room!"

Yuri Valenkov, Soviet foreign minister, smiled and shrugged, inspecting the dusty arms of the narrow chair he occupied, its stuffing evident like uncombed tufts of gray hair.

"You think that's what we have, immediate problems with Soviet power?" he asked.

Didenko rubbed his hands through his thinning hair

and then cleaned his spectacles intently. The room was blurred, the expression on Valenkov's face indistinct; the manuscript on the desk hazy.

"Oh, I don't know, Yuri—!" He replaced his spectacles. Valenkov was watching him curiously, in an untroubled way. "I just—wanted to talk to you. Yes, I think we do have problems, or we soon will have. Now that Irena's—not here. She was the motor for so much that we're trying to do!"

"I thought he coped quite well at the last Politburo meeting—considering what's happened, how he feels . . . what is it? You don't agree?"

Didenko shook his head. "No, I don't—but I do, yes, that's the trouble. He is coping very well with his grief. He's got himself under control. It's just that, well—"

"What?"

Didenko looked across the room and caught sight, in a diseased old mirror, of himself, a stooping, rather shambling figure with furtive eyes. The sight of Yuri's comfortable rotundity offered reassurance against his anxieties.

"Well, it's just as I said, Irena was the motor, *his* motor—"

"That's hardly fair. He was Party secretary in the Ukraine before they even met, never mind married! Not to mention your part. You've been with them—him—for years. You've put in a lot." Valenkov sighed, his hands raising dust from the arms of the chair, so that he coughed and then grinned, wafting his hand theatrically. He cleared his throat, then added: "I think you're exaggerating if you're worried about him. He can carry on. I'm sure of it."

"No, you don't understand me—!"

Valenkov flushed slightly, and his eyes narrowed.

"Sorry. Enlighten me." Then his good humor reasserted itself. "And try not to patronize me, Pyotr! Just because I wasn't one of the 'Holy Trinity,' just a supporting player."

"Sorry, Yuri. I agree with you one hundred percent. He *was* Party chief in the Ukraine, under Andropov, who brought him on. He was a rising star under Brezhnev, for God's sake, while you and I were keeping our heads down and doing our best to toe the line." His hands were waggling in front of him, as if over a conjurer's black top hat where all the words he needed were hidden. "But he was on the way up, he was marked out by Brezhnev, then by Andropov while he was still head of the KGB!"

"We've all got those skeletons, to a greater or lesser extent. Even Irena was a success back in the Dark Ages. Even if *we* weren't, it doesn't make us better people. Or give us any greater purity—we were *all* alive in the bad old days!" He grinned at Didenko, who did not respond except with a scowl. "Don't sulk," Yuri warned avuncularly. "What *are* you worried about, really?"

"I'm worried by some of the things he said, and the people to whom he listened, at that last meeting. No more than that, granted, but *that*."

"You mean being polite to old Lidichev and the marshal and proposing that Chevrikov is voted back into the Politburo? Necessary, if you ask me, civil unrest being what it is. Is that all?"

Didenko shrugged. Like a banker refusing a loan, he thought, seeing himself caricatured by the mirror.

"Doesn't sound much, I know."

"Well, what's he been saying to you, lately?" Valenkov pulled a cigarette case from his overcoat pocket, and a gold lighter. The smoke was acrid in the dry, cold room. Valenkov looked about for an ashtray, then observed: "Vladimir Ilyich had no vices," and flicked ash onto the poor remains of a patterned rug. He looked up solicitously at Didenko. "You worry too much, old friend. You always did, though."

"Perhaps. But Chevrikov on the Politburo, Lidichev's big pal! And a goddamn reactionary—*what* a fucking reactionary! You know what he's been doing to the KGB! They call him Beria out in that glass monstrosity they call the Center, and that doesn't bode well!"

"Look, neither do events in the Baltic republics, in the Ukraine and Georgia, and God alone knows where else!" Valenkov puffed furiously at his cigarette, its smoke drifting between Didenko and his dim reflection. "Especially in the Moslem republics. You want the army and the KGB run by a saint at a time like this?"

"You saw the reaction I got to my proposals for—"

"What you were proposing was tantamount to *independence* for Lithuania and Latvia, old friend!"

"It's what he and Irena and I worked out, Yuri! He let Lidichev screw me into the floor over it—*it's not the time, Comrade,* was his only remark!" He rubbed furiously at his head, his hair straying into a vague halo. He paced up and down the room, but always beside the table, as if there was some tonic there, a restorative. "It had all been planned. But you know that, you'd been briefed."

"And spoke up on cue."

"And he took no notice—blinked as if he was surprised, even offended, and let Lidichev make me look like a hick from the sticks!"

"Your pride's hurt—"

"No! I don't mind that, really. I don't even mind Lidichev's childish accusations about the cult of personality and all that guff about individualism. I *mind* about Nikitin and where he thinks he's going. He's a closet conservative—!"

"Rubbish!"

"It isn't rubbish. Irena was like a *conversion,* in his case, a blinding light. I've always known it, I suppose— at least, suspected it. But I never thought he'd be a backslider, not once we got the show on the road and it *worked!*"

"Lidichev and the others say it isn't working, though, don't they? They're asking—"

"I know what they're asking for! The application of the brake! Well, perhaps they needn't worry. The car they want to stop hasn't got an engine any longer. It might just come to a halt of its own accord, long before it runs out of road."

He slumped into a chair and dust rose chokingly around him, as if he were somehow mummified, and disintegrating now that the wrappings of *glasnost* and *perestroika* and Irena had been removed. His cheeks felt heated and his collar tight. The ugly, expensive wall- paper, masked by grime, seemed to enclose him, make the room boxlike. Didenko leaned forward.

"Secretly, he feels Lidichev and the army and the KGB are right when they want to use the big stick, keep the republics in line, especially the bloody Moslems. Don't *you* feel that? Aren't I right?"

Valenkov rubbed ash from the astrakhan collar of his dark overcoat, keeping his eyes averted. When he even- tually looked up, it was to shrug expressively and mur- mur: "I don't know, Pyotr—I really don't. You know him a lot better than I do—" It was said utterly without envy. "—but couldn't you be exaggerating? You lost Irena, too, my friend . . . you know what I mean." Di- denko shook his head, but he sensed the flush rising from his neck to his cheeks. "You're a little bit devas- tated, too. Maybe you're imagining things. And we must take a firm line in—"

"Why? Why must we? It's the logical conclusion of everything else, surely?"

"What? *Independence*—for every piddling little republic with a few dissatisfied customers! Whose crazy idea was that?"

Didenko's forehead felt damp as he rubbed at it, tracing his deep frown. Lenin's stiff, aloof bust glared at him from a niche as if he, too, disapproved. But that was wrong... The sense of history of that place, he decided with an effort, was no more than the sense that no one came there.

"It's—logical," he announced as if remembering a complex, half-understood argument. It was difficult to avoid the returned sense of excitement, of heated, almost joyous debate between himself and Nikitin and Irena, as they had mapped and sketched the future. Power to *do*, not just power, had been one of their epigrammatic mottoes. "If you're embarked on reconstruction, and you're going to do it with openness, then if independence is demanded, if it's what's really wanted, it has to be granted."

"He'd never allow that. I don't—well, it's not that I don't believe you and Irena would have... but not Nikitin, surely?"

"He would have done—but that's just my point. *Now*, he won't. She'd have been behind him like his conscience, prodding him down that road."

"And you, too?" An element of mockery in Valenkov's tone stung Didenko into looking up, his eyes hot. Valenkov raised his hands, palms outward. "No offense."

"None taken," Didenko replied. Even Yuri thought it was about power, he concluded prissily.

"Look, Pyotr, I'm not in favor of becoming just *Rus-*

sian again, some third-rate banana power welded onto Europe. Nikitin won't do that to us."

"Exactly. He's a strong man. Lidichev thinks so. But he'll decide to be strong in the good, old-fashioned way."

"He can't put the clock back."

"If he's convinced that's the way to be strong, he will." His own features stared inadequately out of the mirror, beside Lenin's strength in the niche. "The more they accuse him of hesitancy and weakness, the more he'll resort to his old instincts and follow where they want him to go. *Backwards*. He used to willingly lock people up without trial, you know, ban the underground newspapers—*control* things. Now she's gone, I know he'll go back to the old methods!"

"Maybe he'll have to. They're actually *killing* people in Tadzhikistan—non-Moslems, even KGB officers. Think about that. Anyway, I'm not in favor of abandoning the role of the Party, old friend, even if you are!"

Valenkov lit another cigarette. He'd ground out the first one on the exposed floorboards near the rug. He blew smoke towards the ceiling.

"If that's what is required—" Didenko began.

Valenkov shook his head vehemently. "You and Irena, you must have been high on something—or certifiable." He grinned complacently. His overcoat was open, revealing his expensive Italian suit. His shoes shone of supple leather. Stop that, Didenko told himself. They aren't signs of decadence! "Nikitin isn't going to abandon the Party's role in history—" Valenkov's voice and features were without irony, without cynicism. "—and nor should he. I think you're exaggerating—and *dreaming,* old friend!" He sighed. "For God's sake, we haven't got goods in the shops yet to satisfy new expectations, the damn factories aren't operating as they should, we can't build decent housing—and you want to break up the Union! How the hell could we do *anything* if we fall apart into little, squabbling republics and countries now?" He shook his head in amusement.

"Look, you'll only get it all back into the shape you like by using the old methods. You'll have to have *all* of it back again!"

"Never in Moscow—don't be ridiculous."

"And what about Tadzhikistan? The Ukraine or Georgia? Doesn't it matter there? The army's on the streets and the KGB are arresting people for breathing! And it's being done with his approval—at least, he hasn't expressed any disapproval!"

"It won't happen."

"I hope to God you're right!"

"Then do something, Pyotr. Talk to him. Persuade him. I'll support you, most of the way, though not on this ridiculous independence thing."

"I'll try..."

It had not been a good idea to come to that room, Didenko decided. It had been a theatrical gesture; or a kind of psychological stiff drink, to steel himself. Like too many stiff drinks, it had made him dizzy and caused his head to lurch clumsily. Valenkov thought him a dreamer, out of touch with reality. Or someone carrying a torch for Irena, dazzled by her. Well, you were, he told himself. Besides which, carrying the torch would be unpopular, and might be...well, even dangerous. To his career, his position. This room, coming here, had been a visit to some monument to a past war. Lenin's table, Lenin's spectacles, his pen, the glowering, certain bust. A testament to nerve and courage that emphasized his own weakness. It had been so easy, all so *possible*, with Irena!

He muttered: "I only hope he'll listen to me."

*   *   *

You don't need to check, you *know*—

The moon, almost full, slid through gaps in the cloud, and the mountains marched white-flanked into the distance. Kabul's dim glow was behind him, the open expanse of dirt, tire-rutted, pocked by snow and mud, was between him and the stone and mud shack and the tumble-down, corrugated garage shed. He had been there for perhaps as long as an hour and a half, crouched in the shadow of a thin, gnarled tree that dripped melting snow on his head and shoulders, the Kalashnikov cradled as gently as a child in his crooked arms. His feet and calves and thighs were cramped, icy.

You don't need to check, you already know. Silence reigned around and within the shack with its tilting roof and thinly curtained windows. The occasional stiff, unnatural shadow silhouetted the curtains. The cow's udder was bulging in the narrow, ramshackle shed leaning against the rickety garage for support. No one had milked her since the evening. No one was being allowed outside to do so.

And yet he could not leave, could not just walk off into the darkness. What he pretended was calm, good sense; recovery time was a terrible absence of will and energy. He could not *accept* that they were inside, that this place was a trap; that he was cut off from the two dilapidated vehicles in the garage. So he remained squatting beneath the thin tree, hearing its branches murmur and rub in the breeze, its few remaining leaves rattle like foil, while his body became gradually colder, more numb. Couldn't accept it . . .

. . . because he had no idea what to do next. He must look, despite the fact that there were the rutted marks of recently moved cars, clear in the moonlight and sparkling with frost. Wide limousine tires. And a small, stiff pond of marks near the shack that were footprints.

He rose slowly, unsteadily to his feet, bending to rub his calves into life, the rifle dangling beneath his chin from its strap. He straightened up, hesitated, then stepped out from the tree's shadow into the moonlight. His head snapped back and forth as he moved in a slow, low crouch across the icy ruts, the open space, his hunched shadow moving jerkily beside him. The mountains seemed enlarged by the moonlight that bathed them.

He stepped on something which crunched metallically, not like frozen mud. His breath soughed in fright and he remained rigid, the sensation of burning in his foot, his imagination filled with momentary pictures of one-legged men, footless children, limping women. He kept his foot still, though his leg began to shiver. And looked down. He bent like a drunk picking up spilt coins, carefully, until his hand touched around his boot . . . *antipersonnel mines detonate on contact or proximity*, he told himself, but could not believe it. Found—

—foot raised, hand shakingly clutching the thing, hand opening unwillingly . . . Bug. On his muddied hand lay a tiny microphone. They'd sown the open space with them, so certain were they he would come, so extravagant of means. He looked up, waiting for the door to open. Yes, there were others, lying in the freezing mud, sparkling bigger than the frost particles. Dozens of them.

Run—he stared at the crushed bug in his hand—run.

He moved as light spilled out, immediately masked by bulky shadows. The night was filled with shouted orders. He thought he saw Harrell, even Gaines from the British embassy, before he was whisked aside like a cape. Frost and microphones crunched under his running feet. Someone saw him, and yelled like a huntsman. A flare burst into the air, illuminating everything in their eagerness to be certain of him. The garage's tin wall buckled from his impact and his breathing drowned out their noises. He could not see his own footsteps as the white flare died—would they? He looked wildly about. The place was isolated from other shacks and huts. The sand and snow and frost would betray his bulk if he fled across the open space. The corrugated tin quivered with his tension. Harrell was yelling instructions, cursing the man who had fired the flare. Gaines was already seeking compromise, restraint; Harrell dismissed him with a single expletive.

The full-uddered cow shuffled in the lean-to, stirring up its scent and the smell of trodden, soiled hay. It lowed quietly. He sensed them scattering, heard one car engine from some distance away, saw headlights flick on, move closer to bathe the scene. The cow was unsettled, odorous. If he moved, moved at all, they had him. If he remained, they would find him. The cow shifted, rubbing its flank against the wall at his side. The smell of the shed reeked from the open upper half of the door. Almost without decision, much as a rat might have scuttled for that dirt-smelling straw, he heaved his body over the bottom half of the door and rolled almost beneath the cow's rear hooves.

It stamped on his side, winding him, then moved protestingly off, to skulk against the shed's far wall. Hyde rubbed his side and waited for his sight to adjust to the close, fetid darkness...

...and saw the two bodies bundled at the bottom of the door, heaped like dung against the mud wall, one on top of the other, limbs intertwined. The man and his son. Where were the women?

It doesn't matter—! His body began a traumatic shivering, however tightly he wrapped his arms across his chest, enfolding the rifle. He stared at the bodies of the two men he had known, who would have helped him; one face stared towards his in the leaking moonlight, a black third eye through its forehead.

The cow moved back over him, shuffling, beginning to snort and stamp and shiver, an image of his own fears. Its swollen udder hung just above his face, leaking warm milk. The cow's tail swept and twitched as at a plague of flies.

Voices—

Harrell's, which he newly hated but which increased his shivering. The cow grunted, hot-breathed, stamping its hooves as he burrowed into the clinging, filthy straw. Something scampered quickly away from his hand. He tasted the nausea at the back of his throat. The cow stamped on his calf, numbing it. Its noise drew them. The dead Afghan stared at him.

"Check the garage—carefully! That cow shed—check it out, asshole!" Harrell. Gaines muttering somewhere more distantly like an ineffectual conscience. A torso leaned over the lower half of the door, a flashlight poked and prodded at the shadows. Hyde saw his leg, still numb, exposed, one of his hands, too.

The cow banged against the wall of the shed, shuffling over, onto Hyde. More milk leaked because of mounting panic. The flashlight washed and shifted.

"See anything?"

The cow shuffled away from Hyde's side, having kicked out at him with a hind leg. He bit his lip to stifle his breath, any cry.

"That cow's mean."

"See that?" Flashlight on the swollen udder, the swaying hindquarters, just above Hyde's straw-covered face. "Maybe you'd be mad, too, if they didn't milk you. And she's got maybe too much in the way of company."

"How come?"

Hyde did not, could not breathe.

"Those two—the Afghan gooks, dummy. They're just inside the door, remember?"

"Sure."

The cow's hind legs shuffled closer to Hyde. His side ached, his leg burned. The cow kicked him again, on the shoulder, just missing his head.

"He ain't in there."

"We should check it out, like Harrell—"

"Want to play with Daisy there?"

"Not much."

"Then he ain't in there—right?"

"Right."

The flashlight winked out. Footsteps. Hoof against his temple, stunning him. The cow barred his way now, its dun flank heaving, eyes wild, mouth foamy, the long horns tossing, beginning to gore at the straw as if pitchforking it aside from Hyde.

He reached up, remembering with a huge, dizzy effort. Squeeze. The cow stamped, shuffled, gored. The tip of one horn slid across his baggy trouser leg, tearing the material. Squeeze. Both hands. Firm but gentle. Milk spurted intermittently, then regularly from the teats; spraying him, the straw, the dead men.

Gradually, the cow settled, hooves almost still, head well away from him, staring out through the doorway. Headlights washed the shed's walls as he worked rhythmically, his arms beginning to ache as he reached up, squeezed, pulled, reached, squeezed—his mind numbed. Voices came and went, huge; momentary shadows caught in the headlights; the occasional flicker of flashlights. Harrell cursed frequently; ordered the two cars immobilized, *but good,* and that chilled him—and disturbed the placid cow for a moment as he ceased milking. Cars moved away, tires squealing, engines loud.

Eventually, the cow's milk was exhausted. Its head had begun nuzzling, grunting in the straw. He rolled away from beneath the contented, hardly stirring animal.

In a while—the cars now out of the question, the men dead over there in the corner—he would, must slip away. *South . . .*

Harrell had shouted that, in answer to an unheard question, during another moment when he had stopped milking and the cow's hoofs had begun stirring again. *He'll go south—Pakistan—I tell you, it's south.*

And it would be. There was no other or nearer way out. Harrell would be waiting, certain he would come. *South.* There was no choice.

BRITISH GAS, the flank of the van proclaimed, white lettering on blue, with the more modest declaration, GAS, all but revealed beneath the newer stenciling. Shares were down and complaints up, both to a remarkable degree; hence the sudden patriotism, presumably. Clicking his tongue, Aubrey crossed the wide pavement to the Cabinet Office's Whitehall entrance, avoiding the trench and the overalled diggers bobbing up and down within it. Red-and-white barriers, warning signs, a smell of gas, half-uncoiled rolls of bright yellow plastic piping. Autumn's last leaves scuttled against every obstacle, hurried by a small, gritty wind off the river. After Alan's funeral, and despite the jet lag, Aubrey was eager to recommence his new responsibilities. The past few days had rendered him like the new headmaster of a good school struck down by flu during his first bout of reforming zeal. There were threads unpicked, all sorts of embarrassments and delays . . . and now they were digging up the road outside!

A pneumatic drill began, making his shoulders flinch as the sergeant on duty at the door saluted him, ushered him inside.

"Good morning, Sir Kenneth!" he was shouting.

"Good morning, Fred!" Aubrey shouted back, smiling and grimacing at once. Behind him, his car pulled away.

Leaves rattled against the door in a pause in the drill's attack on the pavement. Tidiness and priorities insisted. He was impatient as someone helped him off with his coat. There was JIC; Godwin's business; a meeting with an unfrosted PM the following afternoon; a meeting with Longmead; and a High Table dinner at his old college on Friday.

He stumbled over the rucked carpet in the corridor. A man in a pair of blue overalls knelt by one of the ancient cast-iron radiators. Water stains on the carpet, a chilliness in the place. He turned back towards the duty sergeant.

"Replacing the central heating, Sir Kenneth—I'm afraid."

The inevitable use of hammers. Floorboards stacked like firewood near the green baize door through to Number Ten. He shrank from the noise, hurrying into his office.

Untidiness. He felt every new creak of the floorboards, like the approach of some maelstrom of feelings and demands. Alan's death and his niece's character were only just below the surface and the intrusion of the Gas Board scratched and wore at the patina of a long night's sleep and an ensuing cool orderliness of mind. The past few days had really worn him out. He *must* get down to some proper work!

Gwen smiled as if battling severe dyspepsia. The banging in the corridor was horribly audible in her office. Perhaps in his own office...?

He exchanged quick pleasantries and accepted her solicitation regarding the funeral in San Francisco. He all but snatched at the sheaf of filed reports she handed him, with her typewritten summary attached by a paper clip.

"Half an hour, Gwen," he insisted. "No interruptions."

"You'll want to send Sir David a congratulatory message on his new appointment?"

"David—? Oh, yes, draft—no, I shall see him at college on Friday, I'll tell him then."

"Yes, Sir Kenneth."

David Reid—young David, a cabinet minister at forty-one, and after a successful business career. David's mother will be so proud...

Then he remembered that Reid's mother, Mary, had died the previous year. But the thought hardly interrupted the sigh of gratitude with which he closed his office door.

The drill's noise seemed to seep up Downing Street with a lurking, malicious intent. The hammers in the corridor were clearly audible. Aubrey hurried behind his desk like an eager shopkeeper and sat down, opening the first file at once, even as he studied the digest initialed by Gwen. JIC meeting agenda—later...drill and hammer...GCHQ SigInt reports...nothing attractive... drill and hammer, louder...USSR—photographs—at long last!—of the October parade through Red Square, and the rankings along the top of the Lenin Mausoleum. He pushed his spectacles against the bridge of his nose and leaned over the splayed enlargements, fingering the columns of explanatory type that accompanied the grained, shiny prints as he did so. Yes, Nikitin looked weary. Chevrikov, who had changed horses and now rode with the conservatives in the Politburo, was standing next to him, not Didenko or the foreign minister ... mmm. Some changes already? He picked up a magnifying glass and Nikitin's scowling, cold-pinched face almost disintegrated into its component dots. He sighed. He must come back to this. He needed a great deal more than was here, have young—who? Ah, yes, one of Peter Shelley's brightest protégés. Have Peter in, too, and a lot more information. He suspected the PM would be asking for projections from JIC before very long. He scribbled his notes on a pad. In a moment of relaxed concentration, drill and hammer sounded.

Alan slipped into his awareness like a burglar and Kathryn was there, too, with that detached, self-sufficient air about her; she was drowning, but clinging to disdain and not to the lifebelt.

He continued with a conscious effort, forcing himself to concentrate on new South African interference in Namibia—par for the course, despite that place's new, if partial, independence. He turned the file quickly aside, and glanced once more towards the edge of his desk where Nikitin glowered back, looking ill. He looked worse than in the photographs and videotapes of Irena Nikitina's funeral, supported then on either side by daughter and son-in-law. The girl had been the image of Irena, fur-coated and -hatted against the chill. Nikitin appeared to be losing his battle against grief ... He ground his teeth angrily and glared at the old radiator as the noise of hammering seeped along it, echoing.

Gradually, he allowed work to embrace him once more. Then Gwen was suddenly at the door and behind her a man in a pair of blue overalls displaying a visitor's security pass. A metal toolbox rattled in impatient anticipation. He groaned audibly.

"Sorry, mate—sir. Got to 'ave the rad off, now."

"What—I'm sorry . . . ?"

"Got to." The young, cheerful face was blandly implacable. "Clear out all the old rads and pipework today and tomorrow, it says here." He waved his worksheet. Aubrey flapped an already defeated hand.

"It's all right, Gwen. The sooner they begin, the sooner they'll be finished." He smiled.

"It wasn't the case when we had *our* central heating done!" she replied with surprising vehemence.

"Cowboys," the young plumber commented, turning back Aubrey's rug and laying a garish old curtain beneath the radiator.

"The Gas Board!" Gwen aimed at his back as she closed the door.

Aubrey sat down, at once catching the leaden eyes with which Nikitin regarded him from the photograph. He heavily underscored his note to summon Shelley. The drill's intermittent artillery faded from his thoughts. He opened the next file and Malan's photograph struck him, the man seeming to regard him even though his features were in profile. Water gushed into a big plastic bucket from the old radiator. He looked at the label attached to the back of the print. London . . . ? Malan must have left San Francisco even before himself. The picture had been taken yesterday. Malan at Covent Garden, in a box. The plumber grunted now that the water had stopped dribbling into the bucket. Aubrey recognized James Melstead, retiring permanent secretary and an old friend, next to the South African.

The second print was again of Malan in profile, a daylight shot through a wide window—restaurant, by the look of the table. The man opposite Malan, his dining companion, was familiar. He did not look at the reverse of the print. Not Dmitri Priabin, KGB Rezident in London, who was back in Moscow, there to answer questions and to try to rescue his posting and his career. This chap in the photograph was older. Of course, Priabin's number two, deputizing for him at present. Rublov. That's who it was, Rublov. Aubrey permitted himself a momentary smile. Tony had done well there, closing that pipeline. Two men outside the restaurant and out of focus were noted as KGB security from the embassy in Kensington Palace Gardens.

The plumber tugged the cast-iron radiator away from the wall. The noise hardly startled Aubrey, so absorbed was the old man. Malan, the gold and diamond broker and price fixer between Pretoria and Moscow, was... well, what *was* he doing? He glanced down at the accompanying report, compiled by young Evans. The security reference was that of Godwin's little department. Evans promulgated the Godwin thesis, unadulterated. Apparently, Malan was to be regarded as the key to any new pipeline for high-tech smuggling. Evans called it an *exciting, lucky break*.

He continued to make notes while the plumber began breaking up the radiator with a hammer and cold chisel, presumably along its original sections. The noise thudded in his head but not in his thoughts.

Malan. Certainly the Russians trusted him. Godwin *was* suspicious, mainly on the grounds that many of the companies in which Malan had a financial interest had been *selling* to the Russians for years, openly or on the q.t. Evans had made a request to increase surveillance. Gwen would know which form was required—yes, he could grant that. He ignored any examination of his motives for disliking Malan. In the photograph he was smiling at some remark of Rublov's. He needed to gain some background on Malan's current preoccupations.

He made a note.

Evans had appended one of Godwin's typically hurried, angry reports about some young man in the City selling shares in a small high-tech company and known KGB surrogates buying them up. Aubrey snorted. Godwin suspected collusion; he suspected mere greed. For him, money had never amounted to much, perhaps simply because he had more than enough for his needs. He had been slower than most of his peers, even to reach for power, though he well understood its attractions. But this report he bought wholeheartedly. He made an angry note to step up that particular investigation. There was little doubt that the young gentleman in the City was deliberately undervaluing the shares in order that the KGB might purchase them with the minimum of outlay! The company concerned produced circuitry for the communications systems of the new American nuclear submarines. A prize for Moscow Center to actually *own* it!

He looked at the heaped files, the sprawled pictures, the pages of notes he had made—and smiled at the struggling plumber tugging one section of the dismantled radiator through the door, using the old curtain like the rope used to drag away the carcass of a bull.

Immediately, Gwen was on the intercom.

"Mr. Anders, Sir Kenneth. Highest security." Gwen always announced such calls with a little breathless thrill in her voice. Aubrey looked at his watch. It was—Heavens, five in the morning in Washington! He felt his own buzz of urgency.

"I'll lock the door. Don't let our friend batter it down, Gwen!" Foreboding mingled with his excitement—but this must surely be some other matter? He snatched up the telephone.

"Paul, my dear fellow, it's still the middle of the night with you!"

"Kenneth . . . I'm calling from . . ." There was a mutter of noise in the background, and tinny music, tired and thin. "I'm calling you from my favorite all-night diner!" There was self-ridicule in his laughter, a slight sense of strain, too. "I wanted to call you before daylight, before I got myself back to normal." There was a pause, then Anders growled: "Who is this guy John Frascati? I got my ass chewed off by our great and good national security adviser yesterday just for asking about the guy! And when that happens to me, Kenneth, I want to know why!" Anders seemed more mystified than shaken, but Aubrey asked quickly, his thoughts flying up like sparks. "Why must you call me from a diner in the middle of the night?"

"Because I'm not supposed to talk to anyone off the record about this. But I want to know how and why you got me into this. I'm in this greasy spoon because this call was never made. You'll get a formal negative reply through the London embassy in due time. I'm going to tell you more than I should, and I know you're going to keep asking until I tell you more than they want!" He was breathing heavily, it seemed, as if he had been running. Then he added: "OK? Now, just who is this guy?"

"My niece's lover. A former investigator for your FAA."

"Yeah, and a Vietnam vet, and creditworthy and a college bum in his day busted for marijuana! I know all that—look, Kenneth, I got my ass busted, I got told by a snotnosed *kid* who sat beside the adviser that it was none of my damned business! That I do *not* like."

Aubrey was genuinely puzzled rather than disturbed. He adjusted his half-glasses, rubbed his forehead, frowned at his desk. Nikitin frowned back.

"I asked you a favor on behalf of my niece, Paul, that is all, I assure you."

"The hell with that!" Anders sounded offended and bemused. "I know the guy's address, I know he's not at home; taken off for the hills, I'd guess—except that just the mention of his name was enough. I'm told I have no interest in Frascati—no interest, period. He's someone else's concern."

Anders had reached the point of disclosure, and paused for effect. Perhaps he hoped for illumination or simply the mischief of titillating Aubrey's curiosity. "Whose?"

"There's a group," Anders began, clearing his throat. It was melodramatic, deliberate. "Inside Langley. It doesn't seem to report to anyone. Understand that, not to anyone, not even the president! *They're* the ones interested in your friend John Frascati—why?"

"I give you my word, Paul, I have no idea!"

Aubrey rubbed his forehead, which prickled despite the office's chill. He was unsettled; there was that unmistakable element of black farce, but Kathryn was involved. His reaction was private, filled with foreboding. These damned secret *games* the Americans loved so dearly!

"Are you going down the road to another Irangate, Paul?" he burst out.

"Don't moralize with me, Kenneth—I have no idea, either! I'm not supposed to know. I don't *want* to know. This call is what I owe you, but I never made it, OK? This is strictly none of my business from now on."

"Of course," he murmured with a Pavlovian instinct while his anxieties became more and more lurid. "Where *is* Frascati?"

"I have no idea, Kenneth! Maybe he just got sick of your niece, huh? He isn't home. And I was told, butt out—*sir!* I may be head of Direct Action, Kenneth, but I know the score!" It was anger, hurt pride that had made Anders call. And perhaps a few drinks too many. But this, this was *awful!*

"This group—?" he pressed.

"Sure—this group. They call themselves *Carpetbaggers* . . . maybe it's only a joke, but they don't answer to people. Like God beginning the world, Kenneth, they were wound up and left to tick away—like a bomb! Can you see why I'm calling you from the diner on the outside of town?" Anders had recovered his equilibrium and even his good humor, somehow. The business didn't worry him—he was used to it, for heaven's sake! Vietnam, Watergate, Irangate, Nicaragua—the special little murderous groups had proliferated faster than rabbits! And, meanwhile, Anders was satisfied that he had not been compromised, that Aubrey had no cynical or professional motive for his inquiry, therefore he had off-loaded everything except his pique at being told to— *butt out.*

Almost instantly, Aubrey's thoughts became personal and centered around an image of Kathryn's white, strained, disdainful features.

"What do they do, these *Carpetbaggers?* Why were they set up?" he asked urgently.

"All things to all men—or is that just what they represent? What they do, they call *Tilt.* Like when you want to beat a pinball machine badly. You *Tilt.*" He paused, then added: "And now you know a lot more than I'm supposed to tell you, and I find out you knew a lot less than I'd hoped." A mental shrugging off, a relaxation. Anders added, irritatingly blithe, only his voice tired: "So long, Kenneth. Call me anytime—on any *other* business!"

"Paul—"

The tone purred with a brittle, distant insistence. The knocking through the pipes, magnified by the absence of the radiator, was at once ominous, prophetic. *Carpetbaggers ... Tilt?*

It *was* ominous, he decided. The CIA had played too many—far too many—dangerous games. Their arrogant belief that a few murders, a change of government here and there, the destabilizing of currencies were all part of one's patriotic duty! My God ...

His head ached. He could not remember what Kathryn had told him of Frascati's doings or even his whereabouts when she last heard from him. How was the man involved with this new and nastily secret group?

That was not the question, he reminded himself, trying to recover calm. The question was—were these people interested in Kathryn, too?

The snow-crusted blanket he clutched across his shoulders hid most of the rusty bloodstains on the sheepskin jacket. His stained, baggy trousers were now filthy from the cow shed and the mountains. The donkey stood unmoving, indifferent at his side, as if despising the charade in which it had become involved. The small, reluctant queue of people and vehicles shuffled a few yards nearer the new checkpoint and he dragged the donkey forward. He was icily cold and, as soon as he was still for even a minute, leaned against the unresisting flank of the animal, or against the basket slung across its back. He had thrown away the rifle because he knew they would search the baskets, search him. He was unarmed except for the knife. The snow blew across the road and seemed to fall precipitously away towards the stream far below. The cliffs to one side of the road funneled and whirlpooled the wind. His eyelashes and eyebrows were stiff with snow that slowly froze. His beard was white, hardened like an uncleaned paintbrush.

Hyde waited. There was one small truck leaking fumes the smell of which was making him nauseous, two women in black, two boys with a dozen sheep, an old taxi, and himself ...

... and the two mullahs directly in front of him, turbaned and bearded, and the Afghan police at the newly erected, expected barricade, and the one European in fur hat and topcoat and gloves, still blowing on his hands, his collar turned up but not enough to disguise that he was CIA, one of Harrell's people from the embassy. They had guessed he would come this way—his tired thinking simple and panicky—this shortest road out of Afghanistan, through Mama Kheyl towards the Khyber Pass.

The snow blew like a veil between himself and the barrier. He presumed Harrell's limousine was parked beyond a twist of the mountain road. All he could see were the police cars and an army jeep, old and Russian and canvas-hooded, white and weighted with snow. His shivering had become automatic, continuous. The mullahs had inspected him contemptuously. The narrow, twisting road had trapped him between a wall of rock and the precipice. He had had no choice, lacking the energy and the will to attempt the mountain tracks. He had tried to hot-wire and steal a car in Mama Kheyl, and had failed. The donkey had not offered transport, only disguise.

The truck billowed exhaust fumes as it slipped beneath the raised red-and-white barrier. He and the donkey moved forward behind the mullahs with equal reluctance. The truck vanished around a shoulder of naked rock. The women, now, were questioned, gesticulated at. The police were officious, and glanced continually towards the American blowing on his hands. Hyde was still forty miles from the border. It was becoming impossible to believe in his own escape.

The women passed through the barrier. The sheep began to wander beyond the pole and it slid upwards with an audible creaking to allow the two boys to pursue and arrange them. The driver of the taxi wound his window down, his voice raised against the wind. The mullahs were becoming impatient, studying the American. The wind buffeted Hyde, the snow hard as grit within it. He should have made for Jalalabad, opened out the chances of a car, some vehicle.

He looked down towards the gray slither of the stream. A Russian troop carrier lay on its side, a long way down, as if it had expired like an old animal seeking water. He clutched the blanket closer around his shoulders, holding it like a veil across his mouth and nose. His hands looked too white to be Afghan, filthy as they were. Where was *Harrell?*

The ancient bus had carried him as far as the outskirts of Mama Kheyl before turning back to Kabul. Then, nothing had offered itself except the donkey, stolen from a lean-to against a broken-down hut. A man had lain feverish and unseeing on a pallet in the hut, apparently alone. Hyde had had no compunction about stealing bread, dried meat, the donkey. Where was Harrell? This American might, just might not recognize him, but if Harrell was here ...

The mullahs were at the barrier, and suddenly vociferous. He caught at disruption, at windblown scraps of outrage. Their long hands pointed out the American, who shuffled with uncomfortable, suspicious contempt. The police were berated for delaying the mullahs. Arms waved, anger increased. *Heathen ... why is this man here? Whose orders ... ?* Their bigotry opened like a narrow, illusory window. The boys tidied the sheep as if eagerly collecting gray pebbles on a beach. *Allah ... who is that man, why do you wait for orders from him?* The American had turned away, worried now, attempting anonymity. Where was his transport? Was he alone?

The barrier slid upwards towards the two mullahs, but they were now launched into a small ritual of denunciation. *Europeans—Russians, the heathen Americans—who, who—?*

He nudged the donkey forward, sensing the knife against his ankle as if his skin had thawed. The mullahs regarded him. He bowed his head respectfully—*God is great*—and then risked—

—spat towards the American, who was half-turned away, then shuffled beneath the barrier—

The nearest of the uniformed, greatcoated security policemen moved his rifle as if to bar his way, then was abused by one of the mullahs and his eyes flinched with hatred and fear, ignoring Hyde. The American moved, as if to intercept, but his steps were uncertain, embarrassed. Behind him—*behind* him now!—the mullahs' voices were high with condemnation. Hyde moved forward, aware of the thinness of skin across his shoulders and down his bent spine, heaving the reluctant animal alongside him, pulling it each slow step, it seemed.

The naked rock was almost sheer, knifelike as it jutted into the road.

A black, long car, windows and windscreen white and blank, wipers raised as if in salute or frozen by the snow, sat waiting. He shuffled past it, face averted, slowly moving along the car's whitened flank, the donkey protesting at the wind's renewed force, the flurries of snow chips it threw into their faces and eyes.

Then it was behind, left behind.

His shivering was no longer from cold. He staggered

beyond another twist of the road and halted, resting against the donkey's silent, indifferent, shivering flank. He felt lightheaded, dizzy, blinded by the snow, his hands numb, his feet without any feeling in them.

Forty miles...

The boys were from the next village, if there was a next village. They were fifty yards or so ahead of him, the intermittent bleating of their sheep like a poorly transmitted radio message. He must follow them, must keep up with them, he told himself as they again disappeared behind the veil of snow like mirages. But he could still just hear the sheep and the clucking and shooing of the boys. He must not lose them.

The donkey moved forward as if leading him. He clutched at the basket on his side of the donkey's back with one hand, the other numbly holding the thin blanket across his face and shoulders. The road went unregistered beneath his senseless feet. When he heard them, the small noises of the sheep and the two boys were sirenlike, alluring, but unreal. Transmission was worsening.

He stumbled more and more often, his eyes closed more and more frequently without the prompting of the flying snow and the wind...

...the intermittent, distant, tinny noises of sheep and the high, clear, interrupted voices of the boys...

5

BLOOD AND
VOICES

The telephone's insistence shrugged her awake. She was aware, somehow, that her father had not been there, in whatever dreams she might have endured. Five in the morning, the alarm's illuminated dial declared. She rubbed back the hair on her forehead, the heel of her hand coming away faintly damp, and picked up the receiver.

"Yes?" she croaked, then swallowed. "Yes?"

The ropes and necklaces of lights sparkled beyond the open curtains, the roads and towers of San Jose. A police siren wailed somewhere in the distance and a garbage truck clanged and clattered down on the street.

"Kathy—!"

John? It *was* him and yet she was unable to believe it.

"John! John, thank God—"

"Listen to me, Kathy, please—!"

"Where have you *been?*" It was a wail of relief, her arms suddenly cold and her forehead icy.

"I don't have time for any of that crap!" he bellowed, his nerves quickly raw. "Just *listen* to me, for Christ's sake! I had to hide out, lose them—do you understand? They were looking for me, I had to throw them off!"

It was melodramatic, and somehow insulted her relief that he was still playing conspiratorial games! Where had he been?

"I don't understand you!" she replied, her face heating, her fingers plucking at the cord of the telephone. "Why didn't you call?"

"They trace calls, for Christ's sake!" Then she heard his harsh breathing, as if he were silently counting in order to regain his temper. "Kathy, *please*—I need your help. Listen carefully..."

"You could have *called,* damn you!" It was like striking a child who had wandered off, out of fear. She knew she was being cold...it was because of his independence, his separateness—he had called now not because he needed her, only her *help*. "You could have called. I've been going out of my mind!"

"I doubt that, Kathy, you're a very together lady... sorry. I couldn't call. I kept away from people, places, out in the country. I couldn't trust anyone."

That was it! That damned small animal's fear of people, total mistrust he'd either been born with or learned in Vietnam or some other Godforsaken place.

"You just don't *care!*" she snapped violently.

"Listen, Kathy, forget all that—just bring me some cash, your car—and your gun."

"Why? What the hell do you intend to do?"

"Disappear. That's what I *intend*. I have to think it out, decide what I can do."

He *was* safe. His new calm proved that. The traffic began to be ceaseless. The aircraft were beginning to come in low, lights winking, increasing the pressure of her headache. She tugged at the telephone cord with her fingers, the long forefinger of the hand that held the receiver rubbing small, precise circles on her temple. With an effort, she got out of bed, carrying the phone, and walked towards the window where the traffic semaphored with increasing violence with brake lights and headlights.

She hunched towards the receiver cupped against her mouth. "John, where are you?" Her eyes prickled. She sighed. "What do you want me to do?" An aircraft slumped towards the airport's grid of lights almost with desperation.

"They want to kill me." His calm was that of exhaustion.

She shook her head violently. But *he* believed it. And, if it was true . . . ? Her thoughts cleared of the furniture of their relationship, their mutual history. Just do what he asks, she told herself.

"Kathy," he almost whispered, "this will screw those bastards in the CIA. Sure, I thought it had to be a bomb, until that Russian airplane went down—then I knew there was another way. And now I've found it—proof! I know just what they did—I've seen for myself and I know. And they know I know—don't *joke!*" he warned quickly. "Just bring me what I ask—your car, money, the gun . . . please."

"John, I—"

"Kathy, this isn't some fucking lover's tiff, for Christ's sake! They want to keep me quiet—dead! And don't give me that smart-ass crap about how I never grew up and I'm still a boy at summer camp and someone's spoiling it all for me!" He was silent, then quietly he pleaded: "Just do it, Kathy."

She forced herself not to hesitate; to abandon the large contradiction of his submissiveness as a lover and his utter independence as a person, and said: "Yes."

His relief was audible.

"Where?" she prompted.

"I'm near my apartment. You may have to go in there for me—no, never mind that. Just check it out for me, drive around one or two times. OK?"

"Yes."

"Bring the gun, the car—" He all but giggled. "As much cash as you can lay your hands on. I don't want to leave any more traces with cards. OK? Can you come right away?"

"Yes, I'll come now. That all-night diner, on the corner of—"

"I'll be outside. I'll watch for you. Kathy, I'm sorry I couldn't—"

"I'm on my way—love you," she added quietly, holding the receiver away from her mouth as if shocked.

"Sure—just hurry, girl."

It was he who put the telephone down. The quickening dawn revealed her apartment, which he had shared but which had, oddly, always seemed only her own. She shivered, thrusting down the receiver.

Money, gun, car.

For the money, she need only use the automatic teller machine at the bank; for the car, the keys were on her dressing table. She remembered where she kept the gun.

In the bedside drawer. Together with the condoms, as he had too often joked. Hurry...

*   *   *

He awoke to straw scratching at his face and hands. He was lying on his side and there was the overpowering smell of fresh blood; and squeals and bleats eloquent as pleas. He groaned, then stifled the noise, his hands enraged with renewed circulation, his feet agonized—his mind immediately, fuzzily thankful. He moved, holding his hands in front of his eyes, to be certain. Filthy, aching, tingling; undamaged. His cheeks, too, burned, and he rubbed them, oblivious of caution. He remembered the two boys, the donkey's plodding, the small snow-heavy fleeces wavering in front of him, then blacking out, then the wavering fleeces briefly in focus, then blacking out again . . .

He turned his head to thank the boys and discover his surroundings—warm light, deep shadow, the insistence of straw and dung, the oppression of blood. The lamb hung by its hind legs and blood was draining from its Islamically slashed throat while the dying carcass twitched, just as others that lay around it on the straw twitched, seeping now rather than bleeding. Hyde vomited drily, emptily. Only then did the slaughterman take any notice of him, his large knife shining and wet, his eyes bright, hands red. The two boys watching their small flock slaughtered turned large eyes in his direction.

The man studied the draining lamb for a moment, then crossed the barn towards Hyde, the knife in front of him. Hyde tried to struggle upright, his chin slimy with saliva, and the slaughterman pushed him back onto the straw, nodding. Inspecting. Hyde slumped against a loose bale as if drugged, his nostrils and thoughts affronted, appalled. The Afghan nodded and returned to the lamb, lowering it onto the straw now that the blood had petered to a slow dripping. The remaining living lambs, three of them, were bleating with a kind of horrified, pleading simper.

Jesus Christ . . . Their slaughter strictly according to Islamic law seemed important; another atrocity to add to all the others Hyde had witnessed. But his body would not move, obey him. The boys gabbled. The Afghan muttered in reply.

"He was with Masood. English, I think. There will be money for him."

Hyde could only roll onto his side, exhausted, groaning, his throat gagging, his hand over his nostrils; better to smell the dirt of days.

"Who'll pay?"

"The Americans . . . maybe. The Pakistanis—like your sheep, uh? Maybe the British. He is worth money, uh?"

Another lamb squealed, struggled, was hoisted and slit. Hyde covered his ears, pressing his hands against his head as if to squeeze all thought away like water from a sponge. He did not want to think, could not think . . . money. Sell him. They would take him out of Afghanistan . . . out like the sheep, but still alive in his case.

Hands felt, toes moved, cheeks burned but possessed sensation. Nostrils—he could not close them like a seal against the alien element of the blood-smell. His stomach heaved, again and again. The squealing of the final two lambs filtered through his pressing palms, above the noise of the sea he had created in his ears. He wanted to scream. Wanted to do nothing but scream.

John's apartment was in a high-rise condominium at the edge of a relentlessly spreading high-tech industrial park. Its upper windows were already copper and burning with the dawn. The air was still chilly and she shivered as she turned the car onto the flat, treeless road along which a dozen condominiums stared across at the low-rise factory units. The traffic had thickened. She understood that the temperature was not the cause of the constant shivering of the skin on her arms or the small area of cold in her back. She was cautious, too, unable now to ridicule or dismiss John's anxious paranoia.

Drive around, he had said, *once or twice.* Who would be watching his apartment? Who could hide along this featureless, barren stretch of highway? She felt drawn into some sinister game and had difficulty in remembering that it *was* a game, that his suspicions and fears were those of a child trying to scare her. In a moment, the blindfold would be removed, the other kids would laugh and her hand would only have been thrust into Jell-O and not something slimy and nameless.

She parked the car. Only hundreds of yards away, she could see the lights of the diner, pink and green neon, without promise. The traffic hurried into the maze of factory units, slipped smoothly away from the row of high buildings. She was in the parking lot of the condominium next to John's.

The dampness of her hands surprised her; their quiver disturbed her, and she rubbed them hard together before getting out of the car, dragging her wool jacket across her shoulders. OK, she would walk to the diner—pass his condo, check out any ... surveillance. Crazy—

There seemed to be no one in the rows of parked cars, except drivers who pulled away as she approached or passed. The topmost windows shone brighter with the reflected dawn than those which glowed with electric light. The highway smelled of gasoline and dust. US 101, rushing through modern, sprawling, affluent San Jose. She liked the place. It wasn't as soulless as LA and nowhere near as pretentious as San Francisco. It was without history, almost, something else she liked, its new tawdriness deliberate, functional; masking wealth, energy, brains.

She looked down from the line of condos and away from the spread of Silicon Valley factory units and warehouses. It seemed suddenly darker along the highway. Beyond the diner and the industrial park lay the dark blotch of a winery, the white speck of its adobelike buildings. A Spanish-mission feel.

There was no one watching the apartments. She was angry, grinding her teeth together. She looked back at the city's lights, mostly behind her, then at the traffic, and sensed herself as ridiculous, her esteem stung. This was the last time, the *last* time. No more crap about conspiracies! The moon was a nail-paring low on the still-dark horizon but the Coast Range's hills were becoming pale masses. She passed the last of the apartment blocks, and then the industrial park, too, seemed to peter out, leaving the diner isolated and shabby on the edge of a narrowing, almost desertlike landscape.

The traffic noise seemed louder, as if the diner's parking lot somehow magnified it. She scanned the seven or eight parked cars but could not identify John's.

A small dawn breeze plucked at her sleeves, at her dark slacks and hair, blowing it across her eyes. Music flowed from inside the diner's closed doors, one of last year's hits; country music, insistently normal. She strained to make out the figures behind the low cabin's glass, expecting to recognize his profile, his face looking for her. It was a joke, a damn bad one, too, for Christ sake! She brushed her hair angrily away from her face, her cheeks hot with self-ridicule. Seven or eight cars, the traffic a blur of lights and noise, the diner seedy and the repository of some pleasant but mostly unpleasant arguments. Drinks and tacky meals after quarrels and submissions.

DAVE'S EATERIA, the neon proclaimed, splashing pink and green onto the parking lot of dusty, potholed concrete. The noise of the traffic became irrelevant with the sudden eruption of headlights from one of the parked cars, splashing over her, making her squint—

—his body, she was certain as her stomach lurched, lying beside one of the cars, an old, Day-Glo-painted Chevy with the steel steer's horns on the radiator grille. John, lying less than fifteen feet from the dusty edge of the highway, as if he had crawled—

—car engine. She whirled around. The car's headlights were extinguished now, as if not required, their purpose completed. She flinched as the car drew out of the lot towards the highway.

She ran the dozen yards to where the body—

—limp, as if every bone within the skin's bag were smaller, broken to pieces. Marks on his clothes, dark blood on her hands. His arms sprawled, his neck lolled. His blank eyes glittered at her. Her father's face blinked like a flashing light, then John's, then Alan's, then John's again, the only two dead people she had ever touched. She held his crushed and somehow empty body against her, dead weight, her fingers sticky and touching his beard. The backpack had spilled some of its contents— a map, some fruit, another shirt rolled up as if he were bringing it back for her to wash. Her hands became wetter as her eyes streamed.

The car drew onto the highway, as if satisfied, and moved slowly away. Someone was making a low, keening noise but it didn't seem to be her. Then nausea heaved into her throat as his head, released gently, lolled away and hung, face down. She released the body and it slid into motionlessness. She stood up, gagging, her mouth filling with saliva and tears as she wiped at her face. There was noise, startling her, as the diner's door opened. Her whole chest seemed to have swelled up into her throat and mouth, choking her. A man in a check jacket had left the diner, heading unconcerned towards a truck. The cab door slammed. She could, as she sniffed and swallowed, still smell John's clothes and skin.

The truck's engine fired. The car that had slipped away from the lot returned, sliding back off the highway, drawing towards her. Pausing, assessing, sidelights on, windscreen dark. The sky was pale overhead, golden at the horizon, the hills brown and blotched with green. Nothing seemed to be happening except those separate, small registrations.

She looked down. His mouth was open in a hideous rictus of pain. His body was—

The car watched her. The truck pulled out of the lot, its bulk unnerving against the dawn. Panic rose, broke over her, and she ran, hearing his voice in her head like a shouted warning—*those bastards in the CIA, I can fix all of them . . . I know how they did it, did it . . .*

She dragged open the diner's door, the glass shivering loosely, the fat man behind the counter looking up, his face surprised above a greasy T-shirt and swelling stomach, his hands wiping massively on a towel. A woman looked at her over a coffee cup; one of the men inspected her casually. She had to *see* John's slack and baglike body to overcome the normality of the scene. Had to call the police.

"I need a phone!" she blurted.

The fat man tossed his head towards the far wall. The smell of frying nauseated her. She stared at her reddened hands and fumbled them into her jacket. The woman had returned to her cigarette and newspaper, the man to tapping the counter in time to the record on the juke-box. Something about standing by someone, whatever— she hardly noticed.

"Thanks!" Her panic was exaggerated, the fat man's indifferent glance told her. A woman panicking, not quite real. Nothing to get excited about.

The tiny mirror clouded beside her cheek, her fingers fumbled the number, her small change. The door of the watching car out in the lot opened and a man got out; small, neat, wearing dark glasses even in the dawn. The lot seemed ordinary, expected, the traffic flowing past. Except that she could now make out the small heap of John's body beside the garish old Chevy. Nausea.

"Police Department—can I help you?"

"Ain't seen her around here for a while," the fat man was muttering, nodding in her direction. Dave, it was Dave, she thought, as if only now recognizing him. "Used to come in with a guy—"

"Police Department, can I help you?"

She opened her mouth and the man outside, as if in anticipation, began moving towards the door of the diner; slowly, casually.

Ran me right off the road—tried to kill me, the bastards! I can fix them now—off the road—kill me—

The small lump of John's body—she could make out the checks of the shirt pattern now, and the pale skin of his brow—the car, the man moving towards the diner. It was all real. John's broken, rubbled bones inside his skin, the blood on her hands and clothes, the choking sensation in her throat—was real. They'd killed him.

She looked wildly around. "Police Department? Hey is there anyone—?" She slapped the receiver back onto its rest on the wall, as if there was collusion between the voice on the line and the man pausing at the bottom of the three steps to the diner's door. Dave's glance was a further collusion, the turning heads of the two men at the counter following his gaze were—

She ran into the narrow corridor behind the drab

curtain hanging from brass rings, past the toilets, out through the diner's back door. The sun caught her like a slap across her cheek, blinded her so that she stumbled on the steps. She began running, floundering in her heels, clutching her jacket, head bent. A dusty space, weeds quivering in the breeze, the noise of the traffic just audible above her own heartbeat. There were no thoughts now, just the sensations of running, of heat, dust, perspiration, weakness in her legs, a pain in her chest.

She had no intent to caution, yet she sensed they would be watching his apartment building. She detoured around the back of the condominium, kept close to the walls of the building, came out on the far side of the next high-rise, then walked slowly, casually towards her car as if coming out of the building...

She collapsed into the seat, quivering and exhausted, taking what seemed minutes to find her keys, fumble one into the ignition, start the engine, grip the wheel damply and jerk the car into gear. John's dead face flashed in her eyes like a failing light, just as Alan's had done. The sensation of his broken body pressing against her revolted, tautened her whole frame. Her thoughts whirled. She had no idea what to do, who to turn to. They'd killed him, just as he'd claimed they were trying to do.

The car moved as if of its own volition. The wheel was sticky with perspiration and John's blood. She wanted to wipe her hands, violently. She saw dimly, wetly, the first traffic lights glaring as if there was rain on the windscreen. Her apartment. Her clean, neat, safe apartment was all she could think about. A shower became an obsessive desire. The locks on the door, the curtains; safety. Distance between herself and the diner's parking lot.

The traffic jolted and stumbled through a new suburb,

along wide streets which eventually narrowed and greened and relaxed. She parked her car beneath a dusty tree outside her apartment building, oblivious to caution as she slammed the door and hurried towards its entrance. Into the elevator, sighing upwards, welcoming its whispered speed. The familiar thick carpet in the corridor, which she hardly noticed was empty. Her keys fitting the secure locks, the click of strong bolts.

The door closed behind her, her relieved, exhausted breathing the only noise except for the ringing of the bedside alarm which would have woken her only ten minutes ago if it hadn't been—

She ignored the flashing images of his face, less hypnotic now than in the car, and threw down her jacket on a chair, pulling off her stained blouse with thick, icy fingers. She unbuckled her belt, stepped out of her shoes...

The coffee table's assembled magazines were neat as always, the smoky glass of its surface dustless, unmarked. Its brass feet denting the carpet's thick pile— four imprints beside the ones it now made...

She held her head tightly between her hands, as if she could smell their haste and expertise like sweat or fear. The minor tremor of a search had displaced her furniture, put one picture slightly askew, left a small crescent of clean wood where an ornament had not been exactly relocated. Not burglarized, she told herself unnecessarily. Searched. They had been here, looking for something.

She pressed her hands tighter against her cheeks, hurting her jaw. They'd been *here*—

His lunch had tasted like paper, hardly digestible. Longmead's company had been tedious, their mutual concerns futile. He had scurried back to his office. Gwen had been instructed to man the telephone in case Kathryn should answer the message he had left on her answering machine . . . not in at six in the morning, California time? Her mechanized, distant voice had chilled him, as if he had been listening to some grotesque message left behind by someone—

He had shied from that idea. Now, Gwen was shaking her head as she wiped sandwich crumbs from her desk into a paper napkin. He waved a hand in what might have been acknowledgment or dismissal, and she called after him:

"That young man of Mr. Godwin's is on his way over, Sir Kenneth, Evans—"

"Yes, yes!" he snapped, closing the door behind him. The rug was turned back across most of the room and floorboards had been taken up and stacked. The plumber looked up cheerfully and nodded at him. Copper pipe gleamed everywhere. Two modern radiators leaned against his desk—God, it was ridiculous! As ridiculous as . . . no, not as his foreboding. He could not dismiss that lightly. Not at all, in fact.

"How long is all this going to take?" he burst out, exasperated, expelling tension; which ran back into him at once as if automatically refilling an emptied vessel.

"Weeks, boss," the plumber murmured, his head half-entombed beneath the floorboards.

"Weeks—!" He pressed the button on his intercom. "Gwen—coffee!"

"Yes, Sir Kenneth. For two? Mr. Evans is here."

"What? Oh, yes, send him in." He looked at the plumber's unruffled features. "Weeks?" he repeated menacingly. "Just in *here*?"

"Oh—only a couple of days more in here, guv."

Aubrey looked at his watch. "Please go and disrupt

my secretary or someone else, would you? I have a meet-ing—ah, Evans, come in."

The plumber climbed to his feet, picked up his tool-box, and left, whistling as if to deliberately irritate.

"Sit down, Evans!" he snapped. The young man's broad, florid features crumpled into dismay. "Oh, do sit down, my boy!" Aubrey added in mollification, waving him to a chair near the desk. Behind which Aubrey retreated.

"You wanted a full briefing on Malan, Sir Kenneth—"

"Did I? Yes, I must have. You're familiar with Tony's theories, *and* any evidence . . . ?"

"Yes, sir."

Copper pipe, the new radiators, the stacked floor-boards. Evans's overweight bulk squeezed onto an up-right chair. The silent telephones. He turned abruptly from staring into the white sheen of the net curtains which obscured Downing Street outside.

"What can you tell me about an aircraft accident in northern California, perhaps six months ago?"

"Sorry, sir—I—"

"Have you ever heard of an FAA investigator named John Frascati—like the Italian wine, I presume—who might have made something of a fuss about such a crash? Well—?"

Evans's face was squeezed with concentration, like that of a child wishing to help but thoroughly bemused as to what was expected of it. Then—

—cherubic brightness and a triumphant grin.

"Frascati . . . rings a bell—the name. It was about six months ago. I'd have to check, but I remember a pas-senger aircraft, one of the internal US carriers, flying from . . . oh, somewhere like Portland to San Francisco, crashed near some lake. Shasta, was it?" Again, his features compressed and wrinkled like a deflating balloon. He rubbed his wide forehead, murmuring: "This chap Frascati—there was some fuss when the FAA brought in a verdict of instrument and engine failure compounded by the usual pilot error. He didn't agree. I can't remember why, though, without checking."

"*Was* there anything suspicious about the crash?"

"Only to him, sir."

"Would it have security implications—for *any* reason?"

"I—no, I never heard anything like that." He shook his head. "No, definitely not. Nothing." He smiled, but it faded, withered by a lack of response from Aubrey. Bemusement slipped back across his face.

"Never mind about Malan for the moment. Evans— I want you to find out as much as you can about this accident, mm? On *this* side of the Pond. Don't call up our cousins at the embassy, not for the moment. Ask our CAA people."

"Now?"

"I think so, yes. Leave whatever you've brought on Malan. I'll look at it later. Well—?"

The intercom cheeped.

"Yes, Gwen?"

"Your niece, Sir Kenneth—she seems distraught."

"Quickly, put her through!" Evans had risen to leave, but Aubrey waved him back onto the small, hard chair. Then Aubrey snatched up one of the telephones, his chest thudding as with the efforts of some small, trapped animal. He turned his back on Evans, pressing his right hand against his breastbone, aware that his shoulders would look shrunken with tension to Godwin's young assistant. It could not be helped; he had no appearances he wished to keep up at that moment. The woman's suspected danger frightened and unnerved him.

"Kenneth—" She used his name unfamiliarly, like a word in a foreign language. His stomach was at once watery with relief and new, pressing forebodings.

"Kathryn, you're all right?"

"I didn't know who to call—you left a message on the machine. I called—

"Kathryn, for God's sake, what's happened?"

"They've been in my apartment."

"Who?" He was aware that he had already begun to deceive as well as protect her . . . if he could, in fact, protect her. *Carpetbaggers*.

"I don't *know*. They've killed John!" she wailed immediately after. Chill realization sidled closer, insinuating itself as easily as a snake into a rock crevice.

"Where are you?" he snapped urgently.

"A neighbor's apartment. I couldn't stay there. I have the key—a girlfriend of mine. They'd searched, *been* there! Moved things."

He sighed, ignoring the leaking valve she had become, shock dripping away slowly in tiny, unimportant details. The neighbor's telephone could not be bugged, as undoubtedly hers would be.

"Don't use your own telephone." Then, Frascati's murder swallowed him and he floundered for a moment, until grasping the professional thread to which all else clung. "Is there someone watching your building?" he asked. "Were you followed, Kathryn?"

"Followed?" Silence. She had no inkling. He must get this right, he thought. "Please look out of the window— carefully. Does the window overlook the street?"

"Yes."

"Then please look, Kathryn," he soothed.

"What do I look for?"

"Men in cars—parked cars."

He sensed her walking to the high window, wishing her to be cautious.

"Was anything missing from your apartment?"

"I don't know!"

"Had John given you anything for safekeeping?"

He heard her sniff, swallow, and her voice was rushed and very breathy.

"No, there was nothing like that."

"Anyone down there?"

"Maybe—I'm not sure." Then rage and frustration. "How the hell would I *know?*"

Try to think of her as someone on a ledge that you have to save, he told himself, aware of Evans moving on the small chair, making it creak and protest. Evans sighed, probably out of embarrassment, because he had heard Gwen announce his niece and yet this was an extraction, a tooth-pulling operation; simply, getting an agent out. But, Sir Kenneth Aubrey's *niece?* Aubrey understood Evans's bemusement.

"I understand," he soothed. Her tone informed him that the thermometer of shock was rising once more. She would see the dead body now, be revolted and guilty. He shivered. "You found him?"

"Yes, yes—I went to meet him and he was dead when I got there, he'd been in a hit-and-run, that's how it looked but there was a man watching, who *knew!*" Then the recurring, surrogate rage at their intrusion into her apartment. "When I got back here, it had been *searched!* They'd been *here!*"

"Yes, of course. I understand." Medical, assured, soothing voice. He *had* used it often, and often it had been efficacious. It *had* to be now. "Kathryn, listen to me carefully. Is there anywhere you can go, somewhere safe? I don't mean immediate friends, or your mother, somewhere away from San Jose? And have you credit cards with you? I don't want you to return to your apartment. Is the place where you are on the same floor?"

Dull, leaden aftershock now. Good. "Huh? Why? No, two floors down."

"Did you call the police?"

"I tried to. I couldn't, he was coming—"

"Good. Then don't call them." He swallowed, then continued: "If they can find John's body without your help?"

After a long silence in which he felt hotter, then rubbed his forehead and stared at the glaze of the net curtains, she answered in a tiny voice: "Yes."

Now, the first move in the extraction—despite all the questions he wanted to ask and which she must, eventually, answer!

"Your apartment building—I seem to remember a service entrance? Use that to leave. Don't take your car. Do you understand?"

"Yes."

Aubrey swallowed, then asked as calmly as he could muster, "Have you thought of somewhere?"

"Safe? Yes, it's—"

"No! Don't tell me. When you reach it, call me. Do you understand?"

"That I'm in your world? Yes."

"Kathryn!"

"John said it was the CIA, just like that—as if he expected no better, no different. Is it?"

"Kathryn, I don't know. But I promise you I will find out. And, as soon as I know where you are, and that you're safe, I will arrange for someone to come out—" Shelley could divert someone from the Washington embassy, to fly out; someone armed, no reasons given. His breath seemed small for some moments; Anders's words wormed in his head, noiseless and burrowing, threatening Kathryn.

"What's *happening?*" she demanded, emerging from the slight hypnosis of her trauma.

"There's nothing I can tell you!" he shouted back. "Not at present. Now, Kathryn, please do as I say. Just remember that John was concerned—*cautious*—please act in the same way."

"It killed him."

"Please do as I *say*."

After the silence, she said: "OK. Thanks—I think. I'll call you, then."

"At home. This evening. Wherever you are. You call me every two hours. Please." He tried to sound parental, but realized his lack of experience. And was left silent, waiting.

"OK. The service exit. No car, no luggage. OK."

"Are you ready?"

"No. But I have to try, right? I don't have any choice, is what you're telling me."

"No, my dear, I'm afraid not. I can't calm your fears. They are not unfounded."

"Then what in hell is happening to me?"

"I can't tell you, Kathryn—not at the moment, believe me. I wish I could."

While the connection remained, he was certain she was alive and unthreatened. He could assist with the inevitable bouts of fear and guilt and bewilderment. But, when he put down the phone—

"Kathryn, trust me, please. Go now. Go carefully, I beg you!"

The truck must have jerked to a halt, throwing his frozen cheek against the thick, hard wool of one of the dead sheep. His eyes opened reluctantly and his body protested even the slightest effort so that he was unsure as to whether he had moved at all. His head must have lolled, though. He would not have settled near the dried blood stiffening the wool around the gashed throat of the dead sheep.

Snow puffed in through the gaping seams in the canvas hood of the truck, and where the flaps met over the tailgate. The hand brake protested and the truck was still. His body seemed a long way down from his head and difficult to maneuver. His legs would not part. He was unsure of the position of his hands—a terror of frostbite rushed through him, nauseating his empty stomach more than the smell of old, familiar blood, and the sight of the heaped, limp carcasses of the drained sheep. They had lost their power to revolt him, had simply become his camouflage as he lay—

—hands not coming apart, not coming from behind his back. Legs refusing to move separately. The mound of sheep between himself and the flapping, loose stretch of canvas at the back of the truck where hard white light washed in with the snow. The noise of the wind and the voice of the driver who was the slaughterman. His body pinioned.

He was awake to his surroundings now, the contours and confines of the truck. His fingers and wrists had sufficient feeling in them now for him to recognize the bite of rope or some other material around them. He squinted down at his feet, black against the paleness of a sheep's flank where they rested. Cloth tied his ankles together.

He lay back, hardly more than disappointed. He remembered the slaughterman grinning into his face as he tied his ankles, and the practiced way in which he had flipped him over onto his stomach in order to bind his wrists. Trussing him like one of the sheep. The Afghan had carried him over one shoulder like a sack out to the truck, after the sheep had been loaded, and thrown him down behind the cab, hidden by the mound of mutton on its way to Pakistan, another Islamic society demanding properly slaughtered mutton, and paying better than Kabul. *We go to Peshawar, my friend . . . there, money for them, money for you, I think.*

No need to think. Harrell will buy you all the sheep you can slaughter, son.

Despite that—he groaned weakly—he had fallen asleep! In the back of the careering, bouncing truck, he had exhaustedly slept! He pressed his cheek against his shoulder, as if nursing an aching tooth. He stared blankly at the snow-rimed wool on a sheep's flank. The icy wind slapped the loose canvas of the hood against the side of the truck. His bound wrists and feet were absolutes. He was as much a slab of meat as the carcasses surrounding him. He tried with a futile, dribbling kind of desperation to imagine the border crossing they had reached. He must know it. But it came fitfully, like monochrome patches on old, decayed film stock, grained and flickering.

Outside the wind tugged, and threw the voices of the driver and at least two guards. The checkpoints were just outside Torkhan, in the Khyber. You do know this bloody place! Afghan side of the border. Customs shed, vehicles, hard lighting hanging long-necked over the crossing point. Security casual since the Soviet withdrawal; all good Moslems together. The driver was asking, with exaggerated indifference, about Americans.

"A car, some hours ago . . . why?"

The ritual spitting. "Heathen pigs almost ran me off the road." The conversation dribbled on. His fingertips tingled, his wrists began to chafe against the cloth strips binding them. His feet had become braced against the dead sheep. Snow puffed into the back of the truck, wet on his face.

"Your papers—OK. You can pass." Then the calling on Allah and the starting of the engine.

His thumbs ached with slow-returning blood, his fingers itched intolerably. His feet prickled. He felt nauseous, his head dully revolving. The truck jerked forward, slithering on deeper snow, righting itself like a dog shaking off water. He dribbled bile and tried to raise himself, braced against the sheep's carcass, into a sitting position—then lay back again groaning. The truck slowed, taunting him, towards the Pakistani side of the border.

He rolled weakly over onto one side. His fingers plucked at the top of his boot, able to distinguish its leather from the cloth of his baggy trousers.

The Afghan was speaking poor English, trying to make himself understood. A few words of Urdu, after trying out Pashto on guards who were obviously from the south, not local. He realized that, all of it. As his body twisted away from his hands, his fingertips touched then closed upon the hilt of the small, sharp knife. The heavily accented English continued just behind his head, the singsong accents.

Mutton for Peshawar, the market . . . yes, the monthly delivery. Where is Iqbal, he knows me . . . ah, his first child! The guards were bored but punctilious; an officer must be watching them from the shed; near the stove. *I stay tonight in Peshawar . . . good, good, in order, yes?*

The knife was halfway out of his boot before he realized it. His listening had sharpened, filtering out the wind and the slapping canvas, hearing the creak of a door, the stamp of cold feet, the *slamming of a car door*—

Crunch of heavy footsteps—two men—drawing

closer to the truck. The knife was between his hands like a wafer, his neck muscles taut and his back arched as he placed it, missed, placed, missed, placed it and began to saw at the cloth around his ankles.

Americans ran me off the road. The Afghan was beginning the sales pitch. Hyde sawed raggedly, felt the blade cut his palm, clutched it tighter, sawed.

"We didn't pass you on the road, buddy. You looking for us?"

Harrell's voice puffed through the canvas hood, clear as snow. Hyde held his breath but his hands did not stop. He did not dare look at his ankles, look at whether the cloth might part soon. He winced as the knife sliced flesh.

"Americans?" the Afghan was surprised and wary, closing himself like the drawstring on a bag. The two Pakistani border guards had fallen silent.

"You will assist these gentlemen if you wish to continue your journey." The officer, speaking Pashto. Three sets of crunching footsteps then, not two. He held his breath and listened.

"But I have done nothing!" the Afghan began whining.

"Thanks, Captain—the guy speaks English. We heard. What is it buddy? What's in the truck? In your head? Anything for us?" Someone laughed, but there was an edge of excitement in the sound.

"Nothing in the truck, I swear!—"

"Mind if we take a look?" The cloth parted and his legs flopped, tight with cramp, but apart. All he was aware of were the hands that held the knife still bound together behind his back.

"It was other Americans—an American car, perhaps—!" the Afghan blurted.

Hyde lay waiting for the flap to be drawn back, his face averted, hands useless, legs crying out with bunched calf muscles. The Afghan wouldn't sell him yet because he knew they'd take, not buy ... but the authorities were on Harrell's side.

The flap was dragged back with a whiplike crack against which he flinched. Snow gusted in and beam from the flashlight flew like the snow. Washed over the carcasses. Danced back and forth, touched his shoulder across the sheepskin jacket, traced down the spine of the carcass nearest him, slipped back to his shoulder as if to rouse him, back to the carcass again, then to the sides of the truck, to the canvas hood, then to pick out the gaping, drained throats of the sheep.

"Jesus Christ, the way these people kill their meat!" Harrell growled as the light vanished and the flap slapped back. Hyde wanted to exhale but it seemed too great an effort. "OK," Harrell said at the front of the truck after his footsteps had thudded and slithered past Hyde's head as it rested against the side of the truck. "Just the dead sheep. Shame. Thanks, Captain. You can let the guy go now."

A dismissive command in Pashto, the noise of retreating footsteps drowned by the engine's noise. The rattle of the pole being raised just audible, the skid-then-acceleration of the truck. Moving slowly downhill like an old, uncertain man.

He was utterly drained from tension, shivering with relief. The untied canvas at the rear of the truck flapped and cracked stiffly. He lay still, hands beneath him still holding the knife.

He was—out—out, he thought, as slowly as if deciphering code or morse. He—was—out ... making—for—Peshawar. Harrell was—behind him—now.

Beneath the intermittent words was the sensation that, if he lay still for the next slow hour, he would regain just enough strength to cut the cords around his wrists ... If he did that, before Peshawar, he could climb out of the truck. It was all he had to do, free his hands before they reached Peshawar. He could manage that ...

PART TWO

LARKS' TONGUES IN ASPIC

The lark's on the wing;
The snail's on the thorn:
God's in his heaven—
All's right with the world!

Robert Browning, Pippa Passes

6

A GROUP OF
REFUGEES

The ancient taxi's windows were smeared and foggy, the large, cold stars indistinct in the night; and indeterminate, like the encamped army of shacks and hovels on the outskirts of Peshawar. Aubrey felt himself too old, too closeted, to be nakedly confronted with the ghetto of displaced Afghans who had not returned to their country after the Russian withdrawal. Thus, he was indebted to the darkness, to his own weary jet lag and to Ros's grim, taut silence. Her face was pressed against the other rear window, her breath clouding it like little cartoon bubbles of speech. She was chalkily pale, even in the taxi's dim interior, but almost childlike in expression, looking out intently into the dark. The Afghan boy driving the taxi whistled tunelessly and said nothing of Hyde, though he had been sent to meet them at the airport. His silence foreboded.

He sat back in his seat, the shock of Hyde's incoherent telephone call returning with a recovered strength, as if he would never be able to rid himself of it. Hyde's rage, his almost paranoid suspiciousness, his secretive withholding of information, his reiterated demands to be brought out, all knocked and banged in his head like distraught mental plumbing. Hyde's desperation accused him with undiminished vigor.

He had called Shelley, requested arrangements for bringing Patrick out, rebuffed Shelley's curiosity and refused to allow any spreading of the news of Hyde's survival. Peter had sullenly accepted his strictures, agreed that he would moonlight—as he had said, *like a bricklayer using the firm's equipment to do some private job strictly for cash*—but he had agreed.

Hyde had insisted on one thing ... *Harrell. CIA. Harrell.* It was a hook to draw Aubrey up like a fish. *The CIA killed Nikitin's wife.* Then Hyde had cut the connection, knowing Aubrey would come, that his recovery was assured.

Ros had insisted on accompanying him. Aubrey had not had the stomach to refuse. He wished now, looking across at her, that he had traveled alone. She pricked and accused like a virulent conscience; or, like a mirror, she reflected and deepened his own concern. Both roles were equally irritating to him.

It can't be true, it's insurance, he had told himself again and again. It's exhaustion, it's paranoia; Patrick's at the end of his tether. But Patrick was being hunted because of something he had seen ...

Aubrey sighed. Ros twitched as if struck, then grimaced and returned her attention to the smeared win-

dow. Aubrey, irritated by her manner, wondered what
on earth she thought she could see out there in the night!
Then he sensed the taxi stop weaving and begin to slow.
Through its windscreen, past the boy's shaggy head, the
headlights revealed a group of ramshackle, listing huts,
one or two with corrugated roofs, others badly thatched,
their walls stone, brick, mud, cardboard or hammered
tin still faintly emblazoned with oil company logos and
other commercial symbols. Aubrey shuddered, assailed
for some unknown reason by the sense that he had arrived too late. For what, precisely, he could not say, but
certainly too late. The boy gestured them out into the
night's chill.

Ros, uncertain now, her eyes darting and no longer
intent, clutched her fur jacket around her throat. The
keening, thin wind snatched at her skirt and hair, ruffling
both. Aubrey turned up his collar and adjusted the grip
on his stick. *Get Godwin—you'll believe his version of
what I saw.* It was arranged. Tony had changed his flight
from New York to London to an Air India flight to
Peshawar. He would be in tomorrow. The stars hung
coldly, frozen in the blackness that was littered with
escaping slivers of dim light and low open fires. Aubrey
smelled cooking and dung and dirt. The boy gestured
them ingratiatingly, impatiently towards one of the huts,
more substantial than some of its neighbors. Aubrey
hesitated on the threshold—like the prodigal's father,
he told himself—and Ros allowed his mutually comforting grasp of her elbow. Then he nodded, trying to
smile, and they went in, the Afghan who had opened
the door to them standing aside like a servant. The place
oppressed Aubrey even before his eyes adjusted to the
dim, lamplit room at the rear of the hut, its chill striking
hardly less than the cold of the night, its earth floor

hard, seeping cold through his shoes, the low ceiling just above his hat.

Which he removed. The place smelled—God, but it smelled!—of dirt and unwashed skin and rough alcohol and a sweet smokiness that he only slowly identified. The Afghan and the boy who had driven the taxi left them, closing the door creakingly behind them, as if embarrassed. He and Ros stood just inside the door as if strangers to the room's only occupant.

Patrick Hyde's eyes focused very slowly as he turned his head from contemplation of the stained and cracked wall to look at them. Aubrey, appalled by Hyde's appearance, was unable to speak. Hyde's face was long-unshaven, almost bearded, and the hollows under his eyes were made cavernous by the yellow light of the oil lamp. The bottle he cradled almost stereotypically was clutched further against his chest as if they were robbers. He did not seem to recognize them. His baggy Afghan trousers and shirt were filthy, like the thin mattress on which he lay.

Aubrey felt Ros's large hand plucking at the material of his sleeve. Good God, he thought. He was ashamed of his silent reaction, but could not suppress it. It overcame even guilt. He had never seen Hyde so—what? Finished. Ros's plucking at his sleeve insisted like the tugs of a child requiring comfort, but he could only stare at Hyde. Patrick had been worn out. He stank, was drunk, and was enveloped, Aubrey now recognized, in the scent of hashish.

Hyde raised himself on one elbow like an invalid, a grudging, unwelcoming recognition in his gaze. Then he declined onto his back again with a low, growling snort; as if they had been expected, but only as bailiffs might have been. The room pressed against Aubrey with a greasy, damp touch, and his head tightened, as if it were too full of thoughts. The silence seemed encamped for an indefinite occupation. Aubrey could do nothing but stare while guilt and pity seeped into the room like water through a leaking roof. The hovel was all too insistent in its likeness to Hyde, all too complementary to his wretched condition.

Then, sandpapering Aubrey's already exposed nerves, Ros's voice bellowed, screaming at Hyde as she released Aubrey's sleeve and lunged forward. Hyde cowered away from her. The intensity of her feeling evoked a sharp sensation of shame in Aubrey. She snatched the bottle from Hyde and threw it against the hard mud of the wall. It failed to break and merely leaked from the neck. Then she had grabbed hold of the stuff of his filthy shirt and was shaking him, terrierlike.

"Fucking state you're in, Hyde!" she was shouting, her fur falling from her wide shoulders to the ground. Aubrey all but darted to pick it up. "The fucking state of you—!" She was still shaking Hyde, but her voice was declining into sobs. "—state you're in, you stupid, bloody—"

She seemed to decline beside the filthy cot as easily as her jacket had done. Hyde stared at her as he might have done at some violent intruder; helplessly, confused, then thankfully, relieved. Aubrey watched Ros's shoulders heaving, heard her huge, gasping sobs. She seemed to be wrestling Hyde against her.

"Christ, Hyde—" she struggled to utter. Aubrey saw Hyde's dirt-streaked left hand against her hair make tentative stroking movements.

Aubrey remained watching them for an uncounted time, deeply embarrassed, his guilt and relief having to be coped with. He felt voyeuristic and yet knew he had to stay. Part of Hyde's attention never left Aubrey, as if his embrace of Ros was mere theater. His hands, clutching at Ros's shoulders, seemed more genuine than his eyes.

Eventually, he lay back and Ros perched her weight at the foot of the cot as she wiped her face and sniffed loudly. Hyde's eyes glared balefully at Aubrey. Ros was rubbing—crushing—shreds of hashish and cigarette paper in her large hands before brushing them distastefully onto the floor. Proximity seemed to induce a new calm; she was satisfied, like a nurse whose examination had found only sprains, a torn ligament or two, cuts and bruises. Aubrey could not be so certain. Something impotently dangerous—corrupted?—stared out of Hyde's eyes; something, too, that might be of little or no further use.

"Took you long enough," Hyde said, one forearm over his eyes as if the light was bright.

"I'm sorry, Patrick." He was not certain on whose account.

"Sure. Interested, were you, in the trailer for the big film?" His voice sounded remote, indifferent.

Ros was watching Aubrey now, protectively antagonistic to him.

"Yes, indeed," Aubrey murmured. "However fantastic."

"Oh, it happened. Where's Godwin?"

"He was in the States—he's on his way. Be here tomorrow."

"He'll be able to identify the RPV for you."

"RPV?"

"Remotely piloted vehicle."

"I know what it means!" Aubrey snapped, cursing himself in the same instant. Hyde's mouth opened in a snarl-like expression that might have been satisfaction. His forearm still covered his eyes.

"I know you do." Then Hyde removed his arm and

his head lolled towards Aubrey, his pale eyes hot and somehow anguished. "You've buggered me up for the last time, old man! Just *understand* that, will you!"

Ros's body had recaptured its earlier tension. There was a mutuality of dislike, even hatred, directed towards him from the cot. He felt himself leaning more heavily on his stick.

"Tell me what happened," Aubrey said.

"Oh, you want to know, then?" Hyde taunted. "And I thought all you wanted was for me to be safe!"

"Patrick," Aubrey said, sensing only dimly the route he must take to Hyde's confidence, "you told me that the CIA killed Nikitin's wife—" He ignored Ros's puzzled breathing, her little gasps as he proceeded, even her eventual defensive anger. "—rather a large claim even for someone suffering from battle fatigue, as you so obviously are!"

Ros made to move from the cot but Hyde grabbed her blouse. Shivering with anger and cold, she contented herself in plucking up her fur and wrapping it across her shoulders and breasts.

"Don't take any notice of him—it's just technique. He's *all* technique."

"Patrick—I'm here to get you out. Everything has been arranged—"

"Who with?"

"By myself. With Shelley's help—wait! Peter knows nothing except that you're alive. My God, Patrick, I had to ask his help! I needed papers, money, *assistance*." Hyde was relaxing again. "Now, I want to know what you saw, exactly what happened, how you came to be there and how you came to be here. Because if your information is accurate, then you are in even greater danger than I at first thought." Much greater, he admitted to himself. "Tell me what happened."

While Hyde spilled his information as parsimoniously as a miser, Aubrey was conscious, through his gnarled, thickly veined hands, of the increasing pressure his weight exerted on his walking stick. He was aware of his feet growing colder from the packed earth of the floor; aware of Ros's small habits of self-pacification in stroking the single blanket over Hyde's legs, in brushing imagined specks from her dark skirt, in touching at her hair. Her face had become blotchy and exhausted; and increasingly malevolent as she listened, staring at Aubrey. Hyde's narrative began to increase in tempo. There was a need to tell.

Aubrey felt the successive emotions of gratitude, sympathy, guilt, self-accusation and impatience slide through him as he listened intently. But the pull of those sensations was identical to that on his attention, his intuitions; the prospect and immediacy of danger. However much, now that he was old, he wished he might linger in the cloisters of affection and rest, it was always that acquaintance with risk which drew him.

They've killed the engine of change, switched it off, he told himself. They don't want change. KGB, army, and Harrell—Anders's *Carpetbaggers,* it must be. He was certain of it. Frascati's suspicions were confirmed by Hyde.

He could not but believe Hyde. During the flight from London, he had pondered whether his lurid hints had not been designed simply to ensure his rescue—but no longer. Patrick had seen, had escaped, was hunted. His virulent, burned-out weariness, his chronic suspiciousness, this monotonous diatribe to which he was forced to listen, all confirmed the truth of what he related. The sense of danger grew and crowded as a breeze moved the flame of the oil lamp, enlarging and moving the shadows in the room.

He must get Patrick back to London, as secretly as possible. They would make every effort to kill him. Should he even wait for Godwin to arrive...?

Yes. Diverting Tony out here had been instinctive, but sound. Hyde's whereabouts were unknown. Debriefing was, for the moment, safer here than anywhere. And, looking at Hyde, he sensed that he would not leave this icy, noisome room without protest. Hyde's sullen, exhausted rage had come to rest on that narrow cot. He was withdrawn, contemptuous, filled with enmity towards anyone and everyone who might oppose or threaten him.

Then, without any sense of completion, Hyde had finished speaking. He lay staring at his forearm, ignoring both of them.

"Thank you, Patrick," Aubrey offered. A scowl briefly inhabited Hyde's features. Ros continued to stare with hostility. To her, Aubrey was Hyde's employer, his boss; she was afraid of him on Hyde's behalf.

"Thank you," he repeated.

He was concerned for Hyde, guiltily sympathetic. Greater than that, however, was the pressing sense of danger and the mounting anger he felt rising inside him. The damnable, stupid adolescents! The murderous children! Killing Irena Nikitina because she was perhaps the motor of *perestroika*.

Clever and damnable... and with as many possible reverberations as a stone flung into the middle of a pool. Who was involved? Who had ordered it, or concurred in it?

And on whom could he rely, who to trust? The room pushed against him, its shadows looming. To protect the security of what they'd done, these renegades would go to any lengths. The cliché struck with the insidious realization that there might be no one he could trust, no one he could employ to assist him.

His feet were numb from the floor's chill. His hands gripped each other whitely at the top of his stick. He saw that his enlarged, wavering shadow was that of a bent, frail old man.

Hyde, quiescent, appeared as if he were already dead.

"No, just a vacation. A friend's fishing lodge on the lake. I work for a company in Silicon Valley."

"They need the British now?"

Blake smiled in reply. The remark from the untidy-haired blonde at the store's checkout was unbarbed. Freckles speckled her tan like the markings of a bird's egg. He hoisted the two grocery bags into the crooks of his arms, smiling between the columns of brown paper.

"Thanks."

"Have a nice day."

"Yes."

He walked out of the small supermarket into a cool, fresh morning, but felt warm enough in the de rigueur check shirt and denims. The trip to the store had been necessary; irritatingly, the woman was out of cigarettes and they had needed eggs, bread, steaks. His irritation quickly faded into pleasure at the spruce and pine darkly clambering up the slablike mountainside. The somnolent ease with which the small town went about its business beguiled him. He opened the trunk of the rented car and lowered the two grocery bags into it. As he closed the trunk, he looked up again at the snow clinging to the mountains and capping the sharp peaks.

It was difficult to maintain anything other than a pleasant calm, now that he was away from the lodge and the woman and her incessant questions. He slipped into the seat of the bulky sedan and began tapping the steering wheel with the palms of his hands, unwilling to start the engine and take the dirt road back to the smooth, gleaming lake. The woman would be waiting, wound overtight like a watch spring, almost seeming to lurk in corners of the rooms just to irritate him. Her tension—and what he supposed might be her grief—stifled him, even on the lake's pebbly shore or the jetty from which he fished desultorily.

Were she not Aubrey's niece, he would deal more sharply with her whining—tell her where to get off, so to speak. He liked women and was habitually at ease with them. But this woman held no sexual charm for him; about her was the brittle sensation of metal fatigued and about to buckle. She occupied too much space in the rooms she entered, especially in that cramped fishing lodge. She moved quickly and suddenly, almost as an insect does.

The whole business was beginning to bore him, after Washington. He and Caroline touched power there more openly than in London, and both enjoyed it. Especially Caroline, his wife. Privilege and shopping with her circle of diplomatic wives . . . *diplomatic*, as she never failed to remind him. Not the secret world. There was no excitement for her in that. And, he was increasingly forced to admit, the job was beginning to pall for him. Were he posted somewhere out-of-the-way, a backwater, he might already be seriously considering a transfer to the Foreign Office.

He sighed. Recollection soothed, as if he had reached a decision just by rehearsing old arguments. He started the engine, routinely checking that the pistol remained in the glove compartment.

What do they want? Why did they kill John? The woman's endless questions, bleak as her features as she asked them. He banged the wheel then reversed out into the dusty street, turning the car to head back towards the lodge. Sunlight gleamed from a blind windscreen. He glanced perfunctorily in the mirror as the car reached the end of the single main street and bumped left onto the dirt road. Clear. He whistled softly, which prompted him to turn on the radio. He flicked through country music, rock, a vaguely familiar orchestral piece, a weather update—then settled for the rock station, turning up the volume. *Why did they kill John? What is Kenneth doing about me? I have to get away from here— what is going on?* The slabbed guitar chords quieted the woman's recollected voice. Perhaps—if this was the pitch of excitement that marked his future—then he should seriously think about a transfer, talk to a senior attaché, test the ground . . . ?

Dust filled the mirror. The car bounced and twisted along the forest track, then began the long slow descent towards the lake. He smiled. Yes. Caroline's arguments were beginning to look more and more attractive.

He slowed around a bend, then accelerated. A chipmunk scuttled across the track just ahead. A roadside sign warned of crossing deer. He shivered at the thought of unluckily striking one, the animal's wide-eyed pain— —car in the mirror, bouncing in rhythm to the undulations of the road. Fifty yards back, keeping pace. Its joggling in the mirror was vaguely hypnotic. He shook his head and switched off the radio as if angry with it. The car was unfamiliar, not one of those from neighboring lodges. A dark-green sedan, a Lincoln with a tinted windscreen. Parked where? Across the street from the store. And confidently slow to follow him. He accelerated a bit. The car maintained its distance.

Perspiration prickled his forehead and beneath his arms. His palms were damp where they gripped the steering wheel. His heart plucked in a quick, staccato rhythm. The forest pressed close around both cars. He slipped through a splash of sunlight coming down in slanting lines. The Lincoln passed through it seconds later. Irrelevantly, he looked at his watch. Then at the tripmeter. He was a mile from the lodge.

Lead them away? Take a long route, see if they follow? How did he know they were tailing him? Instinct, or just an imagination newly jolted into activity? He glanced at the glove compartment, opened it and placed the Browning on the passenger seat. It was cold to the touch. He turned up the car's air conditioning. You don't know, he told himself. He was traveling at forty now, the car rocking and bouncing along the track. The hills on the far side of the lake could be glimpsed through openings in the tall firs. There was a turning perhaps a quarter of a mile ahead—take it? Check them out? He accelerated up to forty-five. The Lincoln slipped through another glare of sunlight the same number of seconds behind him as when he had been traveling at thirty.

With the conviction of panic, he was certain. Almost fifty. The Lincoln emerged and disappeared like a mirage in the mirror, cloaked and unmasked by the cloud of dust he was throwing up. Still maintaining the same distance.

There was no time to lead them off, because the woman might already be in danger. The narrow side track shot by and was behind him. Even before he had really decided. Nothing for it now except to reach the lodge.

A reasonableness stubbornly remained. The panic was superficial, to do with the car's speed and his sweating. There was the sensation that the men in the Lincoln were CIA or FBI or some other official organ. Not the enemy. Dislike of Aubrey's niece reinforced that reasonableness. He glanced at the large pistol.

He squinted in the sunlight as the car skidded around on the grassy slope just above the lodge. The morning lake hurt his eyes. The woman opened the door at once, alarmed; with the fear of a child, hardly real. He thrust the gun into his belt and opened the door of the car. The Lincoln had sidled to a halt twenty yards from him. Its passenger door opened. Out stepped a young man in a lightweight, fawn suit, blue shirt. He felt exhilarated now, the woman's hunched, tense body on the porch somehow silly, the lake gleaming and still, the dust settling around the cars as it might have done around two elks sparring during the autumn rut. He raised his hand to wave—

Kathryn saw the pale little leap of flame, twice, from something in the stranger's hands, just in front of where his forearms rested on the door of the green Lincoln. And saw Blake's slim form jolt, then arch backwards, roll across the hood of the rented car and slide awkwardly into a sitting position against the offside front wheel. Then the man in the fawn suit ran towards the slumped body while the car's driver, gun drawn, hurried towards the lodge. Blake's forehead was smeared red. He was cursorily inspected, then both men were running—

—saw the doorway, the bright rugs on the polished floor, slipped, hands gripping the stripped wood of the far wall, then the strap of her purse, then her hands were holding the window frame of the bedroom Blake had been using. She was quivering as she heaved herself over the window ledge, stumbling down onto the grass, which her hands touched, still wet with dew where the shadow of the lodge fell.

She pushed herself to her feet. The nearest trees were damply obscure in her vision as she began running. There were shouts behind her and two detonations like those which had killed Blake. Birds screamed in protest. She grasped at the air in front of her as if struggling to climb rather than run. Then the bole of a tree collided with her left hand and a branch whipped her across the cheek and the sunlight was dappled over her blouse and arms then densely shadowy in another moment. She could hear nothing other than her own exerted breathing. Something snatched at a tree trunk beside her face, making a long, ugly white scar. Her hair, loose about her cheeks, filtered the sting of splinters. She stumbled over roots, her feet pained in the flimsy shoes. Her mind seemed incapable. She saw the flitting images of the two cars facing each other like challenging animals, the gun, the fawn suit, the little spits of flame, Blake falling helplessly and grotesquely; but there was nothing she could call thought. So she ran, and almost at once there were no other sensations than her heaving lungs and stumbling feet, rough bark against her hands, the overpowering scent of resin and the rhythmical slapping of her purse against her thigh as it dangled from its strap.

And the occasional whipping of low branches, their tangling in her hair, or her hair spiderwebbing across her vision to be brushed roughly away like the thin, flying branches.

Her cheek hurt, sunlight blinded her from directly above, pine needles strangely stung her face, their scent filling her nostrils. Her mind thought her body was still running as she rolled down a slope, dizzy, exhausted, her hands cut and bleeding, her knee hurting, her body whirling then slowing.

Water submerged her right hand icily. Sunlight, then blackness—

"Christ, Patrick, someone ought to try hypnosis on you!"

Godwin thrust himself upright on his sticks and fumbled the tiny tape recorder into one pocket of his heavy tweed overcoat. Then he slouched away from the cot on which Hyde, now dressed in denims and a loose sweater, lay like a helpless and accusing invalid. Aubrey followed him out into the winter night. Somewhere, a goat bleated. Aubrey was grateful he could make out nothing of the refugee encampment. It had still been light when they had arrived, he, Ros and Godwin. The slanting tin and cardboard huts and hovels, the few ancient vehicles and goats and scrawny chickens—that permanence of the temporary—had depressed and repulsed him. He did not want to see any more of it. If only he could get them all out of the place tonight! Twenty-four hours in Peshawar was already too long. He tapped his stick impatiently, almost snapping at Godwin:

"He's been through a great deal, Tony."

Godwin lumbered around to face Aubrey. "I know that, sir—but he's so bloody uncooperative he's beginning to drive me up the wall!"

It was true. Hyde *was* beginning to irritate. "What do you think, Tony?" He sighed inwardly. "Does what he says ring any bells? His description of what he saw—does it give you anything to go on?"

Even in the windy, icy darkness, he saw Godwin shrug, leaning heavily on one of his sticks, rubbing his lifted hair with the other.

"Sorry, sir—shouldn't get angry with the silly sod. He always was an awkward bugger." Godwin paused, then said: "Whatever it was, it wasn't Russian."

"Why not?"

"They never went in for RPVs in a big way. The stuff they have is miles behind what they used on that plane. More likely, if he's accurate in what he's describing, it's Israeli or German—even American."

"I see. You can't be more specific?"

"Not without a lot of reference material and a lot of inquiries. Even comparing computer models." He paused, then asked lightly: "Got a Jane's handy, sir? There's two things, really. The altitude at which it stooged around up there, then the way it homed in to bring down a big, fast-moving target. The plane would have been moving at four to five hundred knots. An RPV ought to be able to do about half that at best, maybe only a quarter of the speed. Therefore, the guidance and control systems in the launch vehicle had to be very sophisticated..." He paused, absorbed by his reflections.

"So—what happened to the launch vehicle, afterwards?"

"Could be anywhere. Are you picking me up on the idea that it might be American—because of your niece?"

"Perhaps."

"I'm not prepared to commit myself, sir." Again, his large hand moved as if drying his thinning hair. "My God, I daren't commit myself. It's too bloody fantastic to think about! Shooting her down? I can see why a few army and KGB boys would want to get rid of the 'Tsarina,' but the CIA involved? Christ—!"

Aubrey puffed out his cheeks, then exhaled as if blowing dust from a polished surface. "Do you believe him, Tony?" he asked.

"Yes—that's the trouble. He says she was on her way to Kabul to do some deal to take the heat off the Kremlin and its Moslem republics—and then the army, KGB and the CIA shot her down! Doesn't really matter which RPV they used, does it, sir?"

"It does. Very much," Aubrey stated.

"Why?"

"Patrick lost all the proof he had. If he's to be kept

alive—if *any* of us are to remain healthy—then we must be able to prove what happened. We need what they call insurance in gangster films, Tony. *Life* insurance."

"Strikes me it's a pity Patrick saw what he saw, sir—for all our sakes!" There seemed no resentment on Godwin's part at being drawn into what might very well become a tightening noose; rather he sensed the intrigued, appalled excitement he experienced himself.

"Yes, it is," Aubrey replied. "But he did—and involved us."

"I don't mind that, sir. That's the job." Aubrey realized that Godwin could not believe that anything more violent or conclusive than his injuries could occur to him. They had happened in Germany; they had arisen from the job, as he called it. He had paid; his sticks were his life insurance.

"Thank you, Tony. But, we'll begin with this RPV. I want you straight back to London—"

"What about you, sir—with him and Ros?"

"I'm going to try to get them out tomorrow. I've hired a car as a backup, but really I need to talk to Shelley again about moving Patrick—"

"You ought to get him out soonest, sir."

"I realize that!" Aubrey snapped, then added: "Sorry. But you, Tony, will go straight back and get to work. My niece's young man made a link between the vehicle Patrick saw and a crash in California—and perhaps he died for doing so. You find photographs, details for Patrick to look at, to confirm, by the time I get him back."

He could see Godwin nodding. "Fair enough, sir. I'll try to get on the flight down to Karachi tonight. But, sir—"

"Yes?" Aubrey flinched against Godwin's solicitude.

"I know you don't want me to say it, sir—but you're not really safe here. On your own."

"I know that, Tony—please don't rub salt in the cut!"

"Get him out tomorrow. If you think these *Carpet-baggers* are involved and they've already killed Frascati, then they'll be very anxious to catch up with you-know-who. And anyone he's talked to."

"Yes, yes, thank you for your concern, Tony—!"

"Sir, don't go all waspish on me! You can't cope—*deal* with them."

"I hope not to have to."

"If Gaines just handed Patrick over to Harrell at the drop of a hat, who the bloody hell can you trust?"

"I don't *know!*" It was as if they were violently quarreling now, both heated, argumentative, both convinced of their separate rightness. "I don't know what these bloody fools are capable of! I don't know how they could even exist, never mind influence our service. But they can, they do and they have! There are the three of us, and one civilian, Ms. Woode—and, presumably, Peter Shelley is still to be trusted! Other than that—" He threw his arms in the air, stick dangling from his grasp. "Other than we three, I have no certain belief in anyone or anything! I will move Patrick as soon as Peter confirms our route out. Until then, I'm stuck here. Now, please don't make things more gloomy than they already are, Tony."

"Very well, sir. Just concerned."

"I know that. But, find this vehicle for me, prove it's American, then we can begin to uncover these people—turn over the stones they're hiding under."

"And save our own skins—right, sir?"

"Correct," he sighed. "Correct, I'm afraid."

*   *   *

Aubrey watched the lights of Godwin's flight as it climbed away from the airport, a shadow against the ghostly mountains. When the navigation lights were smaller than the frosty stars, he moved away from the window of his room in the Khyber InterContinental and absorbedly poured himself a small whiskey. The bottle seemed to clatter much too loudly back onto the tray on which it had arrived. He disregarded the tempting ice in the small, fingerprinted bucket.

He experienced a towering sense of outrage that he could not ignore. Yes, he was transferring his own guilt to Harrell and his renegades, but Harrell had reduced Patrick to that pathetic, burned-out creature on the filthy cot with his idiotic stare and his delight in the new Walkman Ros had brought with her. It was even more than simply a question of guilt. It was this, this *invasion* of the body politic by a faction of an intelligence service working like a virus. And a group that planned and executed on this scale—!

Killing Irena.

He shivered slightly, pausing before the room's long mirror. He looked weary, but his eyes burned behind his spectacles as if he was feverish. Good God, he was angry!

He returned to the window. Somewhere over there, beyond the pinprick lights of the airport and its suffused glow, Hyde lay listening to that damn tape machine of his, probably drinking some filthy local brew, utterly worn out. He must get him back to London at once. A long rest. No one must know that Patrick had been found, or that he was back in England. Perhaps he and Ros could use the cottage—?

There was a knock. Ros? He nodded to himself as he walked to the door. He would put it to her now, the idea of the cottage.

The man in the doorway wore a dark topcoat over a gray suit. Shaven, healthy, large-featured, looking down at Aubrey with a sardonic gleam in his light-colored eyes. Hands in his pockets, body confidently at ease.

"Sir Kenneth Aubrey." It was not an inquiry. "Could we talk?"

The accent was American, East Coast. Aubrey was stunned by the realization that it was Harrell. Hyde's description scattered like pieces of a jigsaw, but enough remained to identify him. Aubrey all but blurted out his name, then recognized the danger in doing so. "You—have the advantage of me," he managed.

"Huh? Oh, sure—" Harrell held out his hand. "Robert Harrell, CIA. Based here. Can we talk inside?"

"I—er, yes, I suppose so." He allowed Harrell's bulk to move past him into the room, making it smaller, then shut the door. He gestured Harrell to one of the two easy chairs at either side of a fruit-laden table near the window. Harrell removed his topcoat and dropped it on the bed.

"A drink, Mr. Harrell?" He carefully refreshed his own drink, lowering the bottle as if balancing it on the edge of something.

"Sure—why not? Scotch on the rocks."

Handing Harrell the drink, he lowered himself into the other chair. The airport's glow and the sensation of the scattered, grubby lights of the camp beyond it nagged at his peripheral vision.

"To what do I owe your visit? I'm surprised you even knew of my—"

"London called your people here. I got to know."

"London?" Aubrey repeated, mentally winded. *Shelley?* "I'm—not here in any official capacity. I'm surprised that SIS would take such a close—"

"You're chairman of JIC, Sir Kenneth. People of your

seniority don't take off into the blue with any anonymity. Mm?" Harrell rattled his ice as he swirled the drink slowly, staring at it. "No, I got to know." He looked up, still a young man, vigorous and confident. Like a Mormon missionary at the door, Aubrey thought. There was the bland certainty in the intelligent eyes.

Harrell sighed. "Let's not beat about the bush, Sir Kenneth. You're here because you think you can put your hands on—someone we're interested in, too. A guy of yours, an old buddy, named Patrick Hyde. Right?"

Without hesitation, Aubrey nodded and said: "Yes. That is my sole reason for being here. A personal debt, so to speak." He hoped he looked suitably guilty and ashamed as he stared down at his whiskey, then sipped it.

"Sure, you owe the guy. I know the story." Harrell leaned forward. "Sir Kenneth, *you* know what this Hyde might have done. Why are you trying to help him like this?" The voice soothed. Again, there was the sensation of the doorstep conversation with someone selling certainty. *We understand your search . . . we have all the answers you need.* He shook his head. "You're not denying it?"

"Oh, what? No. You are correctly informed." *Shelley!* "I felt I must—"

"What brought you out here?"

"Rumor—gossip. The fact that Patrick used Peshawar as a base." Did he look sufficiently old and tired, he wondered. Harrell's clear eyes scrutinized and weighed him.

"Then you had nothing definite?" How *much* had Harrell been told by Peter Shelley? Did Harrell know?

"Nothing definite," Aubrey concurred. Harrell appeared satisfied, despite his intense gaze, his evident suspicion. But youth made him contemptuous. A guilty old man confronted him; inconsiderable. It was Aubrey's turn to sigh, a small, elongated shuddering noise. "I— you see, I felt I had to come. It all seems such a damnable mess, doesn't it? Patrick's situation, I mean. First of all, presumed dead—then possibly alive but heaven knows where. I just, well, felt I had to come. I'm sure you can understand that, Mr. Harrell?" Harrell was marginally sedated. Aubrey pressed on. "What exactly do you think happened, Mr. Harrell—in your experience of Afghanistan, and of Patrick? What is it you think he may have done?"

"Done? Maybe nothing, Sir Kenneth. But he was there. I mean, really on the spot when that plane went down. A lot of people would like to talk to him about that. What he saw, what *exactly* happened, how he got away."

"But, you don't think he had anything to do with it, surely?"

"Couldn't say. Maybe no." He smiled disarmingly, shrugging large shoulders, opening large palms. "I got to know him quite well, Sir Kenneth. I don't think he was mixed up in what happened. Others may, but not me. But, if we could only find him, Sir Kenneth—it'd make a lot of things clearer. Settle everything down. Help him, too . . ." He paused, then asked with the same clear-faced sincerity that had been his first mask: "Do you have any idea where he is, Sir Kenneth? Is there a way in which we can help each other—and him?"

Aubrey's gaze pleaded back, stared and became absorbed, then merely tired, his hands closing in surrender on his lap. He shook his head.

"There's—nothing I can do here. If you can't find him, Mr. Harrell, then I have to assume he isn't here. Foolish idea in the first place, quite foolish. Old man's whim. I should really be getting back to London—to my work." He smiled wanly, shading his eyes from the light of the standard lamp feebly with his hand. When he looked up, Harrell's cynicism was momentarily slow to fade from his expression. Aubrey waved his hands. "Yes, I must get back."

"I'm sorry you haven't..." Harrell moved from lassitude to briskness in an instant, standing up and reaching for his coat. "Sir Kenneth, just believe me when I tell you we'll do our best to find him for you."

Aubrey rose with an effort, nodding. "Yes, of course." Harrell was angry, however much he masked the emotion. He had expected more, but had been satisfactorily fooled. Aubrey held out his hand and felt the slight pressure of Harrell's grip.

At the door, Harrell's farewell was perfunctory, his contempt undisguised. Aubrey closed it behind the American, waiting with his back against it, the room indistinct, the square of window seeming to directly overlook the camp which concealed Hyde. His thoughts whirled, then he counted. A minute went by, then another, his right hand still on the doorknob behind his back, his body warmed by little outbreaks of heat. Then he leaned more heavily against the door, and smiled.

And was immediately angry. He had thought nothing during those two or three minutes, yet everything was clear. The telephone beside the bed might be tapped, therefore he would use another. Shelley had been too open, although circumspect, in relaying the story of Aubrey's journey to Peshawar. Harrell did *not* know where Hyde was to be discovered.

He opened the door silently. The corridor was empty. He detected the sounds of a lift descending. He scuttled along the corridor and knocked on Ros's door.

"Quickly, it's me, Aubrey!" he whispered stagily into

the veneer, rattling the self-locking handle as noisily as he could. "Ros! Quickly!"

The corridor remained satisfyingly empty. When she opened the door he at once ignored the still-sleepy animosity in her eyes, the robe tugged around her, held at the throat.

"I must use your telephone."

"Why?" she called after him, closing the door, at once alert. "Why?" She was hovering behind him as he began dialing.

"Why?" he asked, turning to her as the line clicked. "Because I have had a visit from someone who is very interested in finding Patrick—and who means him no good! Now, sit down, Ros—please."

She retreated, unsatisfied but somehow cowed for the moment. The line began ringing. He looked at his watch. Yes, still afternoon in London. The personal number . . . which meant he could at once burst out with: "Peter, why the devil did you tell anyone where I was? What the hell are you playing at?"

"Kenneth?" Pathetic! In a moment, it would be, *It wasn't me, sir, it was someone else!* "You've had a visit, then—?"

"*You* ought to know, Peter! For God's sake—" He turned his back on Ros, hunching himself against any exclamation of hers that might follow. "—what did you mean by telling everyone I was *here?*"

In-taken, shuddery breathing came from Ros, followed by a continuing silence that he was thankful for.

"Kenneth, I was ordered to explain your whereabouts," Shelley replied with surprising calm, even authority. "I was asked by Orrell, my director-general, as to your whereabouts. Dammit, Kenneth, I was even asked by the foreign secretary! You can't just rush off into the blue without explaining—or leaving others to explain."

"Peter, they've already sicked Harrell onto me! Don't you realize the damage you've done?"

"I'm sorry for that. But I just wasn't in any position to lie or withhold information. Is it bad out there?"

"Yes, urgently bad. You told them everything, I suppose?"

"Have they seen Ros—with you, I mean?"

"No, I'm sure not. Why"

"I never mentioned her. It might give you a little room to maneuver. Nor did I mention the telephone call you received from—our mutual friend."

Involuntarily, Aubrey glanced at Ros as the bedsprings creaked beneath her bulk and agitation. He began nodding.

"Yes, Peter, I understand. But it will have to be tonight. The route you're setting up."

"I see. I'll need an hour, Kenneth. Luckily the coast's clear at this end. Friend Orrell went to the Varsity Match yesterday with some old college chums and imbibed a little too freely. He went home early." A pause, then: "Sorry, didn't mean to sound that much like a schoolkid. Give me an hour. Is there anything you need immediately?"

"No, we can manage at this end." Aubrey's confidence seemed hollow, echoing like the international call.

"You'll be all right?"

"Yes, Peter—as long as you hurry."

"Yes. How is he, by the way?"

"Just about all right." Ros's frame twitched.

"That bad?"

"Yes. Now, goodbye, Peter."

Aubrey thrust down the receiver and inhaled very deeply. As he exhaled, he leaned over Ros as she sat on the edge of her bed, still clutching the robe to her neck. At once, there were questions and challenges in her eyes, but he said with simple urgency:

"Ros, just listen to me." There was no moment of hesitation or doubt. She had only to carry out his instructions; the arrangements were simplicity itself. "We are going to get Patrick out of here tonight. But first, *you* are going to bring him here. No, just listen to me, Ros!" he snapped angrily, raising his hand. "You must go because I shall be watched and followed—which is exactly what I want to happen. You are not known to them." He devoutly hoped it was true. "So, get dressed, get a taxi, collect Patrick—then, if we can get our timing exact, you can bring him to this room while *I* keep them occupied!" His face, he knew, was flushed with excitement. Damn Harrell's patronizing attitude! "Well, get dressed. I can talk while you're doing that!"

She got up stiffly from the bed, her grip loosening on her robe. He did not glance at her exposed body in the room's long mirror; he simply stared towards the window to avoid mutual embarrassment. Another aircraft was taking off into the glowing night. Godwin was on his way back; he'd get straight to work on the RPV that had been used to kill Irena.

Ros was dragging clothes out of the fitted wardrobe, her face angry, pale and frightened. She swore under her breath, her lips working vehemently.

He remembered Kathryn, then looked at his watch in the panic of remembering too late. He should have rung two hours ago, just to check, assist Blake in soothing the girl, and try to elicit anything more she might know about Frascati's obsessions.

He picked up the receiver and dialed. Ros was watching him for a few moments before she stepped into a thick skirt. He waited. The summons of the telephone

in that fishing lodge at Lake Berryessa went unheeded.
His anger with himself transferred itself to Ros dressing,
then he became freshly angry with Harrell. One of the
evangelists, one of those who smuggled guns to the dis-
affected in a dozen countries, who killed local politi-
cians, rigged elections, smuggled and sold drugs to
finance the guns and bombs. Always stoking the unrest,
tilting the balance.

The ringing continued. Something had happened.
Blake would not have allowed Kathryn to leave the
lodge, nor would he have taken her elsewhere without
reporting in. Aubrey's anger evaporated. Something had
happened.

"Well?" Startled, he looked up. Ros was staring at
his face and he could only wave a hand feebly in her
direction. The telephone continued to ring unanswered.

7

EXCHANGE OF HOSTILITIES

"For Christ's sake, that guy's just *lying* back there! Anyone could come along any moment—what about the *shooting?*"

An angry shoe scuffed leaves; branches were thrust aside, snapping, startling her senses into awareness. One man blundered about, very near her. The man shouting seemed farther off. Kathryn remembered falling, and stifled the groan that the dizziness of opening her eyes prompted. Her body became aware of its own strain and tension, of aches, bruises and scratches, the jut of twigs and stones into her flesh.

The nearer one called back, out of patience and breath: "It wasn't supposed to *be* like this, you asshole!

You should have ordered the guy to stick his hands in the air, not kill him!" A bird struggled through leaves and crossed the glare of sunlight, a cold, quick shadow that awoke all her nerves. Breathing was difficult, to be snatched. She began shivering. The nearer one exclaimed at the bird's passage, himself startled.

Then the farther one called again: "What do we *do?*" He had shot Blake twice, quickly, she remembered, feeling spasms of nerves shudder through her, exaggerating the dig and crease of stones and twigs beneath her back and side. "Frank, what in hell do we do now?"

"It's all arranged, man! The motive is robbery, right? You remember that? The sheriff gets a call in maybe a half-hour. The guy's dead and there's no sign of the girl. Maybe she did it, or maybe some freak who wandered out of the woods! You remember all that—asshole?"

"I remember."

She could locate through the tremors of her body pine needles, broken twigs and small stones as vividly as if she were touching them with her fingers. Her mouth was open, her throat too dry to swallow. Her hand was numbly cold in the water of what might be a stream. Where her side hurt most vividly, her body had come to rest against the sharp, twisted trunk of a tall, spreading bush. It threw deep shadow over her body—but it might not cover her legs! She did not dare to lift her head to look. She just stared into the webbed glare of the sun through the bush's leaves and through her own hair, which had fallen across her face and trailed into her mouth, threatening to make her cough. Her ears ached with listening to the nearer man, the driver of the car, as he blundered around in the undergrowth and the pines that crowded down to the stream. She wanted to scream. It was tightening her throat, filling her nostrils, placing a strange pressure behind her eyes.

"Frank, what about the shooting? Suppose somebody heard us? Do we want somebody to find the body out in the open, just like that—see the *car,* Frank?"

"Shit, this fucking mud—!" she heard Frank exclaim. Then he splashed in water. She imagined she felt the disturbed ripples wash over her numb hand.

"You all right, Frank?"

"I'm up to my knees in this damn creek, asshole!"

"Any sign of her?"

"She fell this way, right? She's here somewhere." He stumbled out of the shallow water, grunting. She could hear the sogginess of his shoes, their slippery crunch on pine needles. Then he yelled, very close. Her body twitched and jumped as if the ground beneath was being excavated: "OK, OK—! Get back to the damn car. Hide it in the trees, but first, get the guy's body inside the lodge. Understand? Then wreck the place—and anyone who just happens along! OK, get moving. I'll find the woman. Get going, Dave!"

"Sure, Frank!"

Kathryn heard Dave retreating back through the trees. Then there was an artificial silence in which she heard Frank's breathing, exasperation—and determination. Birdsong slipped back into the silence. She began to hear her own taut, shallow breathing and tried to swallow the noise away. Her hair seemed to be working its way farther into her mouth, filling it slowly like sand. She was certain it was moving towards her throat, to make her cough, choke, insist on her whereabouts, tell Frank exactly where to find her. She stared open-mouthed at the sunlight and the webbed, tangled branches and twigs of the bush—

—and a shadow moving slowly alongside her.

The branches leaned, but she could see so much light! He must be able to see her, must . . . The shadow moved on, then paused, draped across her eyes. It twitched and jiggled as Frank looked around him. Sunlight poured through the hole caused by a crooked arm as he stood with his hands on his hips, snorting breath after breath, listening between each one.

His shadow slipped away a few paces, then he halted again. Which way had he gone? The broken twigs and something hard and larger like a stone hurt her back and buttocks. Her legs seemed numb like her icy hand in the water. The branches tilted sideways.

She moved her head, her teeth clenching on her hair to prevent noise and panic. She saw, wetly because she had been staring into the sunlight for so many minutes, her white hand, lying at the end of her arm in the shallow, listless creek. She was lying on a slope, looking *down* at her hand. Orientation seemed a momentous discovery. She moved her fingers in the clear water, could almost make out the slippery smoothness of tiny pebbles with her touch. She found her other hand at her side, dirty and bleeding. She looked at it, raised in front of her face, then pulled her hair softly, carefully from her mouth. Bracing her weight with the reawakened hand, she turned very, very slowly onto her side. A shadow— her own!—appeared mirrored in the creek. She looked at her legs, hidden by leaves and shadow.

She felt nauseous—

Gagging and swallowing, she stared at her own face reflected in the narrow water—a pale, nodding blob surrounded by loose hair, her icy hand clasped across her lips.

Eventually, the nausea diminished. She steadied herself, with her hands on her thighs, kneeling over the water. Then, after listening to the man's intense thrashing of bushes and undergrowth, sensing that he was perhaps as much as thirty or forty yards from her, she carefully pulled her dark hair back from her face and ran her hands, one cold, one dirty, over her cheeks. Her knee hurt. She looked down. She was kneeling on the sharp, heavy stone she had felt beneath her. She moved her knee and gripped the stone, then slipped in a slithering crawl from beneath the bush.

Great bars of sunlight slanted onto the slope down which she had tumbled. She squinted, ducking and moving her head, but caught no glimpse of the man, though she heard him, quietly cursing, muttering, moving bushes, branches, stirring leaf mold and pine needles with his feet. She moved around the bush until it masked her from the direction of the noises—

—he stepped out of the shadow of a tall pine, dressed in a dark, three-piece suit like a stranded business executive, the trouser legs clinging damply. Sunlight caught the metal of the gun in his hand. She thought she heard the noise of a car. When it had been hidden, the second man would return. They would have time on their side, after—

—smoke rising distantly through a gap in the trees, down near the lake. Orange tint to water and sunlight. The second man had torched the lodge, destroying the evidence, and Blake's body. Smoke rose gray-black above the farther trees, tall in the windless air. The man called Frank turned to look at it and seemed satisfied.

He was moving in the direction of the bush again, scanning the ground more carefully, muttering audibly.

"OK, honey—I'm going to find you, honey, don't you make any mistake..." He seemed suddenly relaxed, confident. His eyes scanned the ground, found her slithering, rolling track down the slope, walked beside it towards the bush; which was now smaller, more skeletal as she crouched behind it. She could not move now without being seen. Green, gold, brown, herself black-

and-white, soon visible. "OK, baby, come to Daddy, come on, honey, Daddy's got something for you." He was grinning. He moved carefully, sidestepping down the slope as if he wore skis.

She shrank as the bush did, becoming more vulnerable. Frank was fifteen, ten, seven yards from her, had reached the level ground beside the creek, was close to the bush—

—halted beside it, smiling. As if seeing the bush for the first time. She could smell the fire the lodge had become, as he seemed to. He sniffed, satisfied. The gun rested in his hand, on one hip. He grimaced at the creek, which had soaked his shoes and trousers. Her body felt stiff, clamped by something as real as strong, squeezing arms. His shoes squeaked with water and crunched on the carpet of fallen pine needles as he moved certainly, grinning.

"Come to Daddy, honey. Come on, baby—"

She almost cried out, thought she had, but it was another noise, from behind her. Some quick scamper and squeak from the trees had caught his attention and he moved towards it, almost passing her, his peripheral vision caught by the patch of white that was her face and he turned, off-guard and aware in the same instant—

She rose to her feet—was on her feet—as the bright metal in his hand moved to point at her and his smirk returned. He closed on her at once, left hand reaching towards her, for her—

Slowly, too slowly it seemed, she struck at his head with her right hand, finding the rock's heavy, sharp bulk gripped in it when she swung her arm. The stone struck against his wide-eyed surprise, which crumpled into pain, making his young face older and gray-streaked-scarlet as blood sprang from the gash on his temple. His right hand went on grabbing obscenely across her thigh, then held her knee as his face looked up, hardly seeing her, accusingly. She struck at the hand holding her knee, tearing it. He cried out like an animal. She struck at his face because she hated the dumbstruck, dazed look on it, then twice more at the bowed back of his head. His grip loosened on her left ankle. The dark suit lay still. His white shirt seemed to have acquired a red collar. She dropped the stone beside the dead man. She knew he was dead, and screamed.

And then she was floundering across the shallow creek, her feet soaked. Still screaming, as if to deliberately attract the second man. Stumbling, then running, head bent as if a cloud of stinging insects surrounded and pursued her. Then she was breathing too hard to scream any longer.

Eventually, she became more aware of the ground's sharp hardness through the thin, sodden soles of her shoes; and of the unremembered purse worrying rhythmically against her side as she ran.

Aubrey awoke, startled—no, only became aware, he had not been fully asleep. He came to himself, rubbed his eye sockets hard, pressing with his fingers, spectacles raised onto his forehead. He had been half-dreaming of his mother, which was strange. Perhaps Kathryn had reminded him, or Alan's funeral? His mother in the hospital bed, with that faint but warmer smile which had become habitual and welcome in her last years. *Memories, eh, Kenneth . . . memories.* He had patted her hand, kissed her forehead—jaundiced but less lined—and left. He had not seen her again, and he shivered now, his alarm and concern for Kathryn mingled with the quiet desperation he had felt after his mother's death. Then, he had been a helpless observer; as now, too, in the case of Kathryn.

He had continued to ring the number of the lodge, knowing that Blake would not have left there unless forced. No reply. Disconnected or out of order, *you're welcome, have a nice day,* the operator had told him.

He looked at his watch with a furtive haste. Eleven. He had rung Shelley, barely disguising his panic. Shelley would check—he had not rung back, not yet. It was six in London, Shelley had been about to leave the office for home.

Through the window, the Peshawar night was less noisy with neon and sodium now, its glow less throbbing. Ros was on her way by taxi to the camp. He glanced at the bed. New denims, a clean shirt, a leather jacket lay there waiting for Hyde, after his bath and shave. The hired car was in the hotel's underground garage, waiting, too. Ros and Hyde would be gone by morning, on their way to Rawalpindi.

Blank.

All thought of Ros and even of Hyde simply vanished, like shadows. Even guilt could not focus his attention on the neat little heap of clothing or the window which overlooked Peshawar. He was stunned and preoccupied by Kathryn's imagined, convincing danger. The telephone blurted and he snatched it up with a shaking hand.

"Yes?" It was Shelley. "For God's sake, Peter, what's happened over there?" The window became opaque, like a mirror masked by steam.

"I—not good, I'm afraid, Kenneth. The—someone called the local sheriff, because of a fire at the lodge." Aubrey choked. His mind seemed a vast distance from his tiny, shrunken body hunched on the chair, its fragile weight pressing against the writing desk. "Kenneth?"

"Yes," he managed.

"Blake's body was in the lodge, burned but obviously his, rather than—there wasn't a second body, Kenneth."

"Then they've got her!" he burst out, his frame shivering, his free hand waggling feebly, as if trying to pick up a coin from a sheet of glass. He felt nauseous, desperately cold.

"We don't know that, Kenneth! Look, I'm sending someone up there from Los Angeles now—he should be on his way, in fact. He'll have a right to be there, Blake was one of ours—"

"Find her, Peter, whatever you have to do—just find her, please!"

"Yes. The sheriff says it was an accident, but it can't have been. Our man should be there in an hour or so. Floatplane. He'll report as soon—"

"Yes."

"Kenneth, are *you* ready there, at your end? I've arranged things. They can take the road to 'Pindi whenever they want—is he safe?"

"I presume so," Aubrey dully replied.

"Then get them moving, Kenneth. Soon as you can."

"What? Why—?"

"There are Cousins hopping in and out of Century House at the moment as if it was some fast-food place! And whatever they ask for, they get. They're interested in Patrick, and in your whereabouts and motives. Look, Ramsey's our young man in Rawalpindi, he'll meet them on the road just outside the city, signal with his lights, that sort of thing. But get them away as quick as you can—and get back yourself, Kenneth, as soon as practicable. People want to know what you're up to."

"Yes," Aubrey sighed in reply. He glanced at Hyde's little heap of clean clothes, as if he had left them on a shore and drowned himself. Kathryn's body missing, Blake's burned. "Yes..."

"Call when they're on their way."

"Yes."

He put down the receiver on Shelley's good-luck murmur. His frame felt boneless, slack; exhausted. The certainty of her death possessed him, there was no more
optimistic possibility available. They'd taken her with
them, after murdering Blake. She would not be heard of
again. Idly, he looked at his watch. Eleven-fifteen.

There had been something he must perform, some
task, but he could not remember what it was. He looked
despondently up at the window, which seemed large and
naked. Peshawar's lights pressed against its glass. Why
on earth was he looking at his watch—why?

He grabbed at his stick and thrust himself to his feet,
staggering with misery and haste. He checked that he
had his room key, Ros's key, and struggled into his
overcoat. He was their cover, their distraction, when
they returned, and he was late! He plucked up his hat
and then slammed the door behind him before hurrying
breathlessly towards the lifts. Kathryn clung like a cold,
unnerving mist, but fear for Hyde and Ros and a sense
of duty undone urged him. He was late, damnably late—!
He scuttled like the white rabbit, continually glancing
at his watch, for heaven's sake! The remnants of a supper
lay on a tray outside one closed door, shoes to be cleaned
outside another; the smell of thick carpet flooded his
nostrils. At the lift, after summoning it, he was buffeted
by a dizzy, nauseous weakness, so that he placed one
hand heavily on a fragile, wobbling table which bore a
tall vase of flowers. Water spilled and the flowers quivered, mirroring his pessimism. The lift doors sighed
open.

As he descended, small tics of anticipation and anxiety
jumped over the skin of his arms and hands. He fidgeted,
stamping his feet to dispel his tension. The clicking of
his partial dentures unnerved him with reminders of his
age and vulnerability.

The bland marble floor of the hotel lobby was slippery, so he trod carefully, ostentatiously pulling on his gloves and glancing self-importantly about him. A piano tinkled in the cocktail bar, belying Pakistan outside with its Broadway doodlings. Now, out of the claustrophobic lift, he was able to concentrate on Hyde. He experienced a sullen, necessary determination.

He picked up Harrell's men as a dog might fleas, two of them at once folding newspapers, swallowing down drinks, getting to their feet at different tables on either side of the lobby. Then Harrell—smiling, large, certain—came out of the cocktail bar as if summoned, the saccharine strains of *South Pacific* leaking behind him.

"Just on my way home," he announced, unsurprised. "Going out for a walk this late, Sir Kenneth? You look dressed for the temperature out there."

Harrell's appearance awoke anger and the immediate need to conceal his contempt and determination from the American. "Ah, yes, Mr. Harrell—a late evening constitutional." Aubrey summoned the role of the absent, dithering old man with uncomfortable ease. "My doctor recommends a modicum of exercise."

Harrell's glance was keen, yet one of confirmed preconception. They reached the revolving doors and Harrell shunted Aubrey into one compartment and spun him gently and inexorably out into the windy night before joining him where a taxi's exhaust reeked, reawakening the queasiness of Aubrey's stomach. Aubrey kept his eyes from his watch, seeming content to sniff the chilly air and blink at the flying grit in the breeze.

"See you around," Harrell murmured, his hand momentarily on Aubrey's shoulder as he added: "No, I won't, right? You're on your way home."

"Yes. Tomorrow, I'm afraid."

"Good night, Sir Kenneth. Nice meeting with you."

Harrell loomed off into the flaring sodium, his dark bulk lit then unlit then lit once more; meanwhile, Aubrey realized the two who had hopped flealike from the lobby had become absorbed by the street's shadows. Cars and taxis flickered past like broken film, worrying him as he searched for them. Harrell, now vanished, disturbed him. He had been so *confident!* A woman passing him, scented and furred, evoked Kathryn, but only for a moment. Those emotions were now firmly in check. His own safety and that of Hyde were his sole concern. He swallowed, then looked at his watch in the good light of the hotel entrance, fending off the doorman's persistence regarding a taxi. Eleven-twenty. His haste as he blustered out into the wind would give credence to the idea of a meeting. He must drag them along in his gravitational pull, away from the hotel. But he must hurry now. The timing had been precise and he was late. He strode out, as if blindly stepping off some high ledge, down the wide street in the direction of the airport.

A trishaw, pedaled by a turbaned stoop, then another. The noise of motor scooters. The quick passage of cars with blind night windows. He caught the movement of one shadow walking at his pace across the street, then a second man ahead of him, listing slightly to port, his hand seeming to hold the side of his face. An R/T set? Flying dust pecked at Aubrey's cheeks. The taxi would return this way. He must be clearly visible to them and must give Ros the signal that the surveillance at the hotel was accounted for. She must get Hyde up to her room, washed and changed, then back to the hotel garage and the hired car—all before he returned from his stroll. He had made the timing precise—and he was late.

The man ahead of him continued to lean as if the wind cowed him with insults. The shadow across the street and now slightly behind him continued to drift expertly.

Aubrey required the support of his stick to measure the frequency of his steps, the pretended innocence of his gait. Eleven twenty-three. Could she make Hyde take up his bed and walk, get him out of that hovel? Did she even remember the exactitude of times? His gaze slid across the gewgaws of twenty, thirty smart boutique windows, grilled, hardly reflecting the movements of the man across the street. The brands of subtle perfume, the splayed sweaters, draped furs, the refurbished, acceptable face of the bazaar.

He began to watch the traffic, moving his head in birdlike gestures as if he pecked at winter grain in a garden patrolled by cats. Now, they would assume he was making for some rendezvous. He paused at a traffic light, then crossed in front of a Mercedes, two scooters, a taxi, a small knot of trucks and a white turban hanging over the handlebars of a trishaw. The two shadows would be eager and yet unsettled.

The man behind him accelerated, passing him, while the other man dropped back. Automatons. The light from a street lamp splashed across the front-tail man's raincoat. Aubrey felt revived by the game. His breathing was quick and easy and his chest less tight. Deliberately, he looked up and down the street more often. Harrell's men shifted and halted, changed positions relative to him, mingled with shadows where they could. Eleven twenty-seven. He was perhaps a quarter of a mile from the point where he had instructed Ros to look for his signal. His own shadow divided and fell behind at the next street lamp; his two human shadows moved apace with him, growing always more alert.

Eleven-thirty. He was out of breath but he had reached the appointed square.

So had Harrell's men, halting only moments later than he did. The wind was quickly colder, chilling now that he stood still, the square wide and dusty and empty, its shops and cafés and mosques dark, the occasional car prowling. Beggars shuffled at the corners of alleyways and there was a discernible smell of ordure and decay. An emaciated dog rooted in a plastic rubbish bag at the edge of the pavement near a figure lying curled fetally in the gutter, perhaps only asleep. The moon was thin, the stars distant and icy. He hated the fulcrum position he occupied at that moment, almost as much as he dreaded what Shelley might uncover in California. He made himself look up and down the square, amateurishly. He leaned and squinted towards the more distant shadows in a simulation of anxiety, his stance emphasizing he was expecting someone on foot.

Harrell's men waited as trained people waited, confident and all but invisible in the shadows. He knew where they were but could see neither of them.

Eleven thirty-three, then -four, and -five . . .

As he stood there, he increasingly felt bowed by a weight. His thoughts orbited like massive planets, slow and deliberate; Kathryn, Hyde and Shelley, a telephone unanswered, Harrell, Irena Nikitina's murder, Shelley, Hyde, Kathryn . . .

The taxi entered the square like a fugitive, flitting into the sodium lighting that glared on its tinted windscreen. He recognized it, his breathing became difficult and he tried to ignore its beetlelike progress across the windy expanse. He stood still as it slipped past him. Ros's face. He glanced at his watch and tossed his head, making off at once in the opposite direction, his pace agitated after the stick had waggled twice from his cuff in a jerky signal. He hurried along the pavement, suddenly far more aware of how isolated he was and how close the two Americans were.

"Hurry!" Ros urged, knocking the driver on the shoulder, "as soon as you get out of the square." Patrick Hyde saw her turn to him, her face white, indistinct, as she asked: "Did you see him?"

He nodded. He had seen the dark-coated, small, bent scrap on the pavement tussling with the wind before he slumped back against the seat and Ros's shoulder. He felt the taxi accelerate. Her tension was as oppressive as the air before an approaching thunderstorm. He resented it. It clouded his mind, as did the stupor of silent rage at whatever entered his thoughts.

His head ached, his throat was dry. Superficially, he desired nothing more than a drink, another joint—except that they would not contain or shut out the cohering fragments of his awareness. The lights strung above the wide street flashed like strobes through the tinted roof of the taxi. He stared at them, blinking slowly and exaggeratedly. Ros was large and warm, but with the solidity only of someone appearing in a dream. A drink—three. Tranquilizers. Hashish. He knew none of them would suppress the rising anger, the wild, frightening rage he felt. While he remained in that filthy, isolated room in the camp, he had kept it at bay. But it was already stronger.

Physically, he felt collapsed and stranded like the dead and bloated carcass of a huge fish beached by a storm. But he could no longer regain his mental exhaustion and its oblivion. His realization had form now, had taken shape from the scattered images of the past few days. The pictures in his head were like stones thrown at him, hard and sharp and possessing weight. The young soldier's gashed throat, opening as if with surprise, the children without feet and hands or with skin corroded by chemicals, the body of Irena Nikitina, Harrell, the CIA man he had wounded in order to escape from their car . . . and gradually, the preeminence of Harrell's image, continually welling out of the darkness of sleep and waking.

Ros stirred as he began to twitch with impotent rage. He needed to *act,* to satisfy this mindless, uninterrupted anger. When Aubrey and Ros had arrived, he had tried to surrender to his exhaustion, cling to temporary oblivion. To no avail.

"There!" Ros announced. "No, not the front door— down into the garage! I've got my room key, they'll let you through."

Hyde sighed. Ros was leaning forward, her arm against his tense cheek. His hatred frightened him more than any emotion he had ever experienced, but he could not rid himself of it. Harrell had tried to kill him. He would kill Harrell. The jumble in his head arranged itself into that one neat formula.

The taxi dipped its nose down the ramp to the underground garage. Then it stopped and chilly air came through the window Ros had lowered. He was afraid for her, at her being involved, but it was a minor, fleabite emotion beside the anger which plagued him. He heard a rattle and Ros's strenuous insistence on something. Then the taxi pulled forward as he saw the barrier lift into view through the sunroof. They passed under it. There were hard, occasional lights through the tinted glass.

"Over there, towards the lifts!" The slow, shouted instructions of any visitor to any foreign country.

The taxi came to a halt. He found Ros staring at him before sliding out of her seat with a small explosion of breath. She was impatient with what she thought of as his continuing passivity. It was almost funny.

"Come on, Hyde, end of the ride!" she snapped, her nerves as visible as veins on a warm white arm. She even slapped her thigh as if addressing a dog. Grunting, he slipped out of the back of the car, shaking his head like some amiable drunk, suddenly relaxed by movement, holding his palms outwards.

Ros was scribbling her signature on a travelers' check, resting it on the taxi's roof after quietly cursing in search of cash in her purse. Hyde, too, leaned on the roof, staring at the driver, watching the small oasis of calm spread within him. It might only last for a few moments. He savored it. Ros flourished the completed check, which was suspiciously inspected before being folded into a bulging wallet. The driver got back into the taxi and slammed the door. Hyde moved gently away as if afraid of spilling something. Stepped backwards—

—was slammed against the taxi again, realizing that he had not recognized Ros's alarm quickly enough, her mouth opening whole seconds, it seemed, after the breath had been knocked out of his chest. One arm was pinioned and the cold round hole at the end of a pistol muzzle had been thrust against his head, just behind his right ear. As he struggled for breath, the breathing of the other man against his cheek was hard, confident, louder than his own. Blood rushed like static in his ears. His head lumbered, realization dawning. Ros was moving out of shock into helpless fear. She had only a maternal anger to offer, at best, and it wouldn't be enough. His assailant's saliva was warm to his cheek. Ros's stare turned like a searchlight from side to side. Then he was dragged away from the taxi and held, back arched and arm thrust up behind him, off balance.

"Hi!" his attacker breathed excitedly in his ear. "Welcome home to the farm, son!"

Hyde groaned with the pain in his arm. His awareness flailed about like a hand seeking a weapon. Ros moved behind the taxi and the American yelled at her and waved the gun in Hyde's peripheral vision. Ros backed away as it once more pressed hurtingly against his head.

"Just stay against the wall, lady!" There was a residue of surprise in his voice, as if Ros was unexpected and he had no instructions concerning her. "Who's she, Hyde?" The gun twisted into his temple, just behind his right eye, making it water. His shoulder was aching into numbness and his legs threatened to give way.

"My auntie," he muttered.

"She work for Aubrey?" Hyde shook his head. "Like hell she doesn't! Harrell was right, he said you might just try something this crazy! OK, over there, let's go— you, too, lady—my car's over there!"

Hyde felt nausea at the back of his throat. His eyes were wet and blurred. He was pushed ahead of the American, arm still twisted up behind his back.

"You!" the American yelled at the taxi driver. "Get the hell out of here—go on, *move!*"

He seemed to be pushed further into the hard, dusty light of the garage, rainbowed petrol and dark oil patches joggling in his vision. His feet stumbled and his legs were awkward and weak. The pain in his arm had become no more than a burning, distant numbness. The American's cheek pressed against the side of his head like that of a nuzzling pet or lover, the man's body thrusting against his back and buttocks.

Ros backed away ahead of them, her face a white globe, her eyes wide, her mouth terrified.

"And you, you asshole," the American whispered, breathing harder now. "I'd kill you now only Harrell wants to do it himself. He was specific about that."

Ros collided with the dust-streaked black limousine then clung to it, bewildered. Hyde recognized the American's voice now—he hadn't seen his face—as that of the man who had kept on commenting on his smell in

Harrell's car, on the other side of him from the one he had injured in the rear of the car.

Emptiness echoed in the garage, their breathing magnified to a shell's sea-roar. His weak legs, the smell of his own sweat and terror, the certainty that it was now over.

"Open the door!" the American snapped at Ros. "Open it!" She swung the door wide like a chauffeur, then clung to it again. "Get in, lady!" Ros backed into the rear seat. Hyde's arm returned to pain as the American adjusted his grip.

Hyde fell to his knees, the American's grip on his wrist tautening in surprise, twisting his arm in satisfaction as he saw the defeated shoulders.

"No, you drive, lady—we'll sit in the back seat."

Hyde saw the gun motioning at the edge of his peripheral vision, flapping like a small black bat. Hyde's breathing seemed to have ceased—or his hearing had failed. The only noises were inside his head; screams. The young Russian conscript, the mutilated bodies, the footless, handless children, the blind...

...Ros, stupefied by shock and terror, climbed like an old woman out of the rear of the car and clambered heavily into the driver's seat. Her eyes kept watching him. There was nothing she could do.

"Inside, motherfucker."

His arm was dragged upwards. He lifted his head and howled with the pain—lifted his right hand and the knife from his boot. It flashed in the dusty light and moved once, twice, three times, awkwardly, efficiently. Ros screamed before the American did, his scream-becoming-gargle, then windy exhalation. Blood splashed into Hyde's face, as he turned to look—

Jawbone exposed, windpipe severed, the first awkward cut only a long skin-deep scratch across the man's chest. He fell against the American, whose wide-eyed face crumpled, sliding down the dusty car; new blood splashed on the leather.

Ros went on screaming. The American's hand enlarged. Hyde realized he had dropped to his knees beside the body. The bunch of keys shone in the opened, lifeless hand. Somewhere, the taxi's noise faded in the street. It had taken only seconds, the taxi's squealing tires and acceleration like some slowed-down, deepened sound track, a background to his confused reactions, the American's words and death, Ros's screaming, hands flitting batlike about her face, her skin chalky, eyes black, mouth red.

He felt nausea rise into his throat and was unable to prevent himself vomiting—then shivering with returned exhaustion, the seismic shock waves after the explosion of violence. His head rang with Ros's screams and with the reverberations of what might have been horror. Just for a moment, he glimpsed the scene, and himself, as if he stood back from it. Then the bewildered, half-realizing disgust vanished in the huge urgent effort required to rise to his feet and lean against the car. He wiped blood from his eyes and cheeks; wiped sweat from his forehead; sweat—sweat, was it? His head and thoughts whirled.

"Shut up, Ros!" he yelled, his head threatening to burst. *"Shut up, for Christ's sake!"*

He unlocked the trunk of the American limousine, then bent to the American's slack-headed, boneless body, heaving at it, gripping it beneath the limp arms, dragging it, standing it up against him with obscene and revolting pressure, toppling it backwards into the cavern of the trunk, folding the legs in like those of a ventriloquist's dummy—slammed the trunk gratefully, his breathing a roaring noise again, his eyes blinded with sweat.

One of them, he told himself, one of the buggers less, a bit safer now, safer already, one of the buggers... Again and again. Blood beside a rainbow of spilled oil. He opened the driver's door and dragged Ros from the car because it was easier to do that than to tell her, speak at all—

—silent, except to shout at her: "Where's the bloody rental car? *Where is it?*" The desire, the need to escape lagged far behind his need to outpace his exhaustion. The sense of it dragged at his feet, weakened his grip on her arm, all but prevented him from pushing her ahead of him. He pushed her by leaning against her rather than forcing—he didn't have the energy for that. She resisted, shaking her head, enraged, her cheeks reddened, her teeth ground together. "Where is it?" he shouted again, unnerving her so that she pointed. He saw an Audi, parked apart from the few other cars in the garage, then pushed her on with inadequate effort.

The sickness was in his stomach, at the back of his throat, sweetly, frighteningly. His legs blundered foal-like, his feet senseless of the concrete. Ros fought against his pressure.

"Keys—keys!"

She glared at him, both of them breathing heavily, facing each other like enemies. Then some clockwork mechanism—the terror and shock that had invigorated her—broke, ran down, and she fumbled the key into the lock and opened the Audi's passenger door. Then she threw the keys at him, stinging his cheek. He heard them clatter as they fell.

He snatched them up, and heaved himself into the car. Ros's breathing, as he slammed the door shut, reproached.

"What do you think I *do? Courier for some package holiday firm?*" He could not prevent himself from yelling at her in protest at her wordless accusation.

He stared at his hands on the already slippery steering wheel. His right hand held the car keys in a fierce, knotted fist, while his left seemed clawed, as if holding to some desperate purchase by its fingernails. His hands unnerved him and he began shivering with reaction. It would not soon be over, there wasn't a bolt-hole waiting for him. They needed him silenced, dead—it was their only safety; his lay in more killing.

He forced the key clumsily into the ignition and turned it. The engine roared. Ros's breathing continued to accuse, and distance, him. He put the car into reverse and squealed the tires, spinning the wheel, then accelerating towards the ramp to the street. Ros jerked satisfyingly in her seat.

"Why did Aubrey bring you?" he shouted at the windscreen. "Why did he let you *see?*" His breathing quickened, became gulped and difficult. "What the bloody hell are you doing here? Christ, why did you have to *see?*"

Aubrey should have known better. The old sod had endangered her now, too. He shouldn't have involved her. He felt her disgust and horror as his own, sensing the tension between his need for safety and a suddenly renewed desire for oblivion—drink, hashish, sleep. Emptiness. Awake, there was only the shit to look at and smell.

"Look out for Aubrey!" he snapped as they bucked level at the top of the twisting ramp and he began to study the light, late evening traffic. He turned the car onto the street, heading back the way they had come in, towards the airport. "We're going *now.* Just don't miss him!"

There was nothing he could say that she would give credence or even listen to. She had *seen*. Rage flickered at the back of his mind like a striplight refusing to come fully on.

"I've had *enough!*" he shouted. "Understand? Enough! It was either him or me—I've bloody had enough!"

The atmosphere in the car oppressed like the approach of a storm. She was stubbornly or perhaps helplessly silent and accusing. He needed oblivion soon—to rid him of the taste of self-disgust, and of fear for himself, and of the rage that had killed the American easily, so easily . . .

. . . to last this thing out, finish it, he would need small, black escapes; intervals. And an avoidance of mirrors and reflections.

He was sick of killing, sick with killing. Afghanistan. He was infected. He glanced at his hands as if expecting a disease's stigmata. He'd caught it.

He blinked furiously and drew himself more upright in the driving seat, concentrating only on the street, the vehicles and pedestrians.

"There," he heard Ros mutter, her hand feebly pointing at something.

"What?"

"*There!*" she screamed at him, her face contorted.

Aubrey was scuttling along the pavement, head bent into the wind, hat held firmly on his head, stick tapping. Hyde felt a surge of animosity, but it was too wearying to sustain. He slowed the car with a screech of tires, lurching it towards the pavement, startling the old man.

"What is it?" Aubrey asked, opening the rear door and leaning into the car.

"Get in," Hyde said tonelessly. "They were waiting in the garage. We're going now—get in!"

Aubrey climbed into the car as Hyde saw two men, one on either side of the street, halt before galvanizing into quick movement. One of them passed like a shadow across the lit window of a curio shop, the other moved out from beneath an awning, reaching for something inside the breast of his overcoat. Hyde accelerated away from the curb, swerving out into the middle of the street. Ros screamed. An oncoming truck sounded its horn and the man crossing the street—gun visible in his hand now—hesitated, avoiding collision with the Audi. Then both Americans were visible in the driving mirror, diminishing.

Aubrey had turned to watch them. Ros was shivering, her hands clasped around her face.

"Where?"

"What?" Oh, Rawalpindi—yes, Rawalpindi. It's arranged." His voice was hesitant, choked by the stifling confines of the car.

Hyde merely nodded, blinking now like a drunk to bring the street back into focus.

Then Ros shouted: "He *killed* him!"

"What—?"

"Shut up!" Hyde shouted, dizzy with weariness. She was bringing it back!

Ros was turned to Aubrey, spilling her fragments of narrative, her vile little accusations, her shock. Hyde felt something tightening around his temples. He began to be afraid of not finding sleep in time; he had to stop driving soon, he needed a drink...a smoke—something! Ros's voice thudded in his head, where pressure seemed to be inflating like a scream. Soon, without sleep, hashish, he would no longer be in control.

"Shut up, Ros!" he shouted, in an attempt to release the growing, constricting pressure. "For Christ's sake— shut up!"

He went on colliding with her, with her ordinariness, her stance outside. The collision between them seemed to go on endlessly, like a slowed-down film of a car accident, the dummies flung about inside or though the windscreen. She couldn't, didn't even begin to understand. Aubrey's face in the mirror was chalky, grim.

"Shut up, shut up, shut up..." he kept repeating.

Kathryn watched the still-smoldering heap of wood that had been the lodge from about a quarter of a mile away, her back against a rock. The pines gathered thickly above and around her yet allowed her sight of a stretch of lakeshore and the glittering water beyond the pebbles. The county coroner's station wagon had long taken away the charred body they'd found in the lodge's ruins. The fire department engine turned slowly and then headed back through the trees towards town, leaving only the sheriff's car, which glinted and shone in the sun.

She continued squeezing and massaging her right foot, which was bruised and aching. The few neighbors from the lodges and trailers along the shore had already dispersed and the photographer from the local newspaper had left. It was old news already, just a straggle of gray smoke sidling upwards towards the high sun. She had sat there, unmoving, for perhaps two hours, maybe longer. She was safe, and had been since the one called Dave had bundled the sacklike thing he had been carrying over one shoulder, staggering beneath its weight, into the rear of their car, which had been retrieved from its hiding place. His angry, panicky haste had told her that he was carrying Frank. And she'd killed Frank...

She rubbed her foot harder as the images returned. Slowly, rhythmically, they receded again. Her rubbing diminished, becoming more of a stroking movement.

The memory of the stone falling on Frank's upturned, bewildered face and the gradual loosening of his hand on her leg and ankle intruded less intensely now, more like little bouts of retching on an emptied stomach than a full, gagging nausea. She rubbed more quickly, then slowed the action once more, reinforcing the prosaic. Her feet hurt. A formula or ritual. She had inspected her clothes for dirt, each patch and smear, until she could consider the dried red-brown marks as those made by earth and tree bark. She had examined each of the small tears and plucks in her blouse and slacks, dusting her legs scores of times, only to return each time to nursing her bruised, aching feet.

She had cleaned her face with the folded, inadequate handkerchief in her purse. She was the child walking on the edge of the carpet, hopping over the dangerous cracks in the pavement, switching the bedroom light on and off a dozen times. Containing her terror and nausea.

Frank had been bundled like a sack of groceries—no, with even less care—into the back of the car and it had snarled out of the clearing long before the sheriff had arrived. She had convulsively washed her hands with the same saliva-damp handkerchief, and cleaned her face once more, as the noise of the car's engine had faded towards the town. Eventually, she had tied back her long hair, and generally busied herself.

She was unsure of the time, but it was of little importance. Only the urgency to forget nagged at her. After all, no one knew that she had been at the lodge. Blake had—died alone.

At once, she began inspecting her blouse again, patting her hair back; then she resumed rubbing her feet. Some time later, her attention became absorbed by the slow, then quick approach and landing of a small floatplane on the glittering, blinding surface of the lake. She

watched it swallowed by the glare as it touched down
and threw up behind it a diamond wave. As it slowed,
its wake began to snake and fade. She stared into the
glare of the water, absorbed. The small aircraft's bobbing turn towards the shore, its bright red-and-white
form, was an irritating distraction which drew her out
of the water-glare so that she had to increase the pressure
of her hand rubbing her foot again. Then she concentrated on the floatplane and the man from it who was
collected by a small boat with a quarrelsome outboard
motor. He was landed on the pebbly shore near the lodge
and walked attentively past the ashes and heaped wood
towards the sheriff. Her hand relaxed on her aching foot.

Introductions, shaking the sheriff's hand, the showing
of something, the man's acceptance . . . his feet stirring
among the ashes which puffed cloudily against the
water's light. Minutes passed. The nodding of heads,
then the sheriff slapping the newcomer across the shoulders acceptingly as they moved towards the police car.
She heard the engine catch very loudly, but her attention
to it was broken by another noise. A bird flitted with a
blackbird's squawk from a tree nearby, ending for good
the blank time. The water's sheen was incomplete, too;
ripples were clear through the applied sunlight. She
rubbed her arms, shivering as if she had awoken in a
cold bedroom. The police car pulled away into the trees,
bouncing away towards the town. The floatplane
bobbed at anchor, its colors more vivid, unbleached.
With an effort, she looked at her watch as she smelled
cooking drift up from the shore. She knew she must
move . . . be going—

—forced the admission from herself—*must get away,
run for it*. She groaned with a wailing noise. It had come
back. Dirt-stained slacks, aching feet, torn and dirty
and—*blood*-stained blouse, the ashes of the lodge, Blake

spinning like a slow top about to fail, Frank's white face reddening, his head opening. She pressed back the scream, with both hands over her mouth, her breathing rushing, dragging in her ears and nose, hot on her hands. She turned her head, wanting to be sick. Her stomach had been emptied before she climbed the slope to this place. Her eyes were wet and the lake glared once again, falsely now.

She had to leave . . . and there seemed less to prevent her now. The falling temperature of the afternoon, the empty clearing around the lodge's ashes, the admission of how much time had passed, been wasted—all prompted her. She stood up groggily, pulling her flimsy slippers onto her feet, bending again to pick up her purse. The tiny, soiled handkerchief lay browned and crumpled on the pine needles. She hesitated, then snatched it up before brushing down her slacks, then rubbed her arms vigorously. She squinted now because the falling sun blinded her, making her feel more vulnerable. She rummaged in her purse, found her sunglasses and unfolded them, then put them on as if about to step into a hot street.

She began to descend through the pines, the rocks painful under her feet. She had money, credit cards, her driver's license. She'd rent a car. There was a motel on the edge of the small town, and a garage, she'd noticed from the back of Blake's car—which had been towed away by the police. She moved slowly. The light was blue under the trees, eveninglike and solitary. She heard herself mumbling in time to her footsteps and realized that childhood lay in ambush up ahead of her. Sunlight slanted across clearings, which she began to avoid. The trees seemed to continue ahead of her. Her breathing appeared louder. She forced herself to stop counting her footsteps, attempting to scorn the increasing sense of

vulnerability. The resinous smell of the pines, the scut-
tlings in the undergrowth, the chill of the afternoon,
were all crowding in. She hurried more and more—

—stumbled, fell, scraping her palms and knees, her
cheek striking an upturned twig which gouged near her
eye. She cried out, then stifled the noise. Birds scattered
unseen through leaves. Her whole frame was shaking,
quivering like that of a small, trapped animal. That was
childhood and she determinedly sniffed it under control;
looked at her own blood amid the dirt on her hands,
and on her exposed knee where her slacks were torn—
concentrated . . . until her body stilled and her breathing
was less harsh. Then she got to her feet. The trees had
thinned; the light was yellow beneath them now. She
heard a car and smelled its exhaust fumes. She clutched
her purse beneath her arm and walked out of the trees
onto the road, at once deriding her fears, obeying a new
sense of urgency, aware of the shabby condition of her
clothes.

Straight ahead lay the low cabins of the motel and the
canopy of the garage. She hesitated for a moment and
was angry even at that much displayed indecision. There
was a new, recriminatory urgency pressing at her now.
She had wasted too much time up there on the ridge,
blanking everything out of her thoughts. Dave would be
back, with others. They would find it easy to follow her,
the car described, its registration, her direction. Stop
wasting time!

She crossed the road towards the entrance of the motel. She could not see the Lincoln in the forecourt. Flags
snapped in the newly eager breeze. The lobby was hot
as she pushed through the glass doors. Polished wood
blocks, bright rugs, elk and moose heads glowering, as
if still pained, from the paneled walls. A wolf's head
watched her scan the lobby's occupants, then locate the

telephones near the sign to the restaurant. The smell of polish and big iron radiators. She recognized no one, but stumbled almost physically against the normality of the place, its check shirts and bellhop uniforms, a row of suitcases neatly parked. Everything disarmed and unnerved her. Her cheeks flushed with urgency, with lack of decision. The telephones beckoned.

Could she get hold of him anyway? She despised the way she reached for a man she hardly knew as she might have done for her own father—but had never. She promoted the sense of his expertise, that Blake was his man, that it was his duty to alter her situation. She was already fishing in her purse and then realizing, while the argument continued in her head, that she would need to call collect. She accepted her dependence, garbed as obligation on Aubrey's part.

The operator. The London number. It was late evening there, he'd be home. There was a housekeeper, wasn't there? Hadn't Daddy said so? The heat of the lobby seemed to affect her feverishly, disorienting her. She crouched against the coin box in a grotesque of some anonymous, sleazy messenger, glancing around her with ridiculous furtiveness.

Then she saw Dave—yes, it was him, now in a tweed jacket and gray slacks, both clean—walk slowly across the lobby towards the desk. Her breathing became small, pinched. Two others were with him, alike as Mormon callers. The telephone went on ringing Aubrey's London number.

"Ms. Kathryn Aubrey?" someone asked beside her.

She swallowed in a hoarse, groaning way, her eyes startled wide, the sense that it was one of the three overpowering her, even though she could see all of them at the desk, talking to the clerk, unaware of her crouch-

ing in the shadows of the tiny little passageway where
the phones lined the wall ...

A hand grabbed hers as she made to strike out with
the receiver.

"Take your damn hand—"

He pulled the receiver from her grasp and replaced it.
A man she had never seen stood before her, his face
reddened, his hair auburn, wearing white-rimmed
glasses, and a gray, baggy suit. She tried to pull her hand
free. Her legs felt hardly able to support her. Her only
struggle seemed in her mind.

"Ms. Aubrey, please don't make a fuss. Look, I'm
here to help you—*please* listen—!" She stared at the
telephone he had replaced. "Look, can we go somewhere
while I explain? There's no need to be frightened of me."
He was no taller than she, slimly built, rather insignificant. There was something panicky about him that confused her, as if he mirrored her own sense of being
trapped.

"Let go of me!" she managed to say.

"Please don't make a commotion! I almost didn't spot
you. Bit of a shaker, really, coming after—Blake's body,
or what was left of it ..." Her sense of danger diminished; rather, she returned her concentration to the three
men at the desk, to Dave who was showing something
to the clerk, who was shaking his head.

"What do you want?" she breathed as he released her
hand. She rubbed her wrist. He was between her and
the lobby. The toilets were further along the passageway.
He was staring intently, almost not at her, but through
her at some recent memory. Blake, she realized. His
discomfort disarmed her.

"I was—I've been sent up here to find you, Ms. Aubrey. By London. They told me I might—the sheriff said
when they got there the place was well alight." He

looked directly at her. "They only found the one body—obviously. I didn't have a clue as to how to set about finding you—"

"What do you *want* with me?" The foreground was becoming comical, even farcical: menace hovering over by the desk. Soon they'd turn, look—

"What—? Oh look, I've come to get you away, d'you see?" His manner was prim, schoolmistressy. "I mean, you can check on me with London, I'll give you a number to ring. My name's Mallory—" Dave was exasperated, rubbing his chin violently as he inspected the registration cards the clerk supplied. One of the other two crossed the lobby, scanning the parking lot from just outside the doors, hands on his hips. Effectively, he was guarding the door.

"For Christ's sake, are you with *them?*" she snapped, pointing across the lobby. Mallory turned, more clerk-like than ever, more insignificant.

Turning back, he began: "You mean—?" She nodded.

"The blond set fire to the lodge. He and... and another guy shot Blake—shot him, do you understand?" Her protestations were a slow, quiet scream, relieving the heat and tension. "You're from where—London, right?"

"The consular office in Los An—" He hesitated looking towards Dave engaged in a sharp, quick little discussion with his companion. Kathryn recognized there was a sense of near-decision about both of them. The third man's back was clearly visible through the glass doors. "You mean they—?" It seemed the necessary additional surprise required to induce a sense of jeopardy which, if he did not act on it at once, would become fatal to both of them. "Ms. Aubrey, we should get out of here immediately, if what you say is true—"

"You came in on that floatplane, right," she suddenly

realized. He nodded, his gaze seemingly transfixed now by Dave and his companion. "It's waiting to take you back?" Her panic nibbled at her assumed, effortful calm.

"Yes. Yes, let's go, then!" He turned towards her.

"One of them's outside the doors," she pressed.

"There's a fire exit beyond the toilets." He glanced once more at the desk. Kathryn had begun shivering, but the desire for movement bullied her. "Quickly, Ms. Aubrey, this way ... *please!*"

8

THE UNPROFITABLE PURSUIT OF DREAMS

"Comrade Marshal Kharkov, are you saying that it was a direct order from you that put units of the 105th Guards Airborne Division onto the streets of Dushanbe? Is *that* your work on the screen? Are you proud of it?" Didenko pressed.

On one illuminated screen, almost in the center of the rank of television sets along one wall of Nikitin's vast office, the crowds had dispersed, their riot squibbing into isolated stone-throwing, the occasional gasoline-filled bottle . . . except that the litter that filled the streets was more than paper and rubble in grainy closeup; dead bodies, perhaps as many as a hundred of them, stretched away along the perspective of a treelined, soullessly wide avenue to where a bus was smoldering, burnt out. Many of the bodies were turbaned, many were women; some children. The only moving objects on the videotape now were patrolling BMD combat vehicles that must have been airlifted in. The scene of devastation was just what anyone might reasonably expect if one let a Guards' division loose like a pack of trained, killing dogs.

Didenko glanced at Nikitin, and was shocked at the man's frown, its warning to him, Didenko, for God's sake! Didenko had not intended rounding on Kharkov, stone-faced and boneheaded, but the closeup pictures of the slaughter—for it was nothing less than that—had enraged him. And now here was Nikitin, in collusion with the other three men in the room. Having arrived late, Didenko now felt as if he had blundered into the wrong committee, the wrong place. His cheeks flushed at Lidichev's open contempt and Kharkov's barely suppressed anger. He rubbed his hand through his thinning hair, then closed it into a fist just above his head and said: "How the devil did this happen—how did it get to this?"

"Firm action was necessary," Kharkov murmured, his massive composure reestablished, as if he had been momentarily worried by a wasp.

The image on the screen was of two children in each other's arms, in the gutter, thin dribbles of pale blood coming from beneath their robes. They stared at the sky. My God, the scene could have been *arranged* by some arty film director!

"What have you done, Comrade Marshal—what have you done?" Didenko whispered, but in that room, in that company, he sounded like an actor with a climactic line to speak. But it *was* slaughter. He turned his back on them and faced Nikitin. "Aleksandr Aleksandrovich—Comrade General Secretary—couldn't this have been prevented?"

Nikitin's gaze was shifty and loose for a moment, then his features hardened like a mask. He cleared his throat and announced: "Marshal Kharkov did not act without authority, Comrade Didenko."

Comrade Didenko...? It shocked him, like a small collision that heated his whole body with surprise and embarrassment. He recognized the continuity of his anger, brought in the limousine with him from the meeting of the Moscow City Council—where he had been directly challenged over food prices! *The cult of personality* had been thrown at him like an old slur, by some of Lidichev's conservative hangers-on. He resisted the temptation to turn back to face the old Trinity of conservatism—Lidichev, of the Politburo; Kharkov, of the army; and Chevrikov, of the KGB. And felt that the desk divided only him and Nikitin, not his ideas and Nikitin from the other three.

It was as if he had tumbled into a conspiratorial meeting, its target being himself.

"Marshal Kharkov should not have acted without the full authority of the Politburo and the Central—"

Nikitin interrupted him with what might have been impatience. "There was no time to call a Politburo meeting, let alone a full meeting of the Central Committee— Pyotr." His name was a small concession, a departure from the script. "You must realize that. Twenty people died in riots last night. The—" He glanced past Didenko, presumably towards Chevrikov, the chairman of the KGB. "—police could not control the situation. The army had to be sent in."

"With orders to shoot to kill?"

"Only if and where necessary," Didenko heard Lidichev's somber voice intone. "Party headquarters in Dushanbe was destroyed by fire last night. Order had to be restored."

"The ultimate authority of the Party was on trial in Tadzhikistan," Chevrikov added. It was like some chorus without music from a Stalinist liturgy—a cantata celebrating the achievements of some Five-Year Plan that hadn't put bread in the shops—a farce! He glared at Nikitin as if willing him to contradict the platitudes, but the general secretary outstared him with hard, pebblelike eyes, empty as his spectacles. He's just *sitting* there!

Didenko moved to the window, across the high-ceilinged room that was so familiar and strangely changed by the presence of the other three and the absence—he noticed it sharply for a moment—of Irena; absent from her clocks and paintings and furniture, from the room where they had planned so much; planned it eagerly, recklessly, like children anticipating a holiday or birthday outing...so much to do and so little time.

He stared through the tall windows across the courtyards of the Kremlin to where the surface of the river flickered like thousands of moving, golden fish beneath the lights along each bank, like small candles held in some procession.

Nikitin announced: "Marshal Kharkov as minister of defense is directly responsible for the activities of the airborne divisions, and it was his decision—quite properly so—to send them in rather than...less experienced troops."

"I see," Didenko murmured absently.

The city council session had been no more than a rehearsal for this encounter. He had, since his conversation with Valenkov in Lenin's private room, had only one short and unsatisfactory meeting with Nikitin, where the man had avoided through ridicule and denial any discussion of the direction he intended, the ominous demotions and promotions in the civil service—Didenko's own demotion from his Moscow Party post. But Nikitin had been very busy, hadn't he, with his new cronies!

Don't be childish, he told himself. Spite won't help you ... yet he was so enraged by this meeting, by the images on the television screen—by Nikitin's attitude! Recklessness would be what the other three were hoping for, a dash onto the gangplank so they could pull it away with ease.

"The authority of the Party in Tadzhikistan, especially in the capital, was deeply compromised. We could not allow that state of affairs to continue." Lidichev again. Nikitin was nodding!

Just as I had told Valenkov, Didenko congratulated himself with an empty satisfaction, ridiculously prissy and inadequate in the circumstances. Nikitin had taken the easy way to be strong. Lidichev and the others know him as well as I do, perhaps better, Didenko concluded. "We agreed," he burst out, leaning on the vast desk as one of Irena's small French clocks chimed delicately, "in this room, the three of us ..." He hesitated, registered their flinch of memory, then the solidification of their features into concrete assurance once more, and continued: "We agreed that if the people rejected the Party, so be it." Behind him, one of them actually gasped!

"It was never the intention to renounce the historical role of the Party," Nikitin murmured reassuringly. "That was *not* an option of policy. It couldn't be, in the light of the Party's essential—"

"We *agreed!*" Didenko snapped.

"We did *not!*"

Didenko returned to the window. *Over. As easily as that.* He'd lost Nikitin's confidence, even his shelter, in just five words. *We agreed! We did not!* He felt tears prickle his eyes—ridiculous and embarrassing, but there and quite real. Whatever followed now would be anticlimactic, the tidying of the corpse. He had glimpsed the row of three stony expressions as he had crossed to the window. The reflections of the lights processed along the river.

"Comrade Didenko, you are not seriously suggesting the role of the Party is no longer to be considered?" The Party ideologue, the keeper of its conscience, Lidichev. "The Party is the state, the Party is the future." He cleared his throat like a warning. "There was a simple, definitive need to act in Dushanbe. We, in concert with the Comrade General Secretary, saw the clear need, and we acted."

"Round up the customary suspects—only more than usual this time. Shoot some, to demonstrate the seriousness of your intent—we've been down that road before, far too many times!" he sneered. Hardly a dignified defense of freedom, but it was impossible to stop his thoughts whirling and spinning like flailing arms, or to prevent himself using them like blunt weapons.

"Really, Comrade Didenko," Chevrikov remarked contemptuously, "you underestimate the seriousness of the situation in Tadzhikistan. There have been murders and the vilest mutilations, shipments of arms from the Afghans and, we suspect, from Iran—"

"All right—very well!" He turned to face them. All four of them, acting in concert. "But this is a demonstration of force that you hope will keep the Baltic republics in line and encourage yesterday's men in Moldavia and Georgia! Because of the voices raised out there—" He flung his arm towards the windows. "—demanding the dissolution of the Warsaw Pact, free elections, the end of the Party's unopposed authority. That's what this nasty video—" He pointed accusingly at the screen, whose images continued, causing the others not a moment of doubt. "—shown throughout the country, is all about. A stern warning to behave!"

Kharkov snapped: "The rioting began when two off-duty soldiers were dragged from their car at a traffic light, stripped, beaten and shot with their own guns. I—*we*—considered that situation sufficiently serious to take the action that was taken. If *you* do not, then—" He shrugged.

Another clock struck the hour—it was slow—one with blue numerals, heavily gilded with cherubs, which also adorned the garniture at either end of the long mantelpiece. Irena's clock, acquired from the Hermitage because she said it would remind them that it was *Time to strike up the band.* Cherubs with drums and fifes and other instruments . . .

As the last chime faded in a silvery shiver, he attempted to concentrate his thoughts, then Nikitin's voice provoked a new bout of unreasoning anger.

"Comrade Marshal, you will convey our congratulations to the local commander for his swift and decisive action. The Guards are to be—"

"My God—!" Didenko burst out. And it was as if his own lack of rationality had communicated itself to stolid, massively assured Lidichev. His voice was angry, vivid with conviction.

"Do you realize, Comrade Didenko, the nature of the animal you propose to let out of its cage? It is—*things* are—out of control. We cannot have *chaos,* which is your prescription!"

"You must see that, Pyotr . . . ?" He only saw himself excluded by outdated certainties.

The fire threw up sparks as logs crumbled to gray ash, making their faces seem warm and implacable. And yet he could not, for a single moment, doubt Lidichev's sincerity. Though Lidichev wanted to take Russia back forty years, he believed it was right to do it! It wasn't for the dacha in the woods or the *beriozka* shops or even for the naked power. All of them would call themselves patriots, even as Didenko did, despite the fact that they were so damnably *wrong!* Then as if to display Didenko's irrelevance to their considerations, Lidichev said:

"Aleksandr Aleksandrovich—concerning the republics of Latvia and Estonia—our recommendations are in the digest on your desk—"

"Yes, yes!" Nikitin snapped hurriedly. It was his first moment of discomfort since Didenko's arrival. Then he turned to Didenko. There was a slight flush on his cheeks. "Pyotr, the Party has been forced into retreat everywhere. We didn't survive *Stalinism* to be reduced to anarchy now. You understand?" It was an offer not of complicity but of warning, as Nikitin's eyes darted towards Lidichev and Chevrikov.

Didenko swallowed, then shook his head. Nikitin appeared lugubriously sad, but for no more than an instant, then adjusted his spectacles and looked down at the desk. When he looked up again, he said:

"As you know, there is to be a full Politburo meeting tomorrow. There are—pressures—charges, perhaps, that you may have to refute, I don't say answer, Pyotr Yurievich, simply refute...in the light of certain allegations by the committee of the Moscow Party."

The script was ill memorized, still freshly uncomfortable. But it was one that, with regret, Nikitin had agreed to. The easy strength of tradition. Irena would despise you now, of all times!

"I see," Didenko murmured stiffly and walked once more to the windows. He was aware that he might appear to be shuffling irresolutely to a corner of the room.

He rubbed his narrow chin and brushed his fingers once again through his untidy hair. People like himself had *not* succeeded in the past, things had not changed—things were unchangeable; such an easy, logical step to take, that conclusion. These men of patent and heavy adulthood found his outbursts mere tantrums, childish and petulant. They were challenging him to arm-wrestle for the future. They were weighed down with history while he was freighted with an uncertain and probably dangerous future.

"Strength is required in dealing with the situation in the Baltic republics and elsewhere, Comrade Secretary," Chevrikov offered like a tempter. Didenko's lip curled. There would be no backsliding, no apostasy here!

Nikitin said quietly, urgently: "It is a question of the authority of the Party, Pyotr. *Nothing*—nothing can be done without that."

I knew it, Didenko told himself. I *told* Valenkov! Be strong, they'd advised him. The Party must not be challenged or set aside. And there was no Irena here to whisper in his ear that these were yesterday's men, that real strength was reform and the ability to change. There was only himself, and he was no match for them.

"I—don't believe that."

Lidichev stormed, with the collective authority of most of the century: "*You*, Comrade Didenko, cannot simply give people the means of dissent from the Party without educating them to make a response other than hatred! Don't you even begin to understand what is happening? You show them that they won't be arrested and tried for burning buses, murdering soldiers, ignoring the Party and the police, and you expect them to be *reasonable?* There should be no different sides here—we are talking about the future of our society!" Lidichev's heavy features were white with rage and incomprehension. Even Nikitin seemed surprised by the profundity of feeling.

Didenko was silent for some moments, then he said: "It was never our—*my*—intention to make the Party the focus of resentment and rejection."

"But that is the result of your handiwork!" Kharkov barked.

"I refute that!"

"We are trying to prevent hundreds, perhaps thousands of deaths," Nikitin supplied. "We must not be seen now, of all times, to be less than strong." He really believed it! "We must restore order out there before it breaks down completely." He spread his hands. "That is *all* we are trying to do."

Chin cupped in one trembling hand, Didenko listened and accepted that he was irrelevant. Irena wasn't there, not even in spirit; only the man he had always suspected Nikitin could become without her.

"A Politburo meeting. Charges?"

"Hardly charges."

"It—it doesn't matter . . ." Now all Didenko wanted to do was flee, to get out as quickly and dramatically as possible, and thereby show Nikitin *he* was the one being abandoned, not Didenko. "I—I will submit my resignation from the Politburo before that meeting tomorrow."

The silence was not heavy or charged; it simply reflected their relief.

"And from your position as head of the Moscow Party?" Chevrikov asked.

"Yes!" Didenko snapped. "Yes!"

As Aubrey slowed the Audi in response to the rapid blinking of the other car's headlights, he already felt impatient of anything Ramsey might say, the unavoidable gossip and deference. He was tired, and not simply from the driving. The empty whiskey bottle clinked against the seat mounting behind him as he braked and eased onto the verge at the side of the road. It was Hyde's condition that wearied Aubrey—the drinking that seemed like self-pity; the truculent silence, even toward Ros; and the volatility of his rage. His breathing was like the dangerous ticking of an explosive device.

As Aubrey halted the car his back ached the moment he moved in his seat. His arms, too, seemed wearily old. Hyde had refused to drive any farther the moment the lights of Peshawar had climbed together in a haze behind them and there were no other cars on the dark road. And then he had immediately struggled for the temporary oblivion of the bottle, to Ros's repeated protests whenever she roused from a strained, unsettled sleep. In the mirror, he had seen Hyde consume the whiskey with an appalling dedication.

Aubrey opened the door and welcomed the chill air. Rawalpindi's lights were clustered thickly ahead. The stars hung like huge lamps. A young man in a light suit with a clean-shaven face was beside him at once, as deferential and detached as a servant expecting an old employer to climb slowly into bed.

"Ramsey, sir," he said unnecessarily. Aubrey straightened, hands clasping the small of his back, hearing the betraying clicks of stiff joints. The cold air made his head whirl.

"Yes, yes—good," he murmured impatiently.

He realized there should be a sense of safety inflating inside him now that he had made the rendezvous and was standing on the highway's uneven, dusty verge. But, it evaded him like a now discredited acquaintance. These were Peter Shelley's people, he reminded himself. There was a simple scenario to be obeyed; a morning flight to

London, then Ros and Patrick would be taken directly to Aubrey's cottage . . . his other ideas were illusory.

"Sir Kenneth?"

"Yes?" he snapped at Ramsey, silencing him.

Hyde's pale features lolled against the rear window of the Audi. Even drunkenly still, he seemed threatening as much as threatened.

Other figures moved now, five or six of them. Ramsey persisted, obeying Shelley and London. "We're fully briefed, Sir Kenneth. If you'd all like to leave the car now, we'll dispose of it."

"What? Oh, yes—of course."

Another young man was peering against the Audi's window, where Patrick's face lay heavily. The noise of a radio or cassette player emanated from one of their two cars, lending an impression, in the dark, of confidence without tradecraft. He felt distanced as soon as he heard the one nearest the Audi murmur to his companion: "Hyde—heard of him? Doesn't look up to much, does he? Used to be good, that was the word." Then they giggled like girls with a prissiness accented by their class and education. Aubrey resented them— and the guilt they aroused. What had he *done* to Hyde? One young man opened the door with deliberate speed and made as if to catch Hyde as he slumped—quickly Patrick's hand clamped the man's wrist and drew a small squeal of surprised pain. Aubrey smiled.

"Fuck off, sonny—I'm not your Granddad," Hyde muttered, clambering drunkenly out of the car. Beside him, Ramsey snorted in irritation, with what might as well have been contempt. Hyde wiped his mouth, then his cheeks, rubbing hard, and leaned against the Audi, breathing stertorously. The two young men had retreated to what presumably was a safe distance, still smirking in the gleam of the headlights. Ros got out of the other rear door.

Ros... unforgivably stupid, that, Aubrey realized, however insistent she had been. He should not have brought her. Hyde resented it—not for the mothering and the nagging but for the danger Aubrey had created for her. Hyde felt all three of them now were hurrying along one of those long, hooped, twisting nets used to trap waterfowl. Twist after twist of it, all its length, until they arrived at the dead end, wings beating furiously, where Harrell and his people would be waiting for them with all the certainty and confidence of human intelligences outwitting animal instincts.

A truck rumbled past, its headlights disturbing and revealing, making Aubrey flinch and hurry. The only alternative was counteractivity, which meant handling Patrick; dangerous and unreliable Patrick, driven by survival and rage, fueled by drink. It would be so easy for Harrell to stop him... stop Hyde, in his condition, and alone.

Aubrey ignored the cold, appraising part of himself, lodged on an outcrop at the back of his mind. *He* was angry, too, for Kathryn's sake! They had nothing *but* anger between them, he and Hyde, nothing else that could be employed as a weapon to defend themselves.

Ros took Hyde's arm—he allowed her grip, reluctantly—and they crossed to one of the two embassy cars. Her pale face was angry. Thin, occasional traffic flowed past them. The belying safety of numbers; *mere* numbers. People like Ramsey could not solve his problems.

"—bugger doesn't half need a bath," he heard from one of the young men as they passed, accompanied by a complementary snigger. Then one of them seemed to recall himself to reality and approached Aubrey. "The keys, Sir Kenneth? The Audi, sir—?" He was holding out his hand. The radio was crackling with a kind of protest and one of the two cars winked its headlights invitingly.

"Must be London, sir," Ramsey commented.

"Good!" He handed over the keys. The young man said to Ramsey rather than himself: "Shan't be more than five or ten—old quarry nearby. Water's deep enough. Should do nicely."

As his own, older generation might have said, *A bit of a lark, a wheeze,* Aubrey reflected.

The Audi bumped away down the steep slope on the other side of the verge, its headlights picking out stunted bushes, pot-holes, pools of water. Aubrey sighed and rubbed his chin, then crossed to the Ford which had blinked at him and against which Hyde was leaning heavily, now apparently merely drunk, and around whom Ros fussed and patted and clucked. He paused for a moment and caught the glitter of Hyde's eyes.

The engine of the Audi revved loudly, followed by the crunch and slide of its disappearance. The laughter from the two young men confirmed that Hyde, even in his present condition, was better than this *disastrous* intake! Ros glared at him. Fragments of her garbled, hesitant, appalled version of events in that underground garage in Peshawar nagged at him. She had believed the safari under proper management, that there was no danger—

—instead of which, she'd seen Patrick's heart of darkness . . . the same heart of darkness on which everything might now depend.

Hyde was watching him steadily. It was difficult to avoid guilt, to still regard Patrick as an individual under his authority rather than as a case history, someone beyond use. He shivered in the breeze. Hyde's nature now moved pendulously between nausea and aggression.

He knew Hyde wanted to escape just as vigorously as he wished to kill Harrell.

If Patrick couldn't function for long enough and effectively enough, then none of the three of them might ever be secure again. He wanted to tell Ros that but, as he opened his lips, Ramsey's voice interrupted him and he was glad to be tugged away.

"Sir Kenneth, it's the DDG."

"Yes, yes!" He scuttled past Hyde and Ros. The door of the black Granada was held open and a receiver was thrust into his hand. He was aware of Hyde's back pressed against the front window. A small dish aerial thrust up from the grass verge, like an abandoned mower on its side. Via satellite, he would have secure communication with London. He felt weak and shivery, as if he had run a great distance. He had remembered why communication with London was utterly important.

"Yes, Peter, yes? Any news?"

"—found her," he managed to decipher from the rush of his own breath and the static. "She's OK. Kenneth, are you three safe?"

"Thank God," he murmured, breathless, then he slumped into the car's seat. Then, while relief still coursed through him: "Who was responsible?"

"No idea, I'm afraid. As to your niece, she's stowed as safely as we can manage. But we really should have her safely back here, Kenneth, to talk to her. In depth."

"Yes, yes." He pushed relief aside. "Peter, I'm going to change my arrangements for our mutual friend. No, I'm not clear as to quite how yet, but I'll talk to him." Hence the careful analysis and the guilt, he reminded himself. "Just stand by on that, will you? Meanwhile, I'm very concerned about Harrell's people. They were right behind us in Peshawar. I'm afraid there's now an outstanding debt they will wish repaid."

"I see. Very well, then it's probably best he doesn't return here—*you* would be safer coming directly back, on the other hand. I can also see what you might have in mind for—"

"Yes, Peter, but *I* shall have to decide that. After assessment of capability."

"Is he really up to it?" Shelley sounded disbelieving.

"Peter, just make some alternative arrangements for Hyde! Ms. Woode and myself will come back to London, via Karachi, as per the original plan. But Patrick has to part company with us, I think, as soon as possible. For *his* sake."

After a silence, Shelley said: "Very well, Kenneth."

Ramsey leaned into the window of the Granada. "Sir Kenneth, I think we should be going. There was some surveillance around the embassy this afternoon, nothing to worry about, we weren't followed, but I think—"

"Very well, Ramsey," he snapped, cutting him short, then: "Peter, it seems I must go and so must you. Thank you for looking after Kathryn."

"Take great care, Kenneth—in everything."

"Yes. Goodbye."

He put down the microphone and struggled out of the car's very comfortable rear seat with a twinge in his back. He confronted Hyde, who glared at him with the baleful vagueness of any drunk, anywhere. He was smoking, and the smell was sweet and suspicious. Ros's frosty glance, distant, hardly impinged. She clutched Hyde's arm as he stood in front of him.

"Patrick—?"

"No need to whisper. I'm not asleep. Even if I was, you haven't brought my Chrissie present, have you?" The smoke from the cigarette rose, then flew in the breeze. Hyde snorted with a game-playing contempt. *Tell me the old, old story* he could not prevent from coming into his thoughts accusingly. Ramsey drifted away, as if from a marital squabble. Hyde glared and added, "Well?" Ros grabbed at his arm but he made to shake off her grip, then contented himself with patting her hand.

"You're not secure, none of us—" Aubrey began.

Hyde snorted once more. "Christ, old man, I *know* that! Doesn't take much to know that, mate!"

Aubrey felt a tickle of satisfaction at Hyde's belligerence. Hyde was aware of the intended manipulation and his sarcasm had given permission for it to continue. Then Aubrey experienced a long moment of doubt that Hyde could survive, never mind succeed. Surely, Hyde could at least bring Kathryn safely out? That, if nothing else. If so, Aubrey would have to rely on Kathryn's guiding them to the truth of this business, its connection with Frascati, what Frascati had discovered. He continued: "Patrick, there's someone in America—she happens to be my niece—with whom you must compare notes. There's a connection, d'you see, between what you saw and what she knows—?"

"You old *sod!*" Ros protested, her grip on Hyde's arm tightening. Patrick continued to pat her fingers, and to stare at Aubrey from the sunken eyes above his pale, dead cheeks.

"Oh?" he said. "Is Harrell involved?"

Aubrey hesitated, swallowed, then nodded.

"I'm certain he must be. It's too much for coincidence to play a part—"

"Don't listen to the old bugger! He'll have you jumping through *hoops!* You're not in any state to—"

Hyde was in no way angry with Ros, Aubrey realized; he was merely indisposed to listen. He continued to pat her hand as she kept her grasp on his arm.

"To be secure, we need *proof,*" Aubrey continued.

Hyde followed his words as attentively as an engrossed child.

"Can you believe these guys?" The amusement, which sprang from certainty, deflected any more genuine anger Robert Harrell might have experienced. He watched the fingers of his large left hand tapping at the edge of the desk, making smudges in the dust, then looked up at the day that glared through the window. "Listen, I'm not interested in whether the guy was celebrating his two hundredth birthday, Jack! Just lean on the British and make sure Orrell gets off his duff and stops Shelley from helping the old guy—OK? On my desk, or patched through to the airport, within a half-hour, I want his confirmation that Hyde is *Rogue*—no, don't give me excuses, Jack."

The office was hot and smelled of dust; the air conditioning of the Karachi consulate was inefficient. Occasionally, small birds landed outside the window, their dabbing inspections of the stained concrete sill momentary and disappointing. Before he'd slumped in the swivel chair, which creaked and protested whenever he moved, he'd seen the harbor, the fishing boats almost drowned in the water's glitter, the hazy pelicans and the shimmering inlets and mud banks of the mouths of the Indus. Now all he could see was the sky's empty, almost colorless gleam. The noise of the traffic was muted.

"Sure, Jack—sure I'm sure. Aubrey's on his way here, with the others. They didn't take a London flight from 'Pindi." Harrell had no sense of uncertainty. He fingered the faxed photograph with amusement. What looked like Aubrey dressed as a cleaner boarding the Karachi morning flight had been cautiously identified at Rawalpindi airport. Harrell was certain it was Aubrey. Hyde and the woman hadn't been spotted . . . they might have been disguised among the aircrew, the catering staff, the gang on the fuel tanker? It didn't matter. They were coming. "And Jack—I want you to make sure the British declare Hyde *officially Rogue* and make him *our* responsibility." He listened to the amplifier on his desk, to which the receiver was attached, protest for a few moments. Then he said, hands linked at the back of his neck, seeming to address the ceiling: "Jack, don't think of us as the penny-ante outfit that was started up to keep an eye on the Russians getting out of Afghanistan!" His voice cautioned and instructed rather than reproved. His sense of well-being was virtually unassailable. "You can get it done, Jack—you just have to ask!" He chuckled, shaking his head slightly as at a dubious child. Even the dirt the gathered flies suggested, the dust smell in his nostrils, could not disconcert or irritate him. "Sure you can, Jack. Hyde gets cut off by the British, then we cut him off in a more permanent way. The excuse of Bagley in the garage is enough. He killed the poor guy. Lay it on heavy enough and they'll throw up their hands! You won't even have to try." Protest became acceptance, even amusement. "OK Jack, just keep me informed."

He switched off the amplifier and replaced the receiver. Then he flicked down the switch on the office intercom.

"OK, now get me someone important in Delhi." Just as a precaution; just in case Hyde didn't get on the Karachi flight but headed off on his own or with the woman. Delhi was the surest bet for that. Whatever, he and Aubrey were making for London, eventually. There was plenty of time. But not for everything . . . He looked at his watch, then checked it against the tilted, big-faced clock on one cracked, whitewashed wall. The consulate was a crummy, student-lodging kind of place. "And get my car around to the back of the building right away," he added.

The Karachi flight from Rawalpindi—with Aubrey the cleaner on board!—was due in less than fifty minutes. There was time to make it comfortably. It was impatience, anticipation, that made the time drag.

Then, as if he had been checking every nook and cranny for it, he found doubt. The woman's disappearance in California. Those clowns had killed pointlessly. Sure, the British would usually accept any fiction of drugs, robbery, men from another planet if necessary, but the woman was Aubrey's niece and *he'd* be looking out for her. She, very definitely, had to be found—and soon.

Harrell swung his feet off the desk and shrugged himself upright. The office *was* shoddy, as was the whole place! He was sorry to have thought of Kathryn Aubrey. The sea glittered with an intensity that made him squint; the hundreds of masted and sailed fishing boats were no more distinct than spots on his retinas when he momentarily closed his eyes.

What was it he'd said to Jack? They were no longer the penny-ante outfit the *Carpetbaggers* once were, when it was set up? OK, come on then, fella, shake it off. We're not sleeping under a bridge on the Lower East Side any more. This *can* be contained, easily. As easily as they'd eliminated Frascati in San Jose.

He paused with his hand on the doorknob and shrugged. Then he opened the door, whistling and grinning as he passed the secretary and went out to the elevator. The corridor was slightly cooler, more the efficient artificial environment he expected.

The elevator groaned slowly downwards, stifling without air conditioning. He stood facing the doors, hands in his pockets, shoulders thrown forward as if expecting some challenger to bully into the metal box that contained him. Then the doors jerked back, two of his people at once smartened into a military sort of posture and he waved them to fall in behind him. The heat and the dust oppressed and the light glared so fiercely that he immediately slipped his sunglasses on, still squinting behind their tint. The long dusty white limousine was waiting. Harrell got into the rear of the car, at once shutting out the heat, his face slippery with perspiration. Trishaws, belching old trucks, bicycles, chickens, and small, dark foreign people cluttered the narrow back street. The limousine slipped between and around these obstacles with what seemed like patience.

The sea and the desert became more pronounced as they began moving more swiftly along the divided highway out towards Karachi International. The city trickled away into shanty suburbs. A white bird riding on a black buffalo's back, laden donkeys, an imperious camel. Hundreds of perpetually curious dark faces. Cardboard and tin and gasoline-can homes. Omnipresent dust.

Then Harrell noticed small silver shapes reflecting the sun, coming in to land. Fencing, the terminal and the control tower; parked, newer cars, air-conditioned airline buses, huge stabilizers like billboards; the proximity of Aubrey and Hyde. Harrell looked at his watch.

"That flight on time?"

"Yes, sir—last we heard."

"Check it, and get me the office. My call to Delhi, patch it through." The blurred fencing effectively reduced the glare of sea and desert around him as the car passed beside it. "I want no foul-ups on this, no fumbling—understand?" Nods, murmurs of agreement; the excitement of anticipated action, the more arcane adrenaline of apprenticeship within a special, elect grouping. Ambitious, talented young men. "OK."

The driver was talking to the secretary Harrell had appropriated. If these young men did well, they expected advancement, membership in the special grouping, other postings. The driver said: "Your call's through, sir. Pick up the telephone, please?"

"Who's that?" Harrell asked. "Hi, Rifkin—Harrell. Listen, there'll be a face coming over the fax. I want it looked out for at the airport, and that means right away. British, his name's Hyde...yeah, professional. Sure, you'll get the proper authorization. If he comes in, don't lose him, understand, Rifkin? This is Grade A and beyond. Get back to me as soon as your people are organized. A full report."

He put down the receiver. The limousine turned into the airport and towards the terminal buildings perched like bulky helter-skelters at the tops of long, concrete ramps. Ten minutes, if the flight from Peshawar was still on time. A British Airways 747 sagged down out of the colorless dazzle of sky, taking on form and bulk, its lights less visible than the wispy little trails from its engines. Then the airliner touched down, racing away from them. The car drew up under the terminal's concrete canopy, beside a row of tinted, sliding doors. Beggars and hawkers congregated along the pavement. One of the men with him held his door open.

He listened to Fredrickson's report as he crossed the concourse towards the escalator, picking out the men at whom Fredrickson pointed, nodding occasionally. The terminal was familiar—international—as he made for the observation deck. The bar and restaurant were dotted with white faces among the dark. Almost at once, as they halted at the smeared, tinted windows where the dust and heat seemed to seep through, Fredrickson pointed into the high distance at a shadowy dot, hardly real.

"That's her, Bob—she's on time."

"Sure." Harrell grinned. "There's someone down in Baggage?"

Fredrickson opened his jacket. A thin wire and a tiny earpiece. "All wired up, Bob. Candy from a kid . . . huh?"

Harrell experienced a momentary doubt. Aubrey's reputation was formidable; all based on his *past*, he corrected himself. The doubt slipped away. The distant airliner was subtly more solid in the glaring air. Hyde was in bad shape. The woman was—discountable. Aubrey was an old man. He glanced along the observation windows, and spotted two of his men with field glasses, one of them with a child; nice touch. Look for cleaners—

"—cleaners, aircrew, anyone," he found himself saying as excitement tickled his throat.

"We got that covered, Bob—relax."

"I am relaxed, Joe, I really am." And it was true. The airliner was green-striped and -tailed, a small Boeing. He was relaxed. All the bases were covered. The plane seemed to hesitate above the approach lights, as if sensing his presence, then rushed at the sunlight-hazed concrete. From the plane it suggested a conspiratorial alliance against Aubrey and Hyde, a trap they could not evade.

It slowed towards the end of the runway and then turned into its taxiing run towards the terminal.

Harrell announced: "OK, let's get down there and greet my old uncle coming out West for the first time." He grinned. "If Hyde doesn't get off the flight, you've got Customs arranged?"

"Sure, they'll board the plane. Drugs, gold smuggling, some excuse like that. Who knows? But they'll be thorough."

As he reached the escalator, Harrell turned to watch

the Boeing's nose sliding towards the terminal as neatly
as a head slipping into a noose.

Aubrey felt his tension increase as the driveling, muted
music was switched off. Ros, beside him, was paled by
more than the day's glare outside. Passengers dragged
and banged at overhead lockers or scrabbled beneath
their seats, then queued impatiently until the door was
opened at the front of the aircraft and the light flooded
the doorway. Reluctantly, Aubrey stood up, his cleverness deserting him like sand through loose fingers.

He stepped gingerly down the passenger steps, Ros
behind him. The windows of the passenger terminal were
blind with light, but he knew they would be watching
for him. He wondered how long it would be before they
realized that Patrick was missing; or had they anticipated
that?

The baggage hall was crowded, noisy, depressingly
hot and tiring with the collective weariness of the travelers it contained. As they waited, his nerves prickling
along his arms, he glanced from time to time at Ros to
challenge her hostile silence; or perhaps to discover some
slight signal of forgiveness for involving her and using
Hyde. She had eaten nothing on the flight, despite the
deliciousness of the curried snacks. She had blundered
into a strange, bewildering party hosted by complete
strangers; saw faces she recognized, but those familiar
people were behaving perversely, appallingly. Her silence was her hold on normality, frightened and disoriented as she was in his and Hyde's world.

Their bags wobbled and slid down the chute, then
strolled towards them along the carousel. He snatched
at hers then hurried after his, small actions which exerted
and disturbed him, while the press of disembarked passengers obscurely threatened. He could not believe, mov-

ing with the crowd, that he had had the wit and ingenuity to outrun Harrell—

—who was standing at the passenger barrier. Harrell and at least two others, he could not be certain. The American raised a lazy, confident hand and moved parallel with them on the other side of the barrier. Then he confronted them.

"Sir Kenneth. Fancy seeing you here," Harrell mocked lightly. Just the two of you traveling together. I don't believe I've been introduced to the lady?"

It was more potent than an outright threat, the confidence that glared from behind Harrell's affability. Had the man been wearing a hat, he would have raised it! His voice was like a cat's paw shunting a small mouse with languid confidence.

"Ms. Woode, Harrell, Ms. Woode." Aubrey ignored Ros's dumb surprise, her eyes darting and hands flitting as realization rushed over her. "I might claim a similar surprise at finding you here," he continued, then: "Perhaps you could arrange for someone to carry our bags?"

Harrell's eyes hardened for an instant, then appeared to weigh Aubrey with renewed confidence before he said: "I have a signal—maybe I should say an authorization— from London. You should read it, Sir Kenneth, then we should talk. You could say that really it's addressed to you—opened in error . . . ?" He passed a flimsy sheet of creased paper to Aubrey, who took it with a quivering touch.

It was genuine. Addressed to Harrell, to be passed on to Aubrey. Orrell's personal code, Century House ident, time and date. Absolute priority and unignorable. Everything was perfectly correct. Slowly, Aubrey looked up at Harrell. "You've been busy."

"You want to check this with your guy in London, what's-his-name, Shelley? You want to be certain?"

"Oh, I'm not left in much doubt, Mr. Harrell—but perhaps for form's sake, I should call Shelley and confirm this. Mm?" The effort of calm was taxing, and made the concourse seem hotter, more crowded. Tension sapped him like high humidity.

The public telephones, neat and crowded, were suggestively close. Harrell was watching him in a detached, certain mood. London had disowned Patrick, compounding his own guilt. They'd handed him over—just as Gaines had done in Kabul. He was furiously angry with Orrell, who was stupid and pigheaded . . . and from whom no better could possibly be expected, even on his best day! But the force of his inward rage was reserved for Shelley. Shelley had told Orrell that Patrick was alive, where he could be found, that he and Hyde had made contact!

Rogue, the signal had said. The repossession order on a field agent, his being turned out into the street with his pathetic memories. The signal consigned Patrick to Harrell as the *fit and proper authority in the matter*—the bloody, bloody fools!

Nervously smoking a cigarette, Ros stood like someone expecting a lover to appear or not to. Harrell had lit the cigarette for her with mocking courtesy. Aubrey walked to one of the empty telephone compartments and dialed Century House. Eventually—and Harrell's bulk and power did not diminish while he averted his gaze—Shelley answered the call.

"Peter, what the devil is happening here? I'm being ordered to hand Patrick over to Harrell, of all people!"

"Sir Kenneth, I'm to put you through to the DG whenever you call—do you understand?"

"Never mind that nonsense now! What did you tell them? How much do they know?"

"Kenneth, it was Harrell who informed Sir Clive, not

I! Hyde killed one of their people in Peshawar. The way it was represented to Orrell, he had little or no choice in the matter!" There was the protestation of the child about Shelley's anger. "I was on the carpet as your most likely accomplice, Kenneth—I didn't have to tell them *anything*, they already knew most of it!"

Aubrey lowered his voice. He detested the moment of hesitation and doubt before he said: "Patrick?"

Shelley was at once conspiratorial and familiar, whatever residual tension remained in his voice.

"Delhi. Cass is posted there, he'll sort things out."

Aubrey sighed audibly. "I knew Cass was there—it's why I sent him on, in the hope—"

"I see." Shelley seemed affronted by Aubrey's perspicacity. "Convenient then." His tone altered then as he added: "They know nothing of it. But what can you expect of Patrick—this has to be cleared *up*, Kenneth, don't you realize—?"

"Patrick is not going to simply disappear, Peter, not for anyone's benefit!"

"And for your benefit—what is he being asked to do?"

Aubrey hesitated, then forced himself to say: "One signal to Cass, Peter—quick as you can. He is to ignore *all* signals from London that might follow yours. Patrick knows where he needs to go. On to California. No, don't surmise, Peter! Patrick must not be stopped. And tell Cass that I suspect others might be meeting that flight ...no, Peter, I am not joking. This business is going to hell in a handcart, thanks to people like Orrell!" He breathed in deeply, then added: "Peter, just send that signal and for God's sake keep the matter to yourself! Patrick is in the greatest danger."

"I'm sorry—"

"Hardly *your* fault, Peter!" he snapped out spitefully.

"Oh, I'm sorry, I realize . . . well, I understand that you're relegated to the sideline for the rest of the game, Peter."

"You're coming straight back here?"

"Yes. Pass the good news on to Orrell, will you? I'm sure he'll be most interested!"

Aubrey rang off and walked back to Harrell, his eyes glaring in outrage, his stomach churning. Ros had futilely turned her back on the Americans. Harrell seemed to possess the patience of a clockwork model.

"OK, Sir Kenneth?"

"No, it is definitely *not* OK, Mr. Harrell. Far from it!"

An airport official had drifted away from Harrell as Aubrey had thrust down the telephone receiver.

"Where is he?" Harrell demanded.

"Obviously not hiding on the aircraft! I'm afraid the person you are seeking who was to have been handed over to you like a small package of no importance has vanished into thin air. Do you understand the English argot 'done a runner,' Mr. Harrell? Hyde has done a runner—gone!" He waved his hands dismissively. "Did you expect one old man to be able to keep him in check, if what you claim of him is the truth?"

Harrell was abashed for only a moment, then his grin reappeared. Images of Hyde's briefing, his sullen, condemned-man departure, the sands of psychosis that seemed to be shifting constantly under his feet, all returned to Aubrey. They were like smuggled items to be kept from Harrell's scrutiny. Patrick had gone, that was the one thing that mattered. Harrell had been forestalled.

Aubrey remained expressionless as he announced: "I'm afraid Ms. Woode and myself are merely in transit, Harrell, and we must check in for our London flight. I hope you understand—Ros, my dear?"

Harrell moved to bar his way, then simply shrugged. "We'll find him, don't worry about it."

"Mm. Gentlemen, excuse us please. Ros, I really think we should be making our way—"

He took Ros's elbow, attempting to steer her towards the escalators. She seemed nerveless and uncertain, though she managed to indicate their luggage. Aubrey towed his suitcase on its wheels, and they bundled their cases awkwardly onto the moving staircase. His bent posture and the effort of coping with minutiae in his role as air traveler and old man absorbed his attention. Then, as he straightened, he looked back at Harrell's massive, confident calm.

He almost stumbled at the top of the escalator and Ros caught his hand fiercely. Her grip alone prompted guilt. She, too, relied upon him for her safety. Harrell would know she had seen Patrick, had talked and listened ... would require tidying; removal.

"Thank you, thank you," he blustered so she might not notice the sudden fear, the sense of powerlessness that had made him falter and must be reflected in his eyes. Her face revealed a sense of disaster. She understood what might happen—principally to Patrick but perhaps to her. The set of her lips indicated she had no interest whatsoever in any danger to Aubrey.

Hyde squinted behind his dark glasses, partly against knowledge, partly because of the sunlight glaring in a vast sky and mirrored by hundreds of glass and metal surfaces. He trooped slowly with the other passengers from the Rawalpindi flight towards the terminal, the smell of aviation fuel heady in the hot air. He had no idea whether or not Harrell's people were waiting for him. He did not think so. He was unarmed.

Someone bumped apologetically against him and he

staggered slightly, his temperature jumping nervously. His exhaustion frightened him, as did his dry throat, even after the drinks on the flight. The anticipation of his possible inadequacy disturbed him.

The sunlight on the terminal windows masked everything behind the glass. As he looked down again, the shadows of an alleyway between two concrete walls were almost black, before becoming coolly blue. Then the alleyway seemed blocked by a thin dog and thinner, large-stomached children, barefoot and half-naked. Behind there were the cardboard hovels like dolls' houses, with hammered-flat petrol-can roofs. He heard the crying of a baby. He felt himself shiver at the memories of Afghanistan.

Then he was pushed by the press of his fellow passengers towards the terminal doors, forgetting the alleyway that had opened like a lens on a recurring nightmare. He moved passively, hardly aware that his attention had slackened.

A hand grasped at his sleeve. He was dragged off-balance back from the narrow doors, the light hurting his eyes as his sunglasses fell askew. He turned like an old man. The last passengers slipped past him through the doors.

"Patrick, for Christ's sake—!" Hyde shook his head. Cass's face—unexpectedly—no, expectedly, Cass's face, registering relief and urgency in equal measure. Cass's hand pulled him closer. "They're waiting for you up there, you fuckwit!" he hissed. "Were you just going to walk up there and say hello?"

"How many of them?"

"What? Oh, six, maybe more. Americans. A couple have been here for hours, the rest of them spilled out of an embassy car five minutes ago, running like hell." He began scrutinizing Hyde. "Are you all right? Are you with me?"

Hyde rubbed his face as if washing. Beyond Cass's shoulder, two children stared at them, large-eyed, barefooted.

Hyde nodded. "I'm all right."

"You look half-asleep." Cass paused, then said: "No you don't—you look a lot worse than that."

"I'm all *right!*" Again his temperature leaped unsettlingly. He rubbed his face once more, feeling the palm of his hand filmed with perspiration. "All right..."

"Then let's go. They'll be down those stairs in a minute looking for you. They can't have missed you getting off the plane."

Cass began guiding him towards the alley and the children but he was reluctant to go that way. Yet there was a kind of arousal in his renewed fear of the immediate; in his awareness of the next few steps and moments. *Harrell,* still trying to kill him. That registered and had meaning. He brushed past the two children, then past the shanties, hovels and carton-made homes. He tried not to notice them.

"I've got somewhere I can stow you until I can change your ticket—"

"Why?"

"Either I get you a ticket for somewhere local or we leave the airport another way. They've seen you, I'm certain. They'll watch all the international flights—in *here.*" Cass steered him through a glass door, checking the alley before closing it behind them. He was grinning excitedly, out of breath. "If you leave by air, it's got to be local—down this way, second door on the right, got it?"

Hyde paused outside the door. There was a translation of the Hindi—CUSTOMS: STAFF ONLY PERMITTED. He looked at Cass, who seemed more at ease now, his eyes reflecting only a residue of concern and what might have been disappointment.

"OK, in you go." Cass pushed open the door. The cramped, untidy room was empty, and smelled of smoke and stale food.

Hyde at once slumped into a creaking chair, its material frayed, exposing foam rubber and wood. A cigarette-burned low table, a newspaper opened at the stylized photograph of an Indian movie star, a Customs uniform jacket hanging over the back of a second chair, a small, dusty radio playing sitar music. A brimming ashtray. Cass was standing by the door, watching him like a doctor. A gray metal filing cabinet, dog-eared paperbacks, a battered cigarette lighter.

"OK now?" Cass persisted in a nursing voice.

Hyde glared at him. "How do I get out of here?"

Cass nodded. "I'll get you onto something local, to begin with."

"What if someone barges in here?"

"They won't. They've been paid." He glanced towards the travel bag he had brought. "Don't bother with what's in that till I get back." He grinned encouragingly.

"Still on your world tour at Her Majesty's expense, Cass?"

"I've learned to speak Hindi, I read a little Sanskrit, I can bribe someone at the drop of a hat without wasting the money—I don't get Delhi-belly any more. Some day, it won't all be wasted."

"Some day, they'll call you home to a desk."

"Better that than—well, never mind. I won't be long." There seemed to be something else Cass felt impelled to say. "I've never seen someone declared *Rogue* before." Cass rubbed his chin.

"And you think it couldn't happen to a more deserving

bloke, right?" Hyde gibed. "Don't worry, it doesn't hurt until they catch you."

"Are you in any state to—?"

"No. Does that answer your question? I'm in no state for anything." Hyde was sitting forward, watching his hands clasp each other as if for reassurance. He wasn't in any state to do anything, either. That was the truth. *Get me the proof that will keep us all alive, Patrick . . .* Aubrey, almost pleading with him, for some lost cause. Implicit in it was the permission, *Kill Harrell.* That bit interested him. He was oblivious of Cass, of the stale, dirty room. He sensed the muscles of his face frame a scowl. He closed his eyes, the better to see Harrell. *Get me the proof and you can kill Harrell.* Aubrey hadn't said that; not quite.

He ignored the perspective that frightened him most, the strangeness of what he had become, its vileness. He *wanted* violence.

He could—just—convince himself that it was nothing permanent, that it only related to Harrell, to survival. He'd be OK afterwards, it wasn't cancer, only a benign tumor he would be rid of as soon as this business was over. He would be able to put the strangeness of himself aside—yes, he could believe that—

—meanwhile, there was Harrell . . .

Cass closed the door silently behind him. His palm, as he released the door handle, was slick, damp. He shook his head, as if ridding it of sleep or an unpleasant memory. Hyde's face—the concentration, the fear, the sense of latent violence. How, in God's name, could Aubrey be sending him out on an operation? Hyde needed a sanatorium! The old man had flipped his wig . . . or was really, really desperate.

He climbed the short flight of stairs to the main concourse. His not to reason why, et cetera . . .

He'd picked out four Americans he recognized from their embassy staff and he was suspicious of two more white faces. They might know him. The Brits who were on their way out to make certain that, if spotted, Hyde was handed over to the CIA certainly knew him! Which meant complication, and haste. He moved unobtrusively through the crowds, his glance sliding like a camera across faces, postures, searching for lack of luggage and movement. White faces that were neither tired nor bemused nor lost nor impatient... one, there by the curry stand. Then another, a third—four eventually. The four he had seen running from the embassy car just before Hyde's flight touched down. All of them twitchy as deer smelling tiger, though all were still. Cass halted by the bookstall, at once beginning to browse the new paperbacks, half-bent in posture, his hands in his pockets. Five of them, before another minute had passed; then almost another three minutes, before he confirmed a sixth American. They *knew* Hyde would be on the flight. No one, yet, he exalted, by the grace of God almighty whose servant I account myself, from the British embassy, except me!

Slowly, still unable to pick out either Dickson, his head of station, or Miles, the deputy, he began to drift across the concourse towards the ticket desks. He grinned, then cautioned himself. He remained detached; his present activities were no more real than any others that day. Hyde—even in his present state—would have narrowed his awareness, opened his nostrils and whatever other primitive senses he retained. But, somehow, this wasn't quite real to Cass, not his part in things.

No Dickson, no Miles. He moved more swiftly, eager to execute his plan. Indian Air, he had decided. The light for Boarding was already flashing opposite the flight he had envisaged in his neat little scenario. They'd be queueing out on the tarmac already, dammit—

His blithe excitement slowly dissolved into urgency. A quick glance across the concourse and the clarity with which he picked out the half-dozen Americans, the pressing absence-but-only-just of his own head of station, rendered this situation no longer comparable with watching tigers up in the Ranthambore Park. He had returned from there only hours before Aubrey's call. His temperature rose and he was aware of little beads of moisture along his forehead like those he had seen on Hyde's skin, down in that stale-smelling, grubby little room. Quite real now—real enough, anyway.

There was a short queue at the Indian Air desk and only one tired, unhelpful girl on duty. The Katmandu flight was scheduled to leave in twelve minutes. His temperature continued to rise and his skin became itchy, his movements restless as he joined the queue. His thoughts now seemed more disheveled than the clothes he had not bothered to change after taking the call from Aubrey. He shuffled forward, his eyes concentrated on the flashing light on the Departures board and the swift, digital changes of the clock suspended beside it. Shit . . .

Up to Katmandu, a change of flight to Royal Nepalese, then straight out to Hong Kong—there was a flight leaving late afternoon—then on to San Francisco. There wasn't another suitable chain of flights until tomorrow. His hands closed damply in his pockets, the knuckles showing bulkily through the thin cotton trousers. It would take Hyde less than twenty-four hours, if he made the Katmandu flight . . . which was Plan A, for God's sake, and there was no Plan B to fall back on. The travel bag he had left with Hyde contained a new passport, credit cards, a change of clothes—Hyde smelled in a stale, used sort of way—and the uppers and downers

Shelley had ominously insisted on. Everything Patrick needed except a bloody ticket to Katmandu! The other tickets were in the bag. There were two people still ahead of him in the queue and a short, round man arguing over the fare to Benares—the Pilgrim Express, for Christ's sake—!

Come on, come on . . . Eight minutes, and he'd hardly have time to get back to Hyde, never mind get him to Gate whatever-it-was—Gate Fifty-Two.

Cass felt appallingly unskilled. And remembered unbidden the jackdaw lying in the fireplace, on top of the coal laid for that evening in his parents' lounge . . . years ago. Visiting them for the weekend with his then-wife. Lifting it with appropriate care and the shock of its being alive. Its black eye watching him in the garden as he laid it on the lawn, certain it would not live—hitting it with the trowel, twice, to end its misery. This business was like that, without the excuse of humane squeamishness. He felt hot, nervous, reluctant. Hyde would laugh, would have got this job—

He recalled Hyde's drawn, unshaven face watching him, staring like a photographic negative waiting for development, reality. He shook his head. Once, long ago, even Patrick might have been squeamish over the jackdaw's execution.

"Bloody hell, Phil—I thought it was you!"

Cass whirled round, startled, his features betraying him before smoothing into neutrality. It was Miles, SIS deputy at the embassy.

"Jim," he offered meekly, his voice thick, his hands clenched even more firmly in his pockets.

"I thought you were up in one of those tiger reserves until Monday?"

"Until today, not Monday."

Six minutes, six and a half at the very outside. He

daren't look up at the clock now. Miles's face was affably suspicious. Hope to God he's looking for the fiddle, the dodge, not the mystery. Miles had the trowel, he was the jackdaw. No more than six bloody minutes.

"Booking another little trip? Skiving bugger, you are—bone bloody idle!"

"Oh, no—just some tickets I didn't use, you know ... bloody Indians, eh?" He grinned, only slightly shakily now, his hands still twitching in his pockets but less prickly with tension. His forehead felt cooler.

Miles said: "You out here on the same job as us?" His eyes had narrowed. Most of Miles's gestures and expressions looked movie-derived, but he *was* suspicious beneath that layer of affectation. "Dicko didn't round you up, did he? Come out in your own car?"

The argumentative pilgrim to Benares had moved away with his wife and children, dragging a battered suitcase behind him on a length of rope like a large and truculent dog.

Cass rubbed a hand through his long hair as casually as he could muster. "Mm—just for backup," he murmured.

"And you're taking time off to cash in some plane tickets—tut-tut!" Miles was enjoying what he now seemed to think was Cass's small dereliction of duty. Because he was shorter, and more rotund, he had to look up at Cass. "You don't half take advantage of being one of Aubrey's hand-picked flowers, do you?" Miles sneered. "Just like the bugger we're here about, eh?" Miles grinned malevolently. "Hyde declared *Rogue*— what a turnup for the books! Myself, I hope he does come in this direction—love to see the sod's face when we hand him over to the Yanks."

"I thought I could take a couple of minutes off just for this," Cass said.

"Care to come and give us a hand, would you?" Miles asked, sarcastically.

Cass was standing at the ticket desk now. The clock showed five minutes to takeoff. The flashing light on the board had become constant. Gate Fifty-Two was closed, but they'd let someone through, even now, if—

He could do nothing with bloody Miles standing there! "Can you wait a minute? Might as well, now I've got to the front of the queue." The tired girl behind the desk was becoming impatient, like those in the queue behind him. Go on, Miles, bugger off!

"You can take over my roving commission," Miles taunted him.

"So you can go and have a nice lie-down, is it?"

Miles smirked. "Piss off, Phil. If anyone's a skiver, it's you."

Four and a half minutes. It was too late. He had no idea how to get Hyde away from the airport. By the time of the evening flight to Katmandu, they'd be certain to have swept the entire airport—and come up with Patrick. Miles would enjoy handing him over.

"Let me just get my tickets cashed—I'll catch you up."

"Hurry up."

Four minutes—

Cass turned to the girl. Steeled himself, the idea that had blundered into his thoughts making him hot again. The constant light on the board, the glare through the windows, the swell and tide of passengers. He half-turned and, grinning, said:

"Are you still having it off with Dickson's daughter, Jim? She's still only just sixteen, isn't she?" Miles's face went pink, then greasy along his hairline.

"What—?"

Quickly, Cass said to the girl: "A single ticket for the Katmandu flight—hurry!"

"The gate is closed. You must wait—"

"I don't want to bloody wait!" It was like the sudden, determined, overreacting anger with which he had finally been able to kill the jackdaw. Miles no longer held the trowel. "What the bloody hell are you—?" Miles again.

"You cannot board the flight now," the girl said.

"I *can*. I'm going to bloody well try! A ticket, write it out. No luggage, just a cabin bag. Come on, girl!" Cass waved cash in front of her face. Miles grabbed at his forearm and he turned. "Never mind what you think I'm doing, Jim—forget it. Dickson's daughter, back at her school in Cheltenham or Malvern and boasting about your big chopper! One word about me and he finds out what you've been doing, Jim—I promise you, you dirty little bugger!" Cass realized he was grinning in a wild, overexcited way.

"You're *in* it," Miles realized. "That ticket's for Hyde—he's here!"

"And you'll be in it if you tell anyone anything. Let's both keep our little secrets, Jim—now, fuck off!" He turned back to the girl. "Now, love, take the money and hurry up!"

The girl shrugged and scribbled out a ticket after deftly removing a number of notes from the bundle Cass had placed in front of her—then subtracting the fare from the remainder. Cass snatched up the ticket folder. Miles watched him malevolently. Cass winked at him, grinning excitedly.

Then he began hurrying. The light was constant, the gate closed, the girl counting her bribe. He clattered down the concrete steps, ran along the passageway, and burst into the Customs staff room.

Hyde looked up, startled, from his examination of the travel bag's contents. The bottle of uppers was in his hand and he was regarding them as he might have done a snake. Cass waggled the ticket folder. "Come on, bring the bag—hurry, for God's sake! The gate's closed but if it hasn't begun taxiing they'll let you on!"

"Where?"

"Katmandu—then Hong Kong. I'll explain as we go!" Hyde seemed reluctant to move. Cass shouted at him: "If you don't go now you won't be going at all! The Yanks and our lot are *all* here now!"

Hyde hefted the bag as he got to his feet and passed Cass. Both of them were running a moment later. Fifty-Two, Fifty-Two—they won't be watching local flights, in or out. The flight to Katmandu is always full of scruffy, down-at-heel people like Hyde. They won't pick him out. It had been such a neat, clever plan!

The stewardess, her sari fluttering in the hot breeze, was closing the door behind her and the last long-haired passenger who had queued on the glaring tarmac.

"Thank *God*—!" He all but pushed Hyde through the door, past the stewardess. "Good luck, Patrick— bloody good luck, old son!" His relief was overwhelming. The sweat seemed to soak his entire body. His breathing roared.

The door closed on Hyde's impassive, drawn face as Cass squinted up at the aircraft from the bottom of the passenger steps. The image disappointed. Hyde looked too much like a typical white passenger to Katmandu, that was the trouble; one not capable of very much . . .

Inside her room, even the surf was taken care of. The speaker was high on one wall and she could find no means of switching off the persistent, slurring sound. *Big Sur's surf recorded and relayed to your motel room,* the brochure announced, maddeningly. The double glazing of the patio doors and windows kept the Pacific's breathing outside, dulled to the sound of an insect—so they broadcast it instead! She had only to open the door of the suite and she would hear the real thing.

But then, she had not opened the door for hours, not since lunch had arrived on a tray. She had kept the curtains drawn all day; had watched TV in the opaque dusk of the room, lain on the bed, smoked, picked at her food, stared at the ceiling; a study for some Edward Hopper painting of isolation or bleak, dim urban loneliness.

She could not sustain that illusion, not consistently. Fear nibbled, the recorded surf becoming hollower and hollower as she tried not to listen to it. However much she mocked her imagination, the sound of the surf became more and more like breathing magnified into menace. Each time the tautness held her rigid she had to get off the bed or out of the chair and pace the bedroom and the miniature lounge, back and forth, creating the analogy of a caged wild cat in a zoo. She'd smoked one cigarette after another. The air was stale now, despite the air conditioning, but she was unwilling to open the door or slide back the window. It was dark outside. Headlights from State Highway 1 flashed on the curtains.

Mallory had dumped her in this place the previous day. He'd rung twice since then to check on her. Kathryn wrinkled her expression into contempt and inhaled deeply from her cigarette. He had repeated his endless requests for her patience, soothed her with the anodyne *someone will be coming out from London to escort you away from here ... no, I can't be exact about when this will happen, Ms. Aubrey.* There had been only a minimal satisfaction in telling him to shove it, shouting over the phone. Mallory was, so he said, *filling in the details.* She shivered and rubbed her arms vigorously, then released her flesh because she realized she had begun huddling into herself, back bent, head lowered. She sniffed, stood erect, drew on the cigarette then savagely ground it out in the filled ashtray with its now obscured picture of surf breaking over black rocks and the legend BIG SUR. Mallory had informed her mother—so he claimed. She had wanted to inform Shapiro, make some excuse for not being at the office—but Mallory had said no with authority; strongly enough to make her hesitate. Tomorrow, though, she would have to call Shapiro. Christ, it was her career, after all. She was vice-president of marketing, for God's sake, she was needed.

Frank's bloody face raised itself again and she was at once icily cold. She slumped onto the edge of the bed, arms wrapped across her breasts, hands hurting her shoulders. When Frank's broken features eventually retreated, she expected a moment of relief, but instead John's features waited in ambush. She rocked on the edge of the bed, silently, tears running slowly down her face, stinging her cheeks.

There was guilt, too, but it was less demanding than grief; less appalling. She cried until she was angry with her tears and began to force them back—even to the extent of crossing the room to the TV set and savagely switching it on. A cartoon cat ran into a door a mouse had slammed shut in its face. John's broken body. She could not bear the relentless music and turned down the volume. A stone fell on the cat's head. She watched, appalled, as the cat shattered like a dropped vase. Then, a moment later, was on its feet, intact and running. Unlike John lying beside the highway . . .

The noise of the surf intruded, eventually. She did not know how much later. The cartoon had finished. Sports on the TV. Shaking herself, as if sloughing herself back into an old skin, she got up, crossed to the TV set, and switched it off. Decisively. Angrily.

John's crazy ideas. John's obsession. His conspiracy theory! It had disorganized their life together, made them quarrel, wedged itself between them—now, it had killed him! Dear Christ-in-heaven, his ideas weren't crazy, his paranoia was real!

She lit a cigarette, clumsily and shakily, her outrage refusing to dim or settle. A renewed tear fell into her left hand, warm and electric in its impact. She stared at it, then wiped her hand on her thigh. Emotion littered her mind and thoughts. John's death—his *murder!*— had shattered her solid-seeming life . . . oh, but *Christ*, they should *pay* for it!

She stared at the TV screen. Dimly, her own features stared back at her, hardly recognizable in their rage. Once, she remembered her face had been vaguely modelish, her features aloof above padded, power-dressed shoulders. She was shocked at the woman she now saw. The shock galvanized her into switching the set back on.

Her former self was staring back at her from the TV news. Her features had been cut from some shot and enlarged, so that her pale face and the collar of her suit were all but grainy. Her *face*—? She turned up the volume.

"... the San Jose Police Department revealed this evening that the trail had led them to Lake Berryessa, in the wine country. Kathryn Aubrey, aged thirty-two, is the marketing VP of Shapiro Electrics of San Jose. Tonight, Mr. Shapiro was unavailable for comment. The police department stressed that Ms. Aubrey is not—"

She lunged at the set and switched it off, then once more clutched her arms around her, hearing her breathing as a shivering noise that drowned out the recorded surf. The police were looking for her . . . a statewide hunt . . . her *face* on TV—

9

THE DISTANCES BETWEEN ISLANDS

"Tony, of *course* Patrick's been brutalized! What else under heaven would you expect to have happened to him?"

It was so insensitive, so inappropriate of Godwin to persist with his questions. Quite unreasonable altogether ... Aubrey sighed inwardly, staring out across the leaf-strewn park and beyond the brown ranks of trees to where the city climbed into a smudgy, autumnal afternoon haze. His mind felt as indistinct as the view, his long but fitful sleep leaving him more ragged, with less patience and comprehension. Behind him, Mrs. Grey made small noises as she cleared the tea service, and even her presence irritated him ... and induced guilt immediately as he detected the slight drag of her left foot across the carpet—the last, lingering, permanent memento of Brigitte Winterbach's bomb, meant for him. Mrs. Grey was lucky to be alive—thank God.

He turned to Godwin, rubbing his hand through the poor remnants of his hair, then flapping it apologetically towards his companion.

"I'm sorry, Tony—I quite understand your concern for Patrick. It matches my—" Godwin's face remained sullenly disapproving, and the expression niggled. "Oh, for heaven's sake, Tony, I could not find another way! There was no one else to send because there was no one I could *trust!*" Aubrey had moved across the room to bend threateningly over Godwin's unmoving bulk. "And I could not bring Patrick back with me." He sighed, slumping onto the sofa, his waistcoat unbuttoned, his cuffs turned back. He seemed to himself as untidy as Godwin, and as untidy as the litter of reports, files and printouts Godwin had brought with him; having insisted all day that matters were critically urgent, and could not be postponed. "No, Tony, I could not bring Patrick back. Harrell would have taken him from me like a sweet had he been at Rawalpindi. Good God, Tony, they declared him *Rogue*. How many times have you known that to happen, and under circumstances like these? Orrell's toadying to the Americans has reached new depths! I had no room in which to maneuver." The effort of justification seemed to exhaust him and he lay back on the sofa, listening to his old heart throb.

Godwin cleared his throat but Aubrey ignored him. Then Godwin repeated the noise before murmuring: "Poor sod."

"It is a matter of survival—for all of us," Aubrey remarked, his eyes focused on the ceiling rose and on his distorted, bulbous image thrown back from the brass

chandelier at its center. "Patrick, myself, Ros, even you."
There was a surveillance team guarding Ros's house even
now.

"And what will he be like by the time you've finished
using him—sir?"

Aubrey's hands gripped the stuff of the sofa, creasing
and folding the material of the covers. "I haven't the
luxury to speculate, Tony. And that is the end of the
matter." His voice warned. Guilt was nudging irritation
aside and he could not spare time or thought for spec-
ulation now. He could only *execute*, as he had promised
Hyde he would. Discover, expose, trace. "Patrick must
work out his own salvation with diligence. All our sal-
vations!" He glowered at Godwin, weary of the ceiling
and his own distorted reflection. "This business of the
RPV—are you convinced by your inquiries or are you
still in some doubt?"

Godwin scowled, then nodded in acceptance. The arm
supports of his two heavy metal walking sticks appeared
like manacles above the back of his chair, waiting for
him.

"What about the other things, sir—they have to be
got out of the way . . . ?"

"Tony—congratulations on catching the man at Farnborough. I realize there has been a deal of flak to cope
with . . . oh, very well, have him moved to one of the
houses and I *will* find time to have a talk with him. I
realize we need to exploit this little coup, especially
now." He essayed a narrow smile, which seemed to
satisfy Godwin, then waved his hand towards the litter
of papers strewn on the green carpet. "Get the Hercules
and the flight crew and the technicians and whoever onto
some secure RAF base. I'll deal with the protestations
of the CIA as to our lax behavior. Oh, don't worry,

Tony! I'll give it some of my attention, have no fear... now, the RPV."

"Then—" The content of what Godwin had to say acted like a stopper. Aubrey's attention narrowed, became intent.

"Yes? Well?"

"It is my considered opinion, sir, that the RPV was developed and produced here, in the UK." Godwin's cheeks were pink, as if with effort.

"What? I didn't think we—"

"We don't. That's why it took me some time. Process of elimination. Feeding in everything I got from Hyde. Crossing off the Israelis, the Germans, the French, the Brazilians—then the Americans. Leaving—" Godwin shrugged massively, then stared at his big hands. "... Reid Electronics, finally. Them and no one else."

"Reid—*David* Reid?"

"Yes, sir. Though he isn't anything now except an important shareholder in—"

"Her Majesty's secretary of state for trade and industry, Tony? *His* company?" He willed Godwin to look up, not to deny or equivocate, simply to assert. Aubrey felt breathless, his chest light and hollow like that of a bird, inside which a small pulse beat very quickly. Godwin had delayed telling him, worrying at the question of Hyde's fitness... no wonder!

Godwin plucked up a sheaf of his own large, untidy handwriting from the arm of his chair and tossed it towards Aubrey. "That summarizes my conclusions, sir." He shook his head. "There's no way round it."

"But we don't build RPVs, Tony! MoD set its collective face against remotely piloted vehicles years ago and has never rethought the matter since. I don't understand."

"They part-funded a research program, along with

the Yanks, based here—Reid had the high-tech, the electronics, to develop a new-generation RPV. But costs spiraled and the Americans lost interest, and MoD lost its nerve. Reid was out of pocket, seriously. That was over a year ago."

"I'd never heard of it before."

"Nor should you. The banks and some foreign money bailed Reid out. He climbed back in the ring—they've been taking over smaller companies all this year. But, at the time, it was a real blow." Godwin grimaced. "And the bloody thing worked, too!"

"How can you be certain, Tony?" Godwin's eyes were hooded, suspicious. "No, I'm not concerned on the basis of a private friendship," Aubrey snapped. "But the project was scrapped?" Godwin nodded. "Then there were no RPVs."

"Only production prototypes—test vehicles. Half a dozen completed and being tried out when the cancellation order came. Sorry, sir, but they did exist. Working, full-scale prototypes."

Aubrey climbed heavily to his feet and crossed to the window. David Reid, so recently an MP, so recently and expressly elevated to the cabinet. *His* company? The bare facts concealed more than they revealed, obviously.

"What happened to these prototypes, Tony?"

"I don't know—I can't locate them. I could hardly ask, could I, sir?"

Despite himself, Aubrey smiled. "No, I suppose not, Tony." He turned from the window. "But *I* can, I suppose? Is that it?"

"In a nutshell." Godwin grinned with evident relief.

"Then it's probably a good thing I shall be seeing him at a private dinner party this evening, isn't it? Or did you know that?"

"Gwen told me. She looked in your diary for me."

"Good of her . . . yes, very well."

"I'm not accusing Sir David of anything, not personally, sir—"

"I realize that, Tony. That *is* ridiculous."

He turned back to the window. Ridiculous, of course. But Godwin was convinced, and he trusted Tony. Therefore, David Reid's electronics company had allowed perhaps half a dozen RPVs simply to vanish—and turn up at points all over the globe, in the hands of the *Carpetbaggers!* That was why he felt little shock, only a growing anxiety. Images of blank walls, the sense that he would be treading on powerful toes, that he would find doors closed, all closed in on him. Whatever had happened, no one would be admitting anything! Reid's involvement would be deemed embarrassing, not venal—but even more to be concealed for that very reason. The PM, Longmead and Orrell were all still capable of a quick and certain mistrust of him. Aubrey rubbed his chin vigorously.

Godwin's information further jeopardized Kathryn and Hyde, and perhaps himself and Godwin, too. What should he do? How should he proceed, now? A thin and largely imagined confidence was all he had brought back from Peshawar. Urgency—that was all he could add to it now. The engine of quick, decisive activity.

"Are you certain?"

"Sir?"

He turned to face Godwin. "Are you certain that the RPV was produced by Reid Electronics?"

Godwin nodded vigorously. "Yes, sir, I am."

"Absolutely?"

"Absolutely, sir."

"Then you're moving a big stone, Tony, and I'm not sure what's underneath it. Something that will bite me, doubtless!" Godwin seemed uncertain whether to offer a smile. "Who would listen, things being as they are, if we found anything they should hear, mm?" Aubrey flung his arms up as if in surrender. "But these people will not be satisfied until they rid themselves of my niece and Patrick, at the very least. Of that I remain convinced." He sighed. "Therefore, Tony, I must take your instruction and speak to David this evening. The risk to Kathryn and Hyde is too great, too immediate, to do otherwise." He returned to his place on the sofa and picked up the sheaf of papers Godwin had passed him. "I'd better be fluent by this evening," he murmured.

"Sir?" Godwin offered. "About Patrick . . ."

"What now?"

"Well, someone passed on a rumor that he spends half his nights on leave with that nut who used to be a model—what's-her-name?—of all things looking for stray cats to give board and lodging to! Is he—?"

"Losing his grip?" Aubrey felt chilled, but protested: "Ten years ago, I would have said yes, undoubtedly. Now, I'm not quite certain of such things any more . . . well, is there *more?*"

"All I'm saying, sir, is that people are talking about him as if he's lost his marbles. Makes you wonder what he's up to."

"I do not *know!*" Aubrey snapped. "My task is to keep him alive—him and my niece."

The telephone chirruped, impatient from its first ring. Gratefully, Aubrey snatched it up. Shelley.

"Yes, Peter?"

"You haven't been answering the telephone." Shelley was accusing, pressured.

"I'm sorry, Peter—"

"The cabinet secretary and Orrell want me to arrange a meeting with you at the first opportunity—"

"Then you needn't worry—I shall be seeing both of

them this evening at a private function at the Oxford and Cambridge Club! That should do nicely—shouldn't it?"

After a silence, Shelley admitted sullenly: "I suppose it will do." His gloom seemed unrelieved, and now there was a nervousness added to his mood.

Reluctantly, Aubrey prompted. "What else, Peter?"

"A report from Washington—just an hour ago. There's an all points bulletin out for your niece. The San Jose PD are linking her to Frascati's death and that of Blake. There's no mention of the CIA man she's supposed to have—"

In a quavering tone, Aubrey asked: "Are you quite certain, Peter?"

"Yes, Sir Kenneth. What do you—?"

"Thank you, Peter, I must think about this—thank you." He switched off the cordless phone and flung the instrument down on the sofa, his whole frame weak and trembling. He rubbed his cold cheeks with quivering palms.

"Sir—?"

He turned on Godwin as if on any enemy. "She is to be treated like some *South* American government would treat her, Tony! They have accused her of two murders—they're looking for her now! My God, they mean to see an end to any *embarrassment* she might cause them, and quickly!" He hesitated, almost staggering as if from a mild coronary attack. Then he said: "What can I do, Tony? How in God's name can I help her now?"

"The gun, mate—the gun."

The roofs of hundreds of parked cars and the thousands of windows of the airport all possessed the dull color of steel. Across the Bay, the buildings of Oakland and Berkeley appeared in heavily penciled outline, uncolored. An airliner coming in to land, lights still gleaming, was high enough to reflect the unrisen sun. Hyde felt cold, flurried. The newspaper bearing Kathryn Aubrey's photograph remained thrust under this armpit. His hand shook beneath Mallory's face, the man's overlarge spectacle lenses reflecting the first dim glints from the chrome of parked cars. The air was dark blue, as illusory and dangerous as fog.

"Come *on!*" Hyde demanded, clicking his fingers. Behind Mallory's glasses a nervousness showed, an encroaching sense of his being out of his depth—and something that Hyde did not trust and dare not ignore.

Mallory bent across the car's long front seat and groped in the glove compartment. As he emerged, his hand, upheld behind him, gripped a polyethylene-wrapped package. Hyde thrust him back into the car with his left hand and snatched at the package—his knee in Mallory's arched and struggling back as he pulled away the polyethylene and elastic bands. Browning automatic. The two spare clips fell to the concrete with separate rattles.

"What the hell—?"

Hyde clicked the first round into the chamber with a slight, satisfying snap, then pressed the barrel of the pistol behind Mallory's right ear. The muffled protests and surprise stilled as the back beneath Hyde's knee and hand began shivering. Hyde looked around the car, concealed amid hundreds of others. A few early passengers craned their necks looking for their vehicles; the laughter of a child erupted; a teenage girl hugged her father, who balanced her clinging weight with the suitcase in his right hand. A woman counted along the rows of cars. There was no one else. Mallory's eyes, however reluctantly and fleetingly, had confessed that there were others—or soon would be. It was a setup.

"Where are they?"

Mallory had driveled, all the way from the spectator barrier across the huge concourse and out into the surprisingly chill dawn air, about Aubrey's bloody niece and whether he had had a good flight and what a good little bloke he had been at every moment and that he'd got the woman safe somewhere out at Big Sur—Kerouac, for Christ's sake—and that the woman was panicky now because of the police APB put out on her for murder—and *Look, look here, her face splashed all over the morning papers—every one of them.*

"Where are they?"

The newspaper beneath his arm was bulky, demanding attention. Harrell had decided to stop the game, to become serious. The chill of the parking lot seeped through his thin jacket and shirt, making his cheek shiver with a tic. The place was alien, at once too open and too concealing. His head turned metronomically, his neck aching as he looked back over each shoulder in turn, again and again. The half-somnolent terrors of his dozing-waking flight across the Pacific had dribbled away—and gone. He felt his skin crawl with anticipations, tensions; and was thankful. Feral senses had replaced introspection.

"I know you've warned them, Mallory—don't piss about," he said dispassionately, the barrel of the gun smoothing at the damp lock of hair behind Mallory's ear.

As they had passed the bookstand, he had seen dozens of large books proclaiming in photographs the wonders of California, always the *wonders*...desert, rock, sea, mountains, high buildings; perfect-breasted young women in hot tubs, drinking wine. It was a place he did not know; about which there had been no time to brief him; and which was Harrell's back garden. He shook his head slowly, softly. The parking lot was redolent of gasoline and the noise of an engine startled as the man who'd been hugged by the teenager drove away towards the gate. There were other disembarked passengers now, rattling keys, crunching the gravel or clicking the concrete, slamming doors sharply in the cool, deep-blue air. Lightening air—the highest windows in the terminal buildings were already a dull orange-gold. The lights of an incoming aircraft were dimmed by the daylight.

Furiously, he turned Mallory onto his back and splayed his legs wide, his knee resting on the man's crotch, the Browning lightly pressed into his chest just where his tie was askew and his shirt gaped.

"I know Harrell's people have been told. You'd have been instructed to do that, anyway, wouldn't you?" The Browning was now tapping in a gently urgent rhythm on Mallory's chest. His eyes were owl-like behind the overlarge spectacles. His forehead was very white, damp-looking. "You'd have had to do it, son, on orders from Orrell or someone speaking on his behalf." Mallory's shirt front was heaving like the flank of a wounded animal. Hyde could scent the man's fear, even as he swung his head to and fro. Nothing yet, only the hurry of people wanting to get home . . . no one searching. But they must be there. "You'd have had to do it for your pension and the rest of your brilliant career, or just to keep your nose clean. So, where are they?" He sighed.

Mallory was shaking his head furiously, his hands clawing beyond his head. "For God's sake, *listen* to me!" Mallory was still shaking his head, his voice querulous and yet obscurely outraged, too. "Listen to me, you stupid sod!"

Hyde removed his knee but not the pistol. "Go on, then. But don't hang it out. I might get impatient."

"Yes, they're expecting someone, but not you, just

someone to help the girl. *I* didn't tell them, London did it direct. I just got a bloody signal telling me to cooperate with the CIA if and when necessary—!" His chest continued to heave even though Hyde withdrew the pistol a matter of inches, sitting back on his haunches now, as if in contemplation. He rubbed his face, motioning with the gun.

"Go on."

"Look, I don't know whether London expected you to come, or just someone from Aubrey. But the CIA called them when the APB went out on Aubrey's niece. Out of politeness, I was told. Blake's name rang an alarm bell in London, they accepted her involvement, and I was told to hand the girl over."

"Did you?"

Mallory shook his head. "I've seen shock before, Hyde. The woman didn't kill Blake, even if she did kill one of the two who did! Can I *get up* now?"

Hyde stood up, and leaned heavily on the door, suddenly tired. Harrell seemed omnipresent, too clever and informed not to be around now. "Why aren't they here, then?"

"I'm to take you—no, wait!" Mallory had struggled out of the car and was tucking his shirt back into his waistband as Hyde turned on him. Mallory threw up his hands in protest. "Look! I've hired you a bloody car—the keys are *here!*" He pulled them from his jacket pocket and dangled them. They caught the light. "Look, Hyde, the CIA killed Blake—so fuck them!"

"Go to the same school, you and Blake?"

"No—my brother knew him, OK?" Mallory sneered back, wiping his fogged spectacles. "I certainly don't give a stuff about you, Hyde—" He replaced the glasses and they seemed to calm him, to give him some authority. "*Aubrey* wants the woman. Shelley did want her out, to talk to her. I *know* why the Yanks want her, Hyde. They've already tried to kill her, along with Blake." His hand fiddled with his tie, then he brushed at the creases along the sleeves of his jacket. "They burned the place to the ground afterwards, including Blake's body! Look, I don't really know what happened up there, but her story is a bit more convincing than the idea that first of all she killed the bloke she was having an affair with and then she killed Blake who was guarding her! So, if you think I'm going to feed you to them, then bloody good luck to you, Hyde!"

His accent had reasserted its learned superiority.

Hyde said: "I've been declared *Rogue*. You needn't bother any longer to—"

"Look, Hyde, the woman is Aubrey's niece. If I help save her, with you as my witness, then I'll do myself some good—sometime in the future. Besides, Aubrey must have sent you, so you're still loved by someone. I can't see any pressing advantage in handing you over, or her . . ." He adjusted his glasses. "So, pick the selfish bones out of that little lot."

"You'll go back to London, sometime, smelling of Chanel."

"Quite possibly. Funny, though—I didn't take to her at all—but I don't think I'd have handed her over even if she wasn't you-know-who's niece."

Hyde studied the parking lot. Low sunlight gleamed from chrome and glass. He shivered, aware again of the openness of the place. Mallory was studying him dispassionately, almost incurious.

"Where's this car you've hired for me?"

Mallory handed him the keys, then the folder from Avis. He pointed down the rank of cars.

"The blue Nissan—see it?"

"Yes."

"She's registered under the name Karen Anderson. The motel's called the Dharma Lodge—unsurprisingly. I've marked it on the map in the glove compartment. OK?"

"Has she said anything?"

"About why and wherefore? Nothing that makes any sense to me—but then, that's why Aubrey sent you, isn't it, Hyde? At least, I presume so."

"You? What now?"

"Shall I tell them that you managed to give me the slip—you became suspicious? Will that do?"

"As long as you're convincing."

"I'll try. Is there anything else?"

"I'll call you if I need you. Now, bugger off. And make it convincing, mate, or we'll all be up shit creek."

Hyde snatched up the airline bag and walked away. A DC-10, very low, seemed to hurtle the last hundreds of yards of air towards the runway. Again, he shivered. They were less than a step behind him—almost level, poised to overtake. His decisive violence towards Mallory, the calculated, laconic cynicism, were somehow acted, designed to exude a competence he did not feel. He reached the small blue Nissan, unlocked the door and threw the bag onto the rear seat. The parking lot bristled with hurrying people. It required a huge effort to climb into the driving seat.

The place was again alien, his isolation within it increased by the sight of Mallory's car pulling away towards the exit. Only his heartbeat was urgent, nothing else. His hands greasily massaged the wheel. He lacked time—*any* time. They might have found the woman already. Even if they hadn't, it would be soon...and anyway, what the hell could she possibly do or prove that would keep them both alive?

He had opened the window. The glowing morning air was still vaguely cool. He began breathing deeply and regularly in a futile effort at calm.

What could she *know?*

It seemed a stage set through which he was being hurried, so that the columns and gilding of the Oxford and Cambridge Club in Pall Mall appeared hardly more solid and stable than the rushed geometry of the patterned carpet under his feet. It appeared, too, like an intended gathering—but not for the declared purpose, which was to mark James Melstead's retirement as permanent secretary to the Department of Trade and Industry. James, of course, was beaming youthfully, belying retirement, promising attention and industry to those who already belonged to the boards of the various companies he was to join as a director. Glass slightly tilted as he saw Aubrey enter, a special, close grin broke out on Melstead's lips.

There were others there who had purposely gathered for Melstead's sake—Reid, of course, but Malan, too. Aubrey decided it was Malan's unexpected but wholly explicable presence that imbued him with this sense of conspiracy. Orrell, too, and Geoffrey Longmead, of course. They became subsumed into the mystery and Aubrey could not dismiss it. Orrell and Longmead noticed him at once and began moving purposefully, but it was David Reid who broke off a conversation with a banker and an Arab—the latter clutching orange juice, of course—to take his hand and offer a hot and calculating smile. Aubrey noticed, as Reid turned him aside from the doorway, that Longmead and Orrell seemed content to allow him to precede them in gaining his attention. It again seemed conspiratorial, disconcerting. He felt overwarm, stressed, slightly dizzy.

"Kenneth—" Reid began, after the clichés of welcome. "—I know you're going to want to talk to me at some length about this business at Farnborough—I realize that, and I just want to assure you that you only have to call. It's the most damnable mess!" In response to Aubrey's mild smile, Reid's features became more relaxed, his grin more genuine and reminiscent. Aubrey patted his arm.

"Just let me become *au fait*, David—*au fait*," he murmured.

"Of course, you're just back. Yes. Heavens, Kenneth, as if I needed this just at *this* time!" He was still holding Aubrey's elbow and Aubrey began to resent that younger, stronger pressure, as if he were being seen overkindly across the road.

"Yes—"

"A Hercules full of antiradar and God knows what else and one of *my* people arrested! I told Geoffrey and Orrell how stunned I was—the man has been with . . ." He shrugged, throwing his hands in the air. "God, it isn't really *my* problem any more, is it? I no longer run the company."

"Though you are its majority shareholder, David, and the newspapers would enjoy embarrassing one of Her Majesty's secretaries of state . . . ?"

"All right, Kenneth—I may just be asking a favor of you!" His grin remained boyish, attractive. Political enemies claimed the PM was under its charming spell, Aubrey reminded himself. "Nobody wants—I'm saying this as a friend, relying on our friendship, Kenneth—nobody needs or wants a spy scandal now. Security messing on the floor again—*I* certainly don't!"

Aubrey saw Geoffrey Longmead watching him over someone's shoulder. Clearly, David had been given permission to approach him—to warn him.

"David," he announced levelly, "someone has been giving you the impression that I may have become loose-tongued. There is no need to assume that I shall tell *any* of Mr. Murdoch's newspapers anything at all."

"Sorry, Kenneth—I meant this as an apology." He appeared crestfallen. Aubrey patted his arm.

"I'm sorry, David—feathers ruffled by others. You understand?"

"Sir Clive's awful—I concede." Aubrey glanced at Orrell and smirked, despite himself. Across the room, Sir Clive's heaviness had borne down upon two diminutive permanent secretaries new to their seniority—and new to Orrell's genius at inflicting boredom, it seemed. "Let me get you something to drink—then I must circulate. Keep an eye on James, too. He's likely to push the boat out among his friends."

"A small whiskey, David—thank you."

As Reid moved away, still nodding and evidently satisfied—what the Devil did he assume would happen over this Farnborough business?—Longmead and Orrell closed in on Aubrey.

Malan was watching him, too. Engaged in conversation with Peter Shelley and a senior officer from MoD—where was Giles Pyott, he wondered? Then Orrell and the cabinet secretary had surrounded him.

"Kenneth, what the Devil's been happening? Why haven't you answered my calls?" Longmead was testy; no more than an opening gambit.

Aubrey raised a protesting hand and allowed his features to darken.

"Geoffrey, I have been busy—principally with this matter of Reid Electronics and Farnborough! I do not necessarily have time for your calls whenever you might choose to make them." He smiled disarmingly.

Longmead pursued: "Clive here's been getting all sorts

of flak from Grosvenor Square, Kenneth—*principally* concerning your being in Peshawar. What on earth were you thinking of, dashing off? As you stated, you do have a job to do—here."

"Geoffrey—" A modicum of outrage would serve. "—I owed that young man a great deal. I had to see—"

"And you found him!" Orrell burst like a faulty pressure valve, hissing affront. "The CIA had to tell *me*, Kenneth! You did not. But, where is he now, may we ask?" His sarcasm was pronounced, sharp.

"He did—as the saying goes, Clive—a runner." He shook his head regretfully. "He was a frightened, end-of-tether chap, Clive. Paranoid, especially about being betrayed. And he blamed me for somehow abandoning him. Forgetting him. I tried to bring him back, but there was no way that he—"

"You lost him, Kenneth?" Longmead asked. His eyes narrowed in disbelief.

"I'm afraid he—disappeared. I'd like you to try to find him, Clive—please."

"I've had him declared *Rogue*, Kenneth. I can't change that. My God, he killed two of Harrell's people! Who does he think the enemy is?"

"Everyone, I'm afraid. He really is that bad. I'm just..." Shaking his head. "Just so very sorry it's come to this and so bloody guilty that I might have been able to do something to prevent it." He looked up, eyes damp. Orrell was embarrassed...and Longmead convinced. Thank God.

The cabinet secretary watched Aubrey's saddened expression keenly for some moments. Aubrey watched Longmead. It was a children's game of ugly, distorted faces which had to be maintained until facial muscles ached and skin seemed stretched and numb, in order to win the contest. Eventually, Longmead's expression declined into a sad, dismissive understanding of what he thought of as Aubrey's weakness in bolting like a hare to Pakistan out of affection. Rather silly, that kind of emotionalism, in Geoffrey's world-view.

"Kenneth," Orrell announced portentously, "I hope you understand that this man Hyde must be given up, at once, into safe hands—should he ever contact you at any time?"

"Yes, Clive. I fear there's little chance of it now—but, yes, I do understand."

Reid was hovering with Aubrey's drink, almost engaged in making childish faces behind Longmead's back. Aubrey was invited to conspire, but the room was already laden with too many other conspiracies for Reid's disarming manner to induce enough relaxation in Aubrey to allow him to join in.

"And, Kenneth—this business of your, well, your niece, dammit—?"

"Yes, Clive—yes. You are checking on that, I hope?" Aubrey frowned with concern. "People I know seem to be going to hell in a handcart, don't they?" Then, more seriously, he added: "Someone *is* checking with the police out there, surely?"

"It's in hand, Kenneth," Longmead assured. "I'm quite certain we're talking about a grave error there. Though you should not have used someone from Washington in that way."

"No, I realize that. I couldn't attend to it, the girl was very frightened. I couldn't make head nor tail of it, but—well, acted."

"I really think she is going to have to go to the police, Kenneth."

"Yes, that's best."

"Mallory—I'm checking with him," Orrell continued. "You agree, then? Mallory should—"

"As long as he remains with her."

"Of course."

"And, meanwhile, I'll have a word with this chap at Farnborough. Get the reins back in my hands."

"Good."

At once, as if at some unseen signal, Reid had joined them, proffering Aubrey's whiskey. He sipped at it. Longmead said to him:

"Kenneth's going to look discreetly into this Farnborough affair, David. I don't think there'll be any escape of poisonous fumes—will there, Kenneth?"

"I very much doubt it." Aubrey smiled. "Perhaps you can spare me a moment now, David—to give me some background on the chap? Had he worked for the company for long?"

Reid glanced at Longmead, then across at Melstead, engaged in conversation with Malan and some other people Aubrey did not recognize. Then he smiled easily.

"Years, Kenneth. Years of loyal, trusted service. Quite a shock. Look, tell you what—I'll have his complete dossier sent over to your office first thing in the morning. Will that suit?"

"Fine, fine."

"Time to announce dinner?" Longmead asked, patting his stomach.

"I should think so, Geoffrey. I'll send someone to find out."

Aubrey could not rid himself of his feeling of dizziness, of excitement that was almost nauseous, like some novelist's vision of a young girl's sensations at her first ball, dazzled with color and the movements of the dance. The somehow heightened *scents* of this group—which included, obscurely, Malan, who was still watching him—

all but overwhelmed him. He had never felt comfortable in this place. Now, Kathryn and Hyde had bullied him in off the street. He was here to elicit, find out, they insisted. While Longmead, Orrell and Reid all seemed to toy with him conspiratorially. In effect, they'd blindfolded him, turned him about three or four times then set him off to locate someone by touch. He felt himself blundering about and being giggled at.

Probably, they simply wished to avoid a newspaper embarrassment. David's appointment and knighthood must not be summarily and prematurely tarnished. Doubtless it was no more than that...

Yet, he had learned something. The Reid employee arrested at Farnborough and now safe at one of the country places SIS kept up—had he worked on the RPV project? *Years,* David had said. This prospect was a sufficiently plump and tasty rat to attract his terrierlike curiosity. He'd shake that until its neck broke. The employee had probably spied for Priabin as London Resident. And Malan was linked to Priabin.

And to Shapiro Electrics, too. And Malan was watching him as he might have done a snake at the edge of a South African golf course fairway! Oh, yes, something might well come out of a talk to the Farnborough spy.

He realized Longmead and Orrell had drifted towards more congenial company, content for the present with Aubrey's acquiescence, and with having subtly reminded him of his patently immature approach to the dignity of his office. Aubrey shrugged off the rankling sting of their patronage, and of their tangible disapproval of his errant ways. He raised his hand in the air, advancing on the smiling, clubbable, ineffectual Sir James Melstead. Malan, however, continued to watch Aubrey with an intent concentration. And suddenly the tenuous, almost transparent membrane that linked these people with *his* people seemed very strong, impenetrable.

"Look, darling—I've been saying the same bloody thing over and over again for the past two hours! He isn't going to get you out of this. *Uncle* Kenneth is not your fairy godmother. You're up shit creek and that's where you'll stay unless you can find your bloody paddle!"

Hyde rubbed his hands through his hair, tugging at it with crooked fingers. The room was curtained, and gloomy, like a hot dusk. Kathryn Aubrey continued to flap one white, batlike hand towards him in protest. She had passed through anger, outrage, demand, pleading, and finally, fear, so that now, pale in the gloom, she appeared like someone in retreat; like someone pausing for breath on the edge of something.

On the table lay scissors, bottles, a brush and comb, makeup. The motel's row of small shops and its mini-market had provided them. The woman still rejected the implements.

"For Christ's sake," she murmured, "you *told* me— OK? You told me." Her hands massaged her face with small pecking movements, then she stared blindly at the ceiling. Hyde's patience was subsumed in twitchy anger. It was as if they had rehearsed their arguments during some yearslong marital nightmare, so stale and un-budging had they become. "He *promised* me!"

Hyde, staring at the floor through his fingers, mut-tered: "Don't start all that again, for Christ's sake. You shouldn't believe Uncle Kenneth's promises. Nothing for nothing, that's his maxim. To be safe, he needs..." He broke off, then said: "Oh, ballocks to it! Just cut and dye your bloody hair or I'll do it for you! I don't want to hang around this place much longer." He looked up at her. Her stare was malevolent, her mouth a thin line, her eyes bright and glittering. Sunlight edged around the drapes, spilling through dust motes onto the wall. "I don't give a stuff what you think about me, darling. Just do as I tell you, will you?"

"All he could send is you?"

"Clint Eastwood was busy, OK?"

"That guy who dumped me here wasn't up to much. You're even more like something from a fire sale."

"What did you expect, girlie? A gorillagram in a neat suit?" He sighed. The woman had the capacity to nettle and distract, like a sprained muscle that registered an ache each time he moved. He looked at his watch. "Eleven. Get on with it."

She had been alone for too long, he admitted reluctantly. Things had preyed on her and enlarged until she was numbed by her fears. They'd killed her bloke and tried to kill her. Perhaps more importantly, she'd had to kill one of them. Aubrey *should* get her out—him, too. But her constant whining and lack of cooperation was driving him up the bloody wall!

"You want to leave? OK, so go . . . and do what?" she pouted.

He grimaced. "If you weren't as brainless as a silicone cocktail waitress, you'd be able to *tell* me what to do!" He threw his arms in the air. "This is the big dark wood at the back of the house, you stupid bloody woman! We're *lost*. Let's just try to get out of here alive, shall we? Think, woman—*think*." And then his anger at the slow paralysis of grief and fear her features displayed caused him to bellow: "Think, for God's sake! There isn't any time for anything else—we're right out of time to fuck about! We can't go anywhere. Not until we find out why they killed Frascati!" Her fingers dabbled at her bottom lip and her eyes were wet. He was standing over her as if about to hit her. "What did he *do?* Why did they kill him? He must have told you something. Anything. He was scared, alone, running—but he called you again and again! What bloody *proof* did he have and where the hell is it?"

As if aware of his threatening proximity, Hyde retreated with a jerky quickness. She was shaking her head wildly.

"How the hell do I know what he knew, whether he had proof? *I* don't have it, Mister Hyde!"

"Then who does? He wasn't with you, right? Who was he with, who did he see, where did he go?"

"*I don't know,* damn you!"

"Then guess!" he shouted back at her, his fists raised in furious, helpless frustration.

The telephone startled him like the shock of icy water. His heart thudded. Kathryn Aubrey seemed slapped into fixed attention on the receiver beside her.

Hyde hesitated. The telephone stopped, he heard his own breathing loud and ragged, before the telephone rang again.

"Yes—?"

"Hyde?" Mallory's voice was urgent.

"Yes, what is it?"

"I've just found out—it may be nothing, but—"

"What?"

"The phone company wanted to check the log of calls over the past two days. My secretary didn't bother to ask me about it. An hour ago, they said they wanted to check the phone bill before sending it out. Read her out a list of numbers, including—"

"This place."

"Yes. I wouldn't have given it any thought but the phone bill isn't due for three weeks. I—"

"An hour ago?"

"Yes. Do you think it's—"

"Harrell? Yes." He found himself staring at the bottles and scissors and makeup on the table, then at Kathryn Aubrey. "OK, get off the line." He put down the telephone. "Collect your stuff, including what's on the table, and get ready to leave. I'm going for a look around... don't start *arguing!*"

He eased the door of the room open and the bright daylight bullied in like an intruder, making him squint. Leaning out, he looked up and down the row of doors and windows. A boy with a huge baseball mitt, a large-stomached man in shorts and violent shirt, the hum of traffic from Highway 1 and the etherlike hiss of surf. A car engine ignited, startling him. Perspiration dampened his forehead and his hands quivered. He closed the door behind him and put on his sunglasses; then began to saunter, hands in his pockets, towards the motel's main building.

His breathing became lighter, more rapid and controlled. Slowly, his head cleared of the humid, stormy tension the woman and he had filled the room with. He paused beneath the blue shadowy overhang at the end of the block of suites, leaning against a wooden wall that was warm on his back, the gun now crucial to him, tucked into his waistband beneath his creased cotton jacket. The tinted glass of the main entrance masked the foyer's interior. A blond young man heaved someone's bags from the trunk of a cab, a child protested at being summoned for lunch, two men in gray suits strolled, earnestly in conversation, away from the motel foyer. He waited. The Nissan was parked at the rear of the block.

Eventually...

Yes. A man in denims and sweatshirt washing a Lincoln, elegantly careful with the play of the hose, time and again soaping and watering the same side of the limousine. So that he was always facing the hotel foyer.

Waiting for others. Sponge, hose, sponge, peacock's tail of water catching the sunlight, the hood of the Lincoln, then the trunk, then the windows on the far side of the car.

Hyde moved slowly back along the Spanish-style verandah towards the woman's suite, crossing each archway with an intent casualness, as if a spotlight picked him out. His right cheek quivered. He was sweating again, the urge to hurry difficult to restrain. He paused once, as if remembering something forgotten, even clicking his fingers in realization, and glanced to where—

—the hose was no longer in play, soapy foam dribbled down the Lincoln's windscreen and across its green hood. It was another moment before he caught sight of the sweatshirt with GRATEFUL DEAD '89 emblazoned on it drifting past the bright windows of the motel's minimarket, almost directly opposite him.

Longer before he could trust himself to move with affected sloth towards the woman's door and grip and turn the handle. His shirt was damp as he pressed his back against the door after closing it behind him. The woman's face was a chalky mask, the skin dead-looking. He was filled with a feral excitement he knew he must now trust in place of refined, trained instincts.

Her small suitcase lay open on the bed, with bottles and brushes and the glinting scissors on top of the few clothes Mallory had acquired for her.

"Close that! Is there a back window, or a patio door?"

He twitched back the edge of the curtain beside him— dusty material against his shivery, damp cheek—and at once saw the GRATEFUL DEAD sweatshirt moving towards the shadowy verandah. The youngish man's hand was held carefully behind him, as if his thumb were tucked into his belt where Hyde realized the gun must be.

"Go, go!" But the woman had already gone, along with the suitcase, through into the narrow lounge. Hyde stumbled after her, barking his shin against a low table's edge. Kathryn Aubrey was struggling with double-glazed patio doors out onto dusty grass and a parking lot—he could see the blue Nissan—but the door would not slide.

"There's no key!"

Nor was there. Nor symbols or engravings on the glass to indicate they were strengthened. Hyde listened, hesitating, eyes searching the room, aware they had sat in that other hot and close room for the last two hours, not here where at least there were more easy chairs . . .

He heard the handle of the door being tried.

He picked up the telephone extension and thrust it at the patio door. The inside glass shattered. The woman's breath exhaled like a shout of protest. He heard knocking on the door, the handle being rattled more violently. He banged the receiver against the outer glass panel, and only caused scratches, which appalled him with his own insufficiency. A voice called her name, and Kathryn Aubrey looked through into the bedroom, mouth open. Mallory'd booked her a suite because she was Aubrey's niece. Bloody almighty Aubrey—! The receiver crashed through the glass, then buckled the thin metal of the lock—THIS DOOR IS FULLY SECURED read a notice. He jerked back the sliding door, scraping the back of his hand on jagged glass.

"Come *on!*"

She dragged at her suitcase as a heavy thud crashed against the bedroom door. Exhilaration and weakness, he felt them both as he bundled her towards the Nissan, the sun suddenly heavy, clouting at him like a swinging hand. The woman gobbled for air like a stranded fish.

Wood ripped somewhere behind them. Then a man's voice called for them to stop as Hyde slammed the passenger door, the woman's suitcase bundled onto her lap.

Hyde paused, watching the man in the emblazoned sweatshirt, his young, fair face squinting with intent concentration, his hand still nestling in the small of his back. Hyde slid around the Nissan and carefully climbed into the driver's seat.

"What will—?"

"Shut up."

He started the engine at the second attempt. Then the man in the sweatshirt began running. Hyde put the Nissan into reverse and the tires protested. Dust—hand brake turn, the tires louder, dust thicker, the man in the sweatshirt moving gauzily through it. The Nissan jerked forward out of the dust and the man was hardly more than a blundering form when he emerged from it. Then the car bucked out of the lot onto the highway, fishtailing wildly before Hyde regained control.

"Where are we going?" the woman all but wailed.

"Who bloody knows?" he shouted, then ignored her.

"No, I am afraid that I can promise very little, Lescombe. But you expected nothing more, surely?"

Aubrey's eyes were half-closed—a convincing little ploy, he believed, especially when it masked his own very real tiredness. He sat outside the conventional but remarkably effective glare of the hard light falling on Lescombe, whose suit was creased down the arms and whose clubby tie was askew. The man was jowly, unshaven, balding; cornered and cunning and only very recently convinced that what had occurred was real, and indefinite. The hard white light was old-fashioned, but it fulfilled at least one of the expectations after they were caught of amateurs like Lescombe, who'd no doubt seen too many films and read too many books. Lescombe blinked behind his spectacles, looking slightly more owl-like than in the small photograph in the file opened on the bare table in front of Aubrey.

"I really don't see," Lescombe began, then added: "It's very hard to take this seriously, even after something like *Spycatcher*." A bluff and thin dismissiveness, and easily punctured. Aubrey did not suspect or expect reserves. Lescombe's spying had been too easy and too well rewarded for him to have learned or acquired fortitude. Aubrey ran his finger down the list of Lescombe's trophies—the Jaguar in the large garage, the villa on the Algarve in another name, the time-share in Florida, the other bank accounts. No younger women, just the wife who seemed to be enjoying the additional income as much as Lescombe himself. And the children at better public schools than previously.

"You have the advantage of me there, Lescombe. I'm afraid I haven't read it, though I hear it is one of the most boring books ever published." Aubrey looked up, smiling affably, closing the file as if he had digested its entire contents. "I don't imagine you assumed it would end like this, mm?"

"I am entitled to a solicitor, I take it?" The newly learned confidence of money, the egotism of negotiating previous minor dangers. Lescombe had been young enough when he began to enjoy the money, to relish it. And he was a clever man, highly regarded...

...and had worked, so Godwin affirmed, on Reid Electronics' ill-fated RPV project, scuppered by MoD and the US Department of Defense.

Aubrey shrugged expressively. "Oh dear, had I a pound coin for every occasion I have heard that misplaced confidence." Again, he smiled.

"Bloody ridiculous!" Lescombe blurted. But the nibble of fear was there. "You have to bring charges."

"Of course, of course. This isn't *Spycatcher,* after all, is it?" Aubrey gestured at the file. "But, with your arrest and what we have in the way of evidence, it's surprising you seem so eager to rush headlong towards sentence and imprisonment. Hardly the retirement to the Algarve you planned, mm?"

The man had been woken often, not allowed to rest; been disoriented by noises, by meals at the wrong times of day and night. The loneliness and silence and the pervasive musty, prophetic scent of the old house showed on his skin, like blotches of mold.

Lescombe rubbed his hand across his thin hair and adjusted his spectacles. "No one has mentioned charges, evidence," he protested, as if Aubrey had somehow swindled him. "I deny everything. The whole business is ridiculous, as you will find out!"

"Of course. I am here to do that, Lescombe. Then, eventually, an officer from the Special Branch will arrive to formally charge you, in the presence of your solicitor. Then you will be remanded in custody until a date is set for your trial." Aubrey shook his head with owlish wisdom. "I'm afraid it does not look good—and that is my initial impression, after just a glance. Photographs, tape recordings, statements from your bank, comparisons with your tax forms, your declared savings . . . dear me, there is a great deal of sifting to be done—" Aubrey looked up, compassionately, and concluded: "—it does not appear in the best of health, your future, does it?"

"And—you're here to offer me a deal, is that it?" Lescombe sneered to disguise his interest, his little flush of hope.

"I shouldn't think so, Lescombe. Can *you* find any mitigating circumstances?" Aubrey sighed, murmuring as if to himself: "Priabin will have cut all your contacts by now, I'm afraid. Were you to regain your freedom, there'd be nothing to expect from that quarter."

The silence lasted for some minutes. It wore at Aubrey as abrasively as he thought it might be affecting Lescombe. There was no trace of the wife, house locked up and a note for the milkman, as if she had gone on holiday. Had she been warned in some way? Did he know where she was?

Shelley had told him over the car telephone as he was being driven down to Hampshire that Mallory had lost track of Kathryn and Hyde. Harrell had traced them to the motel, but they had vanished. He had to trust Hyde's eroded and weary instincts... Lescombe's file blurred but he continued to stare at it, his hand cradling his forehead to shield the dim inwardness of his gaze. He had instructed Shelley to tell Hyde just to get her out. They had Lescombe, so now there was an alternative to further endangering Kathryn and Patrick. He shrugged off immediate guilt, as he had learned to do so many years ago. Let it come not when it would, but when he had leisure for it.

Lescombe, then. Open him like a tin of sardines for that thin Czechoslovak cat that Godwin had brought back with him from Prague. He concentrated on the background to Reid's RPV fiasco. Giles Pyott had been evasive over the telephone, but only because it was one of MoD's more arbitrary decisions, with a great many resultant red faces now that Reid was in the cabinet. What revenge they thought a secretary of state might wreak on MoD heaven alone knew! *In a nutshell,* Giles had said, *the machine had been too costly and too sophisticated. What's your interest? Oh, background on this chap at Farnborough, fine ...*

Range, altitude, flight duration, electronic capacities—all as Tony Godwin had claimed. *Years ahead of anything else in the field, Kenneth, but we didn't have a use for it.*

But Harrell had found one, the murder of Irena Nikitina. He knew it, but could in no way prove what had become of the prototypes that Reid Electronics and the other manufacturers and subcontractors had produced for their own trials and those expected by MoD.

Did Lescombe know?

Aubrey glanced upwards through his fingers as they cradled his forehead. The man was staring at him, partly in disbelief, partly in morbid anticipation. His bluff and confidence when Aubrey had entered were a new beginning, a new front, but he suspected that Lescombe was dizzied and made weary by ideas of hope, escape, disbelief, terror. The duty man's report was that he was soft and becoming softer—a balloon falling tiredly from the ceiling on Twelfth Night.

Aubrey looked up sharply. "I'm afraid it's no good, old man," he asserted quietly.

Lescombe's reaction was to glance around the dim cellar, his breathing hoarse. Cardboard boxes, a few dusty wine bottles, a broken rocking horse—a nice touch by Set Dressing, that—a small black lizard just on the edge of the pool of lamplight. There was usually a small frog, too—or was it a toad? Unexplained droppings, dirt, damp. The cameras and hidden mikes, of course, an agonizingly broken clock, Lescombe's dirty mattress and pillow, and a chair that appeared broken by great and futile violence. It chilled Aubrey, but it would be vivid and unnerving to Lescombe. It usually worked efficaciously, especially on the comfortable, those used to life's small and indispensable luxuries. The uncovered bucket in the corner stank, of course.

Calmly, he announced: "Is there anything you'd like

to say to me, Lescombe? Is there perhaps a message I can get to your wife, someone—?" Lescombe's lips were narrowed, bloodlessly forced together. Where was the wife? "Though we're not certain of her whereabouts— do you know?"

Lescombe's face was patchily white as he swayed slightly beneath the hard light. It was easy, too easy, with Lescombe's vulnerability exposed like a nerve in a rotten tooth. The man was only an amateur, after all.

"Do you know where your wife is, Lescombe?" he urged. "Or whether she knows where *you* are?"

Still silence. The tiny black lizard crawled towards a dead fly lying on the concrete floor. Aubrey could smell the damp. He consulted the file blindly, assessing his moment, then he repeated:

"I think she should be told about—"

"No." It was announced in a wet, breathy way. Then the face resumed its waxen, masklike stillness.

There was nothing concerning the wife in the cobbled-together file on Lescombe. He had been stumbled upon and caught largely by good fortune. There was only the information that the bank and building society accounts had been cleared out on the day of Lescombe's arrest. Aubrey tapped his finger meaningfully on a passage in the file he did not attempt to read.

"I really think she should be informed, old man. There's no need for this pretense of a Soviet prison to go on any—"

"*No.*" The same wet noise in Lescombe's throat, the face paler, the shoulders more rigid.

"I think I should insist, old man, for your sake, and hers, of—"

"*No!*"

So easy . . . so unimportant. Lucky to find a man still obsessed with his wife, of course. But no more than one steppingstone across the river that confronted him. All that mattered was what Lescombe could tell him of the RPVs.

"My dear chap, what's wrong with you? You look as if you've seen a ghost!"

"She's scarpered, that's why! Fucked off, no doubt, with her boyfriend!" His mouth was open, as if his throat rather than his lips formed the words. His neck was taut, ropy, his forehead damp with shiny droplets, his eyes bright. His whole body was rigid.

"I—boyfriend, you say . . . ?"

"Yes, yes, *yes!* Her fucking boyfriend! That fucking arsehole of a TV newsreader—fucking *local* newsreader, for Christ's sake!"

His head slowly dropped forward like that of someone falling asleep, his chin pressing into his chest. Damp trails appeared down his waxy cheeks, magnified as his spectacles slipped forward on his nose. His breathing was as strained as that of an exercised horse. Aubrey watched his collapse dispassionately, calculating how the conversation, for there would now be one, might be brought round to the precise topic of Lescombe's career—with suitable slides by way of illustration, of course. He felt quieted for the moment by success.

"I understand, old man," he murmured. "My own wife did the same thing with another man—" Lescombe looked up suspiciously, his face wet, his eyes blurred with tears. He removed his glasses and wiped his cheeks and eyes with his sleeve. Aubrey's features were at their most confiding, most disarming. He shook his head with worldly sadness, disillusion. " 'Fraid so. Years ago. Women, eh, old man? The chap was younger, of course . . ." Had he ever had a wife, would he have held on to her any better than Lescombe had his? No matter—

"Hurts, doesn't it?" Lescombe sniffed.

"Like the Devil, old man—like the Devil. Still, what they say is true, time *is* a great healer. But you're sure she's gone?"

"Are the bank accounts empty?" Lescombe managed to ask. Aubrey merely nodded. "Then she's gone. You'll find her, if you want her, on the Algarve, I expect! I hope it's fucking raining cats and dogs!"

"Yes, well—"

"I hope the bitch gets cancer!" Lescombe yelled at him, with blind, hating rage. Then he subsided into tears once more.

Aubrey let him snivel, then recover, wipe his face, blow his nose. As if cued by Lescombe's misery, the duty man unlocked the door and left a tray on the table. Aubrey felt refreshed by the scent of tea from the brown pot. He poured. "Sugar?"

He allowed Lescombe to drink his tea, then he said with studied casualness: "Should we start, do you think, just by summarizing your career—oh, nothing current, old man, this really isn't the time and place for it. But a quiet talk might help—you never know—distract you, perhaps?" It required a vivid effort to control the tense little tickle in his throat as he recognized the sense of desperation creep back regarding Hyde and his niece.

He cleared this throat. "We'll have to cover this ground, d'you see, whatever course events take. I think it might help if we began now, mm?"

The damp of the cellar was seeping through his coat, meeting another, chillier cold inside him. Lescombe's face was passive for the moment. The worm of knowledge had hollowed him like a piece of fruit. The bank accounts were empty, she was gone; what he had dreaded was true—more real than his capture and eventual prison sentence.

He began rocking slightly on his chair like a hollow doll on a rounded base. His passive expression had become strained, as if his stomach pained him. Collapse and compliance were both imminent, with only the facade left to fall.

Eventually, Lescombe shrugged. "All right." His shoulders sagged, as if his frame had dissolved beneath his flesh. "All right, you can get on with it. Doesn't matter now, does it?" His lips trembled; he could not achieve even the slightest belligerence.

Aubrey nodded sympathetically, repressing his growing excitement. He was aware of all the clocks in the old house moving on together. The mantel clocks, the grandfather clock in the dusty, drab-painted hall with its peeling stucco and plaster, the carriage clock, his traveling alarm clock still in his overnight case. All moving too quickly, swallowing time.

With an effort, he announced calmly: "More tea? Ah, good . . . Now, I'll just switch on this small recorder here, and we can begin." He placed it on the table. Only that clock provided by Set Dressing, lying near the broken chair, was not working. All the others were hurrying—

The crowds had been a mistake, he realized that now. They had seemed to offer safety, but their drift and hurry against the smoky golden light across Monterey Bay confused and disoriented him, rather than those who must be looking for them. The bark of a sea lion beneath the wharf, the smell of fish cooked and uncooked. The seafood restaurant was crowded. They should have stayed in the hotel. He was left with only the coccyx of his professional skills and instincts, the vestigial monkey's tail. It was why he had run for crowds and confusion—he shouldn't have.

The uppers conspired with the beer. He blinked and

stretched his eyes whenever the woman stopped watching him to pick at her food with an idle, preoccupied fork. Her hair was brutally short, and bleach-blond, making her face narrower, even harder. He was caught by her tension as if by a spider's web, made incapable of ignoring her predicament and her nature, however much she angered or unsettled him.

"Are you going to finish that?" he remarked, the sneer easy.

She looked up from the fish, her eyes glaring, laying some obscure but encompassing blame upon him.

"I'm not married to you, Hyde."

He rubbed his hair as if massaging his scalp. "Look, if you've had enough, let's get back to the hotel. I'm sick of this place."

The lights along the curve of the bay had begun to twinkle on as the evening gold dimmed. The restaurant was noisy. Laughter unsettled him.

"That dump? Why should anyone want to go back there?"

"To hide. That's what we're doing, hiding—until we find something more constructive to do."

"Why are you here, Hyde?" She swallowed at her wine. "I mean, why can't you find out what's happening? Why they killed John?" She was leaning forward, speaking urgently and softly. Her free hand clenched and unclenched on the tablecloth; long white ringless fingers, unpainted nails. "They—they tried to kill me. They're still trying. *Do* something—please..." She swallowed, her nails scratching lines on the cloth. She was as frightened as he was.

"I'm trying."

She returned to her food in the same desultory manner as before. Her demeanor stung and vexed him like a rash. Fishing boats emerged from the gray-gold evening, lights at their mastheads, somehow comforting though ghostly on the calm water.

"OK," he announced with an effort at sympathy, "I know you expected me to solve your problem—get you out, I mean. I can't. It's not in the schedule." He raised his hands in a gesture of mollification. "OK, let me explain. A world where we're left clutching Harrell's balls is safe—" He was whispering now, his forehead close to hers across the narrow table, his fingers dabbing at breadcrumbs. "A world in which Harrell no longer exists would be perfect. What's behind it all doesn't matter, except that it could keep Harrell at bay. Or even better..." He paused, then added, looking up: "It might kill him." He sat back, a doctor relieved that he had explained some serious illness to a patient. "And that's what it all adds up to, sweetheart—everything." He sighed, uncomfortably hot across his chest and back, beneath his arms.

Kathryn Aubrey stared at him. Her narrow lips were a single thin, compressed line and her face was pale. The blond hair seemed inappropriately young. Eventually, swallowing, she nodded, her long fingers turning her fork again and again, as if she were wrapping spaghetti around it.

"Yes," was all she said.

Hyde pressed. "Did he say anything to you—give you anything? Papers, notes, photographs, the things he claimed he had, proof—?" She was shaking her head vehemently, as if tinnitus maddened her.

"I told you *no!*" she breathed.

"God, there has to be *something!* You lived with him, he shared your bed—he called you time and time again, asking for your help! What the hell did he *say?* What did he know, what proof did he have?"

She was still shaking her head. "I've told you a dozen

times, Hyde, I don't have anything, I don't know any-thing!" Her eyes were brightly wet. The middle-aged man with his wife at the closest table looked severely at Hyde, on the point of remonstrating with him. *Don't treat a lady that way, buddy.* He could almost hear it. The man's wife was whispering urgently to him.

Hyde stood up and pulled at her elbow. The man at the next tabled stirred—stay out of it, for Christ's sake—and Hyde dropped the tip on the table. Pay at the desk, get out of the place, get the woman out of here. He glared at the man, quelling his intention to intervene, and pulled Kathryn away from their table towards the door.

On the TV screen behind the restaurant's bar he saw a penciled, artist's impression of his own face. He could not hear the newsreader above the restaurant's hubbub. Harrell was too clever to provide a photograph from CIA files. But the sketch was accurate. Then Kathryn's photograph appeared, though she seemed not to have noticed it.

He paid hurriedly, pointing back at his table, not in-specting the bill. The air was warm outside. He held her close to him, though she shriveled from his embrace. He was speaking urgently all the time.

"Harrell knows it's me—just the flavor he needs. Like honey for the bears, do you understand?" She walked stumblingly against him. The sea lions barked beneath the pier, the planking thudded hollowly as he hurried her. "He's looking for both of us now. He knows who we both are. Now what the bloody hell did your dead lover *do* just before they killed him? If he didn't come to you, where did he go?"

He held her at arms' length, her back against the rail. Behind the ridiculous, cropped hair the whole curve of the bay was dusted with the lights of small hamlets, hotels, resorts. He was shaking her by the shoulders, but she seemed unnoticing. He could imagine that his grip on her was all that prevented him from quivering with reaction at his own sketched image looking down from the TV set.

Oh, Christ, come on—give me something!

She pulled away from him, wiping viciously at her eyes, then turned to look out across the bay. The smell of hot dogs and cooking fish, the noise of traffic and sea lions, a silvered aircraft high over the sea.

"He didn't come to me. Maybe he was right not to. This, this *obsession* he had—I didn't believe any of it. That made him angry." There were wet streaks on her cheekbones. "He—he must have known I wouldn't listen to him, so he went to my father instead." He was leaning beside her, hands gripping the rails, steadying him and making him patient. "He went all the way up to Sausalito, found Daddy at that jazz club, made him take him home—stayed the night at Daddy's. But he never came to me, Hyde—not to *me!*" Her guilt was embarrassing. Tears shone.

"When was this?" he asked quietly.

"The week before Daddy's seizure—before . . . they took him into the hospital."

"That's too long!" Hyde almost wailed. "He called you *after* your father's attack to tell you he had proof!"

"How would I know? It's the only place I know he went! What the hell else can I tell you, Hyde? He stayed with Daddy. He'd never done that before, not without me. That's all I know. He went to the club, and went back to the houseboat with Daddy—maybe three, four days before Daddy's last attack . . ."

Hyde could hear his own breathing, harsher than the

traffic noises. A ship's lights far out in the bay passed along the horizon.

It was fuck all ... wasn't it? It was certainly *all!* His sketched image was vivid at the back of his mind, a poster urging him to action.

"Sausalito?" he murmured. "And this jazz club—where's that?"

10

THE FATE OF UNWANTED GOODS

"A mere functionary, my dear chap—a mere cog," Aubrey sighed, smiling disarmingly. Of course, his age and demeanor supported the fiction.

"You mean there'll be others?" Lescombe asked, as if afraid of another desertion following that of his wife.

The cellar's cold seeped into both of them. Aubrey had had Lescombe provided with a thin raincoat, and manufactured a struggle with the duty man out of even that minor concession.

"I'd like it very well if we could *both* just get up and leave here, go somewhere warm and comfortable, where we could talk. But—they insist..." Aubrey waggled a sheaf of paper he had extracted from a blue wallet folder.

"I do not see the pertinence of most of this material, my dear chap, but—there you are." He switched on the small tape recorder between them on the plain, scratched surface of the table.

Lescombe was shriveled—yes, that was the word— by his confinement, by the implicit brutality of those who visited him, who carelessly brought his meals and water, and by the slight regard in which they seemed to hold not only Lescombe but Aubrey himself. He was shrunken like cheap cloth because his wife had done as he had always suspected and dreaded, she had abandoned him. His face pallid, he hunched into the raincoat's scant warmth, and rubbed at the stubble that marked the passage of time.

"Now, you've told me the hows and whens of the business," Aubrey murmured in a kindly voice, "quite voluntarily. That's good, of course, it must help." He did not sound optimistic. "A surge of buying, the interest payments becoming out of hand—oh dear, so classic, I'm afraid—then the approach from someone, a slight acquaintance. Of course, we have him in a sort of custody already—" Lescombe seemed to clutch at that for comfort, his smile acid and inwardly directed. "—but it's too soon for anything he may have said to confirm your version of events."

"He gave me to them, the bastard!" It was a weary anger. Almost at once, Lescombe collapsed back onto whatever inadequate mental resources he still possessed. He waved a limp hand and said: "Get on with it."

Good. Lescombe was now in the position of a marathon runner, sensing creeping exhaustion, clearly envisaging the endless, unpassable miles ahead of him. Aubrey cleared his throat and murmured: "Quite. But, I have this ream of questions that others require me to ask." He shrugged, resenting the ease of the game he was playing and the superannuated image of himself he could so successfully project. "The more you satisfy them—*we* satisfy their demands—I think the easier it will be for you, my dear chap. For example, one of the things they seemed to have plucked out of the air is Reid Electronics' involvement in the RPV project, ill-fated as it was." David Reid had supplied Lescombe's dossier. Lescombe had indeed worked on the project. "Now, I believe you in your dates and circumstances, but they seem to think you might have—"

"I wasn't doing it *then!*" Lescombe wailed. "Christ, I could manage the payments then!" The deflected challenge to his desperate need for probity was working. He was convinced that Aubrey believed in him, and that no one else did. Every accusation and implied insult caused minor eruptions of self-regard. "I worked on the project, yes, but I—I didn't talk about it to anyone."

"Of course. Let's clear it up, then, shall we?" Godwin had stumbled upon precisely nothing. David Reid was out of bounds to him. And David had become a political animal by that time, already resigning as chairman and chief executive. He might not even know, in the aftermath of MoD's cancellation, what had happened to the prototypes. He had been too busy courting the powerful and the banks! So, Lescombe's memory was invaluable. "The project was canceled, wasn't it?" Aubrey pretended to consult the sheaf of paper.

"Yes. MoD crapped on it."

"You see your resentment, my dear chap? They might—" Nodding towards the camera high in the corner of the cellar. "—consider your motive to be disillusion, anger . . . ?"

"No. Just bloody money!" The admission escaped him in a pained exhalation of breath.

"Yes." Aubrey assumed embarrassment. "So, the

project was considered—ah, yes, here it is—too expensive and too sophisticated, mm?"

"It was, for the Household Cavalry."

"So, and again I'm consulting these notes, you surely could have seized an opportunity there? Passed on certain information—?"

"I wish I had! Might have had a couple more years of the high life, mightn't I, before the bitch ran off with that blow-dried cunt!"

"Yes." Aubrey kept his eyes maidenly averted for a few moments, as he asked: "But surely, they suggest, there were blueprints, computer models, even physical bits and pieces lying around all over the place?"

"Why are they going on about it, for God's sake?"

"Narrow minds, I think." He leaned forward and switched off the recorder. An electric complicity seemed to shudder through Lescombe's arm and chest. Aubrey's shoulders appeared to mask his movements from the camera on the wall—to which Lescombe's eyes flickered. Aubrey glanced warningly. "I think they'd like to use all this against you," he whispered, then leaned back and switched on the recorder. Lescombe's suspicion collapsed as it came into collision with his need of Aubrey. "I think you should be very definite in your answers at this point," Aubrey warned. Lescombe moved in his chair, tidying himself. "Now, what happened—to the project's bits and pieces?"

Lescombe frowned in concentration. The silence constricted around Aubrey's temples like a drying thong. The driftwood that Kathryn and Hyde had become to him bobbed back to the tossing surface of his mind, and he willed Lescombe to answer him. Eventually, like a tap having been forced to work again with a heavy spanner, Lescombe did.

"Most of the project was covered by patent or pending

patent or MoD security classification. All the subcontractors here and abroad would have had similar cover. I suppose the *blueprints,* as you call them, are rotting in an MoD basement somewhere—or a Pentagon basement. After all, no one's built any more of the bloody things, have they? So no one was very impressed!

"And the physical bits and pieces—like the prototypes, for example—are moldering in a Reid Electronics basement somewhere?" Aubrey's breathing was light and fast.

"A lot of stuff got shipped back to the subcontractors, I think. It was theirs, after all. All done in a hurry. I think Reid wanted shot of the whole business—we were all sick of it by then!"

"So, the project was scattered around the globe?"

"Germany, parts of the UK, the Italians had a small interest. Massachusetts, California—quite a lot of stuff from Silicon Valley—" He broke off, laughing in an ugly, desperate way. "Christ, the to-ing and fro-ing for a couple of weeks. Buggers coming round the factory floor pointing out *their* special bits and pieces!"

"So," Aubrey began, poised and scarcely inhaling, "the prototypes were broken up into their constituent parts? Shipped off in bits?"

"I suppose so."

"Don't you know?" he asked too quickly.

Lescombe was alerted, but his attention slackened almost at once. He yawned, even glanced at the filthy mattress with a kind of longing. Protest was forming in his eyes.

"No, of course not, no reason at all why you should know anything."

"A couple, I remember were broken up. Cannibalized by us for other research. Some others...?" He shook his head, tired and irritable. "A couple of them, the last we produced, were for the Yanks. Higher proportion of US input, to please the bloody Pentagon! I don't know what happened to those. That bloke was over, that fat bastard from California, trying to claim them—that bloody arrogant sod of a South African stopped them being cannibalized I remember—"

"South African?" The too-bright sun, the too-green lawns, Malan and Shapiro and the coffin being lowered. The rock music from a neighboring funeral, the glare of the Pacific along the horizon.

"Major shareholder. Put funds in, I'll give him that, when the chips were down. The California sod's firm had supplied some electronics."

"Malan? That was the name?"

"The South African? Yes . . . rich man. Probably more crooked than me!"

Aubrey stood up, startling Lescombe.

"I'm sorry, my dear chap, I think you've been through quite enough during the past few days! I'm going to call London—I'm not quite without influence, you know—and get you out of this damnable cellar! When you've had a good sleep, a shave and a bath, we'll talk again. It really is not *good* enough!"

He turned from the appalling intensity of gratitude on Lescombe's face and glared at the camera on the wall. "The interview is over!" he squawked. "Have a line to London ready for me—let me out!"

He turned back to Lescombe, collapsing into loneliness and the faint possibility of hope; into unreality, too. Aubrey nodded assuringly. "No, don't say anything, my dear chap—I'll do what I can for you. Not much, perhaps—but I'll at least try to get you out of here!"

"Thank you," Lescombe said huskily.

Malan—a major shareholder in Reid Electronics, part of the company of white knights who galloped to the rescue after the collapse of the RPV project. And Shapiro...?

"Just for the record—the California gentleman—was his name Shapiro?"

Lescombe nodded. "We'd always done a lot of work for them—they for us, too. Their input to the two models designed to impress the Pentagon was big, or made to look that way—" He all but winked conspiratorially. "—for the generals in Washington. Pity it didn't bloody work out, wasn't it?" he sneered, rubbing his cheeks, then his arms, his hands fluttering back to self-pitying eyes. "The business that would have brought in. Christ, I might have got rich out of my share option. Satisfied the bitch that way!"

His look was one of appalled loss. Aubrey was grateful that the door opened. He slipped through it like a cat.

Shapiro, Malan—two prototypes at least on their way to...?

He held the door open, frantically.

"Lescombe—did they ship them to America, those two prototypes?"

"I don't know," came the thin reply. "There was talk of a desperate last attempt to stage a demo for the Pentagon, to try to save the project—" Aubrey thrust his head around the door.

"Yes? Were they in England or America when MoD canceled the whole project?"

Lescombe shrugged with a weary defeat, immediately preoccupied with the return of fear and isolation. He wore an expression of pathetic eagerness to please Aubrey, in order to detain him. As Aubrey had anticipated, more would come now, and quickly, to avert the closing of the door behind him.

"I don't know...might have been." Did he know anything? Should he have essayed this rather dramatic false exit, or continued to pick gently, inexorably away—? "I can't remember—" There was a quavering plea in his voice. "—whether it was before or after the cancelation that Malan was hanging around all the time. I wasn't on the company *board,* was I?" Resentment spurted, but failed to catch light. The plea for continued company returned, his eyes seeming to pursue something as quick and elusive as a mouse on the cellar floor.

"I see." Fiction would replace fact in a few more moments. Effectively, there was nothing more to learn for the present. "Very well, my dear chap. *You!*" he snapped at the duty man, who seemed suitably chastened. "I want this man to have immediate access to bathing facilities—and to be given a hot meal! At once, do you understand?"

The door closed on what might have been a pale, tearful whimper of gratitude. He hurried along the corridor and up the flight of steps, their ascent marked by smaller and smaller patches of mold. On the ground floor, the grandfather clock confronted him and the late autumn dawn spilled grimily across the checkered quarry tiles of the hall.

"Get Godwin on the phone, at once—hurry!"

His unshaven, rumpled appearance was as effective as if calculated, Harrell admitted to himself. Even the slight unwashed odor he sensed exuding from his clothes and body. It all suggested urgency, industry, the act of descending on the Coast because of displeasure. Los Angeles spread endlessly like a salt desert somewhere inland, below his high, darkly tinted windows. He stood, hands thrust into his pockets and shoulders threateningly hunched forward. He stared down at the hazed white expanse of the city, which he disliked, finding it foreign like an overseas posting; Karachi, Peshawar, the places he had sought Hyde—

—who was now here, in California. With the woman, Aubrey's niece, both of them on the run from him. The office out here had fouled up; had allowed the woman to kill one of their number and to escape the net.

His anger was just below the surface, like a treacherous current. He turned from the window, glaring.

"Listen to me, Becker—you let the woman get away. You have no idea where she is now, where she might go, and you can't lay your hands on Hyde. Maybe you guys spend too much time out in the sun, huh?" He glowered, only partly for his own amusement. The tall, fair man on the other side of the desk seemed to wince. "Now, where are they? You couldn't prevent your partner having his skull opened with a rock, so maybe you can't come up with anything?"

"I'm sorry, sir—" Anger attempted to surface but was held under control. "We weren't aware of the urgency attached to the case—not when Frank ... er, Doggett and me went up there to Lake Berryessa. That's all I can say. You didn't inform us it was all tied in together ... sir."

Harrell grimaced and then turned back to the high view through the smokily dark windows. Somewhere at the edge of eyesight that harder glare was, presumably, the Pacific. The mountains had retreated into the haze. There was only the lumpy salt desert of Los Angeles, its freeways like huge black cracks caused by the sun, the traffic they bore hardly visible. It was hot enough outside for men stuck in traffic jams to start shooting each other.

"OK, Becker—get out of here. Go find the woman and her new friend, huh? They're looking for something on me, on *us*. Something Frascati knew or suspected. They won't be too far away. Go get me an update from the Police Department on the APB that's out on them. You ought to be able to manage that."

"—asshole," he might have heard as the door closed, and he smiled. Then looked at his watch. Not yet eleven. The city looked dried, old, indistinct, as if the sun had been high for days rather than hours.

The APB had been out since five the previous evening. He heard his teeth grinding together as he threateningly approached the borrowed desk and its strewn files and papers, slumped heavily in the swivel chair, the leather warm against his buttocks, and rubbed his hand through his hair, breathing in sharp, angry snorts as in a parody of attempted calm. Hyde had been sent to get the woman out, or to learn what her lover knew. And *they* didn't know exactly what Frascati knew because these beach bums out West had killed him instead of making him disappear!

. . . and he was forced to admit, it had all looked good, looked OK, until the threads that had come loose showed up under forensic examination. As soon as he had learned that Kathryn Aubrey was related . . . maybe he'd been told, but it hadn't been underlined for him! As soon as he had acknowledged that, he'd known there were threads on the operation's jacket, blood under its fingernails, other clues that could be unearthed.

Ahead, you're still way ahead . . .

Gradually, calm. He scanned a digest of CIA reports emanating from Moscow. Without Irena, Nikitin was losing his nerve. Or maybe he was just settling back into an old armchair? Irena had been the *real* radical. They sometimes said all *he* wanted was more things in the shops—not real change. Chevrikov and Lidichev were involved with so many of the moves now. So, it had worked.

He should have been able to say that it was over, that

it was only a matter of time. The one decisive moment of the operation had come and gone, had taken no more than minutes to achieve. Irena was dead. The psychological profiles they had studied, the charts they had projected, the whole scenario, all coming to fruition. Nikitin found it hard to hold things together without the woman's support. If Didenko and maybe half a dozen other key people could be shuffled aside, the whole ball game would work out. He skimmed demotions, new promotions, changes of allegiance inside the Politburo and the Central Committee. The seesaw was tilting the other way. Gravity and inertia were pulling down the conservative end of the plank, just as had been predicted when the operation had first been discussed and analyzed. It had *worked,* dammit!

His big hand slapped down on the desk but even the slow blue fly eluded him, drifting off towards the rubber plant in one white corner, leaning towards the windows with what might have been yearning. He banged the desk once more, then threw the Moscow reports towards the cream leather sofa where Becker's people had squeaked and shuffled uncomfortably as he had berated them a half-hour earlier. He had no need to refresh his memory with positive, satisfying information. His recollections were like barnacles on the legs of an oil rig; weakening rather than pleasing, a danger. He was wasting his time rehearsing success. Aubrey was forensic in his curiosity and Hyde and the woman were his implements. They had to be stopped.

Sighing—breath exhaled fiercely—he again rubbed his hand through his thick hair and drew towards him the untidy file on Frascati. The coffee percolator murmured in the silence now that the fly had settled invisibly somewhere. He got up, poured coffee into a paper cup he'd dragged violently from a dispensing tube, and sipped at it, grimacing. Frascati.

He turned over the pages of background—Vietnam, protests and arrests after a tour of duty, ritual burning of the flag, the marijuana bust, then college background, the loner profile, the FAA post, the assessment of his superiors—the guy was good, no half-assed, gung-ho careerist, just quiet, patient, insightful. Too good.

And the growth of Frascati's obsession, like it was for a woman or money; a physical dependency almost, as if on a drug. The desperate need to prove he was right, the more he was laughed at.

Harrell wandered to the window briefly, squashed the fly against the thick glazing with his thumb and wiped its remains on the held-back drapes. Then he closed the Venetian blinds on the salt-desert city drowning in the heat. Oh, yes, Frascati was one of the pious; the self-believing. Harrell recognized a kindred spirit, not without anger. *This can be contained*, Doggett had told him. *No problem*.

He admitted Frascati's file had lulled him when he'd first seen it. A half-dropout, a bleeding-heart liberal. The photograph, too. Long, old-fashioned hair, a youthful, almost weak face. Sure, it had looked unimportant, no sweat, *containable* . . . but it hadn't been, because Doggett hadn't read in the young, beach-bum features that squinted out of the photograph an honesty that edged into self-righteousness. A belligerent conviction of right gleamed in the eyes, and manifested itself in the mouth and the set of the jaw. His character was there for anyone to see, for Christ's sake! It showed in the guy's war record, his insubordination, his barrack-hut lawyer's protests. The speeches he made in court every time he'd been busted for possession sounded like he was one of the Founding Fathers!

And Doggett and Becker and the other flakes out on
the Coast had written Frascati off as a hippie dropout,
a bum . . .

The recriminations fogged and weighed, like the heat
of the morning between his shoulder blades, but Harrell
continued to indulge them. They'd made the same under-
estimation of Kathryn Aubrey. She was just the woman
who slept with Frascati, important only in that she
worked for Shapiro—but not because she was Aubrey's
niece! The name hadn't touched any tripwires until it
was too late and she was already running.

Harrell flicked the pages of Frascati's file, concentrating on details, absorbing them, attempting to com-
prehend. Frascati had been part of the original crash
investigation team up at Lake Shasta. It should have
been more difficult for them, but the plane hadn't come
down exactly where it should have. Frascati was the one
who was suspicious, for whom things didn't add up. He
wanted to prolong the investigation—*it wasn't a fuel
fire, it wasn't pilot error, it wasn't electrical failure.* His
list of negatives was pages long. At first, Frascati had
come up with a bomb theory. The evidence, though
slight, was there—traces on luggage, fragments of metal
embedded in seats and bodies. Harrell had been able to
get the FAA to lose that—had them leaned on in Washington, too. Then, when Irena's airplane went down,
Frascati guessed—somehow, brilliantly, he'd guessed at
some kind of missile . . . and gone back to the lake to
make certain, even after discreet pressure had closed the
inquiry and pilot error had come out of the hat like it
always should have, the conjuror's rabbit.

Harrell flicked newspaper clippings as if they were
soiled or contaminated. Transcripts of the TV interviews
he had given until the media got tired of his whining
and even the relatives wanted to begin to forget and

Frascati was like everyone's bad conscience or the prodigal they wanted to ignore. Doggett had ordered surveillance—but, because the guy stopped getting into the papers and on TV they'd thought him less dangerous! Just a widemouth, a bag of wind...

...but he wasn't. By then, he'd started going back up to the lake area, nosing around. Harrell watched his fists close quite independently of what he thought was his calm and rational perusal of Frascati's file. He again heard his teeth grinding together and felt perspiration appear along his hairline. It could have been finished, neatly and forever, at any time over the past months. Frascati was discredited, ignored, his hunches just that. Nothing concrete—until he started revisiting the crash site. Until the equipment and the photographs were found in his pickup and even Doggett had been able to make the sum add up dangerously. And then he had the guy killed, only *then!* When he should have been *questioned*.

Even for the last few days of his life, Frascati had been able to lose his tail. He'd only been picked up again because they had begun watching the woman, hoping the guy would come home like a pigeon. He had, and they'd staged an accident that had driven the woman underground. The violence of Frascati's murder looked overdone, even without the medical examiner's photographs, the product of a rage too long frustrated.

Between San Jose and Redding where they'd first tried to kill Frascati, there were whole days unaccounted for. And for more than a week before they spotted him at Shasta.

He flicked the file. Sightings maybe—*maybe!*—in San Francisco, even one in Sausalito...? All unconfirmed. Where had he been? Who *had* he talked to? The big question was, was there anything or anyone out there for Hyde to locate and use? Or was the woman everything he'd come for?

He shuffled the files. None of them bore Kathryn Aubrey's name—where the hell was her file? He snatched up the internal telephone receiver.

"Becker—get the woman's file in here on the double! No, now—find it, then!"

He thrust down the receiver, then snatched it up once more, his breathing audible as if after exertion, the damp along his forehead chill.

"Becker—get me Shapiro on the line, now. The woman worked for him, for Christ's sake, he ought to know what she'll do, where she might go! If he's busy, interrupt him."

Both anger and activity soothed him, made his thoughts somehow more vigorous. Standing up, he ignored the city, pausing instead before a map of the state pinned to one wall. Redding to San Jose, from the north of the state to the center. Frascati'd been running, but he'd had plenty of time. His credit card tracked him southwards like a spoor. His telephone calls... Harrell crossed to the desk and picked up a sheet listing Frascati's card charges, running his forefinger down the list. Meals, a rental car, meal, meal, a motel room... thin evidence during the missing few days, Frascati was being careful, the addresses were out in the sticks. Nothing there.

Harrell went back two weeks, to the other period unaccounted for in Frascati's life, before they found him up at the lake taking snapshots like a man on vacation. They'd followed him and tried to drive him off the road. His movements had been easier to trace. He was still using his charge cards... a cash withdrawal, meals, groceries. A clothes store—the sporting goods shop. Harrell grimaced.

Becker came through the door, distracting him, a file clutched in his hand. Harrell nodded. San Francisco's Broadway . . . a sleazy, nightlife dump. Somewhere good to hide out. But there was no motel bill—cash? Where did he sleep that night—in the rented car, on a restaurant table, for Christ's sake? The place he'd eaten in sounded like some live music joint or other, so he would have stayed late. But not all night. Not unless he knew people there, met someone or was allowed to sack out there? He rubbed his chin, allowing himself the small satisfaction of leaving Becker hovering uncomfortably.

Frascati was little-boy-pure, the Lone Ranger of the FAA. The crash had gnawed away inside him just like Frascati was eating away inside *him*. The charge card was the only confirmation, and he might have lost it or had it stolen. But, assuming he was using it . . . ?

"Where did you go, boy?" he murmured aloud. "And wherever it was, does Hyde know about it?"

He glared at Becker as the telephone rang, snatching Kathryn Aubrey's file from his hand and crumpling the list of charge card expenses as he did so. Becker and Doggett had killed Frascati and had failed to kill the woman. Two screwups. Had the woman known where Frascati went or was likely to go, and had she told Hyde?

He saw Hyde very clearly, then, in Kabul. Strung out, exhausted, cunning. Hyde might not have much left— but his success depended on how much there was to do.

"It's Mr. Shapiro, sir."

"Put him through."

San Francisco's sleazy Broadway district. Some kind of club . . . ?

The black man held her shoulders lightly, with what might have been suspicious, wary hands, and kissed her on the cheek. He seemed prompted to memory by her

presence, his eyes glistening quickly, even as they were
surprised by her appearance, her cropped hair. She was
nudged by an ugly, narrow resentment that the tears
were part of the black man's reproving, surrogate par-
enthood. Her father had always referred jokingly to Sam
as her godfather. She had hardly ever believed it.

"You're in trouble, child," he said, removing his
hands. He was no more than twenty years older than
her, he knew her age exactly—child! She felt hot. The
gloom of the small club seemed tropical. "You come
because you're in trouble, honey?" His gaze belied any
sense of the reproach or moral superiority she suspected.

"I'm OK, Sam—really OK. It's just one hell of a mistake—I can't talk about it." She swallowed. The admission was difficult. "But, I—we need your help. This
is Hyde, Sam." The forbearing wisdom on Sam's features
was illusory, surely.

"I know it's a mistake, child—you don' need to tell
me that. You sure you don't need somewhere, something? A place, money, whatever?"

She shook her head. "We need to talk to you—about
Daddy. When he was last here . . . ?" The urgency in her
voice came from a need to run away, to leave the club
and Sam and the cobweb memories that had begun to
cling in the gloom. She had always and intensely disliked
the place, its atmosphere, context. The place confused
her. Most acutely, it reminded her of her father, with a
force that surprised her. She wished she had not come,
and hurried Sam with: "You can tell us about it, Sam.
We haven't a lot of time."

Sam had shaken hands with Hyde briefly, inspectingly.
And seemed disappointed. He waved them towards a
corner table, leading the way. Hyde drifted behind her.
The day they had spent in the cramped hotel room,
behind the slatted blinds, pressed again, increasing her

headache. Hyde had stared at the blinds, at the walls and carpet, his face grimacing with an effort of containment. She had smoked continuously, picked at food, watched him display inadequacy with the certainty of a posed, photographed image. In heavy, home-going traffic, she had driven them north to San Francisco and the jazz club Sam part-owned and which Alan had haunted.

She winced at the noise of a tenor saxophone coming from the small bandstand at the other end of the grimy, stale-smelling room. Discordant shrieks, puttering runs bullied at her, unnerving the fragile, assumed confidence and superiority with which she had entered the place. All around her glared the evidence of her father's wasted time and talents.

"What time's the first set?" Hyde mumbled.

"Ten thirty, man."

"Is Murray on in good form?" Hyde nodded towards the saxophonist hunched into intensity as he practiced; the music wailing, squeaking, making no sense to Kathryn.

"Like always." Sam grinned, as if some Masonic signal had passed between the two men. "You gonna stay around?" Sam appeared to plead on her behalf and she resented his concern, even for her safety.

"We don't have the time, Sam." She was unable to soften her voice. His look reproved, sadly.

"OK, child." He shrugged. "What is it you want from Uncle Sam? About your Daddy—what?" Cigarette smoke wound up through the single hard spotlight on the saxophonist. A furious run of honks and squeals and a floating, high strain that might have become beauty and warm silences, all threatened to dismay her. The images and memories unnerved her. "You want something to drink, honey?"

She bridled, then simply shook her head. Hyde was staring blankly towards the bandstand.

"Beer," Hyde muttered.

"Sure."

Sam moved away and behind the bar. There was a middle-aged black pianist on the bandstand now and Hyde had closed his eyes. The pianist began to doodle behind the saxophone, and the room and the noise pressed like an invitation to some temporary and sordid liaison. Hyde's closed eyes reminded her of John and his gradual seduction into a passion for this music, a sharing of delight with her father. Yes, John might indeed have come here in desperation or fear and felt safe. Alan would have listened, talked quietly, advised; would have been there for John as she had always known he was there for her. Though she had not come, not often. She shook away the thoughts with a fierce, brief anger.

"Christ, Hyde—what are we going to *do?*" she whispered, leaning forward. His eyes opened slowly. The ordinary and familiar made Hyde's world more frightening. "Don't go to sleep, Hyde, for Christ's sake! Tell me what we're going to *do!*"

"Stay alive. To put it bluntly, Ms. Aubrey." He sighed.

"Get me out of this!"

"What's the matter with you all of a sudden? Pull yourself together, you stupid bloody woman! What can *I* do?"

"Pull *my*self together? Christ, have you looked in a mirror lately?"

"I'm trying to avoid them." He closed his eyes again, concentrating as the saxophone slouched and slid and the piano picked at a different kind of beauty.

Sam returned with two cans of beer. Hyde swallowed as the black man sipped gently.

"What is it you want, honey?"

She breathed in, exhaling slowly, sitting more upright. "We—want to know about the last time Daddy was in here. Did he bring John, do you remember?"

Hyde's can was empty. Sam brought another. Saxophone and piano had changed roles, the high, warm notes from the tenor slithering and caressing, the piano banging at dissonance as at a locked door. Hyde swallowed with undiminished thirst.

"Sure, John was here with your Daddy. Kenny Barron was playing that night—played two of your Daddy's numbers. He liked that—"

"Yes, yes," she responded impatiently. "How long did they stay?"

"I saw them fo' while after the second set started—maybe twelve thirty. They ate here." He shook his head. "Sorry I didn't get to say so long, honey. It was the last time I saw your Daddy." She admitted the resentment she felt at the ease with which Sam's eyes dimmed and glistened. The easy love of virtual strangers, she tried to tell herself, those who did not have to cohabit or be responsible.

"Did they leave anything with you?" Hyde asked incuriously. "A package, anything for safekeeping?" The music ended and he was at once distracted into loud applause.

The saxophonist grinned, called out: "Hey, Sam, who's the cat with the great taste in music?"

"Make sure he hangs around for the set," the pianist added.

Sam was shaking his head, frowning. "No, he di'n leave nothin', honey. They talked a lot—your, I mean Alan's friend seemed to do most of it. Like he was in a powerful hurry to get somewhere else. But he di'n leave nothin' here."

"Where did they go?"

"Kathryn's Daddy took the boy home. What else?"

"You're certain?" she interrupted.

"Sure. I heard them make the arrangement when I was sittin' with them fo' moment."

"What else did you hear?"

"Nothing the boy didn't want me to. I thought it was 'bout you, honey—I'm sorry."

The bandstand was deserted, seeming to prompt Hyde to his feet. "I'll just take a look outside." He breathed exaggeratedly, as if suffering from a heavy cold. Then he stood more upright after shaking himself like a dog. "You wait 'til I get back. Just explain to Sam, who's worried about you, that you haven't robbed any banks. But tell him nothing that would make things nasty for him, OK?" he warned. Sam appeared alarmed, eyes widening.

"So you are the guy they're looking for along with the child."

"That's us. Bonnie and Clyde. But we haven't been here—OK?"

"You di'n need to ask that."

"Sorry."

Hyde studied the woman's face for a moment. In her eyes was a genuine fear of the immediate future. She knew they'd have to go on to Sausalito, to her father's home. He shrugged, angry with her. He couldn't trust her to remain impersonal. Her past—her whole life except the last few days—kept tripping her like snares everywhere she stepped. He crossed the room to the corridor leading to the back of the club and the parking lot. He passed the vile smelling lavatory and the narrow kitchen where a single Chinese stirred ruminatively at the contents of a wok. Then the air was cooler and the deep blue of the sky melded with the reflected, diffused

neon of a hundred bars, clubs, gay joints, live sex the-
aters.

He leaned in the doorway, watching the car. The lights
of San Francisco climbed and dipped and ran in an unreal way, as if glinting from the scales of some huge,
many-backed creature. The Oakland Bay Bridge
stretched out across the darkly invisible water, the headlights of traffic glutinously merging. He listened and
watched with heightened senses, then shivered. The city
seemed about to slither towards the unseen water. He
shook his head. Christ . . .

He rubbed his arms. High up, the stars burned
warmly. The white smudge of fog had begun to nudge
into the Bay.

She didn't want to go to Sausalito, and now he was
reluctant to take her. And it had to be that night. His
thoughts jumbled and raced like children tussling. This
was the only trace of Frascati's movements during the
two weeks before his death, and the man he had gone
to see was dead. The woman hadn't been to Sausalito
since the funeral, and she had no idea whether or not
there was anything there to find. Get out, then. Get her
out as she was beginning to want more than anything
else, take her back to Aubrey like some prize, and then
disappear. Make Aubrey make him vanish. Hide him
from Harrell.

Slowly, as he waited, the rush of his thoughts slowed.
Illusions of safety dimmed. He heard the saxophone
from inside the club, the rumble of traffic from Broadway, the distant booming of fog-horns out in the Bay,
the muted blare of bars, clubs, cafés, shops.

Her obsession with the personal, with her own ghosts
and spirits, had been broken open like an eggshell with
the impact of his world. Her grief for Frascati was jumbled into an ugly heap with guilt. Now, men with guns

and orders had intruded into her life. They'd already killed her lover, and they'd tried to kill her. She dragged at him and he could not cope with her when all he could summon was the fag end of training and instinct; the need to survive. She muddied the clear water of that simple necessity.

So, survive . . . forget her.

He moved to the sloping alleyway that ran alongside the club. Neon shuddered violently at the intersection and the noise assaulted. A drunk lay in the alley, nursing a brown-paper, long-necked parcel. His smell was acute and Hyde was grateful for the small signpost to his senses as he drifted into the haze of light and the blare of music and the shouts of descriptive bulbs. TOTALLY NUDE . . . LIVE SEX . . . THRUST CLUB . . . MEN & WOMEN . . . SEX & DRUGS & ROCK 'N' ROLL. The crowds at once surrounded him and he began to feel unsafe, for the first time trapped by the urban. Hands in his pockets, he moved slowly along the sidewalk, past the glitter and threat of doormen's grins, the feet of drunks, the sprawling handlebars of Harley-Davidson motorcycles, amid the smell of beer and sweet smoke and fast food. Two men, arms about each other, preceded him. A squabble in Spanish, the mah-jongg clicks of Cantonese arguing; the street's vitality drained him. Parked cars with tinted windscreens. He kept his face averted from the street lamps. His hands unclenched in his pockets and he registered the simple, physical signal of returning proficiency. He began to bob and float in his new medium. Harrell, he could now admit, had him close to panic. When the woman was near, her concerns littered his thoughts.

Fords, Lincolns, cheap jeeplike imports, motorcycles. A green walking figure signalled the pedestrians and he crossed the street to patrol the opposite pavement. The breath of a drunk, the high laughter of a gay hustler. Resentment of the place and its atmosphere sufficed to concentrate his attention. Empty cars, locked cars, motorbikes abandoned like horses at hitching rails, some of them splayed on their sides. Hookers in shorts and miniskirts, breasts boiling over their blouses beneath hideously made-up masks of faces. Christ...

Two men kissing in an alleyway, preferring the secret dark. A gray-haired man ushering a much younger woman towards the jazz club, David Murray's name in lights fitful and dwarfed by the yells of the performed erotic. He slowed, pausing beside a shop window. Gewgaws, cowboy hats, dolls, shawls...the car was occupied. It had been the lights flicking on and off twice from the police car sliding down Broadway that had alerted him. The police car moved past him, assured. The parked sedan had signaled back. Someone brushed against him and apologized as he turned, hand raised. He moved slightly closer to the car, bending down as if drunk—

—two heads outlined in the rear window, turned so as to observe the jazz club. He straightened and moved against the glass of a Chinese restaurant, its scents pungent, somehow damply savory.

He paused at the curb, tense and confident. The threat had diminished to two men in a Ford engaged in surveillance. The Ford had not been there when he and the woman had arrived. Until one of the men in the Ford went to look, they were ignorant and discountable. He crossed on the green light, drifting amid tourists, hardly taller than the ubiquitous Japanese surrounding him. Then scuttled into the alley where the drunk was nasally singing as a dog urinated over him, leg cocked dismissively. He paused to study the Ford again.

The passenger door opened, a man got out and

stretched, spoke to the driver and then waited to cross
the street; unhurried, routinely occupied.

Hyde's chest thudded and his forehead was damply
cold. The rented car couldn't be recognized—could it?
Had it been traced? He retreated up the alleyway, stumbling over the drunk's legs and frightening the nosing
dog as the passenger of the Ford crossed Broadway towards the club's front entrance, then paused to study
the alleyway. A hooker propositioned him and was
primly rejected. Hyde envied her dismissive shrug as she
moved away. A hand inside the man's jacket, hovering.

Hyde retreated to the car and closed the door softly
behind him, immediately hunching down into the seat.
Carefully, as if unwrapping jewelery or fine porcelain,
he unfolded the map he had plucked from the door
pocket; and studied the felt-pen rings he had made, each
one around a small town with a tiny airfield. His way
out, he tried to tell himself contemptuously. The gun,
which had become comfortable in the small of his back,
began to hurt. He peered over the sill towards the corner
of the alley, glanced back down at the airfields ringed
in black, then up again at the alleyway and the blue-
purple diffused neon that spilled down it into the parking
lot. In moments, a shadow emerged and the man followed it cautiously. The gun was evident in his left hand
as he used the right to balance himself against the corner
of the wall. He skirted trash cans. Hyde's gun fitted
comfortably in his palm—*he* was comfortable, now that
threat was one man moving uncertainly into moonlight
which threw his shadow starkly black against the white-
painted wooden wall of the club. His fist was clearly
visible, extended and gripping the gun. Hyde's left hand
held the handle of the car door gently. His breathing
was calm. The skin felt stretched across his cheekbones

and around his mouth, but only like a mask that fitted him.

Then the woman emerged from the rear door of the club, squinting into the darkness and the hallucinations of moonlight. She startled the man whose shadow was black and surprised and immediately poised against the white wall—

The suite of offices carried the scent of electricity. As he entered, he impatiently flung down the financial section of the *Times* and its announcement that Reid Electronics had agreed to buy out the government's share of Inmost, the transputer manufacturers. *The Guardian* would doubtless call it a scandal and attempt to embarrass David Reid, HM secretary of state for trade and industry! Godwin looked up from the green flow of words on the screen of a VDT, his features jaundiced by the display. Then he stumped forward on his sticks, his face already creased with anticipation of Aubrey's mood.

Aubrey had slept little; that always made him peevish—but Hyde had established no contact with Mallory or Washington, nor even directly with himself. Harrell had returned to America and was probably on the West Coast now, coordinating the search for Hyde and his niece. Lescombe's collapse echoed in his head like the noise of one of those old, unused, dynamited chimneys falling to earth. He was anxious, unsettled, hot.

"Well, Tony—where are we? What have you got for me?" Godwin's frown might have been reproof. He knew he sounded ill-tempered, but this was all he could do!

Evans was hunched over another VDT and there was a slim, dark-haired youngish man watching him with what might have passed for amusement in different and calmer circumstances.

"Who—?" Aubrey began.

"I've borrowed Terry Chambers from the DS. He's on holiday for the moment. He's reliable, sir—"

"Very well. But what is it he does, Tony, to make him invaluable to you?" Aubrey nodded briefly at Chambers, who essayed a smile which immediately drooped. "Chambers," Aubrey murmured. Evans glanced up and was instantly wise, returning to his perusal of the screen and the sheaf of continuous paper beside it. A pencil protruded from behind his ear, there was a second one between his teeth. The smell of electricity was heady, stifling. Beyond the blinds and the tinted windows, Oxford Street was clotted with taxis and red buses. The offices were twenty floors up in Center Point.

"He was on the team that they sent into MoD on behalf of the PM after the stink over contracts and directorships. You know the enquiry—"

"Yes, yes!"

"He's been very helpful, sir. He's also *au fait* with our friend Malan and one or two other people we're interested in. I think we could wangle a permanent transfer—"

"Not now, Tony!" Aubrey whispered with a kind of desperate urgency, his hand on his chest. He leaned towards Godwin as he continued. "Everything we do this morning has the utmost urgency, Tony. I do not have time to consider minor matters! Now—" He raised his voice. "—where are we in the matter of those damned RPVs?"

"Have a seat, sir," Godwin murmured. "We'll show you where we're up to." Aubrey detected reluctance. Early shoppers moved like a celebratory, black Chinese dragon along Oxford Street, a swaying, dense mass of umbrellas. The taxis gleamed wetly. The noise of the traffic at the lights below them was a thin, whispered complaint.

"Very well, very well."

"Coffee, sir?"

"No—oh, yes, thank you, Evans." He removed his damp-shouldered overcoat and his dark hat and placed them fastidiously over the back of a chair, the hat balanced as in some conjuring trick. Then he sat down, brushing flecks from the trousers of his dark suit. Chambers watched him with what was evidently the contempt of the young and callow! He took the plastic cup. The coffee was hot, its flavor bearable. "Well—proceed." He knew he was being deliberately irritating. All three of them looked weary, unshaven, hunched-shouldered. But Kathryn was out there somewhere—! The guilt swung back into visibility like a returning comet, bright and huge.

"Right, sir," Godwin replied grimly, with an effort of control. Beyond him, the displays changed, slid, melted. Figures, paragraphs, computerized graphics. Godwin's face, large and ruddy, appeared clouded with—knowledge, he supposed; suspicions at least. "Have you got anything for us, sir—first of all?"

Aubrey, after hesitating, shook his head. The past twenty-four hours had been spent—misspent—in contact with Washington and Los Angeles. Although Kathryn and Hyde could not be located, there had been no alarm or emergency signals either, Mallory had tried to assure. Other than that—

"Giles Pyott sat on the MoD committee which canceled the project. He had promised to confirm dates, attitudes and the like—quite unofficially—later today. I spoke to David Reid at some length yesterday. At his London home. He was largely unhelpful, scenting some future and potential scandal. The managing director of his company at the time is now working in America. He was vague." Aubrey felt he was dealing wretched cards. "I spoke to James Melstead also, but he was unable to throw much light on our concerns—what is it?"

Chambers's sneer had broadened and Godwin shifted uncomfortably on his sticks.

"Just Sir James Melstead, sir," he murmured.

"Uncommunicative old bugger, isn't he?" Chambers offered. Evans at once masked an embryonic smirk.

"Chambers!" Aubrey reprimanded primly. "You are speaking of one of my oldest and closest friends!"

"Sorry, sir. But we had a lot of dealings with him when I was attached to the Branch and we were brought in over the awarding of contracts—"

"What are you suggesting, Chambers?" Aubrey's outrage and dislike were equally evident. Chambers's eyes were filled with a condemnatory disbelief that Aubrey could be so naive!

"What has Sir James to do with this business? I turned to him as an informed outsider, nothing more."

"Villa on Majorca. Bought it three years—"

"Terry!" Godwin warned.

"I've had it up to here—" Chambers's hand chopped at his forehead. "—with people like—"

"What is this man doing here, Tony? What *parameters* are you applying to this business?"

"Sir, just wait, will you? And you, Terry, just bottle it for a minute." Godwin's high color stemmed from embarrassment as much as from anger.

Aubrey snorted: "Chambers—I am sure you are highly regarded both by your superiors and yourself, but I do not see the necessity for innuendo of the cheapest kind!"

Chambers shrugged indifferently. There was something offensively stylish about his hair and the check, baggy-trousered suit he was wearing. He leaned with an insolent ease against one of the VDTs, looking like one of those barrow-boy City people they referred to as Yuppies!

"Sir, I'm afraid it's all relevant. Since you were here yesterday morning, a lot of water's flowed—"

"Spare me the anodyne clichés, Tony. What relevance?" The room appeared chillier as the rain on the tinted windows slithered like tadpoles. What did they know? James—?

"Sir, we went through Reid Electronics like the Fraud Squad," Chambers explained in deliberate, inoffensive tones. "The PM wanted to be very sure about her new MP, Sir David. She didn't want to cancel the RPV project—well, at least not just at that moment. However, she was persuaded by MoD and the Pentagon and had to watch Reid Electronics all but go to the wall."

"And?" Aubrey realized he was surprisingly tense.

"Anyway, the banks and some big investors rescued the company. Sir David must have had a lot of pull as a new knight and MP and possible—"

"Facts, Chambers—facts!"

Chambers's insolent expression returned to madden Aubrey. It was as if he were listening to the stilted, notebook style of some grubby private investigator relating a wife's infidelities.

"Yes, Sir Kenneth," he replied heavily, hardly responding to what must have been a warning glance from Godwin. Evans studiously continued to be absorbed in the sheets of continuous paper on his lap. "Foreign investment—quite a lot of the loose money floating around in Hong Kong looking for a home. And the lucrative contracts and subcontracts, mainly defense work. And the ease with which Reid Electronics obtained export licenses without too much inquiry as to the end user's friendliness towards the UK—"

"What has this to do with the RPVs?"

"It's where our friend Malan comes into the open, sir," Godwin murmured. "He had to announce himself as a major shareholder in Reid Electronics. It's rumored he put the rescue package together."

"And did very nicely out of it—at least, Pretoria did," Chambers added.

"And because of James Melstead's never-disguised sympathies with South Africa, you have concocted this elegant little fairy tale of duplicity and guilt."

"It doesn't just depend on that, Sir Kenneth."

Aubrey studied each of their expressions and realized how cleverly and somberly they had led him by the nose. He felt sympathies and curiosities floundering against one another in his thoughts like panicking passengers on a sinking ship. He was genuinely alarmed and shocked. Perhaps he was naive. This was not his world. This kind of duplicity was unfamiliar—if true.

"And—what *does* it depend upon, Chambers, may I ask?" His stick was hard against his palm as he leaned his weight forward. The changing screens, the reams of hard copy, the scent of static, the very constancy of the temperature as the air conditioning soughed and wheezed. The place was unfamiliarly technical, alienly modern. And about Godwin and Evans hovered an air of a conspiracy they shared with the detestable Chambers.

"It's the way into this thing, sir. James Melstead to Malan to Reid Electronics."

"How? Show me." It was an effort to make that demand.

The telephone startled him. Evans picked it up, muttered and nodded, then handed the receiver to Aubrey.

"Sir Giles Pyott, sir."

"Thank you, Evans. Giles, my dear chap—you've news for me?"

Pyott was at his most reticent. "Kenneth, I have checked through the history of this thing. I have what you asked me to find out, but I don't see its relevance to the business at Farnborough. Not for the life of me can I see that!"

Giles had been talking to people. People had, more importantly, been talking to Giles! *Steady on, old man ... what's the necessity for all this information ... ?* Eversecretive, utterly paranoid MoD!

"As I explained, Giles—something Lescombe let slip. I concluded he was not working alone. I wanted to pin him down with exact dates. Especially on that canceled project. That may have been the time he was bought. If it was, then he might have been able to supply them with—"

"I see. And this help? From inside MoD?"

"It could be, Giles—it could well be."

"Very well, Kenneth. I'll have it sent round to you at once. All the dates of meetings and decisions, those present. And I'd better scribble out a list of those who knew, had I?"

"Please, Giles. But send the other material now, would you?"

"Of course. You'll keep me in touch?"

"Certainly, Giles. I'm sorry it's coming home to roost in quite this way."

"Quite. Still, no help for it, if there's anything in that wretched man's story! 'Bye, Kenneth."

"Goodbye, Giles." He handed the receiver to Evans, and watched as Chambers replaced an extension. There was a respectful smirk on his lips. Aubrey felt a coronary pain of distaste and foreboding in his chest and an inability to disbelieve Chambers's somber innuendo. "Very well, Chambers—proceed. Occupy the moments until General Pyott's material is delivered!"

"Malan, sir?" Chambers replied, his narrow cheeks slightly flushed.

"Malan—yes." He recollected, very vividly, Malan and James Melstead in conversation only days earlier at that supper filled with bonhomie and caste and club-bability; and deception—?

Godwin sorted through a sheaf of papers, then handed one to Aubrey.

"That's our calendar of events—as far as it goes."

"I see . . . mm, it is a little sparse, isn't it? Hardly sufficient to support the kind of elaborate structure of conspiracy you're seeming to suggest—Tony?" His voice was sardonic but even to himself his tone sounded half-defensive.

"Yes, sir. But, as you can see, we began with the date of the first article in *The Observer* that sparked off the doubts." His finger tapped the sheet. "April eleventh last year." Evans, as if cued by the gesture or the date, dabbed at his keyboard and threw a blowup of the offending article onto a screen on one wall. ADMIRALS TO SINK REID? ran the headline of a front-page article that had appeared at the beginning of the week of the by-election in the north that David Reid had narrowly won. "No one suspected anything was wrong before that." Godwin looked at Chambers, who shook his head. "Did you, sir?"

"Hardly, Tony."

"On the following day, Reid hit back with a statement picked up by the evening papers and a long interview in *The Telegraph* on Tuesday, two days before polling. The opinion polls were running Labour's way. All of a sudden, the TV and radio boys descended on the constituency in herds, Reid got onto every program in sight and on every front page—and won, just, at two-thirty on the Friday morning. The project was canceled on Friday afternoon. Sir David made no statement, but the company did. Share collapse, bank support, Reid pledging money of his own, the PM outraged in private, et cetera, et cetera. It went on for a fortnight, until the rescue package was announced and a couple of big orders." Godwin cleared his throat. Chambers said: "Malan met James Melstead on the Thursday prior to the article in *The Observer*."

"Why?"

"We don't know, Sir Kenneth. James Melstead refuses to disclose their discussions, except to say that he was being lobbied by various South African companies represented by Malan. All very usual and proper, he claimed at the time."

"And no doubt did not lie," Aubrey snapped. "Well, is there more? What about the RPVs?"

Godwin shrugged awkwardly on his sticks. "We think Sir James may have dropped a hint to Malan, over lunch at his club."

"You *think?*"

"Sir, we need confirmation from MoD—General Pyott—as to who knew the week before. Customs & Excise have confirmed the export of the RPVs over that weekend the story broke. Malan himself went to California on the Monday. We think—"

"None of this tells us what happened to them *after* they were shipped to the States! We knew they were so shipped before we began!"

"We guessed that, Sir Kenneth. *Now* we know," Godwin corrected him.

"David Reid claims it was a last-ditch attempt to persuade the Americans to continue with the project. He approved it, when he heard of it. The decision was taken, presumably, by—"

"Malan," Godwin interrupted. "Had to be."

"And on information supplied by James Melstead."

"Chambers, James is not even within MoD's orbit. He was permanent secretary at the DTI, for heaven's sake!" Chambers shrugged. "Will any of this prove what happened to the blasted devices after they reached the United States?"

"The claim is they were dismantled," Evans offered. "By Shapiro Electrics, one of the chief subcontractors. Another company in which Malan has a substantial shareholding."

With a start, Aubrey realized that the image projected on the screen had changed. He could identify Malan and James Melstead entering the Oxford and Cambridge Club, getting out of the same limousine, in convivial conversation. Their shoulders were hunched against a light spring shower which gleamed on the hood of the Rolls.

"Tony, what is the meaning of this?" He glared at Chambers, then at Evans. There was a date, April of last year, at the bottom of the photograph. "What is it you wish me to learn?" he inquired heavily, the stick trembling beneath his weight as he leaned forward, head a little bowed. "There is something, I take it—something *unpalatable?*"

Godwin cleared his throat like a lecturer, then, as Chambers smirked, murmured: "Sir, this is very serious. We haven't got all the pieces of the puzzle as yet, but—"

"By God, Tony, you'd better be able to make the missing pieces fit!"

"We will," Chambers sneered.

"Chambers—I have no interest whatever in your per-

sonal or class vendetta against some of my friends!"
Aubrey growled, enraged. "Just in the truth. That I can
and will accept. Proof! And it had better alleviate the
situations of Hyde and my niece or you will all three
have been wasting my precious time!"

Methinks you do protest too much, he told himself.
Far too much. But the sense of being trapped lingered
unpleasantly. The dish they were preparing to serve
would upset him.

Evans, tapping at his keyboard, changed the screen.
Malan identifiably at Heathrow, in the first-class lounge
and about to depart, so the legend read, for America.
The click of the cartridge of slides as Evans pressed a
key, then Malan and the portly figure of Shapiro squinting under what could only have been a Californian or
African sun. San Jose, and the date—the Monday after
rumors had begun over the RPV project. Both men were
grinning as they shook hands.

Godwin announced reluctantly: "The Pentagon withdrew from the project on the Wednesday—the signal
arrived at MoD that evening, our time. Hence the hastily
arranged meeting on the Thursday—panic stations."

"You're certain?"

"It only needs General Pyott's confirmation, sir."

"Very well. Proceed." He felt cold now and the static
from the computer equipment stung in his nostrils.

"If Malan was informed by Sir James, then the shipment of the two RPVs to the States was not an attempt
to impress the Pentagon at the eleventh hour, but something undertaken *after* all was lost, because MoD decided to withdraw on the Thursday, such was the
certainty with which the Americans had rejected the
project." Chambers was silently applauding, and smirking!

Aubrey coughed behind his clenched fist. "I see. Mm,

perhaps I *do* see. It has at least the virtue of neatness, and for that I congratulate you." Then he felt himself at an utter loss to continue with irony—to say anything at all.

Evans passed him a sheaf of papers.

"It's an account from someone in the Pentagon—who doesn't know why we want to know—which suggests the RPVs never got as far as any army or air force base. They stayed at Shapiro Electrics, the original consignee." Evans wilted under Aubrey's glare of disbelief and rejection, and returned to the computer printouts on his lap.

The silence was slowly punctuated by the tapping of the raindrops on the windows and by the chatter of the machinery. Aubrey stared ill-focused at the Pentagon report, especially at the dates and certainties it contained. Eventually he said quietly:

"And how, precisely, does this lead to the death of Irena Nikitina in Tadzhikistan? This was twelve months *before* that airliner came down in California—*eighteen* months before Irena's death."

Chambers's eyes glinted and his nostrils dilated as if he scented some slow-moving, already wounded prey.

Godwin answered: "This is a digest of Frascati's investigations. At least, of what emerged when he talked to the press and on TV." He handed Aubrey the green folder, and the old man took it gingerly, with his fingertips. James Melstead—James, he thought, appalled. Even if it were no more than an indiscretion—and it must be, surely?—it may have been the first step on the path that had led to Irena's death and Hyde and Kathryn's danger. And damn Chambers, he had no belief in such minor offenses as indiscretions!

"Thank you."

He skimmed Frascati's file. The inconsistencies with

electrical failure, the damage to the fuselage, the claim of explosive residue—Frascati's insistence, almost manic, that it must have been some kind of bomb. Then his resignation from the FAA, the obsessive appearances on television and in the newspapers, the continual protestations. The official version and the FAA's denials, Frascati's impotent fury, his lashing accusations. The public's growing indifference. The end is silence—

"Do you want to see one of his interviews, where he makes his points?" Godwin interrupted his thoughts.

"What? Oh, no . . . perhaps later, Tony."

"If Frascati was right," Chambers observed, "then they killed a whole planeload of passengers just to prove that the RPV worked."

"I *know that!*" Aubrey stormed, the file shivering in his hands, his neck taut. "I—know that, Chambers. I am not senile, not quite. I—" The telephone startled. He snatched it from Evans. "Aubrey!"

"Peter Shelley, Kenneth."

"Yes?"

"Mallory's reporting he's under surveillance. There's nothing I can do about it, of course, but I thought you'd want to know."

"Thank you, Peter. He's had word?"

"None."

"Thank you." He handed the receiver back and the intercom, as if it had been waiting with mounting impatience, buzzed angrily. Godwin answered it.

"Send it right up, Bill. Yes, Sir Kenneth will sign for it personally." He looked gloomily at Aubrey while Chambers rubbed his hands with greasy, moneygrubbing enthusiasm. Aubrey sighed and attempted further concentration on Frascati's file.

The rest is silence, he corrected himself. Frascati

dropped out of sight, reappearing only to be murdered. He shivered.

The ministry motorcycle messenger was slick with rainy leather. Aubrey signed, then dragged open the Jiffy bag with what seemed to him a vast, reluctant effort. The door closed behind the messenger. Only Chamber moved closer to him, but the flick of Godwin's big hand at the corner of eyesight warned him away. Clumsily, he unfolded the stiff, headed notepaper. Giles's neat, bold hand, written with an old-fashioned fountain pen. The meeting described on one sheet, those present on another. James Melstead. Asterisked as if Giles thought him culpable, too! Explanatory note. The DTI were consulted because of the suspected impact on Reid Electronics of the cancellation of the RPV project. Melstead had supplied details of other deals, orders, exports... prognosis, not good. Melstead had argued against cancellation, but was an outsider. The Pentagon's unequivocal rejection of the project had made MoD's decision a foregone conclusion.

James Melstead. Present, sir—

—time of the meeting's conclusion. James must have had to hurry to keep his lunch appointment with Malan at the O&C Club! He rubbed his forehead.

"Sir?"

"What?" he snapped. "Oh, yes, here you are." He handed Giles's notes to Godwin.

The rain all but obscured Oxford Street and its buses and taxis and the scattered parts of the umbrella-dragon. James, why the Devil couldn't you keep *quiet?* Why blurt it out to one such as Malan—the diamond broker with Moscow, for heaven's sake! Malan's large form under the hot, enameled Californian sky, at Alan's funeral. He saw the man quite clearly, sensed his authority and menace. God, this was the bloodiest journey on which he had ever set out! Friends, loyalties, family all conspiring against him and conspired against. Who, in total, was he fighting? Everyone, including James Melstead?

"What—what do we do next, sir?" Godwin inquired. There was nothing of triumph about his lugubrious, almost shamefaced expression. Even Chambers seemed to have subsided into indifference.

"Do?" Aubrey challenged. "*Do?* Isn't it obvious? I am deputed to interview James Melstead in the fond hope that, if he is indeed guilty of a massive indiscretion such as you suggest, he will confess everything. You three will have your mystery neatly solved. For Hyde and my niece, the solution may not be so easy!"

"*Proof* could stop him," Godwin murmured. "Blackmail? He wouldn't want his president to find out—would he?"

"It wouldn't be convincing enough!" he shouted.

Evans was plainly embarrassed by his outburst. Godwin simply understood.

"No, sir," he murmured.

"Meanwhile, I am to accuse James Melstead of betraying the subject of a highly classified meeting at the Ministry of Defence. He will doubtless confirm the accusation as true and blubber into his handkerchief!"

His private world had invaded his professional life through the looking glass and the two had become utterly confused. He knew James Melstead was the first step along the only path that presented itself to him, and what was the earthly use of his massive authority if not for this? A vigor seemed to occupy his old body. He was not, he decided, in the least reluctant to confront Melstead. Duty and compulsion uneasily conspired. He must find evidence that Malan had supplied the RPVs and their control trucks and equipment, via Shapiro Electrics, to Harrell and his murderous little band who labeled themselves the *Carpetbaggers*.

He must prove James Melstead's criminal indiscretions over lunch and Malan's culpable villainy!

"Ring Sir James at home," he announced, clearing his throat. "Tell him I must speak with him most urgently—arrange lunch if necessary."

Taxis slid along Oxford Street, rubying the tarmac each time they halted. Rain sidled coldly down the windows. His head threatened to burst with impatience, and with fear, as his hands clenched tighter and tighter on the curved handle of his walking stick.

The moment had gone even before his hand touched the door handle. Kathryn, shocked by the man's presence, stopped abruptly, one pale hand touching her mouth, masking whatever call she had intended to make. Hyde watched the man emerge from his own surprise and move towards her. The opportunity had gone. His mind scrabbled for alternatives, his left hand slowly letting go of the door handle.

A rattling noise, the squawk of a surprised cat as the garbage can overturned, the flash of something black-and-white hurtling towards the alleyway. The man's gun flicked up from beside his thigh, then retreated into shadow again. His other hand produced some walletlike identification. Hyde heard the voice but not the words.

The moment's gone. Leave her.

It was a real thought for a long, not-unexpected moment. His cheeks quivered, his body felt heavy in the car seat. He blinked the lack of focus out of his eyes. Kathryn's cropped, albino hair gleamed dustily in the light, her face half-turned from the man. The temperature in the car was misting the window through which he watched. *Leave now. This bit's finished. She was* shaking her head, then shrugging. Her stance was tense but she was managing to maintain an elasticity about her upper torso's movements and gestures that might disarm the man's suspicions. When had he last looked at her picture, the power-dressed image with the long dark hair? Leave—don't pretend she can bluff—

The gun was clenched against his thigh, as he pressed it into his flesh to disguise the shaking in his arm and wrist. For Christ's sake, leave—!

The man continued talking. She answered him desultorily. She even lit a cigarette and blew smoke into the night like an actress. Then the man began listening to his fingertips, evidently pressing an R/T earpiece closer. Nodding, answering into his jacket while she watched, her head twitching in slight, continuous movements. Her glance paid no special attention to the rental car. She did not know where he was, he could just stay hidden, then leave after she was arrested. He even knew the address of the houseboat in Sausalito, he did not need her. His temperature rose jerkily. If Frascati had left anything anywhere, it would have been with her father, on the houseboat. Aubrey's niece was clutching her arms now, growing colder, less able to dissemble. The moment the man looked back at her, he would begin to know— must recognize her. He slipped further down in the seat, the gun dangling uselessly beside the hand brake, his left hand simply pressed against the door.

The man nodded more vigorously, then looked up at the woman. Stay down—

She would be able to see the gun now, perhaps even the glint of suspicion in the man's eyes. His hand twitched at the door handle, clutching but not moving it, his gun resting across his lap, his head raised. Aubrey's bloody *niece!* Christ...

Shadow in the doorway, momentary pause, then Sam's voice, raised.

"I don't pay you to take time-outs, just to wait table and wash dishes. You get yourself back in there, honey, or you don' work here no more!"

Sweat cold on Hyde's forehead, springing from a shocked admiration. Kathryn twitched like a snared rabbit. The man made as if to restrain her as she turned. Hyde eased the door handle, felt the air entering through the crack he had opened.

Identification. "Police," the man mumbled, nonplussed.

"You got something on her?"

"I—just asking a few questions, man. We're looking for someone—"

"You git inside, girl!" Sam warned. Hyde eased the door further ajar, the crack now wide enough to contain the CIA man's body like a frame, the gun aimed at the bulky shadow of the center of his torso. No silencer, he warned himself, but the decision had been made for him. Aubrey's bloody niece . . . Kathryn nodded, grinding out her cigarette with her heel, tossing her head as she moved back through the doorway, her shadow jolting smaller down the corridor before it vanished. "What's the beef, man?" Sam continued. "You Vice?"

"Homicide."

"Nobody killed round here—leastways, not tonight and not yet," Sam commented.

"OK. Listen up. Anyone you don't know—man and a woman—they come here tonight, we're parked out front. You let us know, huh?"

"OK. You expect them?"

"Maybe."

"Man and a woman, right? Young, old?"

"Youngish. The woman's same height as the man.

He's thin, kinda ragged-looking. She's long-haired, cool y'know?"

"I'll keep my eyes open. Say, how come I don't know you?"

"New rosters. I'm new, too." The man had already turned, his hand flapping goodbye. "Be sure and let us know. If we see them and you don't, it's big trouble. Understand?"

"Sure. I don't need trouble from the heat." Sam scanned the lot and shrugged, then turned back into the doorway.

The night air cooled Hyde's forehead. The man's shadow enlarged and dissipated as he walked away down the alley towards Broadway, leaving the city's lights to spring freshly out, except where the Bay was dark.

The woman was a handicap, one who'd survived by the skin of her teeth—and his—this time. They knew about the club, he reminded himself in a pretense at rationality. They probably knew about the houseboat; would be waiting—

She was in the doorway, spluttering like an angry, small flame:

"Where in hell were *you,* you bastard?"

Sam was behind her, his dark eyes contemptuous.

"In the car. Waiting," he bluffed. "You weren't in any real trouble."

"You *creep!*" She was shuddering with rage.

"If they know about Sam, they know all about your Daddy," he pressed, angry at himself. "They'll have the houseboat staked out. Understand? If I'm bugger all use to you, what do we do next? *You* work it out!"

11

THE LUGGAGE OF LOYALTY

The overnight snow had been trodden into rutted slush along the Kremlyovskaya Embankment. Priabin's breath wreathed itself around his face, which was drawn and numbed with cold. Two security guards assigned to him trailed behind. He was, after all, still of sufficient authority to warrant them! His recall had not led to a crossroads where all the signposts directed him to destinations of failure. The deputy chairman had, in broad but enthusiastic terms, adopted his idea for a new pipeline; even if it had come out in a jerky series of inspirations. He shivered with relief rather than cold. Anyway, it *was* clever—it was the kind of thing they expected of him, the brilliant boy-general.

The sky was pearl gray, the river slate-dull, the massive red towers and domes of the Kremlin palaces acceptably severe and frowning. He slipped and righted himself at once—even his fine sense of balance seemed indicative of his luck. He admitted his good humor and indulged it, no longer skating on thin ice. He smiled. He had expected to be catechized, berated, made menial in a small office somewhere remote from the Center—but the Center had been as much in a state of shock at the sudden closure of the Stockholm pipeline and the arrest of Lescombe as he had been, and had looked to him to reestablish agents, pipelines . . . and he had supplied their need.

All you have to do now, he instructed himself, is make the bloody thing *work!* His pleasure remained unalloyed. By tomorrow, he would be back at his desk in London, Rezident once more. He glanced around at his two security men, and realized they had stopped. Other men approached in fur hats and overcoats, not men he recognized, except as a type. More security guards. Who—?

He noticed a thin head and frame beneath a too-big fur hat, spectacles blind from the man's own breathing, the exhalations impatient and yet somehow distressed—

He recognized Didenko, the Moscow Party—*ex*-Moscow Party chief, and sensed his own security men's watchfulness as they stopped to exchange greetings with the two men guarding Didenko, both of whom seemed unconcerned at any annoyance Didenko might display. Resigned through ill health brought on by overwork, the TV news had proclaimed of Didenko the previous evening; it was an item that had hardly impinged upon Priabin's relief on returning from the meeting at the

Center where his scheme had been approved. Didenko didn't appear to be ill. The cold was responsible for his pallor, he was moving easily, the hunched shoulders and the wasted appearance of his body were habitual, his coat hanging loosely on him. The news of his resignation had not been important, not last night, but now it was, somehow. The bulletin had been cursory, barely complimentary; much like the old days.

On impulse, Priabin crossed the slush towards Didenko, to the evident relaxation of Priabin's two security guards, whose conversation with their colleagues at once became more animated. Their smoking breaths clouded around them, and their slapping gloves and stamping feet sounded like the rustling of a polite, rather unimpressed audience. Priabin held out his gloved hand—from which Didenko did not so much flinch as intellectually retreat. Priabin introduced himself, at once dubious.

"I—wanted to express my sympathies on your resignation. Your—illness. Not serious, I—" He broke off. Didenko's glance was angrily curious, as if he suspected he were being mocked. Priabin grinned as innocently as he could and Didenko's tall, stooped frame seemed to relax inside the overcoat, his cold feet shuffling for warmth in their galoshes.

"I—um, yes. Thank you," Didenko managed with an effort to dredge up the words. His breath puffed out in little clouds of impatience and arrogance . . . or maybe bewilderment. "No, I'm not seriously ill," he added.

"No." Priabin glanced up at the Kremlin walls and towers, stamping his own feet for warmth. The laughter of the four security men seemed harsh. "I—I'm sorry that you've—"

"You are?" There was shock in the man's voice, but also genuine surprise, as at something forgotten. "You are, yes." Didenko's gloved hand reached towards his hat in a brushing motion, then hesitated, finding fur and not his scalp. He smiled self-deprecatingly. His teeth chattered slightly—with the cold, presumably. Then he shrugged. "There was—" A gleam shone in his eyes as he removed his spectacles to wipe them; a fierce light, despite the silly, blinking, idiot expression on his face. As he replaced his spectacles and studied Priabin, he burst out: "There was so much more to be *done!* Do you understand me? It's not for myself I'm sorry, it's for not having got things done!" His tone was no longer the prissy, hectoring expression so familiar from his television appearances. His voice was rougher, deeper, truly enraged. He waved a gloved hand at the high walls behind him. "I—we—could have done so much more, you see. Irena and—" He closed his lips as if on a biscuit that threatened to break and crumble. "Yes," he continued after a moment. "Yes, thank you for your solicitations. I am genuinely touched. Good morning, General."

He nodded his head with a slight, stiff movement, all but caricaturing himself, while the aftershock of his outburst seemed to remain in his frame, only gradually fading to stillness. He glared at his security guards, and Priabin signaled to his own men.

"Good morning, Comrade Didenko," he announced in a loud voice and his guards were instantly attentive, murmuring farewells and promises of imminent meetings, their foot-stamping now efficient, demonstrative.

Priabin glanced back once. Stooped shoulders, the large fur hat, the big overcoat—Didenko stumbled, but righted himself awkwardly. Almost a comic figure . . . yet so angry, so profoundly angry; like grief or despair.

*   *   *

"Ah, Kenneth—I'm just lunching from a tray on my lap. Will that suit?"

James Melstead got briskly, almost sleekly to his feet, hands extended. Behind him, through the tall windows, Eaton Square was littered with brown leaves and builders' dumpsters. Skeletal trees struck coldly against a sullenly clearing sky. Aubrey took Melstead's hand, gripping it firmly, guiltily.

Then James's sleekness interposed itself, his smile complacent, welcoming Aubrey into an old men's conspiracy of comforts and assured money.

Smoothing his features, Aubrey murmured, smiling himself: "Excellent, James. Good of you to see me so—"

"You, Kenneth? How can I help? I take it you aren't simply paying a friend's dues? You look—concerned?"

"Nagged at, James—only nagged at."

"Sit ye down, Kenneth. Scotch?" Aubrey's eyes jumped to the mantel clock, glowing with cloisonné, and Melstead laughed. "Sun's well over the yardarm, Kenneth. You needn't feel guilty." He rang the bell beside the fireplace. Aubrey perched on the smaller of the two sofas, opposite the chair from which Melstead had risen. Aubrey almost wished he still had his hat to occupy his hands, but the young butler had taken both it and his coat. Now, the young man poured drinks, then handed Aubrey his on a silver tray. Warmth and comfort and old acquaintance stung Aubrey, as if he intended some felony in that elegant room; stealing one of the Newlyn School oils or even the single Lowry, snatching up the scattered silver and porcelain. The furniture was undemonstratively Georgian.

Aubrey sipped at his whiskey as Melstead returned to his chair, ruddily well, dressed in slacks and a buttoned cardigan—cravat and check shirt. Retirement sat easily on his shoulders.

"How is Alice?" Aubrey asked.

Melstead shrugged. "At one of her soup kitchens or doss houses, I expect. She doesn't always confide in me, since she knows I disapprove." Nevertheless, there was pride in his voice regarding his only daughter. Perhaps she was his vestigial conscience? Alice at shelters for the homeless, Alice with derelicts under bridges and sleeping in cardboard boxes in alleyways. Alice with drug addicts and AIDS victims . . . Yes, even as he deprecated, he was as proud of her as he was of his sons, the colonel and the merchant banker. "Dear Alice—she seems so tired some days, listless." He sighed. "But she won't listen to me. Burning herself out." He studied his sherry for a second, then looked up, eyes gleaming. "And what can I do for you, old friend? Oh, it's sole for lunch, by the way—all right? And I thought a Chablis?" Aubrey smiled as he nodded, almost purring his acquiescence. "Good. Well, and now what?" Melstead asked.

"It's awkward," Aubrey began in his muttered, prepared way, "since it concerns young David . . . well, his company, really. You know my latest brief from Geoffrey and the PM, James. And of the gentleman we caught with his hand in the till."

"But, David's not involved, of course."

"Not directly. But, the effluvium, you know—it wouldn't be sweet, and the fallout might affect him quite seriously."

"All can be smoothed over, surely? We can rely on Geoffrey for that."

"Well, perhaps. But these things have a way of making themselves visible to the naked eye—eventually. With the help of *The Guardian* or Duncan Campbell or some such . . ."

"The BBC, I shouldn't wonder!" Melstead's jollity was slightly excessive, his complacency guarded, as if Aubrey had already declared his real purpose. Pretense was in the air.

"The man we are questioning, James—has thrown open some rather dubious doors." He paused, but Melstead's response was one of mere interest. "There were and are so many sensitive projects at Reid Electronics—especially now that the company's bought out Inmost from the government. But it's in the past that any real source of embarrassment may lie. You recall that RPV project?"

Melstead frowned. "Vaguely...mm, yes, come to think of it, quite well. Caused the company's troubles, of course. I'd argued against the cancelation, but without US support of the firmest kind, the project was a dead duck." He sighed, shaking his head. "David's company was sailing for the reef at a great rate of knots from that moment."

The young butler appeared and Melstead glanced at the wine bottle he held, nodding. A watery sunlight fell across the expanse of pale blue carpet, touching big, complex rugs.

"My problem—one of them, at least—is that project."

"How so? David's company survived. Paulus Malan among the benefactors and eventual beneficiaries, of course. But—the project? What's your mole been saying, Kenneth?"

"Ah, well—there seems an inability to account for the actual physical whereabouts of the prototypes—" Melstead seemed to sit more upright, as if a small, quick current had passed through the arms of the chair into his hands. Aubrey said quickly: "—and I have the distinct fear that something of them may have been passed across to the other side.''

"Is that likely—at all likely?" A slight breathlessness? Melstead's glance was intent, his expression strenuously bland. Chambers's face appeared in Aubrey's imagination, grinning. Aubrey detested the image, and the effort he sensed in Melstead to remain calm.

"I don't know, James, I really don't." Aubrey flapped his hands. He could smell the sole being cooked.

"Another whiskey?"

"Oh, no thank you." Aubrey had offended the laws of hospitality too greatly already, and wished he were not bound to stay for lunch. Disappointment filled him. James was on his guard. "But I'm not making headway. I want to make this thing stick against this chap Lescombe. He's been a positive menace. And I do think he's probably passed the RPV secrets along with everything else he ever worked on or could lay his hands on! But, I want to be as certain as I can be before making any further moves—d'you see?"

Melstead brushed gray hair back from his broad forehead, then rubbed his chin, nodding. "Yes, I do see . . ." he murmured. His eyes moved with quick, involuntary glances, as if seeking a bolt-hole. Aubrey loathed what he witnessed, but was unable to blame himself—or even Chambers, except casually. Kathryn's danger pressed like a migraine and an old friendship was suddenly viewed through the wrong end of a telescope, two distant and unrelated people, like the tiny matchstick figures in the Lowry on the wall. "Well, Kenneth, you'd better explain your theories, and tell me how I can help." The butler appeared, nodding. "Over the sole," Melstead added.

"I took the liberty of laying two places in the dining room, sir," the young butler stated.

"Ah, yes. Jules won't allow trays on laps for visitors, Kenneth! Well, shall we go in?"

Aubrey got up. "It seems perhaps two of the items in question are unaccounted for," he remarked. "At least two. They traveled west not east, of course, in the first instance. I'd like to know where they are *now*—practically priceless in value, I'd say, to the other side." Melstead's hand shivered for an instant against Aubrey's shoulder blade as he guided him through the doors to the dining room. Oh, James! his imagination cried like a betrayed girl in a melodrama. Those machines and their control vehicles had been used to practice then perform the murder of Irena Nikitina.

He smiled as he sat opposite Melstead, fussed with the napkin the butler folded across his knees, gave his attention to the misty green of the Chablis bottle, touched the already straight cutlery on the gleaming table. How *much* did he suspect—how much did he *know?*

He looked up.

"You seem very well acquainted with young Paulus Malan, James. Perhaps you could arrange for the three of us to try to thrash this business out? I really do want to get to the bottom of it. The scandal would be of enormous proportions if it turned out that—"

"I shouldn't imagine for a moment that that is the case, Kenneth."

"I'm as yet unclear as to the details, James. For example, the precise date that the RPVs were shipped to the States seems to conflict with the date when it was known by MoD that the Pentagon had pulled out of the project. Now, this man Lescombe may have had time to make arrangements. I have to be certain that those RPVs didn't fall into the wrong hands—absolutely certain!"

"Of course, of course . . ." Aubrey watched Melstead break his bread roll. Crumbs scattered as his fingers gouged; crust flew. He gripped the bread tighter and tighter in his fingers, as if remaking it into its constituent dough.

My fellow Americans . . . Harrell heard the words, despite the turned-down volume of the TV set, and grinned. He nodded in what might have been mocking acknowledgment at the image of John Calvin at a hundred-dollar-a-plate breakfast rally in Atlanta. The speech had been well received. The president had climbed two points in the polls immediately after it had been broadcast live.

Harrell sat at the dining table in the hotel suite's sitting room and spread butter thickly on a slice of toast. Calvin looked confident as he addressed the gathering from behind a floral-like arrangement of microphones. The glare of flashbulbs exposed no nervousness. The eyes were hardly tired, certainly not wary. His features seemed agreeably framed by the huge image of the presidential shield behind him. Danielle, the first lady, glittered and smiled. As a camera closed on her, Harrell realized it was her eyes that showed the strain. Calvin was still six percentage points behind his rival and Election Day was less than two weeks away.

Harrell chewed on the toast. *The achievements of this administration over the past four years . . .* Harrell snorted with laughter and felt crumbs tickle the back of his nose. He sneezed, still amused. There was a tinge of anger, too, at Calvin—Mister Clean, Captain Fantastic. *We can begin to look forward . . .*

"Only because things are looking so much neater over there," Harrell murmured, then sipped his coffee. "So much more stable, Mr. President. You really ought to *know* what we've been doing for you, Mr. President!"

The mockery stilled and he grimaced at himself as much as at the screen. The enjoyment of secret power was inessential; public acknowledgment was—stupid to even think of it. Whether Calvin or the other guy was the next incumbent of the White House didn't matter as much as the way the Soviets and especially the Moslem republics were now going, compared to the way they were only a couple of months ago!

He watched light glint from jewelry, and stared at the overfrocked women and the sleek men as his lips distorted into contempt. Not for the seal behind Calvin, not even for the man himself . . . just for the indifference, the complacency! These people would turn on him in a kind of outrage if they knew what he'd done, just in case there was ever a problem, a demand for recompense that might upset their pet poodles! Like they made a hero of Ollie North one minute then put him on trial the next! There were two senators, who'd been on the Irangate hearings, sitting behind the white-clothed, altarlike table with Calvin and his wife.

The throwing up of hands, that's what made him sick. The outrage, the morality. Neither Calvin nor anyone else could take a deep bite out of the defense budget or bring troops home from Germany or fund the welfare schemes or balance the budget deficit unless things settled down in the Warsaw Pact and in the Asian republics . . . especially there, for Christ's sake. The whole shooting match was going to hell in a hurry, and Irena Nikitina would have given them their independence, just handing the whole of Soviet Asia over to the mullahs and Iranian influence.

Dear-sweet-Jesus, the woman would have left Moscow presiding over the rump of European Russia, without the Baltic republics or the Ukraine or Georgia— come on, roll up, get your independence here! She had gone ape over *glasnost* and no one knew where it was going to end, except in a long, long period of uncertainty. The Moslem thing was the last straw, though. The analyses and studies all showed that Afghanistan would erupt again, Pakistan would go over to Iran, and the ayatollahs would be running most of southern Asia in ten years!

And that couldn't be allowed to happen. So, they'd gambled on their assessment of Nikitin's character, that he was some kind of closet conservative drunk on *glasnost* and only needed sobering up to see the right way to go about things . . . slow down, a little at a time, keep the Soviet Union together. Chevrikov and Lidichev could, the analysis claimed, control him once there was no Irena.

It was lucky there had been a simple solution to a complex problem. He smiled, his good humor restored. And another thing was the billions of dollars it would have cost supporting all those new, independent countries growing in Europe like a crop of mushrooms and all with their begging bowls held in America's direction! God bless the simple answer.

Now we can begin to do the things our country really needs . . .

"You tell 'em, Mr. President—and it sure is better you don't know what really happened." He raised his glass of orange juice in the gesture of a toast towards the screen. Smiling.

The aim is not to be found out. Doing an Ollie was OK, it was the patriotic thing to do. The dumb thing was to get caught doing it and give the men on Capitol Hill a chance to beat their chests and show the cleanliness of their linen compared to yours!

OK . . . There were two little threads that had come away from the weave—the girl and Hyde. Once they were sewn back in, the garment would look perfect, and new, just as with any good job of invisible mending.

"Today," Harrell announced as violent, tinny applause followed the end of the president's speech. Calvin was raising his hands now, and waving—certainly not in surrender. Danielle was beaming as only she and a few Hollywood stars ever could. Harrell reached for the telephone. "Today it is." Because, he added silently, I am not going to be nailed to a cross on Capitol Hill because of a crazy woman and a burned-out field agent!

"I'm supposed to be using the toilet! Of course he's still here, we're having lunch—! What? No, not that... but the inquiries Kenneth is making seem to point to the RPV project... what? Yes, from this man Lescombe or whatever his name is, the one they arrested as a spy. Yes, yes... Look, Paulus, I can't spend time talking to you now, I simply thought you should know. I'm certain it can be contained, though all he will claim is a pressing interest in the Lescombe affair, nothing more... I see. I—I'm not interested in any—no, I'm not quite accustomed to behaving like this! And you're quite right, I don't much like it... What? No, I have no wish to know what you might intend. Yes, you must act on the information as you see fit, of course... Accessory? To what? Yes, I know my complicity, thank you. It looks at me from my shaving mirror each morning... I must go. Goodbye, Paulus—"

"It is your responsibility to make your brilliant new scheme *work*, Comrade General Priabin. Not this other matter. Do you understand me?"

"Yes, Comrade Deputy Chairman—but I think it's wrong. Malan is only looking after his own skin—making *us* look after it for him! We shouldn't show our hand—not now."

"Priabin, you're lucky your skin's still intact after the screwup in Stockholm—and the arrest of this man Lescombe. You *know* how much he could tell Aubrey, about us and the whole smuggling operation."

Dzerzhinsky Square was slaty, gleaming in cold rain behind the old man's head. His saturnine, heavy, peasant's features were in shadow, but his hands, under the glow of a desk lamp, were curled and knotted.

"I don't think, with respect, Comrade Deputy Chairman, that the danger of Lescombe giving Aubrey everything he knows warrants drawing attention to our *concern.*"

"Malan doesn't underestimate Aubrey, perhaps you do? He wants Lescombe tidied up—and I agree with him. I have transmitted the order that he be taken care of. Is that clear?"

"I—"

"Is that clear?"

"Yes, Comrade Deputy Chairman. It's clear."

The old man got heavily to his feet and moved from behind his desk, hand extended.

"Then it only remains for me to wish you a pleasant flight, and good luck with your amazing operation. A drink? You'll have enough confidence in it to toast its success, General—won't you?"

The old man's laugh rasped like a file.

"Yes, yes of course—!"

The telephone in Aubrey's flat continued to ring, the sound insistent, even shrill. The small, matchlike glow of light into which Hyde hunched illuminated his watch. Eight hours away, it was lunchtime in London and the idea exasperated him. He glanced away from his watch.

A moth spun out of the little pool of light like a flake of skin. He had spent almost two hours ensuring that the houseboat, jumbled blackly with dozens of others against the stars, was free of surveillance. The cars were empty, the windows dead, curtains still. There were no lenses, no microphones, no men. The occasional car or truck had passed, engines fading and not suddenly stopping. The woman was a quarter of a mile away, where the rental car was parked in a sloping side street.

His nerves twitched, sated with negative information. Come on... Out to bloody lunch! Come on...

Aubrey's housekeeper was out, Aubrey was out. He could not try the Cabinet Office, would not try Shelley or anyone else. Couldn't. Only Aubrey's home number was secure for him. The skin-flake of the small, pale moth tapped against the booth's light, knocking out the passing seconds. Shivery in the warm, still-dark morning, he felt angry that his surmounted contempt for Aubrey and paranoid mistrust was answered only by the ringing of the telephone in an empty flat. Aubrey should have been there! Now that the woman's usefulness was at an end, Aubrey must take her off his hands before her collapse became dangerous to him. The phone continued to ring unanswered. Getting rid of the woman would give him some leeway if he needed to disappear, to go to ground. She had run out of steam and was as worn as a recent image of himself.

That image he'd lost in the parking lot when he'd been unable to shrug the woman aside and leave her. He'd somehow passed his defeated, exhausted self to her. It had happened to her quietly, during the drive from downtown San Francisco and the numerous returns he had made to the car as he scoured for a surveillance trap. Uncontrollable tears and shivering. He had measured her decline almost clinically.

The telephone continued ringing and an inordinate anger welled up in him, demonstrating that his old skills and the state of his nerves were only feigned, only acted. He could play the part of his former self quite competently, but only for brief periods and at great cost; a single speech here and there, perhaps a short scene, but never the whole play. He replaced the receiver with an effort of restraint and slouched away from the booth into the darkness between two glowing street lamps. Along the wharf, the black houseboats were like tiny slag heaps. He had to move *now*, ingress and egress, before his nerves frayed and the last adrenaline dribbled away.

He glanced back along the empty wharf, listening to the distant hum of a car fading, then climbed the side street's slope towards the car. Even in dim silhouette, her figure seemed slumped in the passenger seat. He hesitated before opening the door. Her startled face was white as her head turned in violent fear, her relaxation like defeat as she recognized him.

"It's time," he said.

"What?"

"Time to go."

"What did he say?"

"No reply. He wasn't there."

"Can't we get hold of him?" she whispered.

Speaking to her seemed unnecessarily complicated, as if he struggled with a foreign language. His one hand clenched the door handle, the other closed in his pocket; the small of his back irritated by the gun and his shoulders shivery with vulnerability.

"Today. I promise—" He forced himself to remain calm with her. "—as soon as I speak to him he'll do something. He'll accept my assessment." His anger and disappointment clutched his detached, clinical vocabulary.

"I don't want to go there," she pouted.

"I need your help." Even to him, the statement sounded threatening. "You know the place."

"That's why I can't go there!" She held up her hands like white minstrel's gloves in the darkened car, her eyes wide, brilliant. "Can't you understand the state I'm in? I can't help it, for Christ's sake!" She folded her arms, clutching her hands beneath them. There was a kind of—what was it?—dread about her that scraped at his nerves. He felt a bout of tiredness fall like a heavy blanket across his head and shoulders. He bent into the car.

"Look, I'm buggered too, just like you. It's taken too long to check the place out because I find it hard to function like Action Man any more. So, I want your help for an hour, at most. Now, get out of the bloody car!"

She appeared on the point of defiance for a moment, then opened her door and climbed heavily out of the passenger seat, sniffing loudly, repeatedly. The noise irritated. Through compressed lips, he murmured: "It's just an hour. Harrell's people aren't here. There aren't any ghosts, either."

"Aren't there? How would you know?"

"Look, after this, I'll make sure they get you out. Aubrey will do it, if I insist." He pressed the air down with his hands. "OK?" She was shivering again, arms hugged against her breasts, her tall, thin form hunched as if she were on the brink of nausea. She seemed to be struggling to translate his words into something she could understand. "If there's anything in your father's—" Indrawn breath, as if hurt. "—houseboat, or if there isn't, I'll get you out of here, to London. Somewhere you'll be safe." Exasperation surfaced. "Look, I can't say any more than that, for God's sake!"

She looked at him then, but only as if he had slapped her across the cheek. She blamed him, in the absence of others, for her predicament; hated being there, hated his insistence. She was like him in Tadzhikistan, broken as easily as he had been when his Walkman had been damaged and he had thrown it into the ravine. Why in *hell* had Aubrey thought he could use her as an agent?

"We're running out of time." He took her resisting arm and pushed her alongside him, ignoring the pleading expression on her face, the silent working of her lips. Their footsteps padded and shuffled along the quiet street. A radio or hi-fi played mutedly somewhere, heightening his nerves.

They'd already driven along the wharf, not so slowly as to draw attention to themselves, so that she could point out her father's houseboat. He paused, aware only of the wooden pier leading to it, the sense of old wood and its voices, the little cries of alarm their passage would arouse. He breathed deeply, three times, then released the woman's arm and touched the gun in the small of his back, clicking off the safety catch before stepping onto the planking of the short pier. The one-story houseboat sat squatly as if waiting for the first sound. A plank creaked. The tide slopped quietly beneath the pier. The smell of stale food and seaweed wafted on a fragment of breeze.

"Come on." Her first step was silent, the second awakened a plank. Her shivering was audible, rubbing against his nerves like sandpaper. He held his hand behind him as if awaiting a relay baton and her long, cold fingers gripped his, her nails biting. The gun was unconsciously in his other hand.

Beaded strings of lights, the glow of the city. The

Golden Gate Bridge floating above the predawn gray of fog across the Bay, its rows of lights like the superstructure of a great ship. He released her hand as they paused in darker shadow, the houseboat's wooden wall rough under his palm and against his cheek. Random patterns of lights in the high buildings in the center of San Francisco. The wharf was empty of traffic. He pulled at her hand and heard the rattle of keys and her harsh, quickened breathing.

He watched the short pier and the wharf beyond it, the long stretch of street lamps, the occasional light already showing in second-floor windows, the whitening façades of jumbled, untidy houses. A car moved along the wharf and he grabbed at her hand, silencing her. Its headlights were sinister as they trawled the sidewalk, then moved on and away, closing like the eyes of a cat as the car turned a corner.

"OK, hurry."

She turned the locks and opened the door. Emptiness was a distinct scent in the air for a moment. She hesitated but he pushed her forward then followed, closing the door behind him. It creaked like seaweed pressed between finger and thumb, as if pained. Her breathing was harsh, the only sound until he became aware of the sough of the tide beneath the floorboards; it disconcerted, that lack of solidity beneath his feet, the sense of water. As his eyes grew accustomed to the intenser darkness, he recognized the lumpish outline of a piano, near which something dully glinted. A rug slipped treacherously beneath his shoe and he stepped back as if from a snake. The night became square, lighter patches. It would be quicker to use the lights, but too dangerous. Stepping carefully, he dragged the curtains across and flicked on a small flashlight. The shadows sprang out cloudily from the furniture, the rug's colors glowed. The woman was staring at the polished floorboards as if seeing something prone there.

"Is there a safe?" She merely shook her head, blinking in the flashlight's gleam, her face pasty and tragic as a clown's. "Then where?" he snapped. His flashlight slid over a clock on the wall, its short pendulum still, the hands on its large old face frozen at the wrong time. Its not working plucked at his nerves. "*Where?*" he snarled.

She shrugged, bewildered as if in a strange place.

"I don't know." Her voice was phlegmy, thick. "He never—hid anything before."

Hyde crossed the room, barking his shin against an old, sagging chair, and entered the—bedroom, yes. He drew the curtains and switched on his flashlight, wiping its beam across a wardrobe, the large bed, a chest and cupboards. Record sleeves and sheet music lay scattered, as if the place had been burgled, but he sensed that the untidiness was habitual and not recent. An overturned running shoe without its partner in one corner, the stubs still in a metal ashtray bearing the legend KEYSTONE KORNER. Photographs of a dozen jazz musicians—among the most easily recognizable in the last thirty years—framed on the walls. He sensed the woman behind him, shrunken and younger. The skin between his shoulder blades crawled in response to her dread and guilt and desperation. He brushed his hand as at a worrying insect, flapping her presence away.

Drawers, one by one. A photograph of Kathryn Aubrey—there had been a larger, prouder one on one wall in the living room—perhaps the woman's mother. Underwear and shirts, a cocaine spoon? A cigarette-rolling outfit and...yes, taped to the back of the bottom drawer, the small packet of marijuana. He left it in place. The shoes and a single suit, a few pairs of trousers in the wardrobe, a broken guitar. All the time he was

searching, the woman watched the room from the doorway, perhaps hardly aware of him except when he addressed short, angry questions. Money tucked beneath
extra pillows on the wardrobe's shelf. Sheet music, bills,
royalty statements bearing the names of songs that had
become minor jazz standards.

Nothing but fluff beneath the bed and the rug. The
scrape of his nails on the floorboards as he pulled them
aside. Time slipping... fifteen minutes and the bedroom
not finished.

Eventually—

—bathroom. Heart pills, toothpaste, aftershave. A
denture box reminding him of the man's age. The girl
again watching from the doorway, now shivering and
sniffing. Snail tracks gleaming on her cheeks as he suddenly turned the flashlight on her face.

In the living room, the curtains were stained by the
beginning of the dawn. Perspiration sprang out along
his hairline and he wiped at it, cursing. She flinched at
the noise from the corner of the living room where she
had retreated. That angered him, too. He dragged back
the rug and she made as if to protest. Instead, he heard
her teeth chattering and the rub of her hands up and
down her arms, massaging out cold. Nothing. Uneven
floorboards. Piano lid, furniture, drinks cabinet, book-
shelves, a chest of drawers. Mostly envelopes of developed photographs. The curtains lightened perceptibly.
Fifty minutes—

—kitchen. The noise of pans, cutlery, tins and jars.
Nothing. He was hotter now, his hands quivering when
not gripping something, his legs aching and weak as he
repeatedly rose and kneeled. He felt himself running
down like a spring.

Seventy minutes. Nothing. He returned to the living
room, enraged and shaking.

"Where, for Christ's sake—*where?*" She had begun shaking her head even before he spoke. He gripped her upper arms and shook her. Her eyes were filmy with pain and shock. "Where, for Christ's sake, where?"

When he let her go, she slumped against a tall dresser, the saxophone hanging beside her head. She was still shaking her head, not looking at him. He had frightened and beaten a dumb animal; completed her collapse. Shit—

He stumbled on the uneven floorboards as he moved towards her and she cowered feebly against the dresser. Plates rattled softly, threatening to fall. The light from the curtains, her haunted face crumpled like a dirty handkerchief, his own face flickering on and off like a decaying reel of film in his imagination, the floorboards—

He knelt down, touching their unevenness. Rough edge, polished surface, the screws—screws? No nails?—dulled with a thickness of wax polish he could scrape off with his fingernail. There was only the water beneath the floorboards, surely? The one-story building's floors were the planks of the short pier, weren't they? He smoothed at the floorboards, remembering the kitchen drawer in which he had seen a screwdriver.

He returned to the floorboards, resting the flashlight, its light dimmer either because the battery was failing or the curtains were brighter ... Unscrewed the section of floorboard—one, two, three widths, just wide enough for a body to slip through. Lifted. There were more planks beneath the wooden floorboards. But they came away together, and he could hear the susurrus of the slow tide, slopping. He shone the flashlight down on the oily-black water swilling only feet below, then ducked his head down into the cooler air. There was the dimmest of light now even under the pier. He flicked the flashlight carefully from side to side along the weather-proofed underside of the pier. A small rowing boat, moored, canvas huddled at its stern. Nothing else. He felt weak with frustration. Harrell sidled into his awareness; the clock in his head raced. *Nothing, bloody nothing!* he screamed silently, releasing his exhausted, clutching nerves.

He did not look at her in the semidarkness of the room as he sat on the edge of the opening then lowered himself through until his feet touched the edge of the boat, which bobbed away on its short painter. He dragged at it with his heel, then dropped into it, stumbling, rocking its frail, rotting wood.

He heard his own breathing above the tide's, a seashell roar; then he plucked aside the loosely tied canvas. The gleam of air tanks, a dry suit hidden like a crumpled corpse. A metal box like something a cameraman might use. He stared at it, one hand holding the knuckles of the other as they moved, grinding like pestle and mortar. The box was locked.

Gradually, his heart rate dropped and his breathing became steadier. His temperature stabilized. The fading of the adrenaline left his weariness exposed. His throat was dry. He hoisted the box and stood upright in the slop of water in the bottom of the boat, then held the box over his head. She responded to his muffled order and took the cool box, lifting it clear of the opening. He heaved himself slowly, groaningly back into the room. The tide's slurp seemed more audible now that he no longer idled on it. Taking the screwdriver, he snapped at the locks, breaking them easily. Her attention had been caught, but with a fascinated dread of inspecting the belongings of yet another dead man she had known.

Notebooks, tape cassettes, a tiny recorder, a camera,

rolls of film in their little tubes, perhaps a dozen of them, two long-range lenses, newspaper cuttings.

He looked up, grinning shakily.

"Everything," he murmured, sifting the things in the box like coins. "Everything—Christ, it has to be here, the means of stopping it . . ." His voice tailed away. He felt cold now. Reaction shivered through him. It was relief, he told himself.

He unfolded a map in a polyethylene wallet, glanced at it, then slipped it into the pocket of his jacket. Something to savor like an appetizer before the meal that lay in the box. Everything Frascati knew and suspected. Scorched fragments of metal. He remembered the wreckage in Tadzhikistan, laying beached like a decaying whale carcass on the sandbank. Remembered her, too, lying face down in the water in her expensive suit, one shoe missing, her thick hair unraveled. This was how they'd done it, here in the box. Sketches, pages of close handwriting, calculations filling dozens of sheets, an index of the film that had been exposed. Easy . . . He had it—

"Quick!" he snapped. She was staring into the box. He went into the bedroom and returned with one of her father's leather belts. He strapped the lid of the box in place, then lifted it. Her hand lay on his. Her eyes glittered strangely.

"Let me take it," she said.

"If you like." Possessiveness. She struggled slightly, then walked with a leaning gait to the door. The curtains were lighter still. He hurried after her, the dawn spilling into the room, glinting from things as she opened the door. He closed it behind him. She was already hurrying along the pier. The planking muttered and squeaked. It did not matter now, so long as they hurried. She'd tire of the weight of the box in a minute or so; she just wanted it like a talisman and keepsake. "Wait—" he murmured, checking the wharf. People now, a newspaper boy on a bicycle, a trickle of cars, the chatter of radios. Curtains still drawn across in the houseboat next door, sitting flatly on its pier.

Sound of something, like static? Voice? Scratch of an R/T button pressed to transmit or receive. His stomach lurched, his left foot causing the planking to grumble, the Browning's grip slippery in his hand. The woman had lowered the metal box. The light from the cuticle of sun coming above the hills flashed from the box like a mirror signal. He watched her rub her wrist and forearm and bend again to lift it. The cat's claw of an R/T button one more, from, from—

—next houseboat, the curtains still pulled across and dead. A tinny voice exclaiming, then the curtains were pulled aside. The sudden wail of sirens.

The woman was standing halfway along the pier, waiting. Shoulders defeated. Beyond her, Harrell . . .

. . . Harrell could not suppress the grin of pleasure as he raised the bullhorn to his mouth. The jazz club had come up empty, but the surveillance he had ordered on the father's houseboat—beautiful. They'd called him in LA the moment Hyde had been picked up patroling the wharf and the surrounding streets. There'd been no time to search the houseboat, only to commandeer the neighboring place and set up surveillance. But then, Hyde and the woman had found it all for him. The metal box gleamed silver in the sun. He raised his hand as if greeting friends. Behind him, half a dozen people.

The woman was ten yards off, no more, Hyde twenty-five. The door of the neighboring houseboat banged open. Three men, armed. Two pump-action shotguns leveled on Hyde. Harrell's lips tickled with amusement.

"OK, Hyde!" he called through the bullhorn, his voice booming among the houseboats, louder than the idling traffic they were cordoning off behind him. Drug bust, the SFPD had been told and had accepted through political connections.

It was all so easy.

"Move in on the woman," he ordered. "Slow and easy. Keep out of the firing line." Then, through the bullhorn: "Just put the gun down, Hyde. It's gotten out of your control. Move slowly, easy—"

Hyde felt the shivering return, his legs weakly rooted. The men were moving carefully towards Kathryn, but still leaving him exposed to the pump-action shotguns. There were police beyond Harrell, stopping the traffic, taking up positions along the wharf, their sirens wailing down to silence. The sun made him squint and the sweat in his eyes reduced the scene to something viewed through a bright, refracting crystal. The woman was lost. The fucking *box* was lost! The footsteps of the three who'd emerged from the neighboring houseboat were heavy and quick on the planking, only yards away now—

—fired instinctively into the stomach of the leading man who careered back against his companions, arms flung out. They held him like a sudden coronary victim, halted and surprised.

"Hyde—!" he heard Harrell roar. Hyde saw the woman's white and desperate face, her fluttering hands. The metal box and a man kneeling beside it, taking aim. The shotguns were coming to bear like heavy black sticks. "Take him *out!*"

The water struck Hyde's face and chest like something solid, impenetrable. His arm was aflame. Then he was beneath the surface, the water boiling around him, the booming of gunshots dulled. His arm hurt, and burned. The light dimmed and the weedy piles of the pier loomed out of the growing dark. His chest swelled as he struggled to thrust the gun into the safety of his waistband. His head was bursting, his arm on fire.

The light vanishing—

P A R T   T H R E E

THE GOSHAUK IN HIS POWERE

*Ther was the tyraunt with his fethres donne
And greye, I mean the goshauk, that doth pyne
To briddes for his outrageous ravyne.*

Chaucer, The Parlement of Foules

12

THE GARGOYLES ABOVE THE BUTTRESSES

It seemed that the rain dripping from the umbrella and trickling between his coat collar and his skin was the only element of calm. The police cars were idling their engines now to maintain the brightness of the ring of headlights that lit the scene. The rain slanted coldly across their glare. His gloved hand held an ignored cup of coffee as he watched the bodies of Evans and Lescombe being slid into the rear of the ambulance. They had had to remain in the wreckage of the car, crushed against the bole of a tree at the bottom of the embankment, until his arrival; a further small guilt. The noise of the car engines tightened around Aubrey's temples. There was no shred of decency, dignity either, in their being removed from the wreckage whole hours after their murder.

Murder, certainly...

The ambulance doors were shut together softly and he nodded his permission to the driver, then stepped back beside the uniformed inspector from the Hampshire Constabulary as the rear wheels churned and flung mud out of the grassy slope. The ambulance bucked at the top—the bodies were strapped to their stretchers, they could not be spilled—then slid onto the deserted country road, the sound of its engine gradually fading into the intense conversation of those congregating in or near the police cars parked around the site of the crash. Lights were being erected on tall metal poles, red-and-white tape crisscrossed the churned grass and mud. Evans's car, shortened by the impact, displayed a flank deeply injured by another vehicle before it had left the road. And there were footprints of tire-soled boots coming and going.

Murder. Professional, disguised, discreetly done, but murder. Lescombe had been silenced, though Aubrey could not reprimand himself for having Lescombe moved. Whenever he had left the house, they would have followed and killed him. It was Evans's death he regretted. Godwin's colleague. One of his own people—! No, not regret. Evans's death made him angry.

The effect of the cold rainwater soaking his collar from the inspector's awkwardly held umbrella had diminished. There was no dulling recollection of Hyde's telephone call as he drove down from London to—this. Rain washed across Evans's car and soaked Aubrey's trousers above the large, clammy green gumboots they had loaned him. Harrell had Kathryn; Hyde had managed to evade them—*no, I don't expect they think I'm dead, sorry about that...* and was now moving from public telephone to public telephone around the Bay Area, as if grotesquely teasing him rather than covering his tracks. *Soaking wet, hole in my bloody arm, mate, do you think I give a rat's . . . ?* Hyde did, of course, silently cursing himself for walking into the trap at Alan's houseboat. *All I've got's a bloody map!* The evidence—from Hyde's estimate of it—had been substantial, perhaps conclusive. Now, Harrell had all that, and Kathryn.

And they'd quieted Lescombe forever. Aubrey closed his eyes against the headlights' glare and the whitened, blowing rain and the crushed front and empty windscreen of Evans's car; but mostly against a return of the unbearable idea of Kathryn's extreme danger.

"Is there anything else, Sir Kenneth?"

"Mm?" He opened his eyes dizzily. "What? Oh, in a moment or two . . ." The inspector retreated once more into stolidity. The mackintoshed, anoraked forensic people—supervised by a Special Branch chief inspector he did not know—invested the scene, tiptoeing, measuring, photographing. "In a few moments." He dreaded returning to his car and his driver. Hyde would be calling again, soon. The shock of Evans's murder was wearing off, leaving only the acute distress of Kathryn's danger. He had blamed Hyde, in his appalled anxiety—then had apologized. But both she and the proof were lost to them!

He stumbled at the force of his guilt, then struggled up the churned slope to the wet, gleaming road. The skid marks from Evans's tires were clear in yet more headlights and flashing blue streaks from police and ambulance lights. Shattered glass and a detached hubcap, together with anonymous pieces of plastic and chrome, littered the verge and tarmac. A narrow road, in bad weather. The lurch of a heavy truck or large van had pushed Evans and Lescombe down the embankment and into the trees. The police surgeon suggested that Evans had been suffocated using a child's soft toy, from the evidence of fibers in his mouth. A large, grinning lion which had been thrown onto the rear seat afterwards.

Aubrey's chest pained him. The policeman released his supporting grip on his elbow. His car glittered, the rain splashing back from its roof and hood.

"Thank you, Inspector. I shall be here for some while. Perhaps you'd bring me any—preliminary reports?"

"Sir."

Aubrey ducked into the rear of the lengthened black Rover and his driver shut the door behind him. The windows fogged immediately and the driver and the policeman were no more than bulky shadows in the rain. He lit a cigarette and almost gagged on the smoke; nevertheless, he persisted until the tobacco calmed him. His hand was shaking, evidence of his fears. The opposition had outrun him, gone ahead and ambushed his little party, decimating their numbers and strength. He twitched with impatience and tension.

Harrell would use Kathryn, not dispose of her. Aubrey reasoned slowly and deliberately; convincing himself more easily than he had anticipated. She was a trump card, to be played, not discarded; reserved for the moment, awaiting his next move.

Next move? He snorted. Evans and Lescombe had been murdered, that door was now closed. Hyde was injured and hunted, the tensions in him wearing him out. The glowing tip of Aubrey's cigarette wobbled uncertainly. It would have been easier, though not so *productive,* to have brought Kathryn out at once. Now, the cavalier use he had made of her had rounded on him.

He was hotter now. His trousers clung damply around his knees and shins. The smell of his gumboots was faintly nauseating, and there was a wet smell of mothballs from his overcoat. They knew he would send Hyde after her—because he had no proof that would arouse anyone else's interest and solicit their assistance. They knew he and Hyde were without resources and becoming increasingly desperate.

His forehead was slick with perspiration. The cigarette was once again nauseating and he ground it out in the ashtray that clicked shut like a small trap. Patrick had had everything in his hands, just for a moment. But Harrell had outmaneuvered not only Hyde but himself.

The telephone bleeped and his heart leaped, then thudded painfully. He snatched up the receiver, to hear Hyde's breathing as heavy and ominous as his own. He, too, must have looked ahead and viewed the inevitable. Aubrey felt empty of recriminations, shockingly detached.

"Patrick?"

"Yes."

"Is there any trace of—"

"One glass slipper on the staircase, you mean?"

"Patrick—!"

"Don't play the outraged uncle, *sir*. It doesn't become you. Just the usual ruthless bastard will do to be going on with—*sir*." His whole protest was concentrated in the sarcasm of his respect. Then he added: "I don't give much for my chances, by the way."

"Where is she?" Aubrey burst out, his head throbbing. He watched his hand curl and uncurl in his lap like some small, naked, trapped animal. "I should never have involved her—"

"She *was* involved!" Hyde snapped at him. "She knew Frascati, that's all that interested them. For Christ's sake, Harrell killed Irena Nikitina! You think the murder of your niece is going to *worry* him?"

"She was a bystander, Patrick!"

Hyde was breathing heavily; the noise distinct, pessimistic.

It smelled damply of cigarette smoke inside the car. Aubrey rubbed at one of the windows, only to see the rain wriggling down and the face of his driver glancing in, to whom he nodded. The driver wandered off in the policeman's company. The hollow below the embankment glowed like a stage hidden from view.

"What do we do?" Hyde asked.

"These damned people and their damned conspiracies!"

"I know all that. It was in the recruitment brochure. You probably wrote it—no angels in the architecture, only the gargoyles. What do we *do*?"

"Where will they take her?"

"Where do you think?"

"That lake—?"

"Shasta, yes. I would. They'll know by now—or they'll soon find out—what she told me and what I know." Aubrey shivered.

"You have a map, you said?"

"Yes. It's marked, but I don't understand it. But it's where the airliner went down. She'll be there, your niece, if she's anywhere."

"Yes."

He was silent for some time, until he heard Hyde ask, impatiently: "Have you dropped off?"

"What? No . . . I was considering what can be done—at this end."

"And—?"

"I'm not sure." He glanced towards the light-filled hollow, and shook his head. It would be foolish, even dangerous, to tell Patrick about this occurrence. "I—you must locate her, Patrick. I will pursue what we already have in hand, Tony and myself. There are leads here..." Hyde's snorted contempt was audible. Desperation threw up James Melstead like a cork on a wave. It was, after all, his responsibility, the breaking of James Melstead. James knew the dates and the places and the shipments and the people and their purposes—or did he?

"It's my responsibility to trace those RPVs from the manufacturer to Harrell," he announced pompously. "Your job is to locate Harrell. You must describe that map in detail to Tony, link it to the information he has, before anything else. Marks, you said?"

"Initials, crosses—like *Treasure Island*...including the black spot for some poor sod!"

"Very well. Talk to Tony. There may be—"

"Something down there? You're hoping, aren't you?"

"Nevertheless."

"And the woman? What do I do? What's my *priority?* Harrell, proof, or your niece?"

Aubrey hesitated. "Patrick, for the moment, simply *locate* them!"

"All right. I don't have a lot of choice, anyway, do I? I have to kill Harrell, whatever bright ideas come floating along like untreated sewage. Unless *he* goes, we're all permanently in the deepest part of the shit!"

"For the moment, do *nothing!*" Aubrey warned.

"All right!" Hyde snapped back.

Instead of Hyde's image, Aubrey saw that of Melstead. "Patrick, I think I have found the necessary lever. I think I can—get hold of it—before you are forced to act. I counsel patience."

"Never much of a virtue. I have to go, there are too many people about. I'll call in about the map."

"Very well, Patrick. Be careful—"

"Master of the fucking obvious," Aubrey heard, before the continuous hum of the replaced American telephone. He put down his receiver and sank back against the seat, shivering. He had recovered responsibility for the outcome of this business and, although it unsettled him, it nevertheless interposed its bulk between himself and his greatest anxiety, Kathryn's safety. The answer lay here, with Melstead and Malan.

He lit another cigarette and listened to the rain on the roof of the car. Yes, he would break Melstead. Dear James, his old friend, would tell him everything, eventually. The matter was horribly urgent, because of Kathryn—but there was enough time, just enough...

Breakfast at the Savoy. There was a residue of surprise and pleasure, as if it was he who had spent the night in the suite's adjoining bedroom with the girl who was now crooning audibly as she ran the shower. Breakfast in a suite overlooking the river at the Savoy hotel. Priabin almost felt a silly, childish grin as he buttered another narrow slice of toast.

Until he remembered his anger with Malan, and scowled as if he sat opposite a stern parent who was leafing through his school report rather than the digest of his scenario for the new smuggling pipeline. His anger became petulant as he noticed marmalade smeared at the edge of one of the pages scattered around Malan's empty plate, where grease was solidifying alongside the bacon rind. To mask his expression, Priabin sipped at his coffee. Malan had used the KGB to kill Lescombe— in doing so, he'd had one of Aubrey's team killed, too— Evans! If Malan underestimated Aubrey, assumed his emotional reactions were desiccated with age and authority, then *he* did not. Aubrey would be like a hive stirred to anger by a stick because Evans had been murdered. And he was sitting there, opposite the South African, summoned like a schoolboy!

He ground his teeth and shook his head, his hands in his lap as if they had been caned. Malan flicked off his reading glasses and stared at him. Boats moved slowly on the oily Thames behind Malan's broad face, beyond the tall windows. The suite's sitting room was heavy with period furniture and long drapes, ornate with plasterwork and gilt. Like some room in the Kremlin, for God's sake—!

"Something on your mind?" Malan asked.

"You," Priabin jeered. Malan smiled.

"Because I went over your head? Because your superiors trust my judgment?"

"Why the hell my service does your bidding I simply don't understand!" Priabin burst out. He felt inflated by frustration and injured self-esteem; felt, too, that rather despicable sense of safety in the knowledge that Malan would never use the quarrel against him with the Center. Like shouting obscenities when the bully is long around the corner and out of earshot! But he *had* to get it off his chest. "I should have been consulted. You used my people, damn it!"

Malan shrugged. Leaning forward heavily, he said: "I'm sorry your corns have been trodden on, man. The thing had to be done quickly if it was to have the right effect. *You* were in Moscow—saving your bacon after that fiasco in Stockholm...which, all right, may not have been your fault—" He held up a placatory hand. "Look, we have to work together, man. This scheme of yours—" He gestured with his broad palm at the scattered sheets around his greasy plate. "Your ideas are interesting. Now, do you want to talk about it, or cry over spilled milk?"

The man's arrogance was unbelievable! And yet, it

possessed a tanklike, armored authority. He used it almost unconsciously.

"Well? There's a lot more to discuss before I show this to anyone in Pretoria."

Priabin snorted and Malan's eyes flinched into a moment of amusement, then settled to their habitual supremacy once more.

"Don't fuck about with my people again," Priabin snapped sulkily.

"Only if your deputy chairman agrees."

"It was still a bad move to kill one of Aubrey's people," Priabin persisted, his hands on his thighs, his forehead heated and prickly. Malan sat back against his chair, threatening it with his bulk, his terrycloth bathrobe revealing blond hair on his chest and the slow regularity of his breathing. "Lescombe could have been taken care of at any time—even if he'd talked, there was little that would have helped Aubrey, considering what he knows already. It was a bad move."

"So you said, man. *Now* have you finished? Aubrey isn't important—you're too impressed by his old cups and trophies, man. I'd heard you hadn't the stomach for it—" Again, the smiling moment in the eyes, though the lips remained unflexed.

"Look—!" Priabin snapped, banging his fist on the table. The cutlery rattled, and the tiny silver pepper pot toppled like a taken chessman. "My new plan doesn't need Aubrey's vengeful curiosity to contend with, especially not during its initial operation! If for no other reason—and I can't imagine that mere efficiency or protocol would persuade you for a moment—the need for secrecy and low profiles should have influenced you and the deputy chairman." He sat back, breathing athletically, satisfied at the flicker of anger in Malan's eyes and the two spots of pink on his cheekbones.

"Very well," Malan murmured after a long silence. "Very well, man, I apologize. I'm just an ignorant Boer, I wouldn't know about these subtler things—would I? And now, can we get on with what you're here to talk to me about?"

Priabin stifled a sense of resentment at the dismissive, insulting tone of Malan's voice, and said: "What else do you need to know?" To avoid the inspection of Malan's gaze, he buttered another slice of toast.

"What backing do you have for this? It's flashy, clever—"

"You mean," Priabin muttered, chewing on the toast, "it looks too cavalier for the Center to be in favor of it?"

"Just that."

"They are."

Malan shrugged. "It's ingenious. But then, man, you have a reputation for that, eh? It's got your thumbprint all over it. If it works, you'll get all the credit."

Priabin managed to ignore the remark.

"If I put this to Pretoria, and to—other people, then they'll want something in return. Am I to negotiate with you?"

Priabin nodded. "You are. I would have thought you'd be getting a great deal out of it already."

"Look, I'm on my way to Bombay today. That means diamonds. Your people have been dumping diamonds on the Indian market. We in South Africa—" *Effrica*, he pronounced it, and it grated on Priabin's ear. "—will get the blame for what your people are doing. The volume of diamonds illegally passing through the Indian market is being noticed, and they think it's us—when all the time it's greedy bastards in Moscow raising hard cash and disposing of a surplus. It has to stop. Our arrangement was working well. We have to go back to the original quotas for every market outside Europe, or the whole bloody thing will be ruined. I'm going on to Moscow after Bombay, and I expect good news by the time I get there."

Eventually, Priabin concurred: "I think that can be agreed. What else?"

"The share of the profits has been calculated quite cleverly—by you?" Priabin nodded. "It may interest Pretoria, but not me. And you have to deal through me."

"It's not written in stone."

"Good."

Priabin glimpsed the girl through the gap in the bedroom door.

"Anything else?"

"The route you propose isn't officially open to us at the moment. But you know that. That's my job, to open it up, while you take care of the routes from America and Europe through Britain and France—OK. The pipeline through Africa and on to Moscow is more difficult now the Cubans have withdrawn." He looked up, rubbing his chin. "I'm negotiating for a share of everything, large and small, however advanced. OK?"

"You know I can't agree to anything like that, so why ask me? Take it up with Moscow."

"Just to needle you, man. Unsettle some of that bloody cleverness. You irritate me."

Malan hardly acknowledged the girl's departure as she passed through the sitting room, handbag over her shoulder, long fair hair swinging as if she had sprung from some soft-focused television ad. He smiled, however, at Priabin's evident interest as the girl closed the door behind her. Then he stretched with irritating luxuriousness. "I doubt if Moscow will agree."

"I don't. Your plan's too clever and too good to waste. I'll tell Chevrikov that—will that suit you?"

"I know who's buttering my bread, Malan. Does that suit *you?*"

"Fine. We both know where we are."

"We do."

Priabin resented the polite, hard little game they were engaged in playing. He *did* know who his new masters were. Irena was dead and Nikitin, as might have been foreseen, was coming out of the closet as a conservative. *Gradualism* was the new buzzword. He remembered Didenko's sallow, dejected face on the embankment. He'd fallen. Nikitin's two radical angels had been knocked off his shoulders and no longer whispered in his ears, tempting him towards *perestroika* and *glasnost.* Instead, Lidichev and Chevrikov and the other members of the old Pretorian Guard were back at their posts, surrounding the emperor. For people like himself, it had all seemed real for a moment, like the Kennedy administration must have seemed to Americans, all that time ago—*a brief shining moment,* or whatever it was they had called it. Gone, now.

"Something the matter?" Malan asked.

"What? Oh, no . . . nothing wrong. I'll leave you your copy of the outline."

"Just one thing before you go. We need to get back inside Reid Electronics as soon as—"

"Well, you and the deputy chairman might just have made that impossible for the moment!"

"We have to be back in. The company's just bought Inmost, and that means wafer scale technology and transputers."

"I know that," Priabin said.

"Then do something about it, man. Your people and mine will want everything they can get out of Reid now. They'll start pressing you soon, so why not anticipate them? I'll persuade Pretoria, I'll cover you with glory in

Moscow—just get someone back inside Reid, to replace Lescombe."

"I'll see what I can do."

Malan watched Priabin reach the door, hesitate but then apparently decide against any parting comment. The door closed behind him. He snorted and shook his head as if the Russian had left something irritatingly lodged in his hair. Then he looked down at the type-written sheets on the table and could not forbear to smile. It was, indeed, a good plan. Though that Russian boy-general *did* irritate him, with his almost-Western, liberal contempt for Malan's country and its politics. He shrugged and rubbed at his hair, feeling momentarily hot inside the bathrobe. Priabin would do as he was told, from now on. He smiled again as he turned to the window. It amused him to think that Priabin knew noth-ing of the reality of Irena Nikitina's death.

On the oily-gray Thames, a neat blue-and-white launch slipped across the window of the sitting room. A man in evening dress stood holding what must be a bottle aloft, tippling from it at the stern while a girl in a crumpled, satiny party frock slumped against the cabin, legs spread and stretched. A third figure, wearing a white dinner jacket, leaned well out over the rail, ob-viously throwing up. Malan's lips curled in contempt. Christ, this bloody country! He rose from his chair and sat heavily on the sofa, dragging the telephone onto his lap. There were small matters to be taken care of—things the KGB wouldn't do for him now that Priabin was back, firmly ensconced as Rezident.

He waited after dialing, then: "Blantyre? Is that bug placed in the woman's flat?" Doing Harrell's job for him, too!

"Yes." The voice sounded offended.

"Good. I'm not really interested in Hyde or Aubrey.

I just want to ensure that we tidy up properly, for *our* sakes, no one else's. Melstead is the only person who can point in our direction. You understand me?"

"And if Melstead—?"

"For the moment, just keep me informed. Do nothing. Harrell was a bloody fool, to have taken Aubrey's niece. If you'd done it, Blantyre . . . still, man, you wouldn't have, uh?"

"I'd have made sure I killed Hyde."

"That's Harrell's problem. Send my ticket for Bombay round to the hotel before eleven."

"Sure."

"OK, you know where you can reach me."

He put down the telephone, his complaisant mood restored. The drunk with the champagne bottle was weaving along the launch's rail, evidently shouting; a despicable caricature. He recognized the unimportance of the events developing around Aubrey. It was unlikely he would see his niece again, at least not alive. Harrell was not a subtle man. Her fate hardly concerned Malan; she was already in the past like the girl who had left earlier, and less responsive in bed. Kathryn was good at parties, and with business acquaintances—but more like a wife than . . .

He dismissed Kathryn Aubrey as the launch slipped out of view. A board meeting at eleven-thirty, a working lunch with bankers, then the flight to Bombay. He stretched his legs and threaded his fingers at the back of his neck. It was Aubrey's little drama now, no longer his, and already as unimportant as the vanished launch with the drunken Yuppies aboard. For himself it would be easier to deal with Lidichev and the conservatives in the Kremlin. Irena Nikitina had, like Priabin, despised him and his country. Eventually, she might even have reneged on the diamond and gold arrangements between

Pretoria and Moscow. His trip to Bombay was essential because the grasping, stupid bastards had begun dumping uncut diamonds onto the Indian market. He clicked his tongue, then settled himself comfortably once more. It could be taken care of. They'd keep the diamond business in check for the sake of getting their hands on transputer and wafer scale integration technology. Moscow would drool in anticipation.

He laughed aloud. He was on the board of Reid Electronics, but for this new technology he'd have to steal and smuggle the stuff! Still, it was vastly more amusing that way.

His eyes glared open and his hand grabbed instinctively beneath the soiled pillow for the pistol. Traffic noises, the blare of a radio through a thin wall, the Meccano-like structure of the Bay Bridge through the tired slats of the blind. The noise of a quarrel above the traffic and the radio. His heart calmed and he remained staring at the crazed plaster of the ceiling and the unshaded bulb. A door banged, someone grumbled and spat, a woman's voice ranted wearily; a child cried. Black and Hispanic voices. Hyde had fallen asleep with the soft, mounting quiver of a cheap headboard against the wall behind him.

He released the pistol's grip and sat up. The bottle on the unvarnished dresser, reflected in the liver-spotted mirror, was still half-full of bourbon. It was some kind of achievement.

He must have slept for—eight-thirty by his watch—almost nine hours. Cautiously, he studied his hands, feet, sensed the rest of his body, and yawned. His arm throbbed dully. The room's sordidness hardly intruded. He pulled on his heavy suede shoes and tied the laces without feeling his head lurch. His stomach was merely hungry. A woman shouted in Spanish in the hallway, cursing a man's retreating shamble. The child had stopped crying. He tugged the gun from beneath the pillow and slipped it into his waistband at the small of his back. It settled familiarly.

He crossed the narrow room and switched on the battered television. The picture of President Calvin, re-campaigning on the morning news show, rolled then calmed. He turned up the sound and sat at the scratched table, unfolding the map carefully, his hands quivering with what he regarded as no more than anticipation. Calvin was behind in the polls and promising earnestly, somewhere in the Midwest. The room smelled of the one joint he had allowed himself. He sniffed, his fore-finger tracing and touching distances and locations on the US Forest Service map of Lake Shasta. It was crossed and scored by lines, circles, dotted tracks, lettering. Calvin's voice disappeared from the TV behind him and the anchorman's breeziness was immediately unreal. Eastern European rumbles like the noises of a distant and un-regarded storm, then Soviet Central Asia—he glanced around at the television set, which displayed another map, with an expert standing before it, pointing like a schoolmaster at a blackboard. Rioting in Tadzhikistan, troops again called out, more arrests, more bombings. *A firmer line is being taken by the Soviet authorities . . .* Politburo changes in Moscow, old-guard Communists reentering the arena. Hyde thought only momentarily of Tadzhikistan and Afghanistan, then returned to Fras-cati's map. It had begun here, at Lake Shasta. The CIA had shot down a civilian airliner to test the RPV they would lend the Russians to use on Irena Nikitina. It had crashed . . . yes, there. CS had to mean crash site, a shaded area presumably showing the extent of the wreckage. Red shading spilled down the slope of Horse

Mountain, between the McCloud River and Squaw Creek arms of the vast man-made lake. He rubbed his hand through his tightly curled hair, then down his stubbled, dry cheek. There were more marks on the McCloud River Arm, on the shore, too.

There was something about the landscape, even on the map, that struck like a shadow at the corner of his eye. Momentarily, he saw Irena's hair choking her as he turned her face out of the water. He shook his head. The initials *CT* marked with a cross in the McCloud River Arm, something sunken or hidden more than a hundred feet down. A dotted track weaving from the lake to the crash site, another cross without initials perhaps two miles from the wreckage. He stared, but his mind remained empty. They'd killed Frascati for this— along with his dry suit and the other stuff. CT, then, was something he'd looked for and probably found.

Hyde remembered, with the clarity of an envious lover, the little tubes of film, the sketches, the notebooks, all Frascati's evidence...now in Harrell's hands. He clenched his fists on the map as if holding an imagined knife and fork, brutally demanding to be fed. Harrell had the woman, but she was almost *unimportant* beside the evidence he'd recovered!

Hyde sat bolt upright, as if injected with a stimulant. The chair squeaked on the floor's cracked and scored linoleum. Through the drunken slats of the blind, the Bay Bridge lumbered up out of the curls of morning fog. He glared at the map. Hostile territory, enemy position. Harrell—the cross marked and ringed on the eastern shore of the McCloud Arm; no camping site, no marina, no scenic or picnicking spot, no hiking trail leading to it. Frascati had found something there—ringed twice, scored deep into the paper on which the map was printed. He turned the map over. Again, the double ring was much more heavily marked than any other spot, a mark made in anger or excitement. Frascati believed he had found the place they had used, their base camp on the climb to Irena Nikitina's death.

There had been other maps in Frascati's box, perhaps marked like this one. The markings might be even more clearly labeled. Harrell would be there, just waiting, knowing Hyde would not give up or be allowed to give up.

Then he shivered at the cry of a woman, the heavy slap of a hand, the curse of a man. His arm burned as he absently touched it. He took his fingers away from the heavy bandage, grubby from the previous day. Looked at the crumpled, stained denims and jacket he was wearing, the water marks. Remembered diving from the houseboat's jetty, the sensation of pain in his arm, the momentary blackness and the swelling, tearing pain in his chest—until he surfaced beneath a rotting pier . . . swimming from boat to boat along the harbor, breaking into a deserted houseboat. He'd dried and fed himself, having bandaged the bleeding slash across his upper arm. He left only when the police activity had droned away, had become no more than men in dry suits searching the bottom of the Bay.

The arm would hold up. His jacket pocket was bulky with more bandaging. He turned to look at the television to confirm what he had absorbed, that neither he nor Kathryn Aubrey had been mentioned. Harrell's doing. No reference to the incident in Sausalito. The woman protested next door, the man—her pimp, presumably—demanded more money, applied easy, casual brutality.

He got up, touching at the gun, then went out into the bare, grim hallway, his shoes scuffing on the floorboards. The smell of coffee, the murmur of a child, radios and televisions like a slowly gathering crowd. He went down the stairs to the lobby, passed the grubby-shirted porter and smelled gasoline in the warming air outside. Used the telephone charge card Mallory had given him, forcing it into the slot at the first booth; dialed Aubrey's Center Point number. He watched the busy street. Five in the afternoon in London. Doorways and the mirroring windows of crumbling shops and eateries and arcades. The sun glinting on car windscreens. No one looking for him.

"Put him on," he said, hearing Godwin's voice. "And I want everything on Lake Shasta—yes, the crash site, all you know." His temperature began to exceed that of the warming November morning. Windows, windscreens, parked cars, pedestrians, loungers especially. Nothing.

"I'll get it together," Godwin replied with a kind of satisfaction. "Here's Sir Kenneth—"

"Patrick?"

"Who else? What have you got?"

"I've been tied up in a JIC meeting for most of the morning—"

"Don't bugger about with the daily grind, *sir*."

"Patrick, have you located Kathryn? I—she is alive, isn't she?"

"What? Yes, she's alive. Harrell knows I'm coming. She'll be waved like a flag to draw me in. Now, I need information from Godwin. Put him on. I'll keep in touch by telephone. Have this number manned, twenty-four hours every day. Since there's no backup," he added sarcastically. "Sorry about the family name not drawing the attention and all that, but it's me he wants."

"Very well." Aubrey's voice had become small and pinched. Hyde shrugged. Cars, windows, doorways, a blue-and-white patrol car slipping past without hesitation, occupants' heads unturned towards him. "Patrick, I'm sorry that I can't organize—"

"It's a dead-end situation. I wouldn't normally have backup at this stage, would I? Now put Godwin on."

"Yes, Patrick."

Hyde fumbled the map from his breast pocket, flapping it open. He turned it in his hands, crumpling it, staring at the marks, the arms of the lake stretching out like the fingers of some huge, half-amputated hand.

"The map I salvaged, right. Forestry Service, Lake Shasta—you've got one?"

"Yes. Had to nip around to Grosvenor Square—tourist cover, of—"

"For Christ's sake, stop pissing about, Godwin! Either you've got it or you haven't."

"All right, I've got the map."

A man casually approached the telephone booth as Hyde leaned beneath its clear Perspex ceiling. Newspaper beneath his arm. Middle-aged, wearing a coat. Hyde watched as the man drifted past, then scanned the street, relaxing. Nothing. Patrol car returning. He waited. Nothing.

He looked down at the map. "Right. There are a lot of marks on Frascati's copy—want to make notes, dear?"

"Yes, Mr. Hyde."

Hyde was almost frightened, for a moment, at the comfort he derived from what was no more than banter.

"There are the initials C-for-Charlie, S-for-Sugar near Horse Mountain—is that the crash site?"

"Mm . . . ? Yes, that's right." The map crackled open, six thousand miles away. Papers rustled in the background. "OK, what's next?"

The man in the coat was drifting back, now more

attentive to shop windows, doorways, even the traffic, eyes everywhere but on the telephone booth.

"C-for-Charlie, T-for-Tommy, in the lake itself. Any ideas?"

The patrol car had disappeared. Brown Ford, Lincoln, Nissan, Porsche, Firebird, all as before... old green Buick, new, parked thirty yards away on the opposite side of the street. He flapped the map.

"Well?" Hyde barked. "What is it?"

"What else have you—?"

"There may not be time for anything else! What the fuck does C-for-Charlie, T-for-Tommy mean, you silly sod?"

The man in the coat and hat halted now, waggling the newspaper behind his back while he watched Hyde's reflection in a shop window. Standing like a policeman or an army officer. The doors of the green Buick opened, two black men violently garbed—he relaxed, but they moved too quickly to completely disalarm him.

"Patrick—*in* the lake, you said? What's the matter there?"

"Trouble!" The two blacks were moving purposefully now, and the man in the hat and coat was turning to watch him. There was another car, sidling along his side of the street, eighty yards away. "*What is it?*" he shouted, hunched over the receiver.

"C and T could stand for Control Truck, Patrick. You said Frascati had a dry suit—he could have found the RPV's launch and control vehicle in the lake! They must have dumped—Patrick? Patrick, are you there?"

Godwin looked up at Aubrey, small and old against the gleaming, rain-filled evening outside the Center Point office.

"Put down the telephone, Tony. Break the connection." Aubrey said, sighing, moving suddenly with the aid of his stick.

"Is he all right, sir?"

"Tony, I do not know!" Aubrey stormed.

Godwin blanched at the repeated tapping of the stick on the floor. Chambers rustled papers intently as Godwin looked down at the map in his hand.

Aubrey snatched the map away from Godwin, almost tearing it. Rain wriggled down the windows, copious as grief, as he looked towards the home-going crowds, and the glitter of brake lights in Oxford Street. Godwin had shaded the area of the crash, but nothing more.

The blurt of the telephone startled all three of them. Godwin snatched it up.

"Patrick—Christ! What happened—what? Listen, you'll need to know . . . OK, you'll call back, but where was that mark, CT? McCloud River Arm, close to the Shasta Caverns, a little north, reference . . . yes—what? Yes, I'll tell him. 'Bye—!"

Godwin shrugged, but he was grinning, too, as he put down the receiver.

"Drugs bust, sir, that's all it was. He wasn't the target at all." Relief shone on Godwin's high, balding forehead and Aubrey felt himself quiver with relief, too. He felt hot inside his suit. The stick was suddenly more necessary.

"Then he had the nerve to remain where he was—he didn't run?"

"Apparently."

"Good. He'll need it." He cleared his throat. "And this CT business. Where is that?" He knew Chambers was inwardly mocking his formal pretense to indifference, but he could not be more honest in his gratitude at Hyde's continuing freedom. His head already ached with the day's *insignificant* business, for heaven's sake!

The PM had been even more irritating than was her wont, more reluctant and demanding. He reached for the handkerchief in his breast pocket to touch at his brow and found Chambers watching him intently with dark eyes. He merely waved his hand as Godwin lifted the map like the cover of a sacrament. "Well, Tony, where is it?"

"Patrick says—here. There's another cross on the shore, here, but it's unlabeled. Could be a lodge, some kind of cabin or other."

"That's where she is, then," Aubrey observed heavily. "With Harrell." He saw Evans's dead face, and that of Lescombe, both so easily dispatched.

Tony Godwin's anger at Evans's murder had been even stronger than his own. Aubrey had spent a sleepless night, listening to thin traffic, the occasional barking of a dog and the yell of a lout, home-going, waiting for the city to reawaken and excuse his consciousness. Then his day had been, at best, a fumbling approximation of competence; small wonder the PM had been testy, even after one of her habitual, shrill triumphs at Question Time.

"Very well, Chambers—what do you have for us?" he announced, shrugging off his coat. "How have you spent your day, pray?" His caustic tone was all he could summon. Chambers frowned, uncertain.

"First thing, sir, Malan's left the country. Got that from the Branch—we'd asked them to keep a lookout. Flight to Bombay. He didn't contact Melstead before he left."

"Mm." Aubrey leafed through the digest he'd been handed by Gwen as he left his office. "Malan may be extremely important to us, but this isn't his matter, I think. I don't sense his departure is a bluff." Politburo changes in Moscow. The old order reemerging. He looked up, glaring. "Get on with it, Chambers! What of—Melstead?" Detachment, he counseled himself.

"Malan went to a board meeting of Reid Electronics at eleven-thirty, then lunch, then to Heathrow."

"I thought you said he didn't contact Melstead? Wasn't James at the board meeting?"

"No—he wasn't reported anywhere near the NatWest Tower at the time. He was in Dillons, the bookshop in—"

"I know what and where Dillons is, Chambers."

"Then he had lunch at his club."

"Yes? Is his—telephone bugged?"

"Yes. But Malan didn't call him, either."

"Then apparently James needs no more stiffening in his collar," Aubrey murmured. "What else?"

"He went to the library in the afternoon."

"Which one—the British Library, the BM Reading Room?"

"The local branch library in Wembley, the *public* library." Then he added: "Perhaps he just wanted an hour out of the chill, poor old bugger."

"Chambers," Aubrey growled, then snapped: "What followed? What did he do there and where did he go then?"

"Spent about thirty minutes—most of them talking to one of the librarians, bloke about thirty, then he went home and had his tea. That's it. He's at home now. No phone calls."

"Does he know he's been bugged?"

"No. The servant was out when we called. He doesn't know."

"Just being careful," Godwin commented. His sticks leaned against his bulky frame and he seemed to threaten the extinction of the chair on which he was lumped.

Aubrey skimmed the digest once more. Their last and

golden opportunity, planned well before the spring. Malan must have known what they intended after the US airliner was brought down...? Not that it mattered. James would *not* have known, but he had been within Malan's orbit, had done well by Malan. And by now he must have realized. Frascati's claims, Irena's death—must have *illuminated* him! Dear God, Aubrey had spent his own life worrying about his probity, his loyalty to his country, his pathetic attempt at *decency!* And it had taken his old age to teach him that the real shoulders to the world's wheel were power and money and probably sex.

"Do you think Melstead really knows, sir?" Godwin asked. "What the RPVs were used for, I mean?"

"What—?" he asked, startled. Then: "Yes. I ought to doubt it, but I don't."

"He guessed, when they shot down that airliner?"

Aubrey struck the map, now lying on the floor, with his stick. "Perhaps."

"Those bloody *Yanks!*"

"Not all of them, necessarily. God knows, I can't imagine anyone *authorizing* what was done! But it suits America, too, in some ways, the status quo. You can find a *hundred* good reasons if you stir up the bottom of the pond with sufficient vigor!" He cleared his throat. "And none of our speculations is of any assistance. This librarian—who is he?"

"John Hughes," Chambers replied. "He's the assistant librarian. Aged thirty-one. Lives in a squat in Willesden. There's someone ready to follow him home."

"They talked for the greater part of the half-hour, you say?"

"Yes, sir. Heatedly at times, so the report says." Chambers held out the sheet of paper but Aubrey shook his head, then rubbed at his chin.

"You haven't pulled off the man keeping an eye on Ms. Woode, I hope?"

"What? Oh, no sir. Hyde called her this morning, he says. Briefly."

"Good. Very well, find out who this young man at the library is and how he is known to James. Call me if there is *anything* at all to report. Now, I must go home and change before my supper appointment. Tony, what do you have on Malan and Reid Electronics?"

"A lot. His holdings, the rescue package he put together for Reid, mainly through his own and Far Eastern companies and the big banks. All his other directorships and holdings from Companies House—oh, and the date of shipment from Lloyds' Register and the Customs forms—"

"Good. I'll read those in the car—what about Melstead's involvement with Malan?"

"I—I've made a tentative list of all contracts and trade deals that might have benefited from, er, support or influence with the DTI—and MoD. It mostly has a South African bias—" Godwin broke off, his eyes pale. Most of the material would have been compiled by Evans. "Evans's initial work," he murmured, looking away.

Aubrey cleared his throat and remarked with studied neutrality: "And probably an anti-Soviet bias?" Godwin nodded. "A charming irony that James has been used by his imagined friends to help his believed enemies, isn't it? . . . Nothing further on Malan's visit to California just before the project was officially scrapped?"

Godwin shook his head. "There's no way we can check on that—no appearance on the same holiday snap of Malan, Shapiro and Harrell. No trucks leaving Shapiro Electrics labeled CIA. It's a closed door, sir. It has to be made to stick at this end."

"I realized that."

"Our old mucker Priabin was at the Savoy this morning for a working breakfast with Malan," Godwin muttered. "Just back from Moscow. I'll bet they discussed a new pipeline—and probably a way in to Reid Electronics again, now that Lescombe's—" He faltered.

"We'll take up that matter in due course. The RPVs were delivered to Shapiro's company almost a whole year before the airliner was brought down. We'll never know what happened to them before this April. So, let us hope to high heaven that CT means Control Truck, Tony, and that they dropped it into Lake Shasta after it had done its job!"

"You want Patrick to—"

"Go swimming? Quite possibly. Poor Frascati did."

"Didn't do him much good."

"Patrick's a different case!" Aubrey snapped, disturbed. "At least, warn him if he calls again this evening—or whenever. A camera that will work underwater. A diving suit. Everything he might need."

"Yes, sir. Meanwhile—?"

"Meanwhile—" He tapped the papers Godwin had given him. "—James is not going to enjoy his supper unless he sings for it. And, Chambers—that librarian. Find out who and what he is. I don't want him to be part of some escape route!"

She rubbed her bruised arms where they had held her but, because he was watching her with what might have been an amused curiosity, forbore to touch her swollen mouth. Her left eye was watery, difficult to focus because of another swelling. It had purpled in a livid bruise. Not touching her facial injuries was the only bravery she could muster, the sum of her defiance. She had told them about the map Hyde had removed from John's box after he had retrieved it from beneath Alan's houseboat. The crosses and circles and tracks she had glimpsed—God, she'd dredged her memory for the information, too terrified to lie or invent. Harrell petrified her, morally as much as physically. His *force*. He couldn't be stopped. She huddled inside the warm, fleece-lined jacket he had given her. It was in her size. The thoughtfulness of that mocked and intimidated her.

Harrell had everything except that map. The metal box was in the two-story lodge behind them. She stepped onto the tiny jetty. A trout speckled in the glitter of water and pebbles below her, then flicked away at the sensation of her shadow. Harrell could use her to draw Hyde in. Kenneth would send him and he'd come like a beat-up punch-drunk fighter; useless and straight into the trap. Then she'd . . . disappear, too, maybe with her feet tied to the box that contained the rest of the evidence. She walked gingerly out onto the jetty, which creaked beneath her, her back turned to Harrell's unnerving, calm gaze. She began shivering again.

She'd seen the cross on the map's blue lake, she'd confused it with the site of the lodge. The crash site, yes, that had been marked. Nothing else, nothing else, *nothing else!* Eventually, Harrell had believed her, as she had believed herself. Now she shivered violently. Thank God the morning was chilly. She knew there had been another cross, out there somewhere. She looked slyly, a little northwards, beyond the creek that flowed down to the opposite shore. Somewhere there. She was able to envisage the map in Hyde's quivering hands quite vividly now. The image frightened her, as if Harrell could see it, too, in her mind. She rubbed her arms, but they hurt and she desisted. She turned to Harrell.

"He won't have gotten here yet." She knew why she was being paraded out there; not for exercise.

"But he'll be along soon," Harrell murmured, stepping onto the end of the jetty, unnerving her further. He seemed indifferent to the effect he had upon her, and perhaps that was the worst thing, that he was somehow distracted by something more important. And it wasn't even Hyde he saw. "Don't you worry about it, Ms. Aubrey. He'll be along." Harrell smiled. It was a pleasant, open smile, undirected at her.

"He won't if he has the least bit of sense!"

"But there's your uncle, right? And Hyde works for him. He's going to be worried about you—and he doesn't have anyone else he can send. QED." He shrugged, looking up towards the gray and brown cliffs and hills of the lake's western shore, scanning their blank clefts and folds. "No, he's coming."

"And you'll kill him like you did John? Just like *that?*"

Harrell nodded. "I'm sorry it's necessary. Hyde's gotten in the way, just like your lover man. And you. It's not just crap when I say I'm sorry about that. You should have learned to walk away from things that don't concern you."

"Dear sweet Jesus, I've spent most of my life doing just *that!*"

"Shame you broke the habit of a lifetime." He grinned again.

"But Aubrey *knows!*" she protested, holding her hands fiercely against her cold temples. The water slopped lazily against the pebbles and the piling of the jetty.

"Knows what?" he replied, shrugging. "Thinks he knows, Ms. Aubrey. Suspects. But, I'll tell you something. No one will want to know what he suspects. Just so long as no one ever has to look proof in the face, your old uncle can't do a damn thing. I'm sorry to put it that way, but it's the truth. Without you and Hyde and—" God, he seemed to be looking right through her towards the water, out where John's map had been marked with a cross! "—well, let's just say without you and him, there's nothing at all. You two are the whole ball of wax. And your uncle sure as hell knows that."

"You killed all those innocent people! You killed *John!*" Anything, anything to distract him, make him think she was just frightened, just cold and appalled!

"It was—kind of necessary at the time. And the Russian woman. She *was* necessary."

"God *bless* America!" she sneered.

"Probably, Ms. Aubrey—probably. I don't think it would be much use explaining it all to you. You'd resist understanding, for all the wrong—"

"You murdering *bastard!*" she screamed at him, bent in rage, her small hands clenched into fists.

He moved two paces closer and she flinched away, now unable to prevent herself touching her face and its bruises. He smiled and said levelly:

"There's a war going on out there, Ms. Aubrey, though you may not realize it because no one's been on TV to tell you about it. People like me are fighting the war. You're able to sleep and eat and fuck because of people like me, and walk about in a dream. Bronze your fanny and your boobs at the beach, watch the ball game on TV, drink your martinis and chew the olives—all because a few of us aren't asleep, because we're walking around with our eyes wide open. Now, I don't expect you to understand and I wouldn't expect you to agree, but it's true all the same." He grinned. "We don't expect you to thank us—just to keep out of the way."

Her cheeks felt shrunken, perhaps because of the chill in the air or perhaps because of the prospect of more violence. Her head tilted back as if to challenge a blow from his large hand. She forced the mockery. "Hallelujah, I done seen the Promised Land!"

"But, in the words of one well-known black leader of the recent past, Ms. Aubrey—you may not get there with us." He looked up again, scanning the tree line, the bare cliffs, the water, then the lodge behind them and the crowding pines. The sun glinted from the windows of the launch moored to the jetty. There was no way onto this shore of the McCloud River Arm by road, only by boat. Not even a hiking trail. "I think maybe we should go in now, Ms. Aubrey. You look cold."

13

INQUIRIES OF SOMETIME FRIENDS

The waiter put down Melstead's crème brûlée and Aubrey's bread-and-butter pudding, hovered against the barnlike background of the Oxford and Cambridge Club's dining room, then moved away as if on casters. His movements and vanishing lulled Aubrey as much as Melstead's ready, persistent smiles. Melstead's spoon cracked the crème brûlée like the top of a boiled egg. It was so difficult here, as if James had deliberately chosen such a disarming context! Aubrey shuffled his feet, bending his head towards the swimming yellow untidiness of the pudding. At a distant table, a cabinet minister entertained with numerous bottles and lavish movements of his arms. One or two of Aubrey's contemporaries were eating at other tables. The high, gilded ceiling and the mutter of conversation induced, like the claret they had shared, benevolence, a mutuality of pasts and presents. A barrister paused at their table, nodding to Aubrey, greeting Melstead. "Rather a nice little appointment, I hear, James—that American company. Ah, dear, the age of the consultant!" Melstead murmured something deprecatory, dabbing his napkin to his lips, and the barrister slapped his shoulder, nodded to Aubrey again and moved away.

Aubrey awoke as if from sleep. Melstead's shrug and smile were as murky as the bubbled surface of Aubrey's pudding.

"Empty man," Melstead observed wintrily, disproportionately.

"Surely not? His legal eminence, I mean—"

"Noisy."

"You refrained from telling me congratulations were in order, James."

"Oh, merely a supplementary, Kenneth. Something to help keep the wolf from the door."

"Your recent experience no doubt being valuable. I didn't realize they did things the same way in America— their civil service, I mean?"

"No . . ." Melstead moved in his chair in a bunched, taut manner. Aubrey was mystified. His languid probings during supper had been answered easily. Now, simply because his tone was more spirited out of an insidious guilt at time-wasting, Melstead was more alert and evasive. "Export licenses, my experience with various countries, you know . . ." He swallowed the last of the crème brûlée, cracking the caramel between his teeth.

The clock on the mantelpiece showed nine. It was too easy for Aubrey to recall that it was lunchtime in California.

"Well, they're getting a good man, James. I just hope you're not selling your skills cheaply." Melstead's glare of suspicion was unmistakable. "Which is the lucky organization, can one ask?" Aubrey bent his head towards his pudding plate.

"Not that it signifies, but Shapiro—"

"You didn't mention it when we discussed Shapiro Electrics and the company's interest in the—"

"Oh, Kenneth, you know what an old woman you are when it comes to seeing mysteries and sinister causes and links everywhere!" It had begun as a kind of protest, then Melstead had attempted to emasculate the observation, turning it aside with a stroke of his hand, a smile. "Well, you are, you know."

Aubrey continued to pat his lips with his napkin, as if merely unable to see the humor of the remark. Then, neatly replacing the serviette across his lap, he said without looking up: "You see, James, it's probably to do with the fact that you're a close friend. I have reason to believe—"

He glanced up, eyes innocently wide. "—that your friend Shapiro may be somewhat unpleasantly involved in some kind of high-tech smuggling—" He raised his hand to silence a protest growing around Melstead's mouth, twisting with what might have been contempt. "Oh, I know its early days and you'll vouch for the man, but there are a few trails that seem to be leading in his direction. It's more precise than just somewhere in Silicon Valley."

"This is a friendly warning, I take it, Kenneth?"

"No, and perhaps I should have said nothing. Your news took me by surprise, I think that was it."

"Kenneth, your own niece works for Shap—God, I am sorry, Kenneth, I really am! But, you see my point?"

The subject had been broached—thank heaven. Melstead's news had been surprising, his little pat on the head for assisting matters so discreetly and expeditiously!

Melstead gestured to a waiter, indicating the cheese trolley with a pointing finger. He grabbed at his claret glass, looked at Aubrey, then merely sipped.

"I see your point," Aubrey replied almost mournfully.

"Dreadful business for you," Melstead soothed. Aubrey bridled, but willed his shoulders to remain still, his face merely gloomy.

"Not as bad as at first feared, I'm glad to say. Clive Orrell has made some inquiries and I gather soothing noises are being made by various police departments over there. She's regarded as a material witness now, not as the prime suspect." He feigned a small, hurt smile.

"Thank goodness for that. I have felt for you these past days, Kenneth." And it was true, Aubrey realized. Melstead *was* his friend.

The cheese arrived and Melstead deferred to Aubrey, who shook his head. "Not for me."

"Ah, then I'll just have a little of that rather good-looking Stilton—and is that Single Gloucester? Yes, then ... Yes, a glass of port. You, Kenneth?"

"No, thank you, James." A banker passed, greeting Melstead, then a permanent secretary who had been up at Oxford with him. A young man ten yards away raised a hand at Aubrey as if summoning the waiter. A Foreign Office tyro who had carried messages once or twice. Melstead settled to the cheese and biscuits, murmuring:

"Can't stand these pretentious places where they force the cheese on you before the sweet." He smiled broadly.

"Yes. It must be the comfort of the place we come for—the comfort of the faces rather than the drafts."

"You're a little jaundiced this evening, Kenneth?" A flicker of doubt in his eyes.

An angel looked down from its perch above a gilded, dulled mirror.

Aubrey said: "I'm deeply worried about you, James. It's why I was pleased we could have supper."

"Me? You sound like my doctor!"

"Your connections with this man Shapiro, and ultimately with Malan—" He raised his hand, warding off protest. "You see, James—and I shouldn't be saying this to you, not strictly and certainly not yet—" No, you should not. He imagined Godwin's chagrined shock, could he have overheard. He was forewarning Malan and Shapiro, perhaps squandering their entire investigation. Giving Priabin and Malan time and insight. But Kathryn must be his sole and overriding priority. He dabbed at his lips with the napkin. "No," he continued, "I shouldn't be saying anything. You see, there are so many things that link them, and so many other things that link Malan to people like the Soviet Rezident, for instance. Please, James, let me finish." He cleared his throat. "It is not simply a matter of what is escaping from Silicon Valley, or from companies like Reid any longer. The noose is closing, the picture emerging. I have a very certain instinct that Shapiro and Malan are in this thing up to their necks."

Melstead was paler, his gaze intent. The sliver of water biscuit and crumbled Stilton between his fingers quivered.

"Kenneth, this is appalling!" he managed to utter. "If any of this is true, then it's *appalling!*"

"Quite." In the car, traveling to the club, he had realized there was no other, less devastating way in which he could unsettle James. It had to be the smuggling, the theft of high technology, the implications of villainy, even treachery; only then could he move to—

"I'm sure they did something over that canceled project, the remotely piloted vehicles Reid was developing. I'm *certain* of it, James."

"But Malan *saved* Reid Electronics!" Melstead floundered.

"Perhaps that was part of his scheme? He's a major investor in Shapiro's company, too—and in many others with sensitive contracts."

"I really can't accept this, Kenneth." The cheese remained disregarded. "I really think you're barking up the wrong tree this time."

"My team doesn't think so—and neither do I, James. We consider that Paulus Malan has been a very bad boy for a very long time. His links with Moscow over gold and diamonds are too well known to reiterate—and this would appear to be his new sideline." Aubrey was leaning forward conspiratorially, speaking with a hushed emphasis. His hand touched Melstead's, which jumped with nerves. "James, even if forbidden, I must have said something of this to such an old and dear friend. We think Malan had those vehicles transported to America, to Shapiro in San Jose, and that from there they simply disappeared! James, there were components, processes, bits and pieces, systems in those RPVs and the control vehicles that were nothing to do with Shapiro's company! Why were *they* sent back to him? Lescombe told me that—"

"Isn't Lescombe dead?"

"James, you sound like a man preparing a denial."

"Of course not!"

"James, I may as well tell you that I intend to make a success of this business. It was handed me by Geoffrey and the PM like a sanitary post in the Augean Stables, but I intend to demonstrate that my abilities encompass success as well as failure. I am going to have Malan's and Shapiro's heads delivered on platters to the Cabinet

Office!" He glared. There was no necessity to simulate anger.

Melstead appeared to quail, his cheeks blanched. "I see," he murmured after a silence, his knife stirring amidst the crumbled wreckage of the cheese on his plate. The small scratching noises set Aubrey's remaining teeth on edge. His heart pounded as he watched Melstead predatorially. "How much proof do you have, Kenneth, of any of this? I mean, with Lescombe—mm, gone?"

"Some. Not nearly as much as we need, I accept. But some. There *is* a picture emerging and it's not a pleasant one; the faces are familiar to both of us, I'm afraid. What else can be unearthed, and how quickly, I'm not certain. Just confident we'll get there.

"I see."

"James, I should refuse that consultancy with Shapiro, if I were you. And perhaps begin to extricate yourself from any embarrassing directorships you may have taken up."

"Me? You surely don't—"

"No, of course not. But I'm certain you could, if you put your memory to it, recall a great deal that would be useful to me—to us. You lunched with Malan the day the project was scrapped, you may have—"

"No!"

"You may have *inadvertently* let something slip, which could have put him on his guard or speeded things up. The RPVs were slipped out of the country immediately afterwards. Did you discuss the project with Malan?"

"I, er—of course not! I don't remember . . ." His face was flushed now. He waved his hand at the waiter with vigorous impatience. "Coffee, Kenneth?"

"Yes, I think so. A small Armagnac might not go amiss, either. Perhaps you, too. I've loosened my tongue.

Perhaps I can persuade you to do the same?" He smiled, eyes ingenuously wide, hand patting Melstead's on the tablecloth where the crumbs had been shunted into a small, neat heap like a worm cast. "James, I'll help, if there's the slightest need, you know that. You could, likewise, help me, I'm sure." Then he pressed: "The Pentagon scrapped their commitment to the RPV project without even a trial. Those RPVs were never meant to be shown to the Pentagon, it was an excuse to get them across the Atlantic once MoD pulled out—get them over there *intact*. I'm certain of it. You must help me in this, James."

No, he had not known, not at first. That much was certain, and even a relief; or possibly excused his manner of dealing with an old friend. Yes, perhaps knowing there was only collusion and not some irrefutable villainy involved would make the breaking of James easier.

Somewhere, at some time, James had guessed. He now knew how Irena had been murdered.

The dam was foreign, not part of a mental picture that he had carried, waiting for the sense of déjà vu. The more the binoculars roamed, the less the image haunted yet the stronger the recognition. The lower wooded hills falling towards the arms of the man-made, three-fingered lake; the bare, sliced edges of higher slopes; and the distant white-cloaked mountain, Shasta, to the north. No feature fitted the mental image, not exactly. The terrain was kinder, people moved in numbers. And, of course, there weren't any bodies, no Irena lying with her head in the water, no soldier with an opened throat. Nevertheless, he knew why they had chosen this place, Lake Shasta, to prove to the Russians that the RPV was the answer to their reactionary prayers. It was sufficiently like those steep valleys and open stretches of

water twenty thousand feet below the air corridor between the Soviet Union and Afghanistan to suit their
purpose. This place was where they first knew, for certain, that Irena would be killed.

Hyde picked out the writhing twists of the lake's three
arms and Horse Mountain to the northeast, slippery
with sunlight. The McCloud River Arm of the lake was
obscured beyond islands and cliffs and the gray water
above the sunken town of Kennett. The lake, as he saw
it, was bluffly welcoming with dotted marinas, the cracks
of boat wakes in the early light, the sense of people and
tamed wilderness. He glanced down at the map in his
other hand, then back to where the water turned in
between higher, grayer cliffs beyond the bridge that took
Interstate 5 across the lake. Up there, in the McCloud
Arm, would be more isolated.

He sipped at the flask, which contained brandy. Only
to take off the early morning chill! Then put the flask
away.

He had spent the previous day hiring the Japanese
four-wheel-drive vehicle in Oakland, while waiting for
the delivery from Mallory, a sniper's rifle. He'd bought
ammunition for the Browning, the dry suit, the camera,
the supplies, the R/T, the other things.

Redding, a dozen miles behind him, had been struggling awake as he drove through it, the neon signs reluctantly paling, the first cars pluming exhaust. A few
pedestrians moving slowly, tugging themselves into the
day. No car had picked him up, no one had been watching for him.

He turned at the noise of a camper and watched it
draw in cautiously. Even when the elderly couple disembarked and immediately gaped at the view, he continued
to study them until lulled by their amazement and their
air of self-congratulation. Even nodded to their greeting,

then turned back to the lake and the hills and cliffs and gray water and the distant, snow-covered mountain. Interstate 5 was already busy; his concern lay beyond it, where the chilly-looking water wound out of sight, up the McCloud Arm towards the place Frascati had marked but not labeled on his map—he touched it in the inside pocket of his jacket, then returned to the 4WD, leaving the panorama to the elderly couple.

He'd rung Ros. The least he could do. Told her he was all right, *all right, Ros, for Christ's sake*—! She'd know where he was now. It was important to her, like the exact location of a crematorium or the church where the burial service would take place. He joined the traffic on the highway, the wires and stanchions and rails of the bridge across the lake cutting the sunlight into neat slices of light and shadow. The marina was below him, houseboats, launches, fishing boats drawn up or docked for the winter. Hills slipped towards the road, and then came the darkness of a long, twisting tunnel, the strobe effect of the lights set in its roof mesmerizing.

He turned left and the narrower road twisted agilely through shaved and raw-edged cliffs strewn with boulders beside the tarmac. A climb, a dip—he pulled off the road as if the scene below had waited in ambush for him. A lodge away to his right and below him became hazardous. White rock dust swirled around the 4WD for a moment before settling. His boots crunched on rock debris.

Hyde caressed the scene with the binoculars. Smokeless chimneys of lodges and huts, a deserted row of campers, one man idly moving amidst the litter of craft at the Lakeview Marina. The first ferry to the Shasta Caves splitting the skin of the water to his right. To his left, the curl of wood smoke from the chimney of a tall, wide wooden house; the brochures called them luxury lodges. A narrow, short jetty, the house's toe in the water of the lake, a pebbly foreshore, a moored launch. He tugged the map from inside his jacket, crouching beside a large boulder still raw from being blasted from its cliff, and checked Frascati's mark ... yes? Binoculars, map, glasses again—yes. He heard his heart thump dully but more quickly. The house was perhaps as much as a mile away across the lake. Beyond it, Horse Mountain reared up, lacking snow, dark with trees then grimly bald. He imagined—could see?—the swath the plunging airliner had made through the trees on the mountain's flank. Farther north, the water was sullenly gray, despite the sensation of the sun warming his face, glinting from glass and ripple. Map, glasses, map, glasses—just there, the cross and the label CT. The RPV control vehicle. Dumped after use, thrown away; disposable. A large van with a launch rail on its roof and the whole control system of the missle inside it.

He swung the glasses along the opposite shore. That sense of familiarity with the place increasing—Irena's dead, so-recognizable face staring up at him—making the nerves in his arms jump and itch. There was no way in and out of the lodge and its clearing except by boat. The terrain wouldn't have allowed the control truck to have been driven to the launch site. A helicopter must have brought it in, just like the one that had airlifted Harrell's RPV vehicle out of the narrow valley. The helicopter, presumably, had dumped this vehicle in the lake after it had been used.

He sighed. The pattern of it was so easily followed, so easily put together. It had taken Frascati months of luck and searching to prove it. Hyde had allowed himself two nights, the coming one and the following one, to re-prove it. Tonight, in a thousand yards square of gray, sullen water, he had to find the position of the control vehicle, photograph it, then come away with proof. Stay alive the whole of the following day before—

—there . . . coming down the sloping grass to the pebbles of the shoreline. The sun was catching her pale skin. Harrell was behind her. Even when he lowered the glasses and the figures became distant, it was unmistakably them. The woman, Aubrey's niece, and Harrell. Coming out to play—

—show, rather. Harrell walked behind her as she slouched down to the jetty, her shoulders such that there might almost have been a leash on which the American held her. He refined the focus further, but their faces were still too small to define their expressions. The second night, he would have to go in after her. That was inescapable. Aubrey was pissing about with people like Melstead, stabbing at the ground and hoping to find oil. Melstead knew whatever he knew, but there was no pressure Aubrey could apply . . . *my niece has been kidnapped by the CIA, Sir James—isn't there something you could tell me that would allow me to blackmail this man Harrell into letting her go? Please . . .*

So, the woman's life remained in *his* hands—

Balls. It isn't her at all, and it certainly isn't Aubrey. It's Harrell.

For perhaps ten minutes, Hyde enjoyed Harrell's miniaturized figure, his unawareness of Hyde's presence. Harrell was using glasses, too, but Hyde avoided the flash of sunlight from his own binoculars. After thirty minutes, during which the woman had paced the jetty, kicking at pebbles and hugging her arms across her breasts, they returned to the lodge, quickly moving out of sight under the firs long before they reached what he assumed would be the porch of the two-story building. It must be rented; he'd inquire in one of the marinas. He moved back on his haunches until he reached the

4WD, then climbed in. He had seen what might have been the flash of sunlight on a barrel, or simply a sliver of broken glass, and one other figure around the lodge. Which meant they were spread out, however many there were, looking for him, anticipating his arrival.

He turned the 4WD and bucked onto the tarmac. The lodge, the water, then Horse Mountain slipped quickly out of sight in the mirror. He turned onto an unpaved road, hardly wider than a trail, leading north towards the cross on the map labeled CT. He had to stay out of contact with them today, then tonight ...

... for Christ's sake, Frascati, I hope there's only one copy of *this* fucking map!

He awoke, knowing that he had slept soundly, dreaming of his childhood. Then he saw the clock and the darkness outside the room's thin curtains and realized it was seven in the evening. He heard the noise of a radio from another room and the movements of people not yet tired. He managed to sigh with almost-luxury and turn onto his back from his comfortable fetal position. He had dreamed of holidays on the crowded beaches available to Party officials, of summer meadows and the bright flicker of fish in a stream, even recalling his shadow bending over the water, engaged and eager. He smiled, and then swallowed, realizing that even his subconscious was attempting to escape from what he had come to see as a dereliction.

The children never win, not against the adults, he had warned Irena—had he glanced with prescient suspicion at Nikitin, even then? They had been more than usually drunk with success and alcohol. *This time they will,* she had replied gaily, laughing at his seriousness as he lolled in a deep armchair. But she was dead and she had been wrong. Nikitin had come to believe that holding the empire together, the union of republics controlled by the Party from Moscow, was his primary task. Didenko knew it was a genuine belief, one that was ingrained in his mind and reinvigorated by events. The three of them, but especially he and Irena, had been like hyperactive children, hurrying around the Kremlin and the state, never still, changing everything. But now the adults had reasserted their old authority, slapped their legs and sent them to bed . . .

. . . the door had been shut in their faces by Irena's death. His sense of frustration and disappointment caused a tear to dribble down his thin cheek. At that moment, Irena was very present to him in the chilly room, and he was almost prepared to admit that he had loved her as more than a friend. That he had almost worshiped her. But his antagonism towards Nikitin now was nothing to do with Irena and everything to do with what they had set out to do, and what had been slowed and prevented by her death.

He got up from the bed vacated for him by one of his sister's children. He was restless and impatient; afraid, too, that he had somehow been betrayed into resolution by his subconscious, while he slept. The floorboards squeaked under his slight weight. He opened one unlined curtain. The frost had left an eyelike iris in the middle of one of the small windowpanes—perhaps where he had heated the glass, breathing against it earlier as he had stared out into the darkening afternoon across the snowbound fields at the back of the house. A light from the house's main room spilled with a firelike orange glow onto the trodden, deep snow. The bedroom was icily cold. He rubbed his arms vigorously. So many memories from childhood had tumbled through his sleep. And always an adult was there, warning the Young Pioneers to stay well away from drunken peasants laughing in a field, or to avoid the roped-off sections of the beach reserved for very important Party officials. Always they had been told not to stray from well-worn trails and paths.

He smoothed his forehead, inspecting his fingers as if for dirt. His eyes felt damp again. Stupidly. There had always been certainties—don't walk there, don't do that, that is permitted, that is not. Nikitin and Irena must have heard those same cautionary voices as they grew up in the Ukraine; the problem was, she hadn't listened and he had. When Irena had called him to Moscow to become city Party chief, he'd heard those same old whispers, but Irena's laughter had been louder and, eventually, the adults had fallen asleep and their new game had *really* begun!

The recent past clutched at his chest, closing like a fist. They'd cleaned out the Politburo, there'd been *real* elections for the Central Committee, they'd achieved so much else in such a short time—it really had seemed, for a delirious moment, that they'd irrevocably changed everything!

He realized that he was pacing the room in a rage of frustration, rehearsing for a performance. He opened the bedroom door and went down the short, creaking corridor littered with untidy rugs to the main living room. His sister, Sonya, looked up, surprised, even concerned at the expression that must be on his face. Her husband, Vassily, the village schoolmaster, glanced up from his meal and the newspaper, somehow mistrustful, as if Didenko represented a danger.

"I see your friend the general secretary has been invited to America by their president, and to London—nice for him, mm?" he jibed.

His sister was breast-feeding the new baby while the little girl, Natasha, played with a rag doll beside the fire.

She might have been imitating breast-feeding, Didenko was uncertain; he had never possessed much understanding of children and their games.

"What—oh, yes. Yes, I had heard something."

"There was a film of Moslem atrocities on the news," Vassily muttered, his mouth full of food. "Out east, somewhere. About time something was done about it."

"Oh, yes—what?"

"Pyotr," his sister pleaded quietly.

Didenko glared at Vassily's bent head and chewing jaw. My God—!

"I saw the news, too. There were—" She glanced at the little girl, then down at the baby. "—mutilated bodies."

"And what's happening?" Didenko urged.

"More troops. Arrests—"

"The usual answer!" he snapped scornfully.

"What else should they do? They're killing people out there!" Vassily grumbled. "Serve those stupid wogs right they've sent in another two Guards' divisions with tanks, everything. Can't have *that*."

"God, Vassily—" he began, and then at once silenced his outburst, as if he were a climber preserving his energy for the last part of a difficult ascent. For what he knew he must do.

It had been their nightmare, of course, Tadzhikistan and Uzbekistan and Kazakhstan going up like bonfires all along the southern border, one by one, lit by the Afghans and Iranians, and by their own *glasnost*. Estonia and Latvia could be reasoned with—even the damn Georgians could be reasoned with—but not the Moslems. So, the Union must now be preserved in blood and the Party's authority remain unchallenged and unchanged. Nikitin saw it as his mission to preserve the Party—he was just one part of the brain they had all three of them been. But, he was what was left after the lobotomy!

"Sorry, Vassily," he murmured, "you're probably right. It can't be allowed to go on." He hesitated, then added: "I'm leaving this evening, Sonya. I—have something I must attend to." But the fire was warm and the room wrapped itself close to him like a blanket.

"Where are you going? Must you go?"

"It's kind of you, Sonya—and of Vassily, too. I feel better for having come. But there are things that have to be seen to. If he's preparing for a visit to America, then he'll be at his weekend place—" Where they'd planned so many of the changes! "—resting before his historic journey. Whatever, he'll be there." He rubbed his forehead. "There are things I'd forgotten to talk to him about . . ." Vassily sneered and then returned to his newspaper, while Sonya nodded.

Didenko maintained a vacuous, reassuring smile. His heart and spine felt colder. There wasn't anything else to do. That was the meaning of all the childhood memories and his sense that Irena was somehow in that small, cold bedroom. Just like Nikitin, he couldn't learn any new tricks. Before his discreet obscurity and state pension, he had to make one more attempt to persuade Nikitin! He must—there wasn't any Irena to do it.

"There's a bus about ten, isn't there?" he said as Sonya rebuttoned her cardigan and burped the baby.

"Who is Blantyre—that accent?" Aubrey snapped, clicking his fingers. He glimpsed the angry shiver of Chambers's shoulders at the noise.

"Um—Patrick knows him," Godwin offered. "Ex-SAS, ex-Selous Scout from Rhodesia, then Namibia—"

"I believe they still prefer to call it South-West Africa, Tony."

"He's Rhodesian in origin. Our people lost track of him a couple of years ago. He's turned up with Malan—interesting."

"So, James is trying rather desperately to reach Malan by telephone—he's rattled," Aubrey exulted.

The day was darkening over London. An orange patch was fading on one emulsioned wall and glowing like an old fire on the VDT screens. There was a golden-pink strip beyond Oxford Street and the first stars were separated from the sunset by a clear, aquamarine ribbon of air.

"Blantyre works for Malan, and he *knows* Patrick," Godwin suddenly exclaimed. "If he's advising Harrell, then—"

"Malan wouldn't advise Harrell, not at this stage," Aubrey replied, turning back towards the room. "He's cut loose from this business—except, possibly, where James is concerned." Then he cocked his head to one side, listening to the tapes of Melstead's telephone calls throughout the day.

Orrell's blunt, bluff tones—Orrell had already acted on James's promptings and rung Aubrey. *I say, old boy, hands off . . . Can't hang James for a lamb, Kenneth.* Then he had rung Longmead, the cabinet secretary, and Longmead had rung him. *Kenneth, what's in your mind?* Greater bluster, his habitual irritation. *You think James might have been mixed up in . . . ? Preposterous!*

Melstead was panicked. The veldt grass was on fire and he could smell the smoke on the wind. He'd even rung Shapiro, but some instinct had saved him from revealing anything except his concern about Malan's absence. Call after call to badger, plead, berate. Now it was Blantyre's flat, unequivocal rejections, his instructions to remain calm, not to worry, that fell heavily in the room against the counterpoint of Melstead's high, almost hysterical tones.

"Is there anything more of interest?" Aubrey snapped.

"I'll run it on," Chambers replied. The snap of a heavy switch, the whirr of tape, then the switch again. "He called Hughes."

"Who *is* Hughes? How can he be so important? He had absolutely no connection with any of this!"

"All right, all right—sir. I'm only telling you—here it is now."

There was a slight breathlessness in James's voice, but he was calmer, more authoritative in talking to the librarian. "No, just keep everyone away from the place. You understand me, John. No one is to go there, not even you. I—well, never mind why, just make sure. Has anyone spoken to you?"

"Why should they?" A sullen, immature voice.

"I—just wondered. Very well, John. Just remember to inform those concerned to stay away from the flat." The click of the receiver.

"That was the only call?" Aubrey asked. Chambers nodded. "Who was he expecting might call on him, who should now stay clear? Chambers, what part can Hughes possibly be playing here?"

Godwin's features became heavier, as if injected with silicon. Chambers, too, appeared suddenly lacking in confidence, even in his habitual cynicism. "There's no connection to Melstead, of course—" he blurted.

"No connection with what?"

"How Hughes spends his evenings."

The room hummed with machinery. Screens, recorders, printers. There was something ominous about Chambers's expression that reminded Aubrey of the look on Ros's face as she had listened to him an hour earlier. He knew he had been *insecure* with her, but it was Patrick's life, and his guilt had obliged him to explain, to reassure. Anyway, after they had found the bug in her flat, he felt himself obligated, almost coerced into frankness. Chambers's expression was unnaturally lugubrious, his eyes like those of someone out of their depth. Godwin, very obviously, was staring at a sheaf of continuous paper on his lap. They looked ridiculously like two schoolboys being cajoled or threatened into some confession of misdoing!

"And how, pray, does Mr. Hughes spend his evenings?" He turned to the window, but the ribbon of aquamarine had darkened and the golden-pink glow was gone, too. He heard Chambers open a file, almost caught the slide of glossy enlargements being shuffled—a murmur from Godwin that might have been the mere clearing of his throat. Then Chambers was beside him, his hands filled with photographs; night images, flaring with street lamps and shadowy with moving figures and vehicles, some of them ghostly with infrared film. Hughes stared up at him in closeup from the photograph on top of the little heap.

"It's just a selection," Chambers murmured. There was anger now behind his diffidence. "They're labeled." He retreated with an uncharacteristic scuttle.

Hughes had been tailed by the Branch all the previous evening and night, all that day . . . yes, there were one or two daylight shots, the grubby street, the boarded-up windows of the squat behind Hughes as he presumably left for work . . . arriving at the library, eating sandwiches in some minuscule, bare park, an out-of-focus pram and mother beyond his bench. But, the majority of the shots came from the previous night. Times, places—Aubrey recognized that one, Euston, then one outside the Victorian cathedral of St. Pancras, then one at King's Cross. They were like a tourist's photographs of everything he saw and did on his visit to London: the station, the taxi, Piccadilly Circus, Leicester Square. The playbill of a theater, a cinema's neon blandishment, an alleyway somewhere. He glanced at the scrawled writing on the back of one photograph. The Embankment, the water black beyond the flare of the lamps, image after image glowing or burning with lights behind and beyond shadowy figures. Hughes's face recognizable in many of the shots, his figure familiar after a while.

"What are these supposed to tell me?" he said, addressing the suffocating tension of the room. Neither Chambers nor Godwin replied. Feet were shuffled, a chair squeaked as one of them moved on it.

Hughes at Euston, in a tube station, in an alleyway where men were huddled into cardboard boxes or wrapped in newspapers and polyethylene garbage bags; Hughes in Leicester Square, on the Embankment, in another alleyway, Hughes caught in a car's headlights... And the other faces, of those he spoke to, those in whom he seemed most interested, were so young. Male and young, boys.

"What are these pictures meant to convey?" he asked, sensing the protest in his voice, the attempt to distance himself from a growing, vile realization.

"Sir, we can't be certain, but—" Godwin began.

"The Branch is," Chambers insisted, tired once more of reticence. For him, the matter was settled.

"These boys," Aubrey protested.

"Two of them were ten, another eleven," Chambers recited. "Supposed to be in care—some bloody care, leaving them on the streets for someone like Hughes!"

"You mean he was soliciting these—children?"

"Enrolling them in his club, more like."

"Hughes is—"

"A pedophile. He's never been caught, but—"

"And for you the conclusion is obvious!" Aubrey stormed, the photographs quivering in his hand. "It is beyond *doubt* that James Melstead is also one of these, these *loathsome* individuals!"

Chambers stared stonily ahead, beyond Aubrey's shoulder. Godwin studied the floor. Aubrey turned away, pacing along the window, his stomach queasy with revulsion. His head whirled with gross images as he glimpsed the photographs, which he was unable to put down, as if his finger and thumb had become stuck to their glossy surfaces. Chambers's voice droned, maddening as the sound of an insect buzzing around Aubrey's head.

"They were offered money, he'd taken their names, arranged to see them ... *explained* what was involved, that they'd be looked after, better than sleeping rough. They'd find friends. Hughes isn't on anyone's files, bit of a surprise. He's the link man, the pimp for a group of people ..."

Aubrey waved his hand feebly and Chambers fell silent at a growl from Godwin. *A scandal,* David Reid had feared that in the afternoon when Aubrey had seen him at the ministry. *I don't need a scandal over those bloody RPVs, Kenneth. I'll help in any way I can, of course— I can't believe either James or Paulus are involved in any way.*

And now this, this—! If Malan knew any of this—he must have known!—then James would have been an easy prey to blackmail. Dear God in heaven, this was *appalling!* Vile, filthy— unforgivable ...

... too real. Aubrey had needed a lever, a key to open Melstead like a door—not a cesspool in which to drown him.

"No—no, Chambers, there's nothing here that suggests the slightest involvement by James in any of

Hughes's activit—" Chambers's stony contempt was evident, his lip curling in cynical confirmation of old prejudices. "You can't show me *any* link, dammit!"

"He warned Hughes to keep away from him!" Chambers shouted, his chair clattering over as he got to his feet. "What more bloody proof do you want? Your friend Melstead likes little *boys!* That creep Hughes gets them for him!"

"I refuse to accept—"

"It's what you've been looking for, the way to open him up! Your bloody niece is in the shit—*sir.*"

"Tony, do you—do you believe any of this?"

"I—I can't discount it, sir."

"And neither can I," Aubrey sighed, turning to the window once more, tempted to press his burning forehead and cheeks against the cold glass. It was too, too awful to accept. Corruption, greed, sexual deviancy—yes, all those. Motives for using people, blackmailing them, getting them to cooperate. There wasn't much he could be taught about human venality. Until now. James with *children!* Aubrey could not escape the mounting heat of his own body, the flare of shame in his own cheeks.

"You've got to put it to him, sir," Godwin muttered.

"I—" He wanted to shout at the top of his voice, but merely murmured: "I know that, Tony. I realize that." Chambers made a snorting noise, satisfied. The room's tension suddenly diminished, as if a powerful current had been switched off. But in himself, there was no relaxation, no sense of relief. How could he even mention it?

James was—unknown. An utter stranger. Vilely contemptible. Corrupt beyond the meaning of the word. He raged inwardly, pacing the room as if to outdistance comprehension. It was something with which he should not have to deal. In his world, men died, betrayed, were callous, brutal, greedy, stupid—but somehow this was *too* awful. And too close. As if, turning in his newspaper to the remoteness of the foreign news, he had stumbled upon child abuse, rape, torture; then casual brutality, utter indifference on another page, a page concerning England. *Home News*. He was usually able to place everything in perspective by returning to his own more recognizable world—but this!

He shuddered. If James had some secret, knowing connection with this creature Hughes, then it must be exploited to save Kathryn. Nothing was more obvious or more difficult than that.

"Something's come up that changes things."

"Blantyre, I was asleep. I have an early flight to Moscow in the—"

"I'm sorry. You needed to know. They found the bug in the woman's flat a couple of hours ago."

"How?"

"Aubrey went to call on her. They swept the place just as a routine precaution. When they found it, they did a full sweep. We're out of contact."

"It's not really my—"

"It is your problem! I've told you, man, you're underestimating these people, Hyde and the old man. Because people like Melstead tell you Aubrey hasn't got weight to throw around, you believe them. Aubrey was with the woman for more than an hour—you think he was just taking tea?"

"You know the woman—you say you know Hyde and Aubrey. Why would Aubrey tell her anything?"

"Because he would have. It's the only way she would play it. Hyde tells her everything—he always did. Why do you think he bothers calling her?"

"What else is happening?"

"Aubrey is having Hughes tailed—I'm almost certain. Hughes leads straight to Melstead. Melstead telephoned my number half a dozen times today. He's close to panic and Aubrey hasn't even begun on him yet! For Christ's sake, Paulus, can't you see this could blow up in your face, man? Are you still there?"

"I'm thinking about what you've said, Robin—I'm thinking!"

"Don't take too long."

"Robin, I don't like this *interference*—it's too basic."

"Aubrey doesn't mind getting his hands dirty."

"I don't want my hands to be in the picture at all. Why hasn't Melstead been able to stop this?"

"Because Aubrey's using his brief from the PM to hide behind. He's only supposed to be going after the high-tech side of it. You had Lescombe killed, Paulus. Got your hands dirty there."

"That was the Russians. It's why I didn't use you. It shouldn't have led anywhere. Damn Harrell for taking Aubrey's bloody niece, man. That's the real cause of all this hassle!"

"So, what do we do about it?"

"You're saying Hyde's woman will know where Hyde is, *and* what Aubrey knows about Melstead? Hyde still isn't my problem, he belongs to Harrell."

"Then just give Harrell the edge!"

"He's got that—what, nearly a dozen men out there. Hyde's on his own, man!"

"Maybe, but if Harrell knows what Hyde's instructions are, what he's doing and exactly where he is, then he can finish Hyde before—"

"Aubrey wouldn't have *told* the woman! I don't believe that!"

"He took her to Peshawar. She already knows what's

going on. Aubrey *trusts* the woman, Paulus. He's got a soft, guilty spot for her. He'd have told her to ease his conscience. Believe me!"

"How can it be done?"

"The surveillance on her is light—one man, most of the time. She goes shopping . . ."

"I don't want a repeat of the mess Harrell's created."

"You won't get it. Ros knows me, I know her. You *need* intelligence on Aubrey, you don't have a lot of choice. It won't come home to you. The Yanks will get the blame."

"Not if she knows you they won't."

"Then I'll just have to be freelancing for the CIA, won't I? Well?"

"I don't know—"

"Melstead knows an awful lot about *you*, Paulus. You need to know whether Aubrey's getting to—"

"All right. Just keep it away from me, Robin—far away."

"It will be. I'll just have a chat with Ros, then decide what to do with her afterwards."

"Be neat."

"As always. Tomorrow. I'll call."

14

REALPOLITIK ON RYE

Horse Mountain. Hyde watched from his perch above its gouged flank as the man cautiously entered the clearing the plunging airliner had made. He was dressed in a check jacket and a hunter's cap, his trousers laced into high walking boots. Hyde clutched the sniper's rifle against his chest, its barrel resting along his cheek, his arms folded. Below him, the man was caught by the high sun which glinted from his binoculars and the rifle he carried. Flies hummed around Hyde; two butterflies circled the man below.

Hyde watched for five minutes, then the man was gone, his slight noises audible as he brushed through a hidden thicket. It was the first of them Hyde had seen for perhaps an hour, excepting the small launch that had idled out on the gleaming lake, signaling flashes of light from a pair of binoculars as another of them looked for him. Hyde squatted with his back against a warmed rock. Tiny yellow and purple flowers struggled out of cracks and crevices around him, amid the lividness of green and orange lichens. Lake Shasta was a polished metal shield. He squinted out at a mail boat slowly moving northwards across the place that was marked on Frascati's map. He had already found a fingernail of pebbly shore between high, difficult rocks where he could enter the water. The 4WD and the dry suit, air tanks, lights and camera were all hidden on the opposite shore.

A small ferry plowed across the lake, taking late tourists to the Shasta Caverns. He lifted the water bottle to his lips and sipped. It shivered against his teeth and he held his hand and arm up to inspect them. The tremor slowly disappeared. He looked down again at the cracked, shipwrecked trees around the clearing, the great scorch where the airliner they had shot down with fifty-odd people on board had plunged into the mountain. The track it had made was shaped like some great, curved, ugly sheath for a weapon.

There was another cross marked on the map and un-labeled, up somewhere behind him. Perhaps it had only been Frascati's hideout while he reexplored the crash site, but it should be checked out. Nobody in Redding had rented out the lodge to them—they owned it. The slim barrel of the FN rifle, with the infrared nightscope and daylight telescopic sight, rested against his cheek and he rubbed meditatively against it as a cat might have done. In five hours, he'd seen the man in the clearing, the launch, two others clambering away from the lodge into the pines—and Harrell and the woman on the jetty.

There must be at least two in Redding, though he hadn't seen them, and another two on the opposite shore. No more than a dozen, couldn't be...

He remembered there had been someone who could have been one of Harrell's men, at Holiday Harbor Resort, where the ferry to the caves had come from. He cradled the rifle more tightly. *I can't get hold of one of those for you,* Mallory had protested. *Just get me one of NATO's new sniper rifles. You can probably buy one round the corner!*

He yawned, surprising himself. He felt lighter, unencumbered. It was even difficult to remember Aubrey at all clearly, which was a good sign. He was simply a phone number, a series of reports to be made to indicate his progress. It was the thankful, temporary amnesia of all agents on shut-ended operations. Only the immediate, the sensory, was important.

There was Ros, of course. She was like an insurance application he always posted at some mental airport. He always talked to Ros, always called her. And invariably asked about the cat, Layla, as well.

Ros had been diffident about Layla when he had called the previous day, and he did not understand why. Ros and the cat were like photographs carried in his wallet— the kind the befuddled traveler always tried to interest the whore in. They were always retained as a token, a remembrance, that he was still himself, still human, whatever it was he was doing. Sadly, he had forgotten them in Afghanistan, for long stretches.

But there were no phones, he told himself, tossing his head. The sun caught his hands and he moved the rifle into the shade of his body. He wasn't allowed to carry pictures, letters, anything of his private self, just in case. So, he had learned to substitute talk for memory. Even Aubrey knew he always called Ros. He told her as much as he could, when he could, and she listened in order to know where to send the flowers. But she'd been reluctant to talk about the cat . . .

He shivered, trying to shake off the mood, and studied the lake. It was down there somewhere, the RPV's control vehicle. One grainy, floodlit picture would be enough.

Two nights.

He rose into a bent crouch. An osprey swept overhead, moving like paper on the breeze down towards the lake. He noticed the scratch of a black bear's spoor in a patch of soft ground. Slowly, he moved upwards, leaving the outcrop, keeping to the thinning trees, his shadow as broken and intermittent as his silhouette. The rifle was across his back, beside the pack. Periodically, he checked the map against the terrain. Occasionally, there was the flash of sunlight on glass from the launch on the lake. A thin wisp of smoke straggled up through the pines, just where the lodge would be. He checked the trees and rocks and air around him continuously, almost tasting the place with his senses; chameleonlike in his camouflage jacket and trousers, he was prepared, almost ready.

The cave was small and empty, masked by brush. Frascati's occupation of the place was only evident in the slight scorching of scattered stones, half a bootprint that might not have been his, a cigarette end. He sat in the darkness, watching the lacework of the brush and leaves moving on the wall near the entrance.

He ignored the whimper at the back of his head and rubbed his cheek hard against the rifle as he cradled it. The cave smelled of earth and damp and, fancifully, of Frascati's obsession. Eventually, he got up, went to the entrance and parted the thorny brush carefully, listening, expecting to be made aware of other people.

Noises came to him from away towards the lake, even the distant hum of traffic on Interstate 5. He heard one animal kill another somewhere below, in the thicker trees. A falling rock rattled—innocently, he decided, letting his breath ease out. Then, eventually, a scrape, a slither, the click of metal touching rock. Suddenly, the noise of breathing—

—that close, Christ. Above you, he told himself. Moving down cautiously, one man. He listened beyond the immediate noises and the blood that drummed in his ears. One man. Hyde's throat was tight, his lips curling back from his clenched teeth, his shoulders thrown forward so that he was almost off-balance with the ferocity with which he waited. The footsteps and scrapings halted beyond the screen of brush and he saw the bulky silhouette of a man in a padded jacket. The shadow of his arm, raised to wipe his sleeve across his brow, fell through the masking leaves and branches onto Hyde, making his skin shiver. He leaned forward as if to pounce through the brush. The man turned to face the cave, evidently aware that it was there; an open, reddened face, blue eyes, cropped blond hair. He held a hunting rifle at his hip, the barrel drooping relaxedly. For him, this was routine, part of a set patrol. Hyde heard his breathing relax, smelled the cigarette smoke a moment after the heavy, old-fashioned lighter's cover had snapped shut. It was difficult to wait, to accept the inactivity—

—so that he welcomed the first movement towards the cave, the use of the rifle's barrel to push some of the thicker brush aside, the peering expression as the man's eyes blinked into the darkness, squinting in concentration, attempting to discern rock, shadow, filtered sunlight.

Hyde swung the butt of the FN rifle instinctively,

and a thin branch snapped and absorbed the force of the blow. The man stepped back, alert, eyes enlarging, rifle barrel coming to bear, its butt pressed against his hip. Hyde stared at the branch he had snapped, stunned—

—fell aside as the first three shots splintered wood, ricocheting from the rocks just above his head, whining in the cave. He covered his head with his arms, waiting for the impact of a stray bullet. Sunlight fell across his hands. He looked up at sudden shadow, the man's bulk was struggling through a gap in the brush. A curse, recognition, the glint of sun on the hunting rifle—

—his own rifle fired twice, held almost clumsily so that the recoil hurt his ribs. Branches snapped under the weight of the man's body as it sagged and was then grotesquely held almost upright by the thick brush. The head lolled, the face stared at him, then the eyes rolled sideways, no longer open in surprise and terror. Hyde held his ribs where the butt of the FN had bruised them. Slowly, his hearing returned. A bird calling in distress outside, the stretch and creak and snap of twigs supporting the man's dead weight. A lack of other noise, no breathing except his own ragged sounds. He climbed to his feet, using his back against the rock. His legs felt weak, the aftershock of panic trembling through them.

He put down the rifle and pulled the man's heavy body through the brush into the cave, tearing the fabric of the padded jacket. He dragged the man to the back of the cave, then ignored the body. He snatched up the FN and his pack, the water bottle rattling against the rock, then eased himself through the gap at the edge of the cave mouth. The wispy strands of padding caught on the twigs were irrelevant. They'd find the body anyway. Doubtless they'd heard the shots. He squinted in the sunlight, looking hurriedly around him, especially higher up the mountain . . . then below, towards the outcrop where he had rested, and the clearing. And saw the check jacket the moment he adjusted the focus of the glasses, emerging from the wateriness of grass and sunlight. The man's face was shadowed by the R/T he was holding against his cheek. Then, as he watched, the man hurried into the trees, moving upwards in his direction.

The crack of an engine starting, then the high-pitched noise of its acceleration. He swung the binoculars towards Lake Shasta, scanning across the glint and muddle of water. Found the small, sleek white gull shape of a tiny seaplane drifting ahead of its wake away from the shore. Must have been hidden by trees or the fold of a creek, he hadn't seen it from the other side of the lake. It turned choppily and accelerated, leaving a diamond spray falling away from its floats as it took off, rose, began to bank in a semi-circle towards Horse Mountain. Hyde tugged the map from his jacket, listening intently before the roar of the plane covered all other sound. Nothing. He checked the map, then the landscape, and moved away from the cave, down the mountainside, following a narrow, irregular track along a paring of ledge. Shadow fell across his hot cheeks and perspiring forehead and he looked gratefully up at the filtered sunlight. The roar of the small aircraft loudened. He moved further into the trees, watching the intermittent scufflings of his progress in the needle mold and the scar of mud left on one outcrop of rock; regretting every signal of his passage.

The aircraft's noise billowed above for a moment and the trees swung aside—he darted against the rough bark of a fir—then the noise diminished, the engine note changing as the pilot banked and began to turn. The man in the clearing would be halfway to the cave by now, moving recklessly, traveling much quicker than he was. There was the single trail, along a narrow river valley towards the Squaw Creek Arm of the lake. Every map showed it; Harrell's would too. Hyde had left in a tiny inlet the small launch he had hired from a broken-down marina on the Sacramento River Arm. None of his equipment was stowed in it, but he needed the boat to get back to the 4WD's hiding place.

The river flashed and boiled beneath him. The trail wound apologetically along the cliff side...just there. He moved within the cover of the trees, paralleling the trail until the land folded down towards the river. The aircraft passed overhead once more, then insect noises emerged out of it like a quiet echo of the engine. Then the voices; one of them crackled and distorted by electricity. The other one was commenting almost lazily.

His hearing was attentive as the aircraft drifted into its lazy turn on the other side of the gorge. The water's noise was only another background. Then the R/T crackled into quiet. They were in that direction, thirty yards away, no more. Two men. Deeper into the trees— *not* between himself and the trail.

He slithered between thin, elastic branches, stepping carefully. Ten yards, twenty—the voices began to fade, moving away from him to an outcrop that overlooked the trail. He avoided the sunlight that streamed smokily across a tiny clearing. A twig cracked, pine needles rustled. After checking the map, he moved on. The river twisted just ahead, out of sight of the two men. The aircraft droned closer, passed with a quick, cold shadow across another clearing where felled trunks were stripped and piled, then its noise diminished. The sunlight fell across him like an accusation as he moved out of the trees and began climbing awkwardly down towards the trail. His watch was, repeatedly, close to his face. Two-thirty. He moved on down a thin, crooked scar in the cliffs, hearing the aircraft noise louden once more. Its white belly flashed above him. He must wait for it to become darker. He was less than a mile from Bear Cove, where the track reached the Squaw Creek Arm, but the trail lay like a pale, visible scar along the gorge; exposed and exposing.

His feet wedged against an outcrop. Cool rock seemed to encompass him, forty feet above the trail. A bush straggled out of the rock, masking him. He leaned against the pack and looked up. He would not be seen from above or below. To the north, beyond the lower hills, cloud was massing around Mount Shasta, lowering like a huge dust cloud thrown up by some explosion.

Remaining still had become harder than movement. He began to wonder whether it was just an excuse, whether the apparent cleverness of hiding and waiting was nothing more than a mask for exhaustion and nibbling fear...

Three o'clock. A man in a pale windbreaker was moving along the trail, inexpertly studying the ground for marks. It was easy to imagine he recognized the man. The seaplane was like a pale gull against the approaching clouds. A thin, chill wind had sprung up. Staying where he was became more difficult for Hyde with each step the man took.

The glossy enlargements lay on the walnut table like accusations against himself now, Aubrey thought, rather than against Melstead, who was out in the hall talking loudly over the telephone to his daughter, Alice. It was as if Melstead's words related Aubrey's hints and allegations, and Alice were berating the old friend who had become hostile. Chambers had insisted on the enlargements, the enhancement of shadow and light in the surveillance pictures. And they *were* unnerving: lost, knowing children's faces like those of wizened dwarfs, scruffily innocent or simply cold with the night . . . and Hughes's omnipresence, the seductive urgency or feigned sympathy of his two expressions so easy to interpret. Melstead was arranging dinner with Alice—no, a late supper the following evening. Alice was the organizer of some shelter for the homeless and was on duty . . . Aubrey sighed and rubbed at his forehead as it prickled with perspiration. It almost seemed that Alice was expiating her father's sins with her charity work. He remembered the lively, spoiled darling she had been as a child. Melstead had been past forty, his wife all but past childbearing—and they'd conceived and produced Alice. Boisterous, selfish, exhibiting charm like a new toy when it suited her; then this deep, apparently lasting conversion to Christianity rather than the Left. *Saint* Alice, Melstead had called her in a tone of pride.

Aubrey detested the thought that Alice would know *he* had been the messenger of disgrace.

Then he heard, quite distinctly: "You know that young man Hughes—you introduced me to him . . . ? Yes—Kenneth's here at the moment, sends his love, of course—but there may be trouble for that young man, up ahead. No, not directly, I don't think so—" Melstead's voice was amplified slightly, as if he had turned to face the door of the lounge so that Aubrey might hear more clearly. "—yes, perhaps as a result of that . . . I'll ring off now. Explain tomorrow—yes, take care, my darling—"

Aubrey heard the telephone receiver being replaced and muffled footsteps coming down the long hall towards the lounge. Sleet spat against the tall bay windows where the heavy drapes had been left undrawn. He felt physically nauseated and could not look towards the scattered photographs. Alice could not know Hughes? It had to be an outrageous, daring bluff from beginning to end—surely?

That wasn't the cause of the nausea. It was the evidence of love given and returned and his own role as an agent of demolition that sickened him. As Melstead reentered the lounge, renewed confidence shining on his forehead and cheeks, Aubrey willed himself to think of Kathryn. Alice—Kathryn. A simple equation. Melstead was saving himself, *he* was saving Kathryn. Melstead's next words angered him.

"You heard that, of course, Kenneth? First thing that came into my head when I recognized the young man. Did at once, of course. Horrified by the images there." He gestured with the glass he had taken up but Aubrey shook his head.

Melstead poured himself a second whiskey with a steady hand, and only the slightest clink of decanter against crystal tumbler. As he turned back to Aubrey, his arm seemed to indicate the room's furniture, its paintings and Adam fireplace, the rugs and hangings as if gesturing at defenses that remained unbreached. "I was concerned, Kenneth. I felt obliged to shift and palter, as someone once said—to avoid your questions." He was talking freely, only slightly too quickly. Aubrey remained silent. "But I'm afraid I couldn't keep it from Alice—not from her. I'll try to dress it up as something to do with security, of course." He had stood with his free hand resting on the back of the armchair. Now he sat down with a feigned ease that Aubrey was compelled to admire. He smoothed the knee of his trousers as he crossed his legs. There was no *atom* of doubt that his fiction would be accepted, the matter closed! All his former nervousness was gone; he was exploiting a duplicity that would have done credit to an experienced intelligence agent. But then, he did have a secret life, a deep cover, did he not? "Now, what do you intend doing about this young man? I can see how you thought I might be a better recipient of this information than—"

Aubrey's head was pressed by a hard, tightening band, so that he put his fingers to his temples. Then he shouted at Melstead who, at that instant, seemed inflated by complacency and cleverness: "James, I have *heard* the telephone calls! I know this man is an acquaintance of *yours*, not of Alice!" It was difficult to catch his breath. Melstead seemed to visibly deflate. Rage coursed through Aubrey; he was angry with the subtle wealth of the room, with the sleet staining the black rectangles of the windows, with the photographs on the walnut table! He dashed his hand towards them. "It's gone past pretense, James. There is nothing, nothing you can say to deny your—" He conjured the word with his hand. "—your *complicity* with this creature Hughes."

Melstead sat on the edge of his armchair, the remainder of his whiskey quivering in the tumbler. The rubicund health had vanished from his face, yet there was still that damnable impregnability in his eyes, the assurance that he was beyond reach.

"Kenneth, what are you saying?" His tone was level, almost threatening. But he swallowed at the whiskey quickly, the glass making a small click against his teeth. "What the hell are you accusing me of?" He looked down at the enlargements with malevolence. "Is this some kind of demented persecution, for God's sake? I'm your *friend*, Kenneth! This unspoken something— you're trying to link me with—with *that*?"

Aubrey felt the relief swell in his chest. James had denied everything, there was some other explanation—

—no other, he instructed himself. Kathryn was suddenly in his thoughts and the photographs of Alice on the piano diminished. There was only Kathryn's peril and the ugly, accusing enlargements on the table between them.

"James, it has gone too far to be covered by a few expressions of outrage and an appeal to friendship," he said quietly. Melstead was watching him from narrowed eyes. He occupied the room now like a transient hotel guest rather than its owner. The traffic through Eaton Square hummed beyond the windows. "You called Hughes, more than once. You instructed him to keep everyone away from some place you did not name. Known to him as well as yourself. Some *other* dwelling. You broke contact with him—as if the two of you shared a secret, were part of some network. And that—in those pictures—is the purpose of the network." Melstead was shaking his head. Aubrey pressed on. "You are engaged with Hughes in this vile business with children, James— God knows how or why, but you are!" Melstead appeared about to protest. "No, James, denials are of no use whatsoever. But..."

Melstead's gaze snapped up hungrily from a study of the enlargements. And yet the expression in them was anger, even contempt. Reserves of certainty remained. He was remembering his world, his circle. Longmead, Orrell, cabinet ministers, the powerful and the wealthy; even newpaper proprietors. He felt he could not be damaged, not irretrievably.

"Ridiculous," he murmured, as if seeing Aubrey merely as a nuisance.

"No, James. Vile. Ruinous."

"You think so?"

"James, I have never been more certain in my life."

"And what concern is it of yours, Kenneth?" Melstead flung back, whiskey spilling onto the back of his hand and his trousers. He brushed at the stain savagely. "Do you think *harm* is done, Kenneth, in your Victorian prissiness? Do you really think harm is done?"

A clock on the Adam fireplace struck eleven, sweetly.

"James, I have to tell you that I shall order this man Hughes to be arrested. I shall interrogate him personally. When he has made a full confession, I shall then ask you what I wish to know."

The room, in the ensuing silence, seemed quite small, airless. Melstead's fear and contempt pursued each other like quick clouds across his features. Then he said: "I don't quite see why you are threatening me, Kenneth, except out of some kind of misplaced disgust."

"Yes, I am indeed making threats, to which I intend to adhere, because I am certain you have full knowledge of what happened when MoD canceled the RPV project. No, wait—I am convinced that you were instrumental in their passage to America. I am also certain that, should you assist me in this matter, then the evidence of those photographs and whatever this man Hughes may say . . . will go no further." He breathed deeply, angry with the bargain he proposed, the wizened innocence of the faces in the enlargements accusing him now, as he had used them to accuse Melstead.

Melstead's face was again chalky. The contempt had vanished, the confidence, too. There was only fear, remaining like the most stubborn and irremovable of stains.

"Why must you know?" he blurted.

Aubrey banged his fist on the soft arm of his chair. "Because a lunatic has my niece! Because I can stop him harming her only if I can bring him down! And *you* have the means of helping me. That is why I am prepared to make this Devil's bargain with you—" He caught at his breath, sharply. "—and promise you that the matter there on the table will not be pursued." He leaned forward in his chair. "It is the best, the only hope I can offer you. The only bribe." He almost felt he was still pleading, that his accusations and suspicions were unfounded. Their thirty years and more of friendship lay assassinated on the carpet between them, near the photographs.

Melstead brushed his hand across his hair, his gesture as posed as if he were before a mirror. Another, less assured man looked out from his eyes. Then, after a long silence, he said: "Kenneth—" He cleared his throat and began again more strongly. "I can't help you."

"In spite of—?"

"I *can't*." He appeared to be gagging on guilty knowledge. His expression affirmed everything, especially his terror of Malan.

"You must. It's the only course open to you."

"I can't, damn it! I've told you I can't. Now believe me!"

"Then you realize what they did? You understand everything James?" Melstead said nothing, his mouth dropping in admission. "Very well, James. I do not have the luxury of time—thus, neither do you. If I may use your telephone? Thank you. I shall instruct my people to arrest Hughes tonight."

The tortoiseshell cat lay on the vet's table, its fur drowsy and damp with drugged sleep. The vet fiddled with the x-ray enlargement on the wall, as if fussing over an arrangement of flowers. Ros's big hands, the rings flashing, stroked compulsively along Layla's flank as the cat's dull eyes stared at her, seeming to resent the crooning noises Ros was making; or simply afraid of the ugly gurgling sounds her throat made.

"... broke her foreleg because of the cancer ... can't pin or mend it—the bone's like putty."

Ros heard herself saying: "She doesn't seem in pain."

"Soon," the vet replied. The cat had become aware of the traffic along the Earl's Court Road, or perhaps it was just the blank square of night window behind Ros.

"Christ, he's so bloody *fond* of this cat," Ros muttered. "He's had her for bloody years."

"...make the decision for him."

Ros's vision was blurred. It was not simply that she felt helpless, the cat's form seemed so small and unresisting on the table. The room smelled of dogs. Ros looked up into the young vet's bearded, patient face. "Christ, I don't know what to *do*—!" she blurted and at once began stroking the cat more fiercely as it stirred at the anguish in her voice. The misshapen shoulder where the cancer lodged was disguised when Layla was lying down. Ros had seen the limp a week before and attempted to ignore it.

Now, she couldn't. She glanced furtively up at the x-ray of the sleeping cat, the cancerous, broken leg stretched out, attached tenuously to the cat's body by a sliver of bone and gristle. "Oh, shit."

Hyde would be incensed. Any decision was the wrong one. She felt as drugged and lumpish as the cat appeared. Layla had subsided into trust under the anesthetic of her hands. Outside, around the corner, the Special Branch sergeant Aubrey had assigned to protect Ros was waiting in the car. Thinking of that focused the image that the soft sports bag in which Layla had always been carried would be zipped tight, if she said—

—she couldn't, for Christ's sake, Hyde would kill her!

Just popping up to the chemist's up the road. Present for the wife, her birthday, the sergeant had announced, locking the car before walking her to the vet's doorway. A dim, grubby light had burned behind the colored glass in the door as she had rung the bell.

Ros was desperately trying to escape all responsibility. Christ, it was bloody *agony!*

"All—all right," she muttered.

"She's a very old cat."

"What difference does that make!"

Layla was bedraggled and small on the table, her staring, unfocused eyes blackened by the drugs. Layla's fur was especially damp on her broken leg where the anesthetic had caused her to dribble. The vet snipped gently at a patch of fur on the cat's other foreleg. Layla stirred. Then he filled a syringe. Ros glanced at the x-ray and found only a further confirmation. Layla mewed dully and struggled to move. Ros crooned more urgently, as much for her own sake as the cat's: *Christ, Layla, I'm sorry—Hyde, I'm sorry.*

The needle, a tiny struggle, a huge black accusing stare; quiet. Ros's eyes filled with tears.

After checking that her heart had stopped beating, the vet said: "I'll get a blanket—you've a car?"

"What? Yes."

He lifted Layla's body and went out of the room. Mechanically Ros bent and scooped up the zip bag out of which the cat's head had poked as it inspected the world every time Hyde took it—*had taken it*—anywhere. There was fur on the table—fur on Hyde's carpets and bed at home, on her bed, too. And there was the hole the bloke in the ground floor flat had dug in the garden after she had had the phone call about the x-ray. She still hadn't been able to come until now. Her breath must smell of brandy. There at least had to be a spot she could point to when Hyde got back and say, *I buried her there.*

Layla was shockingly heavy as the vet put the wrapped body into her arms. The zip bag lay open-mouthed on the table. The vet held it as tenderly as she held the cat's weight, then lowered the body into the bag. He slowly zipped it closed. The noise was like fingernails dragged down a window.

"I'll see you out."

Ros almost stumbled on the steps, the streetlights and headlights dazzling like a shimmering curtain through the unavoidable tears. She held the bag as if it contained explosives already primed.

She turned blindly out of the gate onto the Earl's Court Road, then turned again at the corner where the car was waiting for her, wiping her face furiously all the time, the skin wet and stretched beneath her eyes.

"Hello, Ros. Ms. Woode—good evening."

The voice belonged to a stranger. There was a hand on her arm. Layla's weight dragged at her other arm.

"What—?" she blurted. The man's face was wetly indistinct, even under the street lamp on the corner. She felt obscurely afraid of him; bulky, tall, assured. The accent—? "Get off me."

"You don't remember me? We've met before." South African? She heard it through a muddy, distorting pulse of distraction.

"Look, I haven't—"

"Where is he, Ros?" The man's grip had tightened on the sleeve of her fur coat, almost as she had convulsively gripped Layla's fur as the needle was inserted. "I know you'll know. He always told you things. Some friends of mine in the CIA want to know what he's told you."

"Get off me—" She wriggled her arm. Her bracelets jingled but he did not release his grip. She looked twenty yards up the side street towards the car. Inside it, she could see two shadows, not one. "Christ."

"Your friend's occupied." The traffic, released from the lights at the underground station, rushed past them, pressingly close. Two men drifted past, talking excitedly in high voices. The man pulled her against the wall at the corner. "Now, Ros, if you tell me here, I'll leave you alone. Otherwise, you'll have to come with us. OK?"

"Blantyre—you're that bastard Blantyre!" Ros blurted, recognizing him. "Get your bloody hands off me, you shit!" She struggled, almost tearing her sleeve free of his grip. He pressed against her, his voice a hoarse whisper.

"Well done, Ros. Now, you're going to have to come with us. We don't want an ugly scene, do we?"

The pavement seemed deserted. Even the traffic had been corraled farther down the Earl's Court Road, at the junction with the Old Brompton Road; the waiting cars as noisy and impatient as horses.

"I don't know where he is!"

"Of course you do, Ros—he's called you, Aubrey's been to see you. He's in California, Ros, I know that much. Now, what's he going to do?"

He was pushing against her so that she was being urged up the side street towards the car.

"Your bloody bug! What were you doing in my flat, you shit? Get off me!" She groaned as the zip bag swung against the wall, then against a parked car's door as she struggled. One of her rings caught Blantyre's cheek, scraping it dark in the sodium glare. He clutched at it, releasing his grip. Ros stumbled, then ran heavily, blundering back onto the Earl's Court Road, his footsteps already behind her. The traffic rushed past, solid as a blurred wall.

She ran across the road, dodging the thinned traffic, the bag swinging wildly in her efforts. She heard traffic behind her, saw Blantyre lurching back onto the opposite pavement, out of its path. Ros hurried, her heels clattering, beginning to echo as she turned into a dark garden square. His shoes echoed, too, as she stumbled alongside the railings of the gardens. Her heart was shocked and violently grieved as a cat bolted across the road directly in front of her.

Blantyre was thirty yards, no more, behind her. The zip bag banged silently against the railings as she turned to look. Oh, *Christ*—!

Twenty yards. She stumbled and fell. Footsteps beat louder like the noise of a drum. Then his breathing was audible above her own, his shadow between her and the closest street lamp. The zip bag rested beside her, awkwardly lumpy. Blantyre was grinning and holding his cheek as he leaned over her.

"Listen to me, you fat, ugly bitch!" he growled breathlessly. "Just tell me where he is and what he's doing in California. Tell me now and you can go straight home! What orders has Aubrey given him, Ros?" He kicked her in the side. Surprised shock masked the pain for a moment, then her ribs burned. She clutched her side as he knelt by her, holding her face in one hand, squeezing at either side of her jaw. "Don't piss about with me, Ros. Hyde must have told you I'm a sadistic sod—didn't he?" He shook her face until her teeth seemed loose, her thoughts loose in her skull. She glanced at the zip bag. "Come on, Ros—what orders did Aubrey give that Australian arsehole?" He raised his hand, smiling. "Otherwise, the scenario's rape and murder. It was going to happen outside your place, in the gardens there, but here'll do—make a noise and I'll break your bloody neck *now!*" He dragged at her arm. In terror, she allowed herself to be pulled to her feet. "But it needn't be like that," he purred.

Ros reached down for the zip bag.

"Leave that." He kicked the bag aside with his instep, as if it were a football.

"You *cunt!*" she bellowed. Blantyre hit her, knocking her back against the railings.

There was a yell, then a single shot, a warning. Another shout, the crackle of a transmitter. Blantyre's shadow, leaning down to her—

—gone. The policeman's breathing, his hand on his knee as he doubled over, his gun in one hand. Blantyre's retreating footsteps.

"Christ, I'm sorry, Ms. Woode! I'm really sorry! He was in the car when I got back—" Breathing in raggedly. "God—just took me by surprise . . . fingers up his nose in the end, got away—who *were* they?" The R/T crackled with a voice demanding further information. "Barkston Gardens. Two men, one in my car . . . yes, yes, quick as you can." He studied the dark garden square, then bent down to Ros once more. "Who was he?"

"Tell Aubrey," Ros grunted, holding the zip bag in her lap, cradling it, "it was Blantyre—someone called Blantyre. He's desperate, tell Aubrey." The yell of a home-going drunk startled both of them. Ros began shivering uncontrollably. "Tell him now," she insisted. "He wanted to know about Hyde. He's Rhodesian, South African, something . . ."

Then it no longer seemed important. Slowly, carefully, she unzipped the soft bag, opened the blanket and touched fur. Layla's body was still warm, the fur dry and soft once more.

Bear Cove was gray and deserted in the slanting, driving rain that had soaked him. He eased himself between two split shards of rock. The small launch was below him, tossing like a nervous animal on the wind-distressed water. The waves were choppy, insistent. He wiped his sodden sleeve across his forehead. Low cloud obscured the hills on the opposite shore of the Squaw Creek Arm.

There was only the empty, flecked water and the moving curtain of rain. Dusk glowered.

He had seen two rain-soaked men sheltering in a tight clump of firs, half an hour earlier, and had left the trail to skirt them, then rejoined it half a mile from the cover.

As he moved closer, he could hear the launch's hull grinding against the rocks. He was feverish with wet and cold. He folded his numb hands tightly beneath his armpits. The butt of the Browning, when he had last touched it inside his jacket, had felt lumpy, awkward. The FN rifle clinked against a rock as it swung in front of his chest. He stilled it, paused, then continued to move down the cleft to the paring of pebbly shore where the launch ground and complained. Lightning flashed hazily behind the cloud, away to the north, like an aimless searchlight. The rumble of thunder hastily followed the light. The storm was moving closer.

He heaved at the spike he had driven into the pebbles to moor the launch, but could not move it. Untied the sodden blue rope and flung it into the bow, pushing the launch against the angry bustle and tear of the swell, then clambered aboard. The boat lurched and bobbed violently, nuzzling the shore then the rocks that had hidden it, as he tried to start the engine. Huge raindrops splashed on the engine cowling. More lightning, then the thunder in a muffled outburst of rage. The engine fired weakly, then its consumptive note strengthened until it was too loud, alarming him as he reversed the launch out of the cleft of shore. The wind pulled his jacket up his back like a violent hand, away from his shoulders, around his face, and cuffed him with stinging rain. He turned the launch and jerkily slopped out into the lake. The boat sloshed with water. His hands were white on the wheel. Lightning, then the engine's din drowned by the thunder. Then the engine noise came back, seeming to boom off the cliffs.

He rounded the shoulder of the cove and the wind thrust the boat askew. The rain parted for a moment. There was someone standing on the rocks above the tiny inlet. Hyde all but raised his arm in an offensive, derisory salute; there was something exhilarating about the weather that made him feel reckless. Rain swept back across the scene, obliterating the armed man, the transmitter clamped against his white face. Hyde cocked his head. It must be too bad for the seaplane to be flying. He'd lost sight and sound of it a little after four, had assumed it must have returned to the other arm of the lake to refuel.

He squinted ahead, through the murk. The rain was cold on his neck and pressed the jacket and thick shirt soddenly against his skin. The western shore appeared momentarily, disappeared, reappeared minutes later. He saw his passage as a dotted line on the memorized map in his imagination. He had studied it for almost an hour, knowing the storm was coming. It was two and a half miles directly southwest to the boat landing at Ski Island. Once there, he could take his bearings again for the McCloud River Arm. He glanced at the compass, closed its tiny lid, then left it dangling outside his shirt. He listened for other boats, the noise of engines. Lightning splashed a dull gleam on his white hands and the thunder was almost instantaneous. There'd be no one out on the lake in this.

He caught a glimpse of the shoreline, wet gray cliffs looming out of the rain, too close, and he heaved at the wheel, changing course with a huge effort. The shore disappeared in the murk. Almost dark. Lightning once more, ripping down like a great, livid injury to the cloud.

Thunder at once. The rain ran into his eyes, down his body, its blows heavier, more dispiriting.

His eyes were dazzled by light. The thunder did not follow. Light splashed again. He heard the sound of an engine, saw the flank of their big launch swinging out of the murk, the searchlight mounted in the bow spraying its gleam beyond him, the shapes of two men beside it, armed, the noise of its engines drowning his own. Then the rain folded behind the launch. It had come within twenty yards of him but he had remained unseen as it rushed hungrily towards Bear Cove. He heard its engines diminish. Lightning obscured the glow of its searchlight, then thunder deafened him, booming overhead.

He looked at his watch, judging the distance he had come. Looked at the fuel gauge, at the compass, towards the invisible shore. Looked again at his watch. The wind was hurrying him. He would make Ski Island soon, then another hour on the lake would bring him into the McCloud Arm—but the wind would be against him there, heading north. He had hours, though, he told himself, hours...

He'd have to dive in *this*, or worse. Jesus wept. He'd be alone on the lake...and that was no comfort at all. None. He eased back on the throttle as the cliffs came out of the rain and lights prickled in an almost-complete darkness a little way off to port. Ski Island.

Strangely, he knew something was wrong with Layla, and that thought was colder than his other preoccupations. Ski Island's slightly sheltered inlet embraced the small boat and he shrugged at the wind as if to shake its grip away. Something was wrong with the cat—why should he think that? He let the engine idle, flicked on the pencil beam of his flashlight and studied the map as best he could in its plastic envelope.

*   *   *

The wind banged against the walls of the lodge and Kathryn hunched into herself, elbows resting heavily on the wooden table. Harrell sat opposite her, speaking into his R/T. Another man—Becker—sat behind her. He was lolling on the sofa in the shadows near the fire, which flickered and belched because of the downdrafts. The large lamplit room was murky with wood smoke.

"OK, call it off for tonight—yeah, come on home. If he's still out on the water, which I doubt, he can have all the freedom he wants, for the moment." Kathryn winced at the grin he gave her as he put the R/T down heavily on the table. "More coffee?" he inquired. She shook her head. After that initial and only beating, his politeness was unfailing and appallingly unnerving. Harrell sighed, stood up, stretched. She hated the ease with which she flinched at his slow, casual movements.

"You still haven't caught him, have you," she announced, realizing that she sounded like a child whistling in the dark. Hyde's continued freedom was her only consolation.

Harrell shook his head. Only his eyes were unamused. "It won't be long. Nothing's more certain than the fact that Patrick Hyde's going to be sitting here right next to you, maybe tomorrow, maybe the next day. Or lying on the floor, making a mess of the rugs." Becker laughed, then yawned.

Kathryn thrust her fingers through her cropped hair until the skin of her forehead was stretched, aching. Then she held her hands against the back of her neck because they had begun to quiver again. Not because of Harrell, who had poured himself more coffee and returned to his seat opposite her, not even because of her own brief, unavoidable future...but because stillness, imprisonment, the inability to escape or subdue her imagination, had caused subsidence. Rather, the runaway vehicle of the recent past had collided with a brick wall and shattered to pieces. *Her* past had crumbled, become mangled, injuring her in the collision; it had killed John. Her world had been changed long before John and then Hyde had invaded it with *their* world, long before her uncle had used her as he had. Her past had been a cheat, a conspiracy to defraud. What a God-awful *mess* everything had become.

John had asked her about Shapiro—she'd told Harrell as much. Asked about the RPV deal, the money Shapiro stood to lose. That afternoon, before the storm, she'd volunteered that information. It didn't seem to matter any longer how much she told Harrell now that she had told him about Hyde; except that she had still retained that extra cross on Hyde's map, kept that safe. That was Hyde's only edge. Unless Hyde succeeded in whatever it was he intended, then not very much at all mattered. She was lethargic with the collapse of her world.

She held onto her neck and said: "You planned it all the way ahead?"

"Planned what?"

"You know what."

"No." He shook his head. "Surprised? Ms. Aubrey, we bought those weapons because we collect items like that, just in case. Never know when they might come in handy, or where. Your uncle may think it was all planned a long time ago—probably does—but we made a purely speculative purchase." He grinned. "Which makes the fact that it's the thread that brought your lover man and now Hyde after us kind of amusing— and annoying." He rubbed his nose. "I guess we imagined they might come in handy south of Mexico somewhere—at first. Then we got an approach from some people over there."

"And you hired out like the A-Team," Kathryn snapped, letting her hands fall to her lap and curl there, as if she wished not to touch herself. They allowed her to shower, to change, even to use makeup; she wasn't dirty, perhaps it was just the grubbiness of their company or Harrell's words.

Harrell grinned. "You're just a power dresser from the Sun Belt . . . you're not even really an American. You think you can tell me things?" His good humor—along with Becker's chorus of snorts and smirks—was relentless. "This little group was formed to play the world's policemen. People like us are doing the best we can. That's all there is to it. You're talking like someone prewar, Ms. Aubrey. Maybe it's your English uncle. He's out of date, too. Your cry is *I don't want to get my hands dirty*. I'll just tell you, Ms. Aubrey, that we are all involved. So, when something like this comes along and you can see the clear advantage of it to your country, then you expect to have to do it. That's it, and that's all of it." He shrugged luxuriously.

"God bless America."

"You've said that before."

His ease, his candor, etched her own fate very clearly. Before he had begun to talk to her, out on the jetty and later indoors, her future had been like an iron bar being heated in a fire. Now, it had been used to scar her and she felt its pain. She suppressed a shudder, yet he seemed to sense it and smiled.

"So," she continued, "you just concluded that things would go wrong over there and took the lady out of the game?" It seemed important to continue the conversation. It distracted her, at least.

"We judged that they wouldn't succeed over there. We had the example of the Baltic states and the southern republics. That was some mess. *No one* wanted any more trouble or instability. Things were becoming serious. No, don't smile in that superior way, Ms. Aubrey. It's the plain truth. It was geopolitical, not just about a few people. The US wants to reduce its presence in Europe, maybe in other parts of the world. How could we do that while it was breaking up over there? It had gotten past just applying the brakes. The thing had to be stopped. That's what people like you never understand. Your uncle doesn't. The geopolitical."

"So you shot down an *American* airliner full of innocent people, just to try those damn things out?" Reluctantly—or perhaps gratefully—she was drawn into the passion of a heated debate, into some kind of closing speech for the defense. Perhaps it was his contempt for her that stung. "You killed your own, Harrell—that's what it all comes down to!"

"I regret that. I don't expect you to believe me, but it's true." He looked towards the window behind her, above Becker's lounging head. Kathryn shivered. It was still down there—something was.

She shouted: "You killed John, too, for the same reason!"

"I regret that, too. We gave him time to get tired of it, but he didn't. The people over there wanted us to be really *in*, taking the same kind of risks as them. Prove it, they said. On your own people. We did. It's just good security when *everyone's* got at least one guilty secret."

Kathryn sat back, her face stretched taut, the skin somehow deadened. She was appalled at his blasé narration, not its content so much as its tone. His level, unreflective air; his pronouncement of acceptable, believed certainties. John was passed over as an incident, nothing more. Like the Russian woman.

Images of her father crowded in; his goodness, the sense of how much better he was than anyone else she

had ever known. Images of John, too; of the way she
had hurt him, even the way she hadn't helped, had let
him die. Her eyes were moist. Harrell seemed puzzled.
To deflect his now embarrassing interest, she snapped:
"What was your father like?"

He seemed surprised, then answered: "The American
dream father, I guess. We're still close. He lives in a
white-painted frame house behind a picket fence up in
Connecticut. He's patriarchal and kind and wise...he
really is, Ms. Aubrey, and I love him." He grinned. "So
you see, I'm no monster."

"People like you never understand that maybe people
like me don't want you to do the things you do on our
behalf."

He flapped his arms in a dismissive shrug.

She heard the tramp of feet on the lodge's wooden
porch, then the door sprang open and the wind chilled
the room, as smoke billowed from the fireplace, wrea-
thing the elk's head mounted above two hunting rifles.
Up there, she thought. Hyde's face, surprised in death,
next to the elk, then her own face next to Hyde's.

She shivered with cold and fear. She knew she must
try to escape—do *something* to help herself. The thought
was clear and precise, even amid the smoke and coughing
and mild curses. She must try to get away.

"Six forty-two and the subject is on the move." Chambers stretched behind the wheel of the Escort and
grinned. Then his stubble rasped against the radio mike
before he thrust it back into its clip on the dashboard.

Thirty yards away, Melstead had emerged from the
door of the cream-faced Eaton Square house. Chambers
felt his dry, stale mouth dampen at Melstead's obvious
furtiveness. The camera slid up between his eye and its
subject, and the shutter clicked; the motor whirred on,

time and again. The suggestion of dawn lay beyond the
bare trees of the square like a pencil line made grubby
by a smearing finger. Melstead walked briskly along the
pavement and drew something from his pocket. He was
opposite the small Vauxhall he used in London, now
that there were no official cars. Chambers put the camera
on the passenger seat of the Ford and slapped the steering
wheel as if breaking a horse into a gallop. His eagerness
was palpable, he felt freshly awake.

Godwin's voice cracked from the radio.

"I won't lose him," Chambers snapped into the mike.
The Vauxhall pulled out from the line of parked cars,
towards him, headlights glaring across the Ford's windscreen. "He's on his way, Tony—he's on his way," he
breathed, then started the engine and tugged at the
wheel, turning the car out and around, reversing as the
Vauxhall's brake lights winked. Then he began to follow. "Out of Eaton Square, heading east into town," he
murmured, his excitement hard to dissemble.

Jesus, how he'd waited for this. Almost two years, to
stuff Melstead good and for all. That old fart Aubrey
had said his pal Melstead would not be panicked, had
argued against the tactic. But Aubrey had been wrong,
had clung to the old school tie only to find it had rotted
through. *The blind, characteristic prejudices of your
class,* someone had once told him. Well, up you, mate—
this bastard up ahead shags little boys!

"Turning into Ebury Street," he murmured mechanically, but was unable to swallow the hard, tight lump
in his throat, or rub his damp palms dry on the wheel.
"Grosvenor Gardens, moving north."

The walls of the gardens of Buck House on his right,
the Vauxhall steady almost a hundred yards ahead of
him, its pale color flashing out beneath each street lamp,
the dawn struggling with low cloud away beyond the

palace's bulk. More traffic at Hyde Park Corner and the great arch and Apsley House. The Vauxhall slipped into Park Lane. The billow of an Arab's garments in the early dawn breeze, on the steps of the Dorchester. The flash and clutter of brake lights, amazingly, from the first parked coaches of early Christmas shoppers disgorging near Marble Arch too soon for the shops to be open. Someone lying as if wounded on the wide pavement, a huddle of old clothes. The Edgware Road, the first cafés burning grubby lights. His excitement registered landmarks, street names.

This will do you a lot of good, Terry, old son ... but he had to court Aubrey, had to be—as Godwin said—careful with the old man. But was Aubrey a stayer? Orrell didn't like him, and Chambers wanted to get into the SIS mainstream and quickly. Didn't want to work for years with an old man and a cripple, however clever they—

—admitting it, then? The present company doesn't allow you to shine, does it? He snorted, began pummeling the steering wheel at traffic lights, the Vauxhall drawing away and turning right onto the Marylebone Road. Where was he going? The Vauxhall vanished and he felt a chill possess his chest and stomach as Godwin's voice crackled from the radio: "Where are you, Terry?"

"Bloody Edgware Road—traffic lights!" he snapped.

"Have you lost—?"

"I bloody haven't! I'm not losing this bugger, mate!" Not bloody likely. Turned into the Marylebone Road— *where?* The traffic was thicker, a strip of dawn beyond the skeletal trees and grubby buildings. *Where the fuck was he?* Traffic lights again. He groaned aloud—it was going to be so bloody *simple,* for Christ's sake! Red Alfa, black Porsche, three bloody BMWs, a ratty godforsaken Datsun from the year dot, the tarted-up fake van from a flower shop... Vauxhall! No, bloody *blue* Vauxhall. Green—

—horns barked crossly behind him as he swung into the inside lane and overtook two taxis and a truck, then slid back into the outside lane—hands slippery on the wheel. Traffic lights—for Christ's sake, traffic lights! He slapped at the wheel, heaving his shoulders in impotent rage. The black Porsche drew up beside him, the young, fair-haired driver grinning at him.

Melstead—where was he, where was he going? There was no bloody suitcase! He hadn't taken anything with him, so where was he running?

Oh, yes—Chambers was certain. His whole manner, the slope and movement of his body, the quick darting of his head, all suggested he was running to somewhere.

"Terry!" Godwin seemed to be whispering. "Terry, are you still in contact?"

"Christ, yes!"

Green—he shot forward, well in the rear of the Porsche. A BMW nuzzled alongside and he accelerated, weaving in front of it as if on ice, then back into the outside lane having overtaken another truck that had turned out from Baker Street. Oh, Jesus, you bastard, where *are* you? Baker Street—had he turned left? Gloucester Place, he could have slipped up there!

"Terry, you'd better not have lost touch—" God, the bugger was whispering now! Shit, his thoughts wailed. Lights green ahead—Park Crescent. Aubrey lived around here, didn't he? His panic was such that he all but anticipated the old man's angry figure to appear at the passenger window and wave his stick in admonishment. "Hughes is being stubborn. The old man's very angry—" *I knew that!* "—Hughes thinks he's invulnerable. Just don't *lose* Melstead."

Lights red. He screeched to a halt. The Porsche had slipped the lights easily—Yuppie bastard! Oh, *ballocks!*

The pale Vauxhall, Melstead's profile identifiable, turned left into Albany Street and disappeared. He felt elation, then concentrated hatred of Melstead. He flicked on his indicator and waited, his breathing as loud as static from the radio.

"I've got the bugger," he murmured, though not to Godwin.

Aubrey had called Melstead three or four times during the night, *just to clarify certain matters, James,* or *just to inquire whether you now have anything to tell me, James* . . . rattling the man. Because they hadn't been able to locate Hughes until a couple of hours ago. Godwin had told him just after five; they'd picked him up when he returned to the squat. Aubrey had wanted to steer clear of Melstead, just take Hughes to pieces and get at the truth that way. But the old man had been badly unnerved by the attack on Ros Woode and by Hughes's nonappearance.

Green. He slewed across the traffic, heard the groan and scrape of impact, the blare of horns, and then he was in Albany Street, wildly searching for a glimpse of the Vauxhall.

He slowed opposite a small, weedy parking lot in Osnaburgh Street. Melstead was walking unconcernedly away from the Vauxhall, a suitcase in his hand, his dark overcoat buttoned, his trilby firmly on his head. Umbrella, for God's sake, like a walking stick militarily marching beside him! He'd had a suitcase ready in the trunk of the car, then . . .

Got you, you bastard. He drew into the curb and got out of the Ford. The air struck cold on his face and hands, and his breath steamed as he looked towards the Wren church that was the SPCK's headquarters. He locked the door, fed the meter, and hurried after Melstead, who was strolling—bloody hell, *strolling*—towards the Euston Tower with its copse of aerials and transmitters.

Melstead had panicked, just as Chambers himself had suggested. He sneered in self-congratulation. The excitement had returned.

He was fairly inconspicuous following Melstead, even at this time of the morning. Spicy smells teemed from an Asian delicatessen. A newspaper shop emitted dirty striplighting and cigarette smoke. Where *was* Melstead going?

Chambers crossed Gower Street, sliding across a taxi's hood as easily as a matador, hurrying after Melstead's broad, erect figure. Euston? He'd need time to ring in—hadn't told Godwin he was out of the car, oh who cares. Melstead was firmly in view, unsuspicious. Chambers's mouth kept widening in a silly, satisfied grin. Was Melstead meeting someone—did he think he was meeting Hughes? He hadn't called anyone since midnight, when he'd tried Orrell at home and got a frosty answer from an awoken Lady Orrell. *Clive's not here, James.*

Melstead turned right towards the sullen portico of Euston. Taxis slipped down into a tunnel. Chambers's stomach tightened at the sight of a row of telephone boxes, all but one empty. He really should call in. Did Melstead have a booking, even a ticket? The man's unknown destination and motive angered him. Vanity and outrage mingled. *This will do you a lot of good—don't lose him.* Melstead entered the station's vast concourse. The bums and drifters and tramps had risen and left, the station was busy with the earliest commuters of the day, the first of the departing businessmen. Melstead headed for the newspaper stand and Chambers relaxed.

Telephone. A clear glass booth with a direct view of

the newspaper stand. Melstead had hitched up the side of his overcoat, searching his pocket for change. Chambers slipped into the booth and dialed the Center Point number after pressing his phone card into the slot. Godwin answered at once. Melstead plucked up two newspapers, lodging them under his arm. Laid down change. He hadn't bought a ticket yet.

"Yes?"

A group of commuting businessmen had half-obscured Melstead at the stand. Melstead moved aside and removed his trilby, looking up at the Departures board.

"Euston. He's got a suitcase, looking at the board now. Hasn't got a ticket, I don't think. What do you want me to do?"

A pause—Melstead standing, trilby back on, suitcase at his feet, papers tucked beneath his chin as he removed his overcoat. He heard Godwin murmuring to Aubrey, presumably, then: "If he's leaving town, you'd better detain him. Do it *gently,* Terry. Just tell him Sir Kenneth would like to talk to him again this morning."

"OK."

The small knot still around the stand, a scattering flock of commuters from one of the platforms swelling the numbers in the concourse. Open overcoats, briefcases, cellular telephones, newspapers. A disheveled tramp slumped near the croissant and pastry bar below the Pullman Lounge. He saw Melstead's dark overcoat, trilby, suitcase underneath the Departures board. Godwin had rung off, Chambers could almost see Melstead standing as he had been a moment before—

—almost.

He lurched out of the phone booth, holding on to the door to stop himself overbalancing in his renewed panic. He scanned the platform entrances, the ticket counter, the newspaper stand, the flower seller, the book shop, the croissant bar, the blank windows of the upstairs lounge, the tube escalator—*trilby, dark overcoat, for Christ's sake!*

Then he realized. The overcoat had been removed. Melstead had known, at least suspected. Now, he'd vanished.

Chambers began running towards the newspaper stand.

15

THE SECRETS
OF ALL HEARTS

He knew the woman would be becoming increasingly desperate, knew the fear she would now be experiencing. It wasn't simply his own concerns, his rage that despite the map reference and depth indication Frascati had scribbled on his chart, he had not located the control vehicle's wreckage. No, it wasn't even his own mounting despair as he sat huddled into the long, padded coat, his back against a rock, checking and rechecking his diving plan. It was the woman across there—

—a light sprang on in one of the lodge's windows, startling him. He stared at it, mesmerized, until it was once more switched off. The noise of their patroling launch, on the other side of the McCloud Arm, was perfunctory and intermittent above the sound of the wind, which dragged great starlit holes in the clouds. To stifle thoughts of the woman, he studied his watch once more and shivered, as if he had exactly measured the amount of extra nitrogen in his blood. He must wait another fifteen minutes before he could safely reenter the water. The bottom time that would then remain was no more than thirty minutes before he would have to begin his decompression ascent, then take another, longer enforced rest which would keep him ashore until after dawn. He clenched his fists slowly, unclenched them, repeated the gesture as if exercising. Why bother to go back in? He wouldn't find it anyway. So why bother . . . ?

But Frascati had found it, it was down there! he raged, wrapping his arms around himself, bending forward as if to vomit then rocking gently to and fro, nursing his frustration. Frascati had marked it on the map, it was *down there!*

And you can't find it . . .

And the woman over there . . . The only good thing was that Harrell had no idea what had been marked on Frascati's map, otherwise the launch would be on this side of the arm, looking for him. He huddled over the pencil beam of the flashlight, again rechecking the diving plan he had tabled in a tiny notebook. He couldn't risk staying down as deep as fifty meters for longer than half an hour—it couldn't *be* deeper than that, otherwise Frascati wouldn't have found it!

It would be daylight before he could go down again. This would be the final dive. By tomorrow night, the woman would have broken like an egg and Harrell might have found him.

The anxiety that they might spot the buoy from which the diving line descended nibbled for a moment, then became quelled. The windy darkness, without a moon, blackened the distressed surface of the water. Their launch puttered towards the jetty in front of the lodge and a trick of the wind carried the bump of the boat's flank and raised voices. He did not bother to lift his night glasses to this eyes. They'd been moving up and down the stretch of water in front of the lodge for most of the night, searching the wooded, rocky shoreline with a thermal imager, he presumed.

He heard the door of the lodge bang in another slanting gust of wind, and lights sprang out once more. Through the night glasses, he had counted seven of them. He had not seen Harrell. He looked at his watch, then got up and began changing the regulator from the used air tank to a new one. He had thirty minutes, perhaps forty at the utter limit. He had scanned the crevices, the drowned beds of small streams, the rock faces—and found nothing. He'd searched an area hundreds of meters square, to a depth of fifty meters, crisscrossing the cliff face. It was there, Frascati's map proclaimed, but it remained invisible. If it was deeper than fifty meters, then he'd never find it. He heaved the air tank onto his back, adjusted the straps, checked his buoyancy compensator, his depth gauge, watch, lamp, the camera and electronic flashgun, the dry suit...replaced his face mask, then fitted the mouthpiece of the Aqua-Lung. Carefully, he flopped across the pebbles to the water's edge, began to wade, then swim. The wind tugged at his head as the currents pulled at his legs. He reached the buoy, paused, then began descending the diving shot line, flicking on the lamp. The rocky cliff slid more and more dimly towards invisibility. The dry suit began to squeeze and he pressed the valve on his chest to bleed air into it, flicking himself downwards past twenty meters, then thirty with increasing speed. Twenty-eight minutes remaining. The lamp's beam wobbled across the slope of the cliff face. When the gauge showed fifty meters, he clipped his own line to the diving shot line. His previous two dives had traced the same pattern as he now began, once at twenty meters, the other at thirty-five. He checked his compass, wiping the lamp in regular sweeps across the drowned landscape. Tumbled rock-falls, the cracks of old watercourses, a twisted, nude tree. He reached the limit of the line and turned.

Twenty minutes remaining. The beam of the lamp, in which silt rolled like fog, slipped across something that evoked a sense of structure. His breathing quickened before he could calm it. He moved closer. A gaping hole, the suggestion of parallel lines, the twisting feel of a path, then the corner of a small building. His disappointment was intense even as he was drawn towards the place. The doorway gaped. The chimney was intact. He floated above the cabin, experiencing a strange sense of claustrophobia, compounded by the alienness of the element in which he moved. Then he drifted towards the doorway, the beam of the lamp glancing across the shreds of curtains at the windows. *Eighteen minutes!* He kicked himself free of the place's spell, moving on. The darkness seemed more intense beyond the feeble lamplight. His breathing increased. He regulated it with a greater effort than before. It was down there—

—unless Frascati had scribbled lies on his map, driven to forgery to support his increasingly disbelieved and untenable theory. Hyde paused, treading dark water. The lamplight circled him like a threatening fish. He believed he could sense the water's cold even through the insulation of the dry suit. He felt isolated, sensed the pressure of water above and around him, the uncertain black depth of it beneath. His head seemed tight, as if filled with the pressure of the increased nitrogen in his blood. His awareness of time being lost was that of a dreamer rather than a participant.

Then, the image of Harrell emerged, almost as if the man were actually swimming towards him, releasing Hyde from his paralysis of will. Frascati had been certain; Harrell had killed him because there was something down here.

Hyde began moving again, more urgently. Fifteen minutes remained. A cave that must once have been behind a waterfall, a long ledge where people might have climbed, even walked. Harrell had been able to keep the FAA quiet, whatever the wreckage had told them—but not Frascati. It was down here, where the airliner, presumably, had been intended to crash and be lost instead of scattering itself across Horse Mountain. Now, the control vehicle was down here somewhere...

Eleven minutes. He turned once more, going down beyond fifty-five meters, moving more and more urgently. Ten minutes. A large rockfall, a submarine avalanche. The flashlight washed back and forth across it as he moved closer, entering a narrow defile that must have been carved by a quick stream and which twisted like a snake. Light glanced back from a thread of something in the rock—mica?—then flashed back again as from a mirror. Cautiously, he stood on a large rock, floating as if time was irrelevant—seven minutes—moving the lamp rhythmically, carefully. The depth was greater than Frascati had indicated, but then the rockfall might... it couldn't be down here, not—

—buried. By an avalanche.

He moved closer, sensing the narrowness of the twisting gully, the looseness of rocks, the silt drifting up into the lamplight as a rock rolled away from the slightest pressure of his left fin. Something swordlike, thrusting perhaps six or seven feet out of a strewn jumble of rocks and shards coated with silt.

The rotor blade of a helicopter. Light reflected from silt-patched Perspex which curved with the exaggeration of a baby's skull. He thrust rocks aside with his fins, kicking in slow motion, the rocks rolling slowly, softly into the darkness. He dipped forward, wiping at the expanse of cockpit he had uncovered. There had to have been another rockfall since Frascati's discovery. Perhaps it had been half-buried when he first found it . . . buried enough for Harrell to decide to leave the wreckage where it was. An army helicopter . . . the water and fish had bared almost to the bone the face that stared up at him. Hair floated lazily, all but detached from the blackened, rotted features. The limp, half-vanished body was clothed in the rags of US Army fatigues. There was a cursory moment of revulsion, then only excitement. Five and a half minutes—it had to be longer now, whatever the risk.

From the shape and bulge of its cockpit, Hyde could tell that it was a large army lifting helicopter. There would be other bodies inside. It had come down—had to have—while . . . but Frascati had labeled it CT, not with an H for helicopter. The control vehicle that had launched the RPV would have been brought in and out of Shasta by helicopter, just as it had in Tadzhikistan. A mirror image. The truck *was* down here, down . . . it might have slipped fifty meters deeper because of the avalanche. A rock rolled across the Perspex, moving like tumbleweed in a wind. Silt billowed into the lamplight. Four minutes—no, he had to make that at least ten now. And another half-hour before he reached the surface— his air was OK, time, time . . . Daybreak waited on the surface, as tangible and dangerous as if their launch hovered above.

A twisted, distorted length of lifting gear snaked across the strewn defile. The lamplight followed it as if tracking a darting fish. Somewhere, somewhere...He calmed his breathing again. Bubbles roared silently past his face mask. The big helicopter might have become wedged into the gully, then safely buried. Harrell couldn't have had it raised and removed during the summer anyway, not in full view of hundreds of tourists.

Hyde spent another three minutes skimming back and forth along the defile, the lamp busy as a mole, burrowing amid the debris of the avalanche. Then the silted edge of the truck, colorless, dented, seemed to materialize from the rocks. He rolled one away, then another. The launch rail was buckled, the roof of the truck scorched? Yes, scorched by the ignition of the RPV's engine. He moved through the silt as if dragging aside gauzy curtains, his hands slithering and smoothing, pushing small boulders aside, finding the rear doors, locked still, then the front compartment, the driver's door. The silt eddied around him, stirred by the movement of the rocks and his own escalating current in the water. It *was* here—he had it now, almost all of it.

On the driver's door, he spotted the sick joke of an aircraft silhouette with a superimposed black cross, symbol of a confirmed kill. He paused, his lamp mesmerized by the obscene badge. Irena's face flashed before him, hair in her mouth, the RPV control truck, the launch, the Russian airliner falling out of the darkening sky, the mirror image lake thousands of miles away; the airliner here, passing overhead between Portland and San Francisco, this *thing* here waiting for it, tracking it, locking on, being launched.

Almost unconsciously, he had replaced the lamp with the Nikonos underwater camera and its clumsy, heavy-headed electronic flashgun. The scene flared—four, five, six times. Then the blackened face of the dead helicopter pilot, grinning into the camera, then the army markings on the fuselage, then the launch rail and the scorched roof of the control vehicle—twenty, twenty-two, -four, -five. The IR film was good enough, the wide-angled lens was sufficient, the detail would be clear, just dull and matte, even of the ravaged face of the pilot...

The flashgun continued to fire, detonating surreal images of the dark, silty water and its evidence. He had it now, all of it. It would be enough. There was nothing more he need—

—the woman...

He continued using the camera, the stream of bubbles rising past his head.

Aubrey placed his fingertips against his forehead, glancing through them at the clock on the wall. Twelve-fifteen. He felt weary; not so much because of the sleeplessness of the previous night, more because Hughes remained unshaken, confident he could rely upon whoever it was he knew. His replies and sullen silences and outbursts of anger suggested there were cards he hadn't yet played. And Chambers's intolerant outrage was stifling in the room, too; as was Godwin's silent patience or heavy movements. Even the thin noise of the traffic below where Oxford Street met the Charing Cross Road wore at Aubrey. But, primarily, it was the passage of time on the broad-faced clock on the wall that affected him.

He had questioned Hughes for almost six hours. He had been as skilled and persistent, as much the puppeteer, as he was able. But it had been like a demonstration, a reconstruction for training purposes. Hughes had told him nothing; had not even begun to be really afraid.

"Where is Sir James Melstead, Hughes?" he repeated

for perhaps the hundredth time, sighing audibly, his hand still masking his expression. Beyond the windows, a November midday was uniformly gray. The lights were on in the room.

"I don't know," Hughes replied. "I'm not his keeper."

"No, simply his pander," Aubrey sighed once more. "We know that you must have a precise idea as to his whereabouts. Where was this place you were warned to keep away from?" He looked up at Hughes. "Where is it?"

Hughes shrugged insolently, like some troublemaking pupil confronted by a master without authority. There would be no impressive discipline of fear here! Even the barely subdued hatred and violent wishes of Chambers, so evident to himself, had failed to erode any of the specious, blind confidence with which Hughes countered them.

"I don't know what you're talking about. I want to call my solicitor," Hughes replied.

Chambers growled, his chair scraping on the floor as he stirred.

Hughes blinked, once. "I have a right to see my solicitor. You can't hold me here."

Aubrey banged his palm on the desk that separated him from Hughes, whose only response was to brush the long hair from his face.

"I know that there is another flat somewhere in London, Hughes!" he roared. "You know where it is. It is a place he could go to—where you and others doubtless went—to, to perpetrate whatever disgusting and *illegal* acts you favor! James Melstead, I presume, owns the place. It must be where he has gone now, to avoid arrest." Again, the flicker of Hughes's eyelids, just once. "Oh, yes, make no mistake, Hughes, I intended Melstead's arrest and the facing of criminal charges when he disappeared. I presume he realized that. Please understand my complete seriousness in this matter."

Hughes was still resilient. "You wouldn't have been able to make it stick—any of it."

"How many judges involved?" Chambers snapped, grimacing. "You're certain you'll get the right one, are you, you little turd?"

Chambers moved, scraping his chair behind Hughes, who flinched momentarily.

"Terry—sit down," Aubrey ordered. "I'm handling this." He sat more upright, leaning forward across the desk. "You have spent too much time at the coattails of people you consider powerful. However, contrary to your presuppositions, it would not require much effort to ruin you, personally." Again, he sighed, shaking his head. "Powerful men with secret vices are the most unreliable friends a person such as you could have, Hughes. I'm surprised you fail to understand that simple fact of life." Dutifully and with relish, Chambers chuckled loudly.

The telephone rang. Hughes's shoulders twitched, but these reactions were slight, insignificant. Godwin went into the adjoining office to answer the phone.

"I don't believe that," Hughes said to Aubrey.

Godwin reappeared in the doorway, lugubriously shaking his head. The Special Branch search for Melstead had not located him. Chambers, and the support team that had been rushed to Euston, had elicited only that Melstead had been seen leaving the station rather than boarding one of a half-dozen trains. He had seemed to be retracing his steps, but his car remained in the parking lot, now under surveillance. Melstead had, effectively, vanished. And Hughes remained unscathed by his present situation. Perhaps he sensed Aubrey's own urgency and had decided the storm would soon blow itself out.

"I should, were I you," Aubrey persisted. "You may have notebooks—" The eyes blinked. "You may feel that what you know, what you have done for these people, will be your best protection. These powerful men may well be afraid of scandal, publicity . . . but they will be most afraid of your power over them, should you ever remind them of it." He spread his hands. "I am asking you only for Melstead. In exchange, you may remain silent concerning—" He grimaced. "—the activities of your vile little circle. For yourself, there will be—minor charges."

"And if I refuse?"

"Then there will be more serious charges. You alone will suffer, and heavily. I promise you that much."

"Christ, let me kick the shit out of him—*sir!*" Chambers raged behind Hughes, shuffling his feet. Aubrey watched the man's eyes. They blinked again, as if slowly photographing the scene. He could see no hairline cracks, no implosion of assurance. Twelve twenty-five. Ludicrously, his stomach grumbled with hunger, even as he reprimanded Chambers.

"Calm down, Terry," he soothed. "You know I do not approve . . ." His voice trailed away tiredly, unconvincingly. Chambers actually did want to inflict violence. And, in the end, it might be the only way. But, not yet. Twelve twenty-six. Four-thirty in the morning at Lake Shasta. How *could* Hyde rescue Kathryn?

Hughes must snap like a twig!

"Was it when his wife died? That he began . . . ?"

Hughes smirked and shook his head. "Long before," he murmured, his eyes glittering with pleasure at Aubrey's disgust. "It isn't *sinful,* or an anomaly. It's something we think of as perfectly normal—" He was disconcerted momentarily by another growl from Chambers.

Aubrey snapped: "Tell me where he is, Hughes! Tell me that and you may even be allowed to pursue your hobby! If not, then I can assure you that child molesters are given short shrift in our prisons—whether the attitude of the criminal classes to people like you is morally justifiable or not. You will not be given time or space to debate the issue, I'm quite certain."

An overloud squeal of tires, as if amplified, interrupted him, suggesting an accident. Godwin glanced at the window, at Aubrey, then nodded lugubriously at the back of Hughes's head. Then he lumbered to his feet and moved to the window. Hughes shivered visibly, and turned to watch Godwin. A hooting horn. Aubrey stared anxiously towards Godwin, who nodded again, then announced: "Some poor sod's been hit by a Porsche. Must have tried to jump the lights. He isn't moving..." Godwin left the window, shaking his head. There had been no accident. "Poor bugger—still, I suppose he couldn't have known much about it." He returned to his chair. Hughes turned back to face Aubrey. Well done, Tony.

Hughes was unsettled. No more than that, but it was a beginning.

"Things would not be pleasant for you," Aubrey murmured.

On his cue, Godwin interjected. "On the other hand, we could make it an open prison. With privileges—couldn't we, sir?" Aubrey paused, then nodded reluctantly.

He said: "We would have to make certain it didn't look as though you'd bought such a concession, of course. As for James Melstead, there would be other matters that would effectively cloak your involvement. You do understand us, Hughes?" Twelve thirty-five.

"I understand you. But, I don't know anything." Yes, he was unsettled—but nothing more serious than that. He saw his future only through the narrowest crack in the door. The door would have to be opened further, perhaps by violence; something Aubrey detested.

"You know everything, Hughes."

"I want to see my solicitor. I know my—"

"Rights? You ceased to have those from the moment you were brought here. From the moment you became involved with Sir James Melstead. From the moment you aroused the interest of ourselves and Special Branch. I'm certain you find it relatively easy to believe that this country is well on its way to becoming a police state. In your case, the future has already arrived. Unless you answer my questions, you will become one of society's victims. Of that, be certain."

Hughes, as Aubrey studied him, seemed to have recovered some of his imperviousness to his own future. He continued to believe in the efficacy of powerful friends.

Twelve forty-one—

Fifty-six meters. Bottom time elapsed, already a minute beyond what he had allowed. He watched the wreckage of the lifting helicopter and the control vehicle glare out in the flashgun's light, then recede again into darkness. The water seemed more dense with silt, as if it clung to his dry suit and face mask. There was a euphoria—was it the nitrogen? He wanted to grin, even laugh; was that success, merely? He released his hold on the camera and gripped the lamp again, flashing it on the closed doors at the rear of the truck. Depth, time, the compass reading, all like stern admonishments now—and easily ignored. Yet, in the darkness between the flash dying away and the switching on of the lamp, there had been a moment of disorientation and a hardness in his throat; another warning. He ignored it, inspecting the door handles. The scratches he wiped clean of silt might have been caused by the crash, or by Frascati attempting to break the lock. He picked up a sharp rock, his arm moving in slow motion, the noiseless impact flicking him away from the doors. He held on, stirring silt with his fins, banged again. Bubbles rushed. The darkness pressed against his shoulders with the pressure of the water. Go up now—

—not yet. His head felt tight. He wasn't deep enough, breathing an air mixture, to suffer oxygen toxicity—it was the nitrogen. The doors opened slowly, dreamlike. He let them fall back and drifted into the interior of the control vehicle, raising the camera, the flash igniting, glaring on the screens and upturned chairs and ruined charts and wall maps hanging askew in rags. The control console, the firing panel.

Then the whole truck moved, slithering angrily away from the light, it seemed. Hyde was upturned, flung slowly against a swivel chair, then one wall of the truck. The doors swung closed behind him with a cavernous, distant sound. He spun slowly, rebounding from hard surfaces, from roof, wall, floor. Then the truck settled, rocks banging like violent intruders on the closed doors. He gripped the edge of a console, blinded by the disturbed silt, his head spinning, his fear minimal, his desire to laugh frightening. Depth gauge—yes. Watch . . . broken. He felt panic bubble like laughter, like nitrogen. He pushed against the doors, which did not move. Then he remembered the weight of rocks that had fallen against them.

And laughed. His mouthpiece drifted away, its fury

of bubbles like a visible, helpless giggling in the lamplight. Slowly, with a vast effort of will—his head light, floating—he reached out and recovered the mouthpiece; studied it, his lungs aching... then very, very slowly returned it to his mouth; breathed. Bubbles laughed around him, probably at the slowness of his brain, or at the black panic he experienced because the water's darkness had walls now, enclosing him. His lamp washed across keyboards, dials, recorders, trackers. He was locked inside the control vehicle, aware of the vastly reinforced roof required to withstand the temperature of the launch, aware of the extendable length of railway clamped on the roof... the roof was there, where the wall should be. The launch truck was also the ground control station. Reasoning, see. Memory quite clear. He recalled looking down on an identical long truck in Tadzhikistan. At last, able to think—see! he taunted himself.

He swung the lamp back and forth. No point in using energy yet, he had to control his panic. If he had to open the doors, he would need that panic, just before it killed him, rather than the nitrogen or the bends or just the box in which he was trapped. A blank section of wall, above a row of consoles. He kicked towards it, rebounding, then gripped the edge of a console. The suit had sprung no leaks, the seals were intact.

He cast the lamplight around, as if scattering seed, and located a chair, gripped it in both hands and backed towards the doors. Then launched himself. The black glass bulged and broke as he rebounded away from the shards, dropping the chair. Then he moved forward, picking the glass gently away from the frame. He slipped through the window into the control truck's cab, twisting carefully, gripping the door handle, easing himself out of the truck.

Easy—

Relief bubbled furiously. He propelled himself away from the control truck. The photographs of the interior of the truck clinched everything—the laser target designator, the brand-name equipment, the recorders and consoles and printers and cameras and screens. *Reid Electronics. Shapiro Electrics*...He remembered only now that he had seen them. Sperry, IAI—the Israelis—half a dozen others. Any one name would do. Any one frame he had shot would do! Elation—

His watch was broken.

Panic, black and inescapable. He kicked upwards, upwards, faster, faster—

No!

He slowed, draining himself with the effort, his head loose, light like a balloon. He hovered, the wreckage invisible below him in the darkness. Depth gauge—fifteen meters. He oriented himself slowly, like a simpleton, arms outstretched, turning gradually as if surrounded by tormentors. Then swam upwards—the line had gone from around his shoulders. Appalling to realize he had not even known until he had looked for it. He stopped at a depth of ten meters, his body heavy, tired, seemingly filled with nitrogen, or with some heavier gas. He must stage decompress for five minutes, then at five meters down for another twenty minutes. Then he could surface.

And wait. Wait to discover the symptoms of decompression sickness. Or not. He had no idea how fast he had come up to fifteen meters. Nitrogen bubbles in the blood and brain. Christ—nothing at the moment. It needn't have begun yet, he told himself falteringly.

Hyde hung in the darkness, counting the seconds, the minutes of his decompression.

*   *   *

"I see...nothing. Yes, of course. Superintendent, thank you. No, no—I don't think I'd like the added resources of the Met, not at present...goodbye." Aubrey put down the receiver heavily. The clock's broad face confronted him the moment he looked up. He heard Hughes eating noisily at a folding table in a far corner of the room. Chambers and Godwin were seated on the other side of Aubrey's desk. It was two-thirty. The afternoon was leaden, already declining towards evening. "No, there's no pretext I can use for a more comprehensive search," he murmured.

"Then leave *me* alone with him," Chambers tempted. Aubrey turned to him, his gaze unfocused.

"What?"

"I'll get him to tell you—anyone could with the right—"

"Degree of violence?" Aubrey said witheringly. The sound of Hughes chewing his sandwich was infuriating. "I don't think so."

Godwin shrugged and said: "It might be quicker, sir—what with the time factor. He thinks he'll be protected—that's all the defense he's got. It wouldn't make him want to endure pain."

"Not even if he's frightened of these people?" Aubrey leaned on his knuckles. Chambers slouched insolently on a chair, rocking back and forth. "What if he's assured through fear of them, their influence?"

"What are you offering him?" Chambers retorted. "Only a threat of a different kind...sir."

"Perhaps." He felt unsettled, his collar restrictive, his clothes tight.

Hughes finished his sandwich and wiped his mouth with the sleeve of his jacket, patterned in a violent check. Then he brushed his long hair back from his face, watching Aubrey with what appeared to be the mildest curiosity. Nothing seemed to threaten him, not even the prospect of prison and its attendant violence. Why, for heaven's sake? Was he so much mesmerized by the power of the names on whatever vile list of customers he possessed?

And nothing from Patrick. It was six-thirty at the lake, almost daybreak. Aubrey's shoulders sagged at the admission. Nothing. Otherwise, Mallory would have been in contact via satellite to Euston Tower. The surveillance on him had vanished, after all.

Yet, even had there been such a call, Aubrey could not dismiss James Melstead's importance. His was the voice people would *listen* to! He had to find James. He strode across the room to Hughes, his stick thudding on the thin carpet. Hughes appeared startled, for a moment. Then his eyes glittered with tense amusement. Aubrey sat down on a chair on the other side of the small, littered table.

"I'm sure you realize they will turn against you, Hughes?"

"What do you mean?"

"They will deny everything."

"They can't."

"Why not? Have you evidence?" Aubrey demanded. *Of course! You damned old fool—!*

"I'll be all right, Sir Kenneth—don't worry about me. I won't even see the inside of a court, with a bit of luck, never mind prison." His South-East accent was casual with so many unshaken assumptions. "They'll look after me. They'll have—" He paused, his eyes narrowing.

"Have to? For *you?*"

"They will."

"Then there is evidence? What kind? Photographic?"

"I'm not saying anything. Just let me get hold of my solicitor, will you?"

A bland, unremarkable, street-clever young man; innocuous. Like a cobra.

"And these eminent and foolish men knew nothing of your gathering of information, of course?"

"I'll be looked after. I know that. I'm saying nothing else."

Aubrey smiled, thin-lipped. There were hard little bits from the whole wheat bread under his dental plate. His head snapped around. "Tony, get the superintendent on the telephone. I think we've been looking for the wrong treasure. Get a warrant to search the squat where Mr. Hughes resides—" No, it wasn't there, not from his expression. "And try a bank deposit box—and his solicitor. Use whatever powers are required, but search everything!" Oh, yes, the look on his face had changed, there was something! "Well, Hughes, we shall see. If I find what I expect, then your degree of safety is lowered to a rather dangerous level—wouldn't you say?"

"There's nothing!"

"Oh, but there is. I was stupid not to have seen it at once. Blackmail. Here was I trying to blackmail you and all the time you had the means to blackmail a dozen, twenty, thirty for all I know!" Two-forty. The first slow creeping of dawn at Lake Shasta. Hyde had found nothing. Pray God Special Branch would. He leaned forward, speaking softly. "When we find your instruments of blackmail, Hughes, you will be alone and naked in the wind. Your only safety, your only power to bargain, will lie with me. And my price will be the location of that flat where James Melstead is now hiding! Do I make myself clear."

The sneer was pallid now, the eyes more furtive. Hughes had been so clever and so safe for so long. All threat had been eliminated from his secret and dangerous world. Until that moment.

Aubrey stood up.

"Have you got through yet, Tony?" he snapped urgently. Godwin held out the receiver. "Do you want to talk to him?" "Yes, yes, I'll do it!"

It was all to have been so simple and straightforward. There had been nothing further to decide after the initial and momentous decision to leave his sister's place, walk to the bus station, board the cross-country service and arrive at this place. He even knew the path through the woods very well.

He had almost blundered into the guard and his challenge; but instead had stood rooted to the spot by shock as the guard repeated his shouted demand in the early evening gloom, two, three times—before Didenko had begun to open his mouth and the guard had fired his Kalashnikov out of fear. The impact of the bullet had knocked him off his feet, back into a snowdrift beneath a pine. The snow had been wet against his cheek, cold to his hands, numbing against his side, where the bullet had started a blaze that agonized through his whole body. The guard's mouth had opened in terror and amazement as he bent close to Didenko's face; his relief was huge when he heard the ragged breathing and gasping that surprised Didenko himself. The snow-laden branches seemed far above his head as he lay there, staring. It had taken him so long, so many hours, so much effort—just to become this dark lump half-thrust into a small snowdrift under a pine tree. Footsteps followed soon after.

His gaze was fuzzy, unfocused. His side burned, then his throat shrieked as they hoisted him onto a stretcher made from interlinked arms and began to carry him roughly out of the trees—all those branches heavy with white, feathery fans... The footsteps on wood, climbing and stamping. Muffled voices, a light flashing in his face and over his body. A grumbled comment. He thought he detected the shock of recognition, but perhaps he had been mistaken. Then warmth, sudden and almost violent on his cheeks, making them prickle. His fingertips, too, wet and tingling. His side burning.

Especially when they removed his overcoat and his jacket, then his shirt. Its thick, checked wool was stained over almost half its area. He gulped in surprise at the amount of blood he had already lost.

It had all been so easy; inevitable, he had told himself again and again on the slow bus journey, assailed by the scent of wet clothes infrequently washed and the damp rubber of overshoes and boots. And garlic once, cheap spirit on another occasion. Inevitable.

He giggled, but even to him it sounded like a wet, choking noise. This was the aspect of inevitability he had failed to envisage. The old, wary, paranoid days had even returned here, and with them the guards and the guns. He heard the rustlings of those who crowded around him as he lay—on what? Something soft like a sofa—the voices were as indistinct and tiresome as the mutterings of his fellow passengers on the bus had been. He resented their flitting or looming shadows, diminishing the light, their feet distressing the bright splash of color at the corner of eyesight that must be a rug. The scent of the wood fire was suffocating, and he coughed. Something dribbled onto his chin and was wiped away, reminding him of his sister cleaning her daughter's food-stained mouth. He wanted to be outside again, beneath the dark, laden arms of the pines, in the cold. His blood rushed in this heat. It was pounding in his head, too, which must be clear, so he could convince Aleksandr—!

"Pyotr—Pyotr Yurievich!"

There was greater light for a moment, then a bulk of darkness bending over him, so that he shuddered with fear. But it was only Nikitin. He nodded slowly and allowed his hand to be taken, not understanding the passion of Aleksandr's voice nor the head-shaking by someone standing just at the very edge of his peripheral vision, which was cloudy, anyway.

"Aleksandr—"

He raised himself a little, but was gently pushed back by Nikitin.

"There's no need to talk."

"Yes—!" It was why he had come. To persuade, to shame Nikitin into his old ways once more. He fluttered his hand in desperation as someone removed his glasses. They had already cleared of the fog that the room's heat had clouded them with. His glasses were gently replaced. Didenko sighed, nodding.

Surely they had loosened his collar? They'd taken his shirt, off, hadn't they? The collar still felt tight. Nikitin pressed his hand and he was content to allow the man to hold it. But Nikitin's tears embarrassed him. That was Nikitin the politician, the man who cried easily. People liked it in him, were fooled by it. For himself, he thought it affected, insincere. Irena had hardly ever bothered to hide her contempt for such tricks!

That was it—Irena. He had come to talk about Irena, about the three of them—had he done that already? It was difficult to remember. The tears were streaming down Nikitin's wide cheeks. It was ridiculous!

"Stop crying!" he snapped. Nikitin sniffed, his features surprised, childishly struck with pleasure for some reason. Then the tears continued. "Oh, stop crying and listen!" Didenko pursued. He coughed, his brow was wiped, then he breathily admonished: "You have to,

have to reverse what you've been doing, Aleksandr...
you can't do it. Just can't *do* it!"

God, that was tiring! He breathed, feeling his back
arch with the effort, his heart thud in his chest. Irena
could have kept him straight, made him do things so
easily!

"Pyotr—!"

He heard the cry quite clearly, though seeing was
difficult—very. He felt a draft of cold air, then heard a
boot scrape on the wooden floor and someone berating
someone else—probably the soldier who had shot him.
How much had he told Nikitin? Had he persuaded him?
He didn't think he could make a further effort, though
he would if it was absolutely necessary.

"Pyotr!"

He heard the cry a second time, but the room was
very dark now, almost as dark as it had been under the
trees, dark as the endless flatness of the countryside
through the fogged windows of the bus. There was something remarkably stupid about what had happened,
something futile and stinking of failure, but he did not
know what. And a sense that they were together and in
agreement, all three of them—Nikitin, Irena and himself. Like always...

He blinked, saw Nikitin's open-mouthed and silent
face for an instant, then there was nothing.

"Yes, it's Melstead. Yes, I'm at the flat...what? Because it was the only thing it occurred to me to do, that's
why! No, no one knows this place...yes, I know you
do. I must talk to Malan. He must help. No, it is *his*
problem as well as my own, Blantyre! You tell him so.
Kenneth Aubrey is not a man to be denied. Why the
Devil did anyone show violence to his niece, for heaven's
sake? What? No, very well, it doesn't matter now, except

that Kenneth is utterly relentless when once set on. Tell
Malan that, if he doesn't already understand the nature
of the beast. And tell him I shall be waiting to hear from
you. Yes, tonight. Blantyre, it *must* be to-night! Now,
contact your employer and let him decide. Yes, goodbye—!''

"Yes, Superintendent, I understand the niceties of
search warrants, the right to privacy, the difficulties we
are laying up for ourselves—but you *must* find what I
know Hughes has deposited somewhere! No, I am not
finicky about what story you tell the National West-
minster bank, since they will not cooperate willingly.
Just get hold of Hughes's safety deposit box and its
contents!" Aubrey calmed his breathing and rubbed
thumb and forefinger along the creases in his forehead.
Then he added: "Forgive me, Superintendent—but it is
five in the evening and I do not believe we have even a
modicum of time, never mind a margin of safety. Yes,
thank you."

He put down the receiver and leaned his weight heavily on his elbows. The small desk seemed to quiver. Tony
Godwin looked as sorrowful as a bloodhound. Chambers sat with his chair tilted back, over near the door
which they had closed on Hughes, who was in the other
room. The windows were locked; but then Hughes was
hardly suicidal, was he? But, such was the malign fortune
of this affair, he might just try and jump!

Aubrey felt restored by derision. Hughes's solicitor,
alerted by the Special Branch's inquiries and demands,
was on his way; unnerved, Aubrey was pleased to admit,
by the vague enormities of *national security* and *the
defense of the realm,* together with hints of blackmail
and extortion. The solicitor would be subdued, just as
Hughes was now; wriggling on their hook . . . but

Hughes was so damned unimportant! Aubrey felt a desire to do physical damage to the man for his perversions, just as Chambers did.

And he had to be with the PM for a wide-ranging JIC briefing and discussion at six o'clock. And it might go on for hours!

The lights of Oxford Street glared against the smudged windows. The three of them seemed to be sitting in isolated pools of lamplight, like strangers in a doctor's waiting room, each with something malignant to be confirmed by diagnosis. He sighed aloud, throwing up his hands. "Where is Patrick, Tony? There must be word by now!"

Godwin reached for the telephone, as if it had rung, then shrugged. Chambers was unsettled on his chair, as if unwillingly restrained.

"Do you want me to try Mallory again?" Godwin asked.

Aubrey shook his head. "No—no, it doesn't matter." He reminded himself that Kathryn's safety, Hyde's life, both hinged on finding the material which would open Hughes like an oyster. Hughes's solicitor was being brought to these offices by Special Branch and would be kept here until they located the vile evidence and confronted his client with it. Then they would learn Melstead's present whereabouts—

But all of this required *patience* and *inactivity*, dammit!

Five past five. His driver would bring his car at five-thirty, to take him to the Cabinet Office. Damn the PM's unfailing attention to detail at a time like this! The JIC briefing could wait—if he had proof he could, indeed, postpone it. But he could say nothing of Melstead for the moment. He drummed his fingers on the desk, evidently irritating Godwin. Good!

The telephone—!

"Yes, yes!" Godwin's face was childishly illuminated with relief. Aubrey felt his throat constrict. "Thank God—at last! Yes, I'll put him on—" Aubrey was already hovering beside Godwin's table. A sheaf of print-out was disturbed by his impatience, and a pencil rolled across the carpet tiles.

"Mallory? Yes, where's Hyde? What? This line is very bad, Mallory—!"

"Sir—" Mallory was shouting from a great distance. "Hyde's found it, sir! He has photographs. Everything was there, just as the map suggested—have you got that, sir?"

"Yes, yes!" he replied breathlessly. "Carry on—"

"The control truck was down there, and a US Army helicopter. It must have crashed as they tried to airlift the truck out."

He felt hot and chill in successive moments, feverish with excitement and satisfaction. "Go on, Mallory."

"Hyde said that the truck showed evidence of having been used to launch an RPV, and the pilot's body is still in the helicopter . . . there was Reid equipment inside the truck, sir—"

After a moment, Aubrey said: "Good. Go on."

"He's given me the film, sir. Which route do you want it to take?"

"Given you—? Where is Patrick now?"

"He's gone back to Shasta, sir. He said by the time you got anything organized, they could all have left. Sorry, sir. He's going to keep the lodge under surveillance from the other side of the lake."

"I understand. Will he make contact again?"

"Yes, sir. Regular intervals, I'm to stay manning the phone in my room . . . what about the film, sir?"

"Keep it safe, Mallory—keep it very safe. I'm going

to talk to Washington now. Anders must fly out, or organize something locally. Just sit tight—I'll be in touch ... well done, Mallory! Tell Hyde well done, very well done!"

He put down the receiver. Godwin was beaming like a new father in a hospital corridor.

"It's all on film," Aubrey murmured. "Everything. It's all over, Tony, bar the shouting! She's safe—and we have the proof." He glanced at his watch. Five-twenty. The PM would just have to *wait!* Thank *God* Kathryn would be safe. "Tony, get me Paul Anders in Washington—now."

16

THE SHOOTING OF WEDNESDAY'S CHILD

"Yes, Paul, I am certain—I can give you whatever assurance you require!" Aubrey was giddy with tension. "Paul, you must act quickly—at once. Yes, my niece—"

His driver sat on a folding chair, cap balanced on his thigh and containing his gloves, his hair ringed by the cap's impression. Aubrey was already late for his appointment with the PM. Geoffrey Longmead had called once, his irritation evident. Anders, three thousand miles away, was boyishly disarmed by shock.

"Kenneth—dear sweet Jesus, Kenneth . . . I have to believe you. But—"

"—you'd rather not!" Even the concern for Kathryn's

danger had receded. He had put limitations of time and duration upon it. Limitations of imagination, too. "Paul, please do what you have to do. It is most urgent. Most. Patrick Hyde has given us the necessary photographic evidence. But he can do no more."

Chambers and Godwin were watching him. The door was closed on the other room where Hughes and his solicitor were in conclave. He had allowed Chambers to explain Hughes's position to the solicitor. There had been bluster, then a need for consultation, but little protest as to unlawful detention, the necessity of charges, et cetera. Hughes was an unimportant client.

"There's an army helicopter down there and the control vehicle—Jesus." Anders's voice was that of a man told of treasure and the accompanying danger. "Harrell—how many people has he got out there?"

"Our man Mallory says Hyde's count is eight, Harrell making nine. One of their number is, I'm afraid, already accounted for."

"Hyde?"

"Yes."

"Where's Hyde now?"

"Back at the lake. He has their lodge under surveillance. Paul, will you act?"

"I guess I have to." Aubrey heard Anders clear his throat; there was a shrug of decision in his voice when he said: "Yes, of course. At once. I'll have to liaise with the FBI, maybe the Forest Service and the local sheriff . . . no, hell, I can take a small team out there, right off. You say the West Coast office is under Harrell's control?"

"I think so."

"OK. Look, Kenneth, I have one-ten, our time. The flight out there will take five hours, maybe a little more.

And I need to organize. So, it'll be evening out on the Coast before—"

"Paul, will you please get things moving. Harrell and his people are using Kathryn as a means of drawing Hyde in. He's been free for twenty-four hours. They want him very badly—" His sense of satisfaction faltered, the ground giving way beneath it. There were more traps and quicksands, he realized. Harrell had as little time to waste as he and Anders.

"Kenneth?"

"Paul, please hurry!" He shivered. Godwin's face had clouded, too, as if he had scraped at the veneer of success, exposing failure. "Harrell will be getting more desperate, I'm certain of it. If they get hold of Hyde—"

"OK, OK. I have your man's number, I also have yours. I can be out there in six hours, maybe a little longer. We can put in at Redding direct. It's OK, Kenneth. I'll clean up the mess later. Your niece and Hyde are the priority. Don't worry."

"Thank you, Paul. If you have to reach me urgently, I shall be at my office number. Tony Godwin is here, should you use this number."

"Sure."

Aubrey put the receiver down slowly, staring at it before looking towards his driver, then towards Chambers and Godwin and the closed door to the second office. He nodded at it. "Make certain they both remain here, Terry. If there is anything urgent, I shall leave the meeting to take your call." The illegalities were irrelevant. Perhaps Melstead was also irrelevant at the moment. But his evidence would be vital later. Anders was crucial now. "You know what to do and say should—"

Chambers nodded. Unlike himself, both Chambers and Godwin seemed disgruntled, cheated. They were restless for conclusion, obsessed still with Melstead. He felt Kathryn was now his nemesis, not Melstead. Not nemesis—God forbid she would be that. He gathered his walking stick and strode awkwardly across the room. His driver opened the outer door of the office.

"I shall get back here as quickly as I can, Tony. Keep the superintendent under pressure."

Acceleration. The crackle of the R/T was audible for a moment and Hyde shivered. He'd watched them smash his tiny launch, then report to Harrell. They'd contained him on their side of the McCloud Arm of the lake. Acceleration. Harrell had shortened the operation's pendulum, making it swing faster, abandoning wait-and-watch in his impatience. Just as Hyde knew the woman would be more and more worn and pinched in reserves and patience, he knew Harrell had become jumpy, eager. Perhaps he guessed Hyde had done something, found something. Whatever it was, they were looking for him more intensely than before; no longer content to patrol, they were hunting.

And they had found his boat and destroyed it. Hyde leaned his cheek against the cold bark of a sugar pine, hunched into a crouch, the sniper's rifle across his thighs. He watched the two men withdraw into the dark trees that crowded almost to the water's edge of the tiny cove where he had moored the boat under gray tarpaulin the color of water. Harrell would be sending reinforcements. Hyde glanced at his watch. Midday. He rose into a bent posture and backed carefully into the pines.

He leaned against the steepness of the slope, clambering slowly in a wide circle that would avoid anyone coming from the lodge to the cove. He paused once, ate chocolate, then moved on. The seaplane moored just beyond the jetty dipped and swayed like a waterfowl.

Their launch rubbed audibly against the jetty's wood. He could hear the footsteps of one of them along the lodge's verandah; glimpsed the armed man in a check jacket occasionally. He settled down, the Browning placed near his right hand on the pine needles, his back against a tree, his rifle against his chest, the knife in its sheath where he could reach across his waist for it quickly. Twelve-thirty. He imagined he could smell cooking. Across the McCloud Arm, a small boat drew a wind-tossed mane of water behind it. Hyde settled himself to greater comfort, using the binoculars occasionally. Shadows flitted behind opaque windows. The man on the porch smoked a cigarette, the wind snatching the smoke out from beneath the verandah's sloping roof.

It was after two when Harrell and the woman appeared on the steps and walked down towards the jetty and the water's edge. The afternoon sky was evenly gray behind sullen white clouds. In the western distance, the rain was like smoke and moving closer to the lake. Kathryn Aubrey was dressed in a bulky jacket and jeans. Harrell was wearing a fawn overcoat, incongruously citified. The guard had followed them. On the wind, Hyde could hear snatches of the woman's voice, Harrell's replies. They sounded as stylized as a married couple who had only strangers' word for one another. Their conversation induced a sense of tiredness, of effort only postponed. His hand clamped on the rifle, near the trigger guard. The woman's voice protested something, her arms waving at Harrell as if throwing small stones. Harrell shrugged and turned away from her, walking along the jetty, scanning the lake and the shoreline, the trees behind the lodge. The guard had bent into his jacket's cover to light another cigarette. Hyde could see the lighter flaring and dying, again and again. Harrell's face was cold from the wind, his eyes squinting, glaring. The woman's face was—

He wanted to lower the glasses, stand and wave, shout to her. Tell her not to. Her face was vivid with opportunity, her gaze moving from the guard to Harrell, to the guard walking towards the shelter of the verandah to light his cigarette, to Harrell staring moodily out across the lake—no, he wanted to yell at her, *no!*

She ran towards the shadow of the trees at the edge of the clearing, her footsteps inaudible. Decision had become panic on her closeup face—white and strained, dark marks under her eyes—the moment before she turned and tried to flee.

His glasses flicked to Harrell's shoulders; still preoccupied, not alert. The guard, lighter flaring, smoke drifting, body turning—

—yell of surprise and anger. Kathryn was twenty yards from the trees, running with wild, flailing arms. Harrell turned, saw her. Began running. The guard was down from the verandah's steps, rifle raised. Harrell's mouth opened but the guard's warning yell was louder, as if he echoed the cry Hyde had wanted to make. Harrell was waving his arms as the first shot passed over Kathryn's head in warning. She halted for a moment, half-turned, but the trees were only ten yards away. Harrell was hurrying towards the guard rather than the woman, yelling. It was inevitable—

Kathryn's body was thrown forward as if she had been pushed in the back by a strong, contemptuous hand. She sprawled on pine litter and tussocky grass. Almost at once, another man emerged from the trees. There had been no need to shoot, he must have seen her already, had moved to intercept her. Harrell tugged the rifle from the guard and flung it away. The other man was bending over Kathryn, raising her against his knee. Her blouse reddened.

Alarmingly quickly, the blood spread like dye. It was already impossible to tell where the bullet had entered. The woman's face was chalky as she grimaced with pain. Then Harrell's bulk obscured his view of her. Fifteen seconds had passed—Hyde had counted each of them—since she had turned and begun to run. The shots had been nothing more than a release of tension, an instinctive response to surprise. Harrell straightened and the other two lifted Aubrey's niece and began carrying her towards the lodge. Her blouse, where the jacket hung open, was red across her breasts and midriff, the collar now strangely white. She was unconscious but her chest was heaving.

Harrell scanned the trees grimly, and Hyde hunched into himself as if he had been seen. They carried her into the shadow of the porch, then into the lodge. Harrell looked back towards the small seaplane, nodded once and then hurried inside.

She was badly enough wounded to need to be flown out. Harrell obviously wanted to keep her alive. The bullet must have passed right through her body, there was too much blood on the front of her blouse for it to be still in her. If they could stop the bleeding, she might—

—was she dying? Hyde shook his head. There was nothing to be calculated or gained from considering that question. They wouldn't bring in medical help, they'd try to take her out. He swallowed drily and wiped his cracked lips. He couldn't move in daylight. She had to be no more than wounded...

He shook himself like a dog. He should have done something about the seaplane earlier, increasing the pressure on them, making *them* feel trapped. They'd try to fly the woman out, be bound to. She was their trump card, they had to keep her alive. But, if she was flown out, he would lose all track of her. She had to stay in the lodge. He had to keep them all together. He kept looking out towards the small, vulnerable seaplane. He must immobilize it.

Whatever Aubrey organized now, after he heard from Mallory, couldn't happen for hours yet. *He* couldn't move in daylight. The woman *had* to be all right. Wait then. They'd be calling the pilot back from the search.

The seaplane and its pilot. Just wait...

"Well, shall we get that smarmy bloody solicitor in, then?" Chambers's smile was shaky, like that of someone denying he was ill. "Thorough, isn't he? Not to mention choosy about the eminence of his portrait subjects." It was the voice of someone attempting to restore some kind of false neutrality to a quarrelsome room.

The videocassettes and envelopes of developed prints lay in a small heap on Aubrey's desk. Godwin was shaking his large head slowly, strands of fair hair falling across his forehead. He looked up at Chambers. "It's a bloody minefield, Terry."

"Only for Aubrey." Chambers grinned more aggressively. "He'll have to sort it out—cancel some of his dinner engagements, I expect!"

"He knows at least three of these people—!"

"*We* recognized half a dozen!"

Godwin continued shaking his head, as if to dizzy himself. The photographs flared in his mind like detonations, garishly lighting a landscape of disgust, shock, even embarrassment. Men arriving in some dingy street, accompanied by young boys, young girls. Men photographed awkwardly but revealingly, climbing narrow stairs, undressing. Glimpses of naked children, naked adults. Identifiable faces. "Jesus Christ," he whispered, brushing his hair back untidily, feeling a tremor in his hands. "Why do they—?"

"Doesn't matter, does it?" Chambers sneered. But even he couldn't help it, he realized, the recurring revulsion and nausea. It was difficult to dismiss the imagery contained in the brown envelopes. The videocassettes—no, he didn't want to study those, not at the moment. "Let's show our legal friend the pictures of the judge, shall we? I think they might give him a clue that he's drowning, don't you?"

Chambers crossed the room to the door beside which the Special Branch detective stood, noncommittally; except perhaps for an occasional glance at Chambers that was almost amused; wisdom inspecting innocence.

"Mr. Knowle—would you step in here a moment, please, sir?"

Godwin glimpsed Hughes, perched anxiously on a small chair, before his view was masked by the dark overcoat and height of the solicitor. Chambers closed the door on Hughes. Knowle was suspicious, prepared to be affable or challenging as circumstances required. Yet nervousness had slipped into his eyes like light through an ill-drawn curtain. He was beginning to blame his client for the difficulties he foresaw. He had been prepared to wait with Hughes without much protest, in anticipation of a warrant he must have suspected was not on its way. Conveyancing was, perhaps, more his métier? Godwin smiled, indicating a chair. He felt more relaxed now, soothed by his own superiority to the solicitor and the anticipation of the man's collapse into cooperation.

"I'm afraid," he began, Chambers tensely at his side like a dog on a choke chain, "that matters are a little more grave than we thought, Mr. Knowle." Who at once appeared younger, having removed his heavy-framed glasses. His eyes stared out like those of a young bird. Godwin cleared his throat. "The charges we shall be bringing against your client will be very serious." He held up his hand, continuing: "They will include blackmail as well as soliciting children for immoral purposes. Obstructing our inquiries in a matter of national security, of course..." Knowle looked as if he suspected some trick; there was even a moment when he seemed to gather himself for an outraged diatribe. Godwin found silken threat less easy to simulate than Aubrey did. But his blunter forebodings seemed sufficient to disarm Knowle, who, even now, having replaced his spectacles, looked young.

"You can substantiate at least some of this, I assume, Mr.—er, Godwin?"

Godwin nodded, leaning his upper body forward. The flimsy desk quivered under the added pressure. Chambers opened one of the envelopes.

"Recognize the subject?" he asked, handing two photographs to Knowle—

—who swallowed satisfyingly and fiddled with his spectacles. Then he said:

"I don't see that this has—"

"Listen, Mr. Knowle," Chambers interrupted, "these were in *your* safekeeping, on *your* client's behalf."

"What the Devil do you mean by—?"

"Don't waffle—*sir*. You recognize His Lordship, just as we do. We haven't got time to piss about, have we, Mr. Godwin?" Chambers remarked sarcastically. "See, we're being frank with you."

"I had no idea."

"Well, perhaps not, Mr. Knowle." Godwin smiled. "But your client has information that we require very urgently, in the interests of national security. We think you can persuade him to give us the information in exchange for—*lesser* charges." Godwin spread his hands on the desk. "Some kind of quid pro quo, anyway, Mr. Knowle. Depending on the degree and immediacy of your client's assistance."

"National security," Knowle murmured, dropping the photographs on the desk from his fingertips, which he then rubbed together. "Should—should my client assist you in your—"

"We want an address, that's all for the moment," Godwin said. "Your client knows which address. Ask him for it, Mr. Knowle, and then I think you and he might be able to go home, for the time being."

"An address?"

Godwin nodded. Knowle hesitated, his aftershave expensively and more stringently present in the room, his forehead shiny. Then he nodded. "Very well. I see no reason why my client shouldn't assist you to that degree, in exchange for—"

"Just get the address, Mr. Knowle."

Chambers grinned as the solicitor left the room. "I shan't have him deal with my parking tickets," he murmured, picking up the telephone. "Do I tell the old man?"

"The superintendent first. He'd better put some people on the lookout. I'll tell Sir Kenneth—if the PM will let him come out to play for a couple of minutes." He looked down at his desk. "Put those bloody pictures out of sight, will you?"

Two minutes later, Knowle opened the door and reentered the room. The Special Branch officer seemed to impassively approve of the progress of events.

"My client—"

"The address, Mr. Knowle?"

"It's a place near Euston. Above an empty shop on the corner of Drummond Street and Cobourg Street."

"Number?" Knowle supplied the number.

"I consider that my client has been very helpful, of his own free will."

Chambers waved his hand. "Save it!" he snapped. "Superintendent? OK, here's the address . . . Yes. Put surveillance on the place. Yes, yes, I'll inform Sir Kenneth." He looked up at the clock on the wall, just as Godwin was doing.

Nearly ten-thirty. Godwin was aware of the gap of hours since Aubrey had left, which they'd spent fiddling about getting bank managers away from their dinners or someone else's bed, having had their superiors leaned on! It seemed now as if they had wasted those hours.

"Get the old man quickly," he murmured. "Then get round there as soon as you can. Hughes has had us going for too bloody long!"

Ten o'clock by his watch, from the light of the lamp across the dingy, windblown street. A Pakistani grocery shop was still open, beyond the lamplight, and two customers had gone inside a few minutes earlier. Nothing echoed in his head now except the passage of time. His acute sense of it made him weary—but that was better than other anticipations, other sensations. He clasped his hands together behind his back, feeling them fumble for one another. His heart thudded as a car passed along the street, seemed to slow but then maneuvered to avoid barrier-marked work on the drains, before disappearing.

Melstead attempted to move away from the corner of the window, but the darkness of the room behind him seemed oppressive, something tangibly keeping him pressed against the curtains, staring down into the street. His left arm was numb. He felt cold, despite the flat's heating. He was aware of the empty shop below him as vividly as if he heard the scurrying of rats or mice down there.

God, how he hated this place!

His mind assumed an expression of contempt, like an observant, aristocratic bystander. He had used this place quite willingly, he had loaned it to others in the circle. It had been their enjoyable—brothel, for want of a less accusative word. He owned the place, for God's sake! He had not hated it until now, when it had become a hiding place rather than a place in which to receive and store pleasure, love. Kenneth had merely gaped at him when he had denied there was harm done or intended. But then Kenneth was strait-laced in so many ways... and as incorrigible and inescapable as some ferretlike creature, once put on someone's scent. Even an old friend—perhaps especially an old friend. Kenneth clearly felt betrayed in some obscure and righteous way.

It was Kenneth's condemnation, Kenneth's proximity, that had altered his perception of the place, made the street outside seem sordid and shabby. The flat, had he turned on the lights, was redecorated, carefully furnished; not to overawe but to relax, a place to enjoy and for enjoyment. But now he kept the room—and all the other rooms—in darkness. Loss of identity? Of the appurtenances of an identity thrust on him by people like Kenneth, perhaps. Not that he was ashamed or guilty—no. For what reason should he be?

Afraid, yes. Of exposure to those who would point and condemn—

—where was Blantyre, for God's sake?

Five past ten by the grubby lamplight shining on the face of his heavy gold watch. The children had been fed, cared for! he silently cried out in protest, the voice so loud in his mind that he clasped a hand loosely over his mouth, afraid he had shouted. He rubbed his forehead, then clasped his hands together behind his back once more. Good God in heaven, they were urchins who had run away from home! They knew what it was that was asked of them, they were not Dickensian children with shiny faces and white frocks or sailors' suits! What the Devil did Kenneth think *happened* here? Often, they were allowed to stay for days at a time...

Six minutes past ten. This was unendurable, this waiting! Where was Blantyre? Hughes—untrustworthy, despicable, clever Hughes—might throw in the towel at any moment, for heaven's sake!

It did not matter where he was taken by Blantyre. There was money abroad, there would be other money. Malan would see to that. He needed only to get as far as the port or the airfield or the car ferry or whatever means they had arranged for getting him out of England. The remainder of his life would be easy anonymity, an old age in the enforced sun. Even South Africa...there were lots of places that appealed, just so long as he evaded Kenneth for the next few hours.

The two customers came out of the Pakistani's shop and paused under the lamplight. He pressed closer to the window, trying to make out their shadowed features, so expectant and anxious that he needed to use the lavatory. Was it—?

There was one sharp regret, one intense, recurring pain—Alice. Not simply her knowledge of...this place, things here, his secrets...but the certainty of her condemnation, her vilification. The saintly Alice, his daughter, would never forgive or understand, of that he was certain. She idealized him too much. Idealized her dead mother, too, just as he did. Now, she would think of him as somehow staining his wife's memory, in vile, copulatory images defiling her mother. He doubted her anger would ever lessen.

One of the two men beneath the lamp looked up. He heard his old, shallow breathing quite loudly in the silent room. It was Blantyre! Thank God...

Blantyre spoke to his companion and then stepped off the pavement, crossing the street with long, quick strides. Once he was with Blantyre, he would be safely out of Kenneth's grasp. The doorbell rang, expected and startling. He smiled and hurried into the hall, banging his shin against the leg of a chair in the darkness. He rubbed it as he pressed the video entry phone into which Blantyre had stared without speaking.

Below him, he heard the door open and close again...

They'd been inside the lodge, six of them, for more than twenty minutes. Then the guard who had shot Kathryn emerged, pausing on the steps, then walking hesitantly out into the clearing, his head turning back and forth like that of an overwound automaton. He called back towards the lodge. The rain obscured the far side of the McCloud Arm and the clouds pressed down. The seaplane looked white and small as a gull, tossing on the disturbed water. The launch banged spasmodically against the jetty. The pilot was inside the lodge. The rain drove in beneath the trees, drenching Hyde as he watched the guard squinting into the rain, scanning the strip of pebbly shore.

She was carried out in Harrell's arms—clever. Hyde released the pressure of his finger on the trigger of the FN rifle and heard his own disappointed exhalation. Her face was clown white, even to the red mouth, her limp body wrapped in a bright blanket. She was unconscious. Harrell's expression was grim as he hurried towards the shore, an armed man pressed close on either side of him, like a dictator's bodyguards. The pilot overtook the huddled group, the sheepskin collar of his leather jacket zipped up around his cheeks, his shoulders shiny and bent with the rain. Another man remained on the steps of the lodge, his breath smoking.

Hyde had difficulty regulating his breathing. The rifle was icy against his cheek as he knelt beside the bark of a tree. His attention became absorbed by the slow flopping of Kathryn's head as it hung over Harrell's arm. She looked as small as a child rescued from some highway carnage. The first man was on the deck of the launch, steadying the boat for the pilot, then for Harrell and his burden. He was aware of the tick of seconds in his head, aware of the flap of Harrell's overcoat, stained with great dark patches that in the monochromed, rainy afternoon light might even have been Kathryn's blood; aware of the banging of the launch, the tip and swell of the seaplane—as aware as if he were moving closer and closer to the scene.

Through the telescopic sight, which somehow made the scene less real in closeup, he saw the first shot pluck wood whitely from the launch, near the pilot's hand. The hand flashed out of focus and view, then the pilot's half-turned face was glaring into his eye. The noise of the shots was deadened by the rain. The pilot fell awkwardly, as if clumsily missing his footing on wet planks, then slid out of sight into the cabin. Hyde suppresssed the shiver that hurried through him. Harrell had turned towards him, holding Kathryn across his chest and stomach. Her face flopped into the sight, corpselike, white. Then Harrell began shouting. The man on the launch yelled back, kneeling into the cabin, shaking his head. Harrell, his face strained and even fearful, bellowed for them to go back towards the lodge, himself moving crablike, his head snapping back and forth, Kathryn shielding him from what he thought was the general direction of the shots. He stumbled on the steps, almost dropping the woman. Then the last of them was under the shadow of the verandah. The door slammed shut. Shadows against the windows, then silence.

The seaplane bobbed mockingly a hundred yards from the shore.

Carefully, Hyde sighted on an upstairs window and fired twice. The window shattered, collapsed inwards. Curtains blew damply. They would experience the terror of intrusion, the flimsiness of windows and walls. He fired two more shots into a ground-floor window. The shatter of glass, voices panicking inside. There were two of them still outside the lodge, somewhere in the trees. Harrell would be calling them back; the shots might even have carried, alerting them. No one had fired back from the lodge.

The rain's noise and the spiteful commentary of the wind filled the silence after the shots. He listened, ignoring the lodge, anticipating footsteps, hurried or cautious. Harrell's amplified voice startled him.

"Hyde, you crazy bastard!" the bullhorn blasted from the shadows beneath the verandah's sloping roof. "You crazy sonofabitch, the girl's *dying!*" Even his breathing was audible, a magnified, distorted roaring like that of the sea. "She's Aubrey's niece, dammit! She's going to bleed to death! If she doesn't get to a hospital, she won't see tomorrow, Hyde!" A further roaring of breath, then silence. The echo of the magnified voice faded. Someone would have slipped from the rear of the lodge, perhaps more than one of them, while his attention was distracted with the truth. Oh, yes, she was dying. "Hyde, let someone get her out of here!" Harrell yelled invisibly. "I don't want to be responsible, neither do you! She needs to be gotten to a *hospital,* Hyde. Right away!" The voice taunted him with the facts now. "OK, Hyde, have it your own way. We can't stop the *bleeding,* man!"

Hyde forced himself with a vast effort of will to release the trigger and take the butt of the rifle away from his shoulder. He lowered it and pressed it painfully against his hipbone, twisting it masochistically. Harrell was a clever, clever bastard . . . there would be medical bulletins bellowed out from the shadows, forcing him to follow a required, inescapable pattern like iron filings drawn to a magnet.

"Christ, Hyde, I don't know how you can just let her die!"

Hyde looked at the launch, bobbing solemnly. His anger was bilious at the back of his throat. He could let them take her in the launch. She *was* dying. He could let *one* of them take her to the hospital in Redding, for Christ's sake—!

He raised the rifle, sighted, fired twice. For a moment, the fuel tank seemed unscathed. Then it exploded in a damp, wind-plucked dazzle of flame.

The woman was dead whether he kept her there or not. It was fatuous to believe otherwise.

"Hyde, you crazy man! You just *killed* her, asshole! Now there's no way out for either of you!"

The engine fire on the launch was already dying, the paint work little more than scorched near the stern. Rain blew into his face. His joints ached a little, but there were no other symptoms of incomplete decompression. He should move . . . should really. He wasn't able to see the rear of the lodge, all its windows, its door. The trees crowded around the small clearing and the daylight was dying behind the pall of cloud and the mask of rain. He squinted down towards the lodge. They were cut off, just as he was. They wouldn't call in a boat or anything else until they'd taken care of him.

With an effort, he forced himself to his feet and slung the rifle across his chest. He looked down at the lightless, apparently deserted lodge. He could do nothing before nightfall, however serious Kathryn Aubrey's condition. He cocked his head, listening. There'd be the others, the ones still outside, making their way back, summoned by Harrell. He turned his back on the lodge and moved into the shadows beneath the trees.

Godwin picked up the telephone with his handkerchief draped across his fingers and thumb, dialing Aubrey's number with a pen. Behind him—he'd turned his back on the object of his frustration—the Special Branch forensic officers were moving as delicately as visitors to a stately home. He listened to his own breathing as he waited, increasing its volume to express more adequately the swill and rush of his emotions. He remembered his mother had used to sigh just like that, behind his father's back, behind the chair in which he sat reading the newspapers and ignoring her.

Eventually, after the anonymous, smooth voice of some Downing Street apprentice, Aubrey came on the line: "Sir—we were too late."

"Too late?" he heard Aubrey ask waspishly, as if only half-attending, his thoughts elsewhere. "What do you mean, too late?"

"I mean we got here too late. Sir James is dead." As if to indicate the fact to an audience, Godwin turned to glance at the armchair where Melstead's bulk appeared surprisingly boneless and at peace, his head lolling. The almost empty tumbler was on the small wine table beside the arm of the chair, innocent until analyzed. Melstead's lips were blue.

"*What?*"

"Suicide, apparently."

"Suicide—how?"

"Some sort of poison, the doc thinks. Cyanide, perhaps."

"Is there no sign of violence, nothing to indicate any—?"

"—foul play, sir?"

Chambers, across the room, snorted derisively and called out: "Maybe he did do himself in! Couldn't face the scandal. Perhaps he lost his bottle?"

"Terry, for God's sake!" Godwin growled. Then: "Sorry, sir. No, there's nothing. No evident bruising, no signs he was held down, or the body moved. But he could have had a pill blown down his throat, I suppose. There's no note or anything."

Aubrey was silent for a long time. Melstead stared calmly at the ceiling. Someone brought an armful of videocassettes into the living room.

"Danish, most of them," Godwin heard. "Piles of magazines in a wardrobe, a few clothes. Envelopes full of pictures. Of *kids* . . ." Chambers voiced his hatred of Melstead biliously once more.

Then Aubrey announced, quietly: "I think I can get away within the next ten minutes or so. I'll come directly there. This damned meeting is *endless*, Tony! Orrell and Longmead are trying to engage me in a power struggle, for heaven's sake, at a time like this!" he sighed, then added: "That doesn't matter at the moment. I shall leave them to it just as the PM did an hour ago. But, I shall collect you both there, before we go on to Center Point. We must try to contact Paul Anders. It all hinges on him, now."

"Yes, sir."

He heard Aubrey's receiver put down and replaced his own, thrusting his handerchief into his pocket. Then he stared at Melstead in respose. A slight, concussive blow from someone skilled, enough whiskey over the lolling tongue for credibility, the pill masticated by Melstead's jaws moved up and down by a firm, experienced hand. One bite, two—? Then a little more whiskey. There was hardly any spillage on the shirt front or chin, hardly any smell. And the rest is bloody silence—!

Someone had switched on the television and was inspecting the video recorder. A naked man fondled a naked boy, kissed small, childish genitals, long blond hair, narrow shoulders.

"Turn that fucking television off!" Chambers roared, clenching his fists as if tensing himself to spring at the set, or at Melstead. "Turn it bloody off!"

The image flared and vanished.

"Shut up, Terry," Godwin muttered. He shuffled awkwardly towards Chambers, glowering. He could smell the old scents from the empty shop below the living room. "I'll get in touch with Mallory," he announced.

Godwin dropped his heavy body into the armchair beside the telephone. Ignoring forensic priorities now, he picked up the receiver in his bare hand, dialed the motel number in Redding, and waited, looking at his watch. Eleven-ten. Twenty minutes since they had broken in and found Melstead. Forty minutes since Special Branch had placed the flat under surveillance. Melstead had hardly begun to go cold. If only they'd had the address half an hour earlier!

"Mallory? Godwin. Our end's become—*what?*" Godwin listened, breathed "My God," his face shocked, then frowning with concentration. "When did he call? Ten minutes ago? Then why didn't you—? What? Yes, all right, then. What time's Anders expected—before six, your time, is it? He's *what?* How do you know? Yes, I know it's not your fault..." Godwin's free hand was clenched, white. "No, just stay by the telephone. The old man will want to talk to you!" He thrust down the receiver and glared at it, then at Chambers. "The head of the CIA's Direct Action Staff, Mr. Paul-Bloody-Anders, didn't take off from Edwards AFB until two hours ago!" he raged.

"What the bloody hell is he doing? Aubrey talked to him more than five hours ago!"

"Checking things over, Mallory says." Godwin's big hands slapped down on his thighs. "I should have stayed at the office."

"So you'd have known half an hour ago! So what? It'll take them another three hours, that's all, to get there. If he's got a team with him, they can be at Shasta— what's the matter?"

"Patrick called Mallory just minutes ago. He doesn't have four hours, nothing like that. Kathryn Aubrey's been badly wounded." He shrugged massively, then held up his thumb, turning it slowly down. "He's going to have to go in, now—on his own. If he *chooses* to . . ."

"Christ, *nothing's* gone right with this bloody business from the beginning!" Chambers shouted. "We're supposed to be the good guys. Why can't *we* bloody win for a change!"

Godwin looked at his watch. "It's three-twenty or something like that over there. It'll be dark in less than a couple of hours." There was a specious self-consolation in his voice, then he slapped his thighs again. "Not that it matters a bloody toss what time it is!" He rubbed chin, then his whole face. He looked up at Chambers. "How the hell am I going to tell the old man that his niece might be dying, right now?"

17

THE UNION DEAD

Four-thirty. The light was gloomy even through the im-
age-intensifying sniperscope he was using as a telescope.
The temperature had dropped. Sleet stung in the wind.
The farther shore of the McCloud Arm was obscured,
except for scattered, frail little lights gleaming out of the
murk. It was too easy, and unavoidable, to sense the
woman's deterioration mirrored in the weather. *You
have to wait . . .*

Hyde was squatting on pine litter within a clump of
gray-boled firs, untidily stranded on an outcrop above
and behind the entrance to the Shasta Caverns. He was
a mile from the lodge. The narrow, winding road the
tourist buses used from the shore up to the caverns

twisted like a wet strand of hair up the side of the mountain. He shook the small bottle of pills. They called them "Spring Lambs." He tossed his head, scowling darkly at the plastic bottle. Two of them and he'd be capable of conquering the universe—for an hour, maybe a little more; then he'd run down as quickly and certainly as a broken watch spring. Wonderful. Not yet, though.

He sipped at the almost empty flask. He had collected his pack from its hiding place near the caverns, where he had used the telephone to call Mallory for the last time—last until it's over, he added superstitiously. The brandy ran thinly down his throat, as if it dribbled outside his skin. He flicked on the pencil beam of the flashlight, and studied the map for a moment before putting it back into the pack. He put two spare clips for the Browning into a zip pocket on the breast of the camouflage jacket. Then he scanned the road and the slopes through the sniperscope. The scene was still murky through the image intensifier. He lowered the scope and blinked at the growing evening, tangible as a veil. Then he closed his eyes.

Mallory had got hold of the ground plan of a lodge identical to the one Harrell was using. The verandah ran around the whole building. There was a big room downstairs, three steps dividing it falsely into two; plus a kitchen, larder, lavatory. A cellar under the entire ground floor. Upstairs, four bedrooms and a bathroom. The woman would be upstairs, probably in one of the two bedrooms at the back. Mallory had offered him the brochure, which he'd refused contemptuously. *Can't afford the mortgage . . . it's all right to smile, Mallory. I'm not going to kill you.*

Only Harrell . . . He used the sniperscope once more. The flare of a small, hand-held lamp down by the entrance to the caverns. He watched the lamp moving along the roofed gallery towards the entrance. One man, he presumed, but was unable to make out even a shadow. They might think he'd gone into the caves, and waste time searching for him down there.

Harrell would have kept two of them, at least, on guard at the lodge. No boats had crossed the lake. There were no others Harrell could call in, not quickly enough to matter. There were five, perhaps six men out looking for him, too few to work as a team or in pairs. Soon, they'd move back towards the lodge.

He had to prevent that. He rubbed his arm. The flesh wound reminded him of his own vulnerability, piercing through his new calm. The caverns had been the first place they'd made for, expecting him to need the telephones down there. They had nearly trapped him.

Panicked, he had almost fled into the cave system, before willing himself to run. Remembering that moment, he breathed carefully, regularly, calming himself. He went on breathing gently as he admitted that it was time he allowed himself to be found. That lamp down there. He needed the man's R/T.

He was reluctant to move away from the shelter of the firs, the confidence of altitude and concealment. He raised the sniperscope to his eye again, scanning across the scene. The lamp wobbled back along the gallery, pausing occasionally. It was almost dark now. There was another lamp, perhaps three hundred yards off to his right, bobbing down what he knew was a narrow, steep trail. It was time to move.

He checked the Browning thrust into his waistband, then the knife in its sheath. Struggled to fit the pack across his shoulders and settled it to comfort. Reached for the rifle.

There was nothing more to do or consider. There was a single course of action, one that Harrell would inevitably predict. He sighed, his breath clouding about him before the wind rubbed it away in a magician's trick. The lamp was moving away from the gallery towards the road. The man must feel laziness, and the itch of the growing evening between his shoulder blades.

It was almost five. The day's disappearance had altered things once more. They were isolated now, with the alertness of prey rather than predator, while the past hour had freed him from the sense of being hunted. The closing in of the weather, the gloom, the sleet, had all conspired to insulate him. He patted the small bottle of "Spring Lambs" in his pocket. Later. When necessary.

He stood up. The lamp was visible perhaps a hundred feet below him, moving along the invisible twists of the narrow road. The second lamp had vanished. He breathed deeply, three, four times, adjusting the pack, patting the pistol and the knife, flexing his hands and toes. He heard the wind through the pine branches above his head. Sleet stung against his cold cheeks. Moments later, he had found the track. His boots made little or no sound on the carpet of pine needles; a fir cone cracked once, but the noise alerted only him. In the dark, he grinned.

He emerged from the outcrop and at once saw the lamp moving steadily ahead of him, its pace that of someone jogging lazily. Perhaps Harrell had already called them back. He increased his own pace, moving downwards with the slope of the mountainside, leaning slightly backwards, placing his feet carefully. He visualized the route back to the lodge, over the lump of the mountain just visible against the last grayness of the clouds. Moving steadily lower, he paralleled the lamp, around which the figure of the man carrying it emerged slowly. Yes, he was advancing quickly enough. He would intercept the lamp in a matter of minutes.

*   *   *

There were no appurtenances of the operation with which to distract himself, only the nagging fact that Hyde had broken contact and they would hear nothing more until ... or, simply, nothing more. Aubrey sipped at the vile coffee too-long warmed on the hot plate. His fault. Godwin had offered fresh coffee, but he had not wished even that much communication with either Tony or Chambers. He had just poured himself a cupful. At least, it was hot.

There, a moment of distraction, fussing about the taste of the coffee.

He sat perched on the hard chair near the windows, his vision blurring then refocusing, the lights along Oxford Street wriggling like glowworms, merging, then becoming lamps above an almost deserted street. They could talk to Mallory, of course, any time they wished. But Mallory would call them when Anders arrived. He glanced at his watch. One in the morning, a little after. Anders's ETA at the airfield outside Redding could be as much as two hours away. If the weather worsened, they might be diverted. It was blowing hard in Redding, there was sleet in the air; the forecast was bad.

That was why he had no wish to speak to Mallory. No news is good news; ridiculous, but thankfully the truism clung like a leech. Kathryn was—

He avoided forming the thought, retaining its imprecision. Godwin was at his side, also staring out of the grimy windows, coffee cup in his hand, his breathing claustrophobically near. Chambers was asleep on the narrow camp bed in the other office; furiously asleep, feeling cheated and frustrated.

"You all right, sir?" Godwin asked quietly.

"No, I don't think I am, Tony." Aubrey resented the

intrusion. "I can't see any grounds for optimism. Can you?"

"Only over the evidence. Mallory's got that safe—at least," he added.

Aubrey hesitated, then lit a cigarette. The smoke smelled new and pungent in the office. Aubrey puffed repeatedly.

"Sir, Patrick was missing believed dead when this business blew up..." Godwin's voice trailed off. "I mean—"

"Tony," Aubrey announced heavily, "my niece was *not* involved at that time. She was not *dying* at that time!"

Aubrey got up and moved away from Godwin's oppressive presence. He paced the room, puffing unaware at the cigarette. "I can't even make a bargain, can I, Tony? At this time of night it would be difficult to find a taxi under which I could throw myself in exchange for her life. I am *utterly* safe here, as I have been throughout most of this messy, nasty business. And I am powerless now as I have been from the beginning!"

"Yes, sir." Godwin's tone was dull. "But Patrick's survived this long, and he's got his hatred of Harrell to keep him going."

"But what can he *do?* Unless Anders arrives in time, unless Kathryn is still alive—unless, *unless*...It will all have been a monument to my *professional* ego—won't it?"

"You're feeling very sorry for yourself—sir."

Aubrey glared, muttering: "Am I? Am I really?"

"Yes, sir, you are. Harrell had to—get rid of your niece as soon as Frascati spoke to her, just as he got rid of Frascati himself. *You* know that. Just as he has to try to get rid of Patrick. They're the loose ends, the last bits of wreckage lying around the crash site." He was staring at Aubrey as he spoke. Aubrey was not certain what Godwin saw in his expression, but it made Godwin turn to the window as he continued. "Sorry, sir. It's still true, though. It's still an operation—unofficial, of course, but we do have an agent in the field who has moved into the final phase of the proceedings with a decided and known objective." Godwin turned to him again. "Don't you think he can do it, sir?" Now, Godwin seemed uncertain, his confidence faltering.

Aubrey shook his head. "No, I don't think he can. Harrell's even more desperate than he is—still believing, as he evidently does, that Patrick is the only loose end he hasn't stitched back into the fabric. No—I think Patrick's course of action is futile."

He turned away, wiping his hand across the desk, cigarette ash dropping onto the litter of papers. The printout sheets, files, envelopes, snapshots and sketches; message flimsies, scribbled notes of telephone conversations, all lay as uncoordinated as the whole business had been from the start. It had never been of his volition—in that at least Tony was right. He had blundered into a room halfway through a discussion, after decisions had been taken; and had stumbled each step thereafter. The whole affair was like a bleak, gray, grubby little cocoon, just like the intact length of ash that lay across some note scribbled by Godwin.

Melstead was dead—Kathryn was dying. Patrick was acting out his role and probably his nature, but to no fruitful purpose. Oh, it was bleak, no doubt of it, and its cost was too high, far too high.

"Damn these people and their insane dreams and *games!*" he growled, violently grinding the stub of his cigarette into an ashtray. He felt hot as his heart puttered, making his whole frame quiver. Godwin's expression was irritatingly sympathetic. "Damn Harrell and his lunatic associates!" he continued. "How could they, even in their wildest dreams, have conceived that scheme of theirs?" He shuffled almost guiltily towards the window where the night was as old and tired as he was. You damnable old fool, he told himself, looking along a deserted Oxford Street, hearing Godwin creak on his sticks, perhaps in embarrassment, as he moved away. He swallowed with difficulty.

As he thought of Kathryn, he felt appallingly weak, as if with some virulent form of influenza. Everyone was certain she was dying—was perhaps already dead. Patrick was going in after her—because Anders was *late*.

"I—shall hold myself guilty, Tony," he announced. "Not that it will do either of them the least good! But I *am* guilty—and it's too damn late now to do anything about it!"

Godwin cleared his throat audibly, but said nothing. There was, Aubrey recognized, nothing to say. Nothing whatsoever.

The lamplight came wobbling up the winding road towards him. Above the wind he could hear the scrape and step of the man's boots; could see his form coming nearer. He could feel the rock which hid him under his palms, feel the knife at his fingertips, feel the sleet on his stubble and cheeks and in his eyes, feel the purchase of rocks beneath his feet. There was another flashing lamp hundreds of yards away to his right, higher up, blinking its way through thick pines, and a third down near the shoreline, casting to and fro. Three of them, three more at most somewhere else, out of sight and mind.

Fifteen yards. The man was cursing the weather. Hyde's nostrils widened as if the noises were scents. Ten yards. Nearing the great split boulder beside the road.

The man's face was turned towards the rock, out of the windy sleet. Hyde moved his feet carefully. The wind renewed its keening. The man was level with the boulder, his lamp following the white line down the middle of the narrow road, the light bobbing innocently. The knife scraped softly along the rock—

The man half-turned, a yard beyond the boulder, the lamp coming up and glaring in Hyde's eyes. The knife flashed in the light and then the lamp's beam flashed up at the clouds and remained raised like a struggling arm for a moment, then fell and began awkwardly rolling away like something severed, extinguishing itself.

Hyde lowered the body to the road, cleaned the knife quickly and casually on the man's parka, then sheathed it. He lifted the man and dragged the body behind the boulder, then knelt over it, searching the pockets of the parka. Spare ammunition, billfold, chocolate—the casing of the R/T. He raised it close to his face, inspecting it. Satisfied, he scrabbled back into the wind and scooped up the man's M–16 rifle, then hurried back behind the boulder. He could use the M–16 more effectively at close quarters than the FN sniper's rifle. He'd leave the FN here, with the body. He checked the man's pockets once more, finding his wallet and ID—Becker, was it? He risked the flashlight's beam, just for a second. A blond-haired, fresh-faced young man stared into the camera, his flesh tones ruddied. The image bore no resemblence to the wet, pale blob of the face beside him. Becker— David Becker...he glanced at the photograph once more, then at the corpse's face before switching off the flashlight. He looked like Kathryn Aubrey's description of the other man who had attempted to kill her; who had killed Blake. Quid pro quo, as Aubrey—had he ever been forced to joke about killing—might have said.

Hyde sniffed. What did he call himself when he reported in, *Dave* or *Becker?*

Excited enough and talking to Harrell, it would be *Becker,* he decided. He crouched behind the boulder as if guarding the corpse from wild animals, the M—16 held comfortingly against his cheek. The lodge was three-quarters of a mile away, down towards the shore. He could make out the lake now, duller than the cloud, patterned by the wind. There was a long, narrow, oil-black groove in the hills which eventually opened out near the lodge. Thick pine and fir marched down the slopes of the gorge towards the lodge. He studied the luminous dial of his watch—five-twenty. Time to report.

"Sir—" Don't forget the Mormonlike courtesy! "—this is Becker, sir, up near the caverns. Are you receiving me, base?" There'd be a code word, perhaps. And he sounded excited, breathless. But Harrell needn't become suspicious.

"Becker, what's wrong?"

Harrell's voice, something crooned in his thoughts. Harrell. His frame jumped with nerves. He held the R/T slightly away from his face, allowing the wind's noise to intrude, then said quickly, his accent overemphatic: "Becker, sir—just coming away from the caverns, believe I saw—I think he's doubled back, sir, gotten behind me. Thought I saw a light back down on the gallery. I'll go check it out, sir, but I'm requesting backup."

There was a momentary silence in which Hyde felt his heart beating wildly, then he calmed himself with the realization that even if Harrell became suspicious it wouldn't matter. He'd still send the backup—their job would be to either kill him or bring him back. Harrell was compelled to divert men to the caverns.

There seemed no doubt in his voice when he replied:

"OK, Becker, take it easy. Don't go inside and out of R/T contact until the backup arrives. Understand?"

"Sir."

Harrell announced: "OK, the rest of you out there, converge on the caverns. And stay alert *and* alive." Someone chuckled as Hyde closed the channel. In the round little spyhole of the infrared night sight he took from the pack, he saw the pale gray wash of the nearest lamp begin moving more quickly, descending towards the road.

He checked the body. It was concealed by the boulder and darkness from anyone passing along the road. Only by a freakish accident or as the result of a thorough search would it be found before morning. He paused, watching the descending, feeble light, then he ducked in a crouch across the road and slipped down the pebbly, steep gully on the far side, the wind masking his noise even from himself, the roll of pebbles, the clink of the rifle against rock, his breathing.

If they all closed in, they'd be a mile away. Every yard they moved towards the caverns and every yard he moved towards the lodge gave him more time. The gully dropped sheer into the narrow gorge. The wind's noise lessened. He could distinguish the water, hear the dribble of rainwater from the gully down the rockface towards the stream. The lamp along the shoreline had vanished beyond a promontory. Another lamp was moving up the gorge towards him—no, two lamps, like the headlights of an approaching car. The water rushed a hundred feet below him, hidden by trees. The shaggy outlines of hills, sharp and mounded, surrounded him. The lake was a little less dark than the trees. The lamps were bright and continued moving towards him.

Hyde scrambled down the slope, colliding with the fir boles to break his speed, his arms and back protesting, his breath puffing out indignantly each time. The men's voices loudened above the water's noise. Hyde crouched into the shelter of small, littered boulders, turning onto his stomach to watch the now-quick progress of the twin lights, splashing out in front of the two men he could not distinguish in the inkiness beneath the trees. Then the lamps were beyond him and haloed two hurrying figures. The lights scrambled and bounced and stuttered up the slope towards the road. After a few more seconds, the only lights were across the lake, blurrily coming through the mist of sleet and rain.

Hyde got to his feet and began hurrying, following the slope downwards, his night vision sufficient to trace the thin, unswollen stream as he pushed through the trees along the bank. There was no one between him and the lodge now, which was no more than half a mile ahead. He glanced at his watch, pausing for breath. Five forty-five. Making good time.

Steep slopes enclosed him on either side, like a tunnel roofed by the trees. The defile was narrow, with the sensation of narrowing further rather than opening out as it neared the lake. The wind was no more than a thin noise, a hand distressing the highest branches. The stream gurgled. His blood thudded in his ears. Occasionally, he paused and bent down, seeking some glimpse of light from the lodge. Nothing on the R/T, not yet . . . in moments, perhaps, they'd report they couldn't locate Becker, but then they'd cast about, think, delay . . .

He was making good time, whether the woman was still alive, or not.

He paused. Filtered light coming through the trees. A halo of it. Coming from the lodge—

—Harrell's voice, loudly squawking from the R/T in his pocket. A bird cried and flapped above him, startled.

*   *   *

"Yes, his ETA's been stretched because of headwinds, sir." Mallory's nerves bubbled in his stomach. Aubrey was angry, tired—and shockingly defeated, it seemed. His mood dampened Mallory's own enthusiasm. Hyde's rolls of film were snugly in his pocket. Of course Aubrey was worried about his niece, perhaps even about Hyde, who talked and acted like an automaton most of the time but was nasty enough for what he had to do. Mallory resented the inference that his excitement was out of place.

"How long now? Will they be able to land at Redding?"

"The weather is getting worse, sir—but the tower says yes. Mr. Anders's flight should touch down in—oh, another fifty-five minutes."

"How long after that?"

"Oh, sorry sir, you mean how long will it take him to get up to the lake? There's a helicopter standing by—two, in fact. If I brief Mr. Anders at the airfield, or on the way—" The tension was pleasurable. He swallowed. "—then it's no more than a ten-minute flight, sir."

"Very well. A little over an hour. Thank you, Mallory. Good night." It was as if the pessimism, the *Weltschmerz*, was deliberate. It irritated Mallory. God, the Fifth Cavalry was only an hour away! It couldn't go down the drain in that time.

"Goodnight, sir," he said to a humming line.

The wind banged a door somewhere, rattled the window. The whole motel seemed to creak quietly. It suggested something fragile, unsafe. Mallory's sense of well-being evaporated in a moment, just because of the wind—ridiculous. Or was it because of Harrell?

He'd listened to Harrell's instructions and demands, then smashed the R/T so that its noises wouldn't betray him when he moved closer to the lodge. Since Becker had been uncontactable, they'd assumed he must have gone into the Shasta Caverns, yet he had been ordered not to do so. Doubt was setting in like a change in the weather. He had heard them yelling distantly into the hollowness of the caverns, and had sensed their suspicion and foreboding when there was no reply. Harrell had not ordered them into the cave system, and probably wouldn't. He'd order them back.

It was time. He'd swallowed the two pills and the renewed confidence they'd induced was a tangible pleasure. The lodge was thirty yards away, with no surrounding trees. He crouched near a pile of logs, shiny-wet, the wind nuzzling hollowly through the gaps and spaces. A generator hummed faintly. There was a light in the kitchen, and a more shadowy light upstairs, in one of the bedrooms; where Kathryn must be.

Adrenaline coursed nauseatingly through him as he realized she must still be alive. Otherwise, why the light? No one else would be in bed.

A snatch of voices on the wind revealed that there must be two men at the front of the lodge. Hyde ducked back into the shadows of the woodpile as one of the guards came around the corner of the verandah. The man moved slowly, pausing often, keeping back in the shadows. Two outside. He was almost certain that there was only Harrell left inside—and the woman. The verandah creaked beneath the guard's weight. The sleet blew against Hyde's cheek and hand.

A shadow on the kitchen blind, then the movement of another figure upstairs, hardly thrown onto the curtains. Four of them, then. Harrell's shadow, he had no doubt, had wiped fleetingly across lamplight in that upstairs room. He clutched the M-16 against his chest. The guard moved along the verandah past the kitchen blind, his shadow momentarily black. Then he was once more only a drifting, fainter shadow against the rear of the lodge. He paused at the corner, then moved out of sight.

The kitchen light was extinguished.

Hyde removed his pack, then rose to his feet and slung the M-16 across his back. He adjusted the Browning, paused, then fled across the blowing space towards the lodge, hunching against the sleet. The wind plucked at him, almost pushing him off balance before he reached the lee of the lodge and his objective. The cellar. Bending, he heaved at one sloping door. He hesitated, then felt carefully for the steps, located them and moved delicately down into the darkness, reaching for the door above his head. The wind was suddenly muscular and he braced himself, almost losing his footing as the door threatened to slam down. He lowered it gently and heard his own breathing harshly replace the noise of the wind. He could see nothing until he pulled the small flashlight from his pocket and flicked it on. The thin beam dribbled away into the shadows of the cellar. A scent of apples and must. He eased himself down the remaining steps, his pulse thudding in his ears. He stood upright.

A box of apples, red, another russet. The generator hummed modestly. He'd heard it ouside only by a trick of the wind. A catcher's mitt, a baseball, then a football. The walls were dry, gray. The cellar spread and faded into the darkness beyond the flashlight's beam. An exercise bike, skeletal and upended. He moved cautiously, sensing the cellar with his shins, brushing against boxes, cartons, a black rubbish bag, more boxes of apples. Perhaps there was a permanent caretaker of some kind, one of Harrell's people, the apples as much a disguise as the litter of other objects. Footsteps above his head startled him into immobility. He waited, hearing movement again in what must be—the kitchen? No, he was under the lavatory. Water flushed; pipes grumbled, popped and coughed somewhere nearby; the central heating. There was little sensation of chill in the cellar.

He wiped the flashlight beam along the walls. Two minutes he'd been inside. The place was claustrophobic; the bloody pills worked against quiet movement, that was the bloody trouble with them!

Three minutes... Wine racked in one alcove, a sack of kindling in a corner, lagged pipes, the housing of the generator, irritating now in its humming. Then he found the fuse box on the wall and reached up to inspect it. No labels. He moved on and found the steps up to a door beneath which light gleamed in a thin horizon. Moved back to the fuse box.

Rapidly, he tugged at each fuse, pulling it out of the box. The strip of light under the cellar door disappeared, accompanied by a startled voice from somewhere above, then the noise of someone blundering into something, scraping it across a wooden floor. A curse. Then Harrell's voice, easily distinguishable even though muffled, bellowing: "What the fuck's going on down there, Barney? Get some light on!"

"Could be the fuses?" he heard Barney—presumably—call back up the stairs. The cellar door was opposite the lavatory. "I'll go take a look, Mr. Harrell!"

Hyde backed slowly away from the fuse box, dropping the bundle of fuses behind a stack of cartons and the bag of rubbish. They tinkled on the concrete like a scurrying mouse. The cellar door opened and a flashlight's beam washed down the steps, a shadow barely discernible behind it. Hyde placed his hands flat against the cellar wall behind him, carefully aware of the rifle across his back. Barney cursed his way down the steps and raked the flashlight along the wall, his shadow leaning slightly as if listening, then nodding to itself, evidently hearing the hum of the generator, the hiss and bubble of the heating pipes. The boiler came on with a shudder and a quiet roaring, startling the misshapen shadow behind the flashlight. Hyde could smell Barney's clothes, Barney himself, stronger than the scent of apples.

The light fastened on the fuse box and Barney's breathing exclaimed in surprise. He moved closer, the flashlight unwavering, then he dabbed it across the floor in a mopping circle around his feet. Nothing. Back to the fuse box. A pause. Hyde moved. The M–16 scraped against the wall. Barney's head snapped up and the flashlight dazzled at Hyde's face. Hyde jumped, feet first, his whole weight crushing Barney against the wall. The flashlight grotesquely illuminated his features for a moment before it dropped and rolled across the concrete floor. Barney slid down the wall. Hyde rose to his knees, then his feet. The man's head had struck the wall behind him. Hyde scrabbled for the flashlight. Barney was unconscious, his chest heaving stertorously. His head lolled.

"Barney!" he heard Harrell shouting. "Get some fucking lights on up here!" Harrell was still on the second floor.

Hyde knelt by the unconscious man and removed the pistol from the shoulder holster. Anything else? Cellar key. He thrust his hand awkwardly into Barney's pockets, then inspected the keys he withdrew. One of them fitted, get moving—

He stood up, then climbed the cellar steps with the aid of the flashlight, and pushed open the door, which creaked.

"That you, Barney?" Harrell called. Upstairs, there was a flickering light and then the pervasive smell of an oil lamp. "What the hell's wrong down.there?"

Footsteps in the main room, beyond a door. The staircase was to his right. Noises blundered across the living room and someone called out: "What's wrong, Mr. Harrell?" Then cursed at a minor collision. Something scraped on the wooden floor. "Hey, Barney, where are you, man?"

"Barney, what in hell's name are you doing?"

The oil lamp's wavering glow drew closer to the head of the short, straight flight of stairs. There was a hand on the doorknob only feet away and the sense of a body leaning against the door. Feet stopped at the top of the stairs, floorboards creaking.

Hyde gripped the banister and heaved himself up the stairs, ducking low, his legs pounding as if he ran through deep sand. The lamplight glowed around him. Harrell began an exclamation. The living room door opened, he heard a surprised exhalation of breath—

—blundered against Harrell, the Browning in his hand, his other hand clamped on Harrell's wrist. The lamplight danced wildly on the wooden walls, over Harrell's wide-open, shocked expression, over the open doorway of the bedroom through which he propelled the off-balance American, pushing against the man's weight with his shoulder as if bursting open something locked. The flame danced in the heavy lamp Harrell still clutched and their enlarged and crooked shadows wavered like a speeded-up film on the bedroom walls. Light washed over the prone, unconscious woman, over the sheets as pale as her face, over a wash basin and jug. Hyde seemed to be moving slowly now, in an intimate dance with Harrell—

—who pushed him off across the room. A rug skidded beneath his feet and he fell backwards against the bed. A low moan from the woman. Harrell held the oil lamp above his head like a weapon. In his other hand, an R/T was clamped against his lips.

"Emergency—get back here, all of you! Emergency. Get back here—!"

The Browning gleamed sullenly in Hyde's hand. Harrell's gaze was held by it. The shadows from the lamp steadied. The room was calmly warm in its subdued glow, noisy only with their breathing and the answering voice now coming from the R/T.

"Put it down!" Hyde shouted. "Put it down or I'll kill you now!"

The footsteps on the stairs halted. He heard the creaking noise of wood under pressure from a tense, straining body. Hyde got up and moved to the door, slamming it shut then locking it. He watched Harrell shrug and put down the R/T on a small bedside table, lower the lamp there, too, so that the woman's face became jaundiced with the light. Her breast fluttered weakly.

"I'll kill your boss if you come any closer!" Hyde yelled. "Get back downstairs and stay in the living room!" He moved about the room, his shadow looming and shrinking. "Tell them, Harrell!"

Harrell hesitated, then growled thickly: "Dan, do as he says—whoever's out there, just leave us alone. Understand? Leave us alone."

After a while, assent and descending footsteps. The deliberate slamming of a door. Hyde motioned Harrell to a chair he placed against the door, removed the key from the lock, and grinned. "Just in case Dirty Harry's out there. You'll get it first."

"They won't try anything—except to inform the others what's happening here. Fifteen minutes maximum. I reckon that's all you've got, Hyde, before they get back. Then you're trapped here, just like me." He nodded his head towards the bed. "And the lady isn't packed to leave, as you can see for yourself." He arranged his loosened tie neatly down the front of his shirt, brushed his hands across his hair, and assumed a lazy pose.

Hyde walked to the far side of the bed so that it was between himself and Harrell. Kathryn's face was white. He felt her pulse, then gingerly lifted the sheet and blanket that covered her. The crude bandaging was dyed red across her stomach and side. The sheets were stained. He lowered the blanket and felt her forehead. Coldly damp. She was alive—just.

"So?" Harrell sighed, slapping his hands on his thighs. "What now, hero? How'd you get in, as a matter of interest?"

"Cellar." Hyde sat on the edge of a small easy chair beside the bed.

"Knocked out the fuses, huh?" Hyde nodded. "Where's Barney?"

"Sleeping."

"Permanently?"

Hyde shook his head. "It wasn't necessary."

"The lights should be on in just a moment."

Hyde shook his head once more. "They won't do that. It might help me, in case they try something. Oil lamps. They're cozy, don't you agree?"

"What are you going to do, Hyde?"

"Sit here and wait." The idea was troubling. He heard the scrabbling of men moving in the living room. Fifteen minutes before there were—how many? Eight, was it? He shook his head. Their numbers were unimportant and he had more than fifteen minutes. Harrell didn't expect or want to be killed, and they wouldn't precipitate his death. They'd have to plan—slowly, carefully. "Just wait."

"For what? Until hell freezes over? Should I order dinner?"

"For the cavalry, Harrell—for the cavalry."

Harrell's eyes narrowed, then assumed he was bluffing.

"What cavalry, man? Kenneth Aubrey on a Harley-Davidson? Who *else* is on your side, Hyde?"

"You just can't see it, can you?"

"See what?"

"It isn't just me, any more. People have taken an interest in you, Harrell—at last. People like Anders."

"He has no authority—what about Anders?"

Silence from the living room. Only the wind rattling the window and Harrell's breathing louder and more regular than that of the woman.

"Even as we speak, he's flying out to ask you a few questions about what Frascati found at the bottom of the lake." Hyde's joints still ached; the effort of forming his words reminded them to protest. Harrell was listening intently to renewed noises from below, his eyes darting quickly. Then he shook his head. The glow of the lamp failed to warm Kathryn's skin.

"What's at the bottom of the lake, Hyde?"

The creak of wood along the verandah? Hyde listened. A screen door slammed in the wind. Someone's hoarse whisper cautioned. Surely they wouldn't try anything until the others arrived—it would take time for them to nurture recklessness.

"You know, and now I know, too. Soon, Anders will know. There's proof now, Harrell. You're gutted like a fish and you haven't begun to bleed yet. Soon, the pain—*man*." He grinned. Harrell was unbalanced.

"What proof—proof of what?" he blurted.

Hyde tapped the side of his nose with the barrel of the Browning. "You've seen Frascati's little collection of snapshots. I have one quite like it—did have, rather. I passed it on where it would do most good."

The wind banged at the window, rustling the curtains, making the flame in the lamp shiver.

"Bad weather out there, Hyde. Anders might not make it—in time."

The weather *was* bad ...

Hyde sat back in the chair, tight with nerves and adrenaline. He had little or no control over the damn pills. They just seduced the organism into pumping out energy until the supply ran out, then let the whole body collapse. They were no good for waiting, talking. They made him aggressive, itchy for activity. He pressed his arms against the sides of the chair as if imprisoning himself.

"Keep taking the pills, huh?" Harrell mocked in realization. "Your spring's going to run down soon, Hyde. Then I'll take the gun away from you."

"You won't. I only came here to kill you, Harrell. I thought the woman was already dead."

Silence from downstairs. The lodge creaked in the wind. Sleet pelted hard as pebbles against the window. The lamplight sank, almost died, then the flame wobbled erect once more.

"You're dumb, Hyde—putting yourself through all this just out of a personal beef against me."

Hyde snarled. "The only thing that makes *any* of it excusable is the fact that it's personal—don't you understand that, Harrell?" He was shouting. He had alarmed them below and there were footsteps on the stairs. "Fuck off back downstairs!" he warned. "I'll kill him!"

"It's true!" Harrell called out. "Just forget it, let it alone." He soothed like a parent. His blanched expression recovered its warmth in the lamplight.

"OK," Hyde muttered, his mouth filled with saliva.

"Harrell, you just remember that I'm still not sure I'll be satisfied with a million-year prison sentence for you."

Harrell's smile faded and his hands remained still on his thighs. The material of his trousers was puckered with his effort at calm. Finally, he shook his head. "It's time for a deal to be suggested, I guess."

"There'd be no deal between us. Anyway, too many people know now. People difficult to kill—not like her or her boyfriend, or the passengers on a flight from Portland to San Francisco. All kinds of little brown or yellow men don't matter, but they won't forgive you fifty and more Americans dying in the cause." He glanced down at his watch. The others would be arriving back at the lodge within the next five minutes. He forced himself not to think of Anders.

Six forty-five. He heard their voices outide—too soon!—the snappy greetings before the silence and the slamming of the screen door. Then the creaking of floorboards below them. Harrell was smiling.

"There are too many of us now," he murmured.

Hyde shook his head. "They'll take their time—they'll be careful."

"Anders isn't coming, Hyde."

"He is." .

"That Frascati, he was a real asshole, Hyde—you know that." The talk was urgently confiding; a distraction. He listened for movement, heard only the murmur of voices occasionally raised in dispute. "A real asshole. Everyone else could be kept quiet, but not Mr. Clean! Christ in heaven knows how he found out..." Harrell grinned, then said: "Then there was the girl, and then you." He sighed. "Tiresome, like mosquitoes."

Talk below, a continuous, urgent murmur, the occasional noise of movement. Harrell was alert, listening.

Six-fifty. Where was Anders? Mallory had said his

ETA was thirty minutes ago! Bad weather ... Hyde swallowed.

"Things kind of getting on top of you, Hyde?" Harrell asked with the soothing tones of an analyst. "But, then, you walked in here of your own free will, I guess." He sighed.

The wind buffeted at the window, making the lodge creak like a tree. Hyde listened but could distinguish nothing except the urgency of their discussion. No, not as urgent as before—but they were still talking, still there below him. Something creaked outside the door! He stood up, began to move towards the door, opening his mouth to warn off whoever—

Harrell moved slightly, as if flinching from a blow, his head cocked as if to listen, his eyes staring beyond Hyde, his face tight in case someone shot through the door. He was looking beyond Hyde, through him, almost. Another creak outside the door. Hyde opened his mouth, Harrell stared, then began moving very slowly—

—ducking out of—

Hyde turned and fired twice at the window, the Browning roaring in the confined, warm space. A shadow loomed at the edge of the lamplight but only the curtains billowing in the wind rushed into the room through the shattered window. The man perched on the verandah roof, Uzi clutched in his right hand, was dead before he toppled backwards out of sight. The flames guttered, then the wind puffed out the lamp. Hyde whirled around from the window at the noise of something scrabbling near the chest, dragging at one of the drawers, pulling it open—

He fired three times, the gun angled downwards towards the source of the sound. A slumping, slithering noise followed, then a creaking groan ... then silence.

"Mr. Harrell—you all right? Harrell? Mr. *Harrell!*"

Hyde picked up the gun, shaking Harrell's grip free of it. He felt dizzy again until he straightened up.

"Mr. Harrell—?"

"Harrell's wounded!" Hyde bellowed. He touched Harrell's shirt. Harrell was dead. "If you want to keep him alive, get the hell out of it!"

He crawled quietly across the floor towards the bed, until Kathryn's face stared down at him, a featureless blob in the darkness. He felt her timid breathing on his forehead.

With his back against the bed, he could cover the window and the door. He listened to retreating footsteps outside. Harrell's gun was beside him, Barney's gun in his waistband, the M-16 resting against the bed. The woman's hanging face breathed softly, irregularly on the back of his neck. It wouldn't be long. They'd demand to talk to Harrell, and when they realized he was dead, they'd come through the door and the window and it would be over in seconds.

He swallowed. The woman was alive. For the moment. So was he, for the moment. And Harrell was *dead* and that *was* gratifying! Then the satisfaction vanished and he shivered. A minute from now it would mean nothing at all. He couldn't get the woman out, not even himself. Not now that Harrell was dead—great joke, eh, Bob? Last laugh and all that? It was, too.

Bugger Anders...

The screen door eased shut. Footsteps on the stairs, then along the landing until they paused near the door. The creak of the verandah roof which probably wasn't the wind. The easing of a safety catch.

"I want to talk to Harrell," he heard. The absence of respect indicated they already knew he was dead. Harrell might even be bleeding through the floorboards into the living room. Hyde shivered. The woman was making small snoring noises, as if she slept restfully. Pity about her, really—upset the old man, it will. His own death might even disturb Aubrey, just a little.

He waited. Even the wind seemed to hesitate, listening like himself. The first crackle of an R/T, the first bellow or impact against the door, the first shadow framed by the empty window . . .

Instead, the illusory sound of a helicopter—two helicopters. Loudening, becoming more real than the voices outside, which were shouting, beginning to panic; the scuffling noises of someone sliding away down the verandah roof to the ground, the impact of his landing. The noise of the two helicopters merged and became the only real sound.

"The cavalry," he announced without looking at Kathryn, his whole frame possessed by a feverish shivering and huge weariness. "Just the cavalry."

The helicopters dropped closer, their downdraft billowing the curtains. Hyde sat in the darkness. He could no longer feel the woman's breath on the back of his neck. He turned, touched her wrist, her neck, turned her, pressing his head against her breast. No heartbeat, no breathing. Kathryn Aubrey was dead.

Christ, not now, after everything . . . what would Aubrey say?

He knelt by the bed, holding Kathryn's hands, as the helicopters landed.

POSTLUDE

For if you have embraced a creed
which appears to be free from the
ordinary dirtiness of politics...
surely that proves you are in the
right?

George Orwell,
Lear, Tolstoy & the Fool

"Thank you, Mrs. Grey."

His housekeeper smoothed the lapels of his dark over-coat and handed him his hat. His driver had already taken his suitcase down to the car. The sympathy that gleamed damply in Mrs. Grey's eyes made something in him shrivel, shrink away. He could not forget that he had left this same flat, similarly dressed, for his brother's funeral. Now, it was the funeral of his niece, whom Patrick Hyde had failed to save.

He waved his hands at Mrs. Grey to avoid further fussing; further contact, almost. The appalling Harrell and his lunacies had been quietly and firmly buried by Paul Anders. *I'll bury this if you will, Kenneth,* he had said. *You must see it would do no good for any of it to come out?* Part of him—a large part—had wanted everything to come out into the light of day, so that he could protest at his niece's murder... but the colder, professional part of him knew that it must be hidden. Irena Nikitina had died in an *accident*. Full stop. The truth of her death would solve and dignify nothing—similarly with Kathryn's murder. So, *Yes, Paul, I agree...*

About your niece, Kenneth—He had put the telephone down on Paul Anders at that point.

As to James Melstead, he had been killed by one of his... *pupils,* evidently. Longmead, Orrell, the PM herself, had all been appalled. And relieved that there was no security involvement. A private aberration, not political villainy. He had assured them of that. *In such liaisons, Prime Minister, there is always an element of danger.*

And so farewell, old friend. But, once Melstead and Harrell had been tidied away, there had come this dreadful sadness and this clinging, glutinous sense of guilt regarding Kathryn. It was impossible to escape the grief or transfer the guilt, even to Patrick. It weighed on his shoulders now, and he saw it reflected in Mrs. Grey's eyes.

Turning away from her, slightly dizzy with emotion, he opened the door of the flat. The landing smelled startlingly of the new carpet to which everyone in the block had contributed. Mrs. Grey, despite her concern for him, reflexively sniffed, as if unfavorably comparing it with the carpets inside the flat.

"Goodbye, Mrs. Grey."

"Take care, Sir Kenneth."

"Yes."

He turned at the head of the staircase, and assayed a smile. She liked him to look back at her whenever he was to travel by air. Then he quickly turned away from her silent sympathy and descended the stairs.

The mail lay on the mat but he did not disturb it as he opened the door on the chill of a bright morning. The cold struck through his thick coat as if it were tissue paper. A sparrow flashed up from the pavement towards the balcony of one of the flats. After wiping aside her tears for himself and Kathryn, Mrs. Grey would be putting out some seed, as she watched his car pull away.

He climbed into the rear of the car, hardly glancing at his driver. He sat back, head raised, as if escaping rising water, struggling to breathe. As the car moved out into the traffic on the Marylebone Road, one name formed in his mind. *Malan.* The figure who closed the circle. Paulus Malan. He shifted in his seat as if the name burned him.

As the car pulled away from traffic lights, tears of anger and grief welled in his eyes. Kathryn's former lover, Melstead's blackmailer, Harrell's supplier... always Malan.

However deeply he had to compromise his probity and abuse his considerable authority for the sake of personal justice—he would do it. Whatever he was required to do, however long it took, he would achieve that one task. He would destroy Paulus Malan.

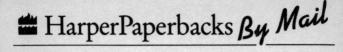